## ABOUT THE AUTHOR

PAUL ABBITT PHOTOGRAPHY

Michelle Holman lives with her family and assorted animals on a lifestyle block in the Waikato. Author of four bestselling contemporary novels — *Bonkers, Divine, Knotted*, and *Barefoot* — Michelle is also the mother of two teenagers.

# *Hand Me Down*

**Michelle Holman**

HarperCollins*Publishers*

**Disclaimer**

All characters in this story are fictitious and have no connection with any actual persons, living or dead. Any resemblance to any person, any similarity of name, place, or events in which the characters are involved, is entirely coincidental.

***HarperCollinsPublishers***

First published 2011
HarperCollins*Publishers (New Zealand) Limited*
P.O. Box 1, Auckland 1140



**HarperCollins*Publishers***
31 View Road, Glenfield, Auckland 0627, New Zealand
201 Elizabeth Street, Sydney NSW 2000, Australia
A 53, Sector 57, Noida, UP, India
77–85 Fulham Palace Road, London W6 8JB, United Kingdom
2 Bloor Street East, 20th Floor, Toronto, Ontario M4W 1A8, Canada
10 East 53rd Street, New York, NY 10022, USA

National Library of New Zealand Cataloguing-in-Publication Data

Holman, Michelle.
Hand me down / Michelle Holman.
ISBN 978-1-86950-871-5
I. Title.
NZ823.3—dc 22

ISBN: 978 1 86950 871 5
Cover design by Priscilla Nielsen
Typesetting by Springfield West
Printed by Griffin Press, Australia

50gsm Bulky News used by HarperCollins*Publishers* is a natural, recyclable product made from wood grown in sustainable forests. The manufacturing processes conform to the environmental regulations in the country of origin, New Zealand.

*For my lovely mum, Iris*

# *Acknowledgements*

When I got the idea for *Hand Me Down*, I did what I always do — thought of a story set in an industry I knew nothing about. Fortunately, my husband came to my rescue; he travels a lot with his job and reminded me that Tash Leckner, whom he used to work with, had moved to the South Island to work at Brookevale Cherries, an orchard in Cromwell owned by her mother, Merryll, and Merryll's partner, Lex McKay. I *love* the South Island, so it definitely wasn't a hardship visiting Cromwell to research this book. Tash's hospitality was wonderful and Merryll and Lex were generous with their time and always at the end of the phone or email to answer questions. Brookevale is a fairytale place, whatever the season, but Merryll, Lex and Tash made it even more special. The cherries are pretty wonderful, too. Lex came up with the name for April's home town. Pisa *is not* Cromwell, although I did borrow the famous fruit sculpture and the annual cherry-pip-spitting competition which is held in Cromwell mall and which I failed miserably at — I wisely retired after my one and only attempt. If you haven't been to Otago, go! It is a beautiful, historic area.

I would also like to thank those who advised me on military matters and helped me with my research.

# Prologue

*O what a tangled web we weave,*
*When first we practise to deceive!*

SIR WALTER SCOTT, 'MARMION' (1808)

Heather Ritchie stood in the tiny nursery of the maternity annexe at Pisa Hospital staring at the baby girl in the plastic cot. The baby was her daughter. She was barely an hour old, grumpy, dark-haired and olive-skinned, and looked nothing like Heather's husband, Grant, thanks to the swarthy, snake-hipped Brazilian barristo she'd slept with on one of her 'shopping' trips to Christchurch last July.

It wasn't her fault that she liked money and dark men who were good in bed. And it wasn't her fault that Grant was pale and boring and the richest man in the small Central Otago town of Pisa, or that he had become infatuated with her and decided he wanted to marry her. Heather Dreyfuss was the only child of the owners of the orchard next door to his. Marriage to her almost doubled the land and cherry trees that Grant owned. Heather also brought Aurora with her, the gracious two-storey Georgian-style house built by Heather's maternal great-grandfather.

Heather wasn't a new millennium woman. She didn't want a career; she wanted to continue her pleasant existence as the pampered darling of a rich man, and she knew the best way to do that was by marrying a man as wealthy and indulgent as her father. She accepted Grant Ritchie's proposal because it made sense to marry him: he was fifteen years older than her and adored her. It was a fair trade. Grant got the kind of wife he wanted, and Heather continued the life she was used to.

Grant was on his way to the hospital to see his new daughter. He was disappointed that he had missed the birth but he'd been away at meetings in Queenstown. Heather had suspected she was in labour when Grant was leaving, but had said nothing. She had even managed to hide her pains from their housekeeper who'd been given the job of watching over her while Grant was away. The baby wasn't due for three weeks, so Grant felt safe to go. The way he had hovered over her had made Heather nervous. It was impossible for her to think of what she'd do if the Brazilian barristo had made her pregnant instead of her husband. When Heather finally admitted she was in labour, the housekeeper only just managed to get her to the maternity annexe in time. The housekeeper returned to the house and packed her bags. Grant Ritchie didn't tolerate mistakes: he would blame her, not his precious Heather, for their baby almost being born in the car.

Heather spoke to Grant on the phone after the birth. He was upset that his child had been born at the small public hospital in Pisa instead of the private birthing unit in Christchurch as he'd arranged. Heather's palms grew damp when she imagined what Grant's response would be when he saw the baby. She'd been dyeing her brown hair blonde for so long that it was doubtful anybody but her hairdresser remembered Heather's natural colour; but nobody would mistake her for an olive-skinned brunette. Grant's adoration was conditional. He was thin, stoop-shouldered and socially awkward, and he had an uncanny ability to see and exploit a money-making opportunity before anybody else. Grant's peers might be jealous of his business acumen, assets and bank account, but his gauche manner and unattractive looks cancelled out any feelings of inferiority they might have felt. Or at least they did until he married beautiful, idle, sly-tongued Heather Dreyfuss. Grant paraded his wife like a trophy, enjoying the looks on people's faces.

Heather looked at the baby's slick dark head, and for once wasn't faking her tears when she sobbed into the phone: 'Grant! I'm *so* … tired! It's — it's *horrible!*'

Grant was sure Heather meant it *was* horrible. His excitement about his new daughter was tempered by guilt about what he'd put his wife through to get her. Heather was his fragile darling, his pampered princess, but he wanted another generation of Ritchies to inherit the extensive cherry orchards started by his grandfather.

'I'm so sorry I wasn't there, darling. Was it bad? Did that bastard take care of you properly? I should have insisted we move to Christchurch sooner so you were closer to the birthing unit.'

'That bastard' was the local GP, Tom Giles. Giles was one of the few people Grant Ritchie couldn't order around, because he was the only doctor in Pisa and didn't rely on Ritchie or Aurora for his livelihood. When she had arrived at the hospital, Heather had briefly been seen by Dr Giles before he was called away to another woman who was delivering. A frazzled nurse had witnessed the birth, made sure the baby was breathing and Heather wasn't bleeding, and had whisked the baby off to the nursery when her mother showed no interest in feeding her. This had suited the nurse; she didn't have time to show a first-time mother how to breast-feed. She was from out of town and didn't know how important Mrs Heather Ritchie was; only that she had screamed the loudest of the three women having babies that night, despite having the easiest birth.

The nurse had bundled up Heather's snuffling, whimpering baby like a mummy and placed her in the cot. 'I think every baby in Pisa is being born tonight. You and another woman have already delivered, and another one is about to. Thank goodness you and the other woman were straightforward.'

Heather had glared at her from her hospital bed. She was surprised at how easy the birth had been, but wasn't about to tell Grant that. Fragile, delicate princesses didn't give birth like third-world women working in paddy fields.

'I'll take her to the nursery. You get some rest and I'll be back soon to check on you. The lady who brought you in has gone. It's a shame — she could have popped in to see you and the baby,' the nurse had continued.

The last thing Heather wanted was anybody looking at her baby. 'I don't want to see anybody!' she'd snapped. 'Put her in the nursery.'

The nurse had raised her brows. Mrs Ritchie was a bitch, and judging by the size of the diamond surrounded by rubies on her engagement ring, next to a platinum wedding band, a rich bitch.

'Press the buzzer if you need anything,' she'd said as she pushed the baby from the room.

Now rising panic had brought Heather creeping from her room and along the corridor in search of the nursery. Perhaps she'd imagined it; perhaps the baby wasn't so dark. Her search for the nursery took her past the tiny waiting room. She was brought up short by the sound of a man's snorting laugh. 'Bet it's your first, eh?'

She peeped around the corner to make sure Grant hadn't arrived yet and saw a dishevelled-looking man with a round, red face and receding blond hair sitting on one of the shabby couches.

His elbows rested on his spread knees, and a magazine lay open between his fat, fuzzy-blond legs. His big toe poked through a hole in one of his battered trainers, and he had a hefty paunch hanging over the waistband of his faded track pants.

Heather's lip curled with distaste.

Hunched at the other end of the couch was Pisa's community cop, Roger Prescott, whose wife, Joy, was having their first child. Heather was indifferent to the misery on Roger's face. She was wasting time; Grant was on his way and she should be doing something to fix things — only she didn't know what.

Roger said miserably, 'They kicked me out. They had to use forceps. I wanted to be with her.'

'You don't want to do that,' the scruffy, blond whale advised. 'What's the point? Nothin' you can do about it. This is my seventh. I saw the first and it turned me up so bad I made sure I missed the others. All Nola does is bitch and swear.' He leaned over and gave Roger a nudge. 'Doesn't do it when I'm giving it to her, though.'

Heather wrinkled her nose and turned away as Roger asked curtly, 'You're not from around here?' He wasn't wearing his uniform, so the man didn't know he was speaking to a cop. As she crept away Heather heard the whale say, 'Nah, just passing through; got relatives in Greymouth. We'll chuck the little 'un in the car and be gone by morning. Nola pops kids out like a sausage machine. One little blondie after another …'

She stopped.

'… they look so much alike I have trouble telling 'em apart. Nola says this is the last, says she's sick of havin' babies and lookin' after kids and she's havin' her tubes done this time.'

Heather studied the baby and pressed her damp palms against her hammering heart. The baby was even darker than she remembered. It snuffled and squealed like a piglet. She looked at the cot beside it and shuddered with relief when she saw that the card in the slot was pink. *Gutsell, baby of Nola.* Heather leaned over the cot and took a closer look at the occupant. The baby was pink-skinned with a tuft of pale hair drying on her forehead and long, feathery, blonde lashes. She looked nothing like the angry, red-faced creature Heather had produced. Heather checked the cards on both cots. Ten minutes separated the births, and the weights were almost identical. She cast a quick look over her shoulder. The corridor was empty.

She had just finished swapping the cards on the cots and the babies' name tags when the frazzled nurse arrived, pushing another cot.

The nurse's face softened when she saw Heather standing beside the cot trying to shush her crying baby. It was being drowned out by the angry squalls coming from the other cot. The nurse smiled. 'Were you worried about her?'

Heather gritted her teeth and jiggled the cot. Changing the name tags had disturbed both babies, but the blonde one was settling faster than the other one, which made Heather even more certain that she'd made the right choice. She gripped the edge of the plastic cot, terrified that the nurse might guess what she'd done but banking on her having been too busy to notice. She needed to get the baby back to her room before Grant arrived. 'I'm taking her back to my room.'

'You should be resting,' the nurse said. 'Go back to bed and I'll bring her to you.'

'No!' Heather said sharply.

The nurse's lips tightened.

Heather forced a smile and softened her voice. 'No, you're *much* too busy. I'll manage.' She rolled the cot past the nurse, stopping briefly to admire the newest arrival, a boy with his father's unfortunate looks and forceps marks on his head. She wasn't interested in the Prescotts' offspring, but she didn't want to give the impression she was in a hurry. 'The Prescotts have a boy — how lovely.'

*Maybe she isn't such a bitch*, the nurse thought grudgingly. 'His father is so pleased.'

Heather pushed the baby towards the door of the nursery. 'I know how he feels: I'm pleased too.'

'Has she got a name?'

She stopped and stared at the sleeping blonde baby. Now that disaster had been averted, having her might be fun. 'I think I'll name her after the month she was born.'

'April?'

'Yes.' Heather imagined rows of frilly pink dresses hanging in the wardrobe in the nursery at home. 'April Annabelle Ritchie.'

# Chapter 1

*Lead me not into temptation; I can find the way myself.*

RITA MAE BROWN

***Twenty-six years later …***

April Annabelle Ritchie-Vincent-Berryman drove the gold Toyota through the gathering dusk into Pisa's main thoroughfare, Aurora Street. The street was named after the house April had grown up in and fled — or been kicked out of, depending on your point of view — nine years earlier.

Pisa had started life during the 1860s when gold was discovered in Central Otago and eighteen thousand miners had flooded into the Carrick, Bendigo and Bannockburn goldfields. The discovery of the precious metal in the nearby Kawarau and Clutha rivers created a mining shantytown which was named after the mountain range that guarded it. When the gold rush ended in 1863, most of the miners disappeared. If Pisa hadn't re-invented itself as a service centre for farmers and the emerging stone-fruit industry, it would have become another ghost town. Its population of two and a half thousand doubled during summer thanks to the influx of fruit-pickers and people coming to holiday at nearby Lake Dunstan. Like most small towns, everybody knew everybody — and their personal business.

April squinted at the glare from the setting sun and adjusted the Toyota's rear-view mirror. Hayley, the car's owner and April's boss, was wedged in the back seat between a bulging overnight bag on one side and a big, round, hard-top make-up case on the other. Underneath her black wool coat she wore a Wonder Woman costume with a thin gold lariat attached to the shiny utility belt, and a pair of red, white and blue 'Stars and Stripes' boots. The belt matched the shaped headband around her forehead. Hayley was particular that the costumes worn by the strip-o-gram and kiss-o-gram girls employed by her and her fiancé, Cliff, be as authentic as possible. They'd stopped in Queenstown to change into their outfits before the final leg to Pisa, and Hayley had been fretting ever since because she'd mistakenly brought the straight black wig instead of the curly black one.

April doubted that the men who had ordered strippers for the birthday party of Aurora's new owner would care if Wonder Woman's hair was curly or straight. For the past seven months, her sole source of income had been what she earned working as a scantily clad waitress and kiss-o-gram girl for Wild Women Do. She had received complaints from clients — and Hayley and Cliff — for refusing to take off her clothes, but none about her hair.

Hayley spoke up from the back seat. 'You look so different in that red wig, April, your own mother wouldn't recognize you.'

*That's the idea,* April thought. Although she had more chance of winning the lottery and paying the rent that she owed on her crummy flat and repairing her even crummier piece-of-junk car than bumping into her real or fake mother tonight. Nola Gutsell, her real mother, was probably still flipping burgers in Greymouth, and Heather Ritchie, her fake mother, had left town right after April had, and returned only once — for Grant's funeral and the reading of his will.

Only Heather would have the gall to turn up at the funeral of the ex-husband she'd been caught cheating on with the orchard manager's son, in Aurora's packing house. Or at least, that was who April said she'd seen Heather with on the night of her seventeenth birthday. And only Heather would expect Grant to remember her in his will. He hadn't — he'd already handed over a sizeable chunk of cash in the divorce settlement to recompense Heather for bringing him Aurora when they married. Pique and the towering disapproval of the not-so-good people of Pisa had sent Heather on her way again. Although she had a hide like a rhino, Heather also had the survival instincts of a rat, and she sensed that a tarring and feathering was all she'd have to show for her visit if she didn't get into her shiny convertible and return to her latest husband. People in small towns tended to have long memories, and the slow demise of Aurora Orchards had affected them where it most hurt — in their pockets.

Unlike Heather, April had known better than to return to Pisa — until now. But her financial situation, and Cliff's decision to pay off a poker debt by providing free strippers for a retired major's birthday party at some old house in Pisa, meant this was too good an opportunity to pass up.

April had stopped believing in luck, fate, her horoscope and that face creams could stop her getting wrinkles. So when she overheard talk in the Wild Women Do office about a booking at an old house in Pisa, she hadn't held out much hope when she asked, 'What's the name of the house, Hayley?'

'Areola,' she replied grumpily. 'And he's Major Tom — like the David Bowie song.'

Latoya, WWD's receptionist and April's flatmate, spoke up. 'You can't use that song. Major Tom is an astronaut and he's dying.'

April didn't care about Major Tom, just the name of his house. 'Are you sure you don't mean "Aurora", Hayley?'

'Nope, I'm sure Cliff said Areola.'

Latoya buried her face in her coffee cup.

April's heart had started thumping so hard she was surprised the front of her T-shirt wasn't shaking. 'Areola is another word for nipple. I don't think anybody would name their house after a nipple.'

Hayley's face fell. 'Oh — perhaps I got it wrong.' She consulted the booking form. 'Oh yeah, it's Aurora. How did you know that? And how am I supposed to find a house in the middle of Central Otago? I wish Cliff wouldn't gamble,' she finished petulantly.

Latoya had done some research on Cliff and discovered that he'd been declared bankrupt twice already. April knew Cliff wouldn't agree to pay for flights to Queenstown, which was the closest major town to Pisa. It was a six-hour drive from Christchurch, but he'd still expect Hayley to drive.

April trotted out the story she'd told Latoya about visiting Pisa in the summer holidays when she was a kid, and offered to drive Hayley's car.

Hayley was delighted. She got nervous driving outside her local area; just thinking about driving all the way to Queenstown had tied her stomach in knots. 'That is so nice of you, April!' Her gaze sharpened, and April guessed what was coming. 'They've asked for two strip-o-grams. Why don't we leave Susie behind, and you can be the other stripper?'

April smiled sweetly. 'I'm still not ready to make the leap from kiss-o-gram girl to stripper. How about I sing "Happy Birthday" to the major and introduce you and Susie?'

Her refusal to strip was a bone of contention between April and Cliff and Hayley. When Cliff had employed her, April had promised she'd graduate to strip-o-grams once she'd got the hang of doing kiss-o-grams, but months later she was still keeping her clothes on. April didn't have a problem with nudity or stripping *per se*; the extra money she'd earn was enough to justify gritting her teeth and taking her clothes off in front of strangers. No, false modesty wasn't her problem — it was the marks on her back left by the buckle on her second husband's belt.

'Oh.' Hayley's mouth turned down. Susie would expect to be paid. 'I can't pay you: it'll have to be a freebie.'

April shrugged, and avoided Latoya's puzzled gaze. She knew how broke April was, but not that something valuable awaited April at Aurora. All April had to do was figure out a way to get it without being caught or recognized.

'I'm not going as Angel April.'

Angel April was Wild Women Do's most popular kiss-o-gram. 'But people love Angel April!' Hayley protested. Her heart sank when April cranked up the wattage on her smile — April's smile grew in direct proportion to her stubbornness.

'I need a change,' April insisted. Thick make-up, a tiny white dress and a set of angel's wings wouldn't disguise her. As soon as the locals heard her name and saw her distinctive white-blonde hair, they'd be on to her. 'I want to be a devil.'

Hayley looked doubtful. April was blonde and angelic-looking. 'I don't think you're cut out to be a devil, April.'

April could have told her there were plenty of people in Pisa who'd disagree. 'I'm tired of doing singing angels and nuns. It's time I explored my bad side.'

'So strip.'

She shook her head. 'I'll make a much better devil kiss-o-gram than a stripper. And,' April played her ace, 'I'll be free.'

April had heard about Grant's funeral and Heather's swift exit from town in a letter from another of her fake relatives: Heather's mother, Rosamund Dreyfuss. Rosamund wasn't a soft, doting mother or a cosy, cosseting granny. She disapproved of the way her husband had spoiled their daughter, and Heather and Grant had spoiled April. Whenever Heather's name was mentioned, Rosamund declared 'Ruined — utterly ruined', before adding 'and my granddaughter is going the same way'.

Heather didn't like her mother, and April was wary of her grandmother and knew not to throw any tantrums if she didn't get her way.

Rosamund didn't try to find April or contact her after Heather had spilled the beans about April's parentage in retaliation for April spilling the beans about what she'd seen in the packing house. Nobody had tried to find her because nobody cared. When Grant found out that April wasn't his, it was as if the previous seventeen years had never happened — he threw her off the property. The arrival of Rosamund's letter not long after Grant's death was a surprise. Four years on, April could still recite its contents.

*Dear April*

*I am assuming you know that Grant died from melanoma last month. If you didn't, now you do. You'll be surprised to receive this letter. I admit that I thought long and hard before writing it. You will also be surprised to hear I've followed your somewhat erratic progress since you left Aurora. Twenty-two years old and already on to your second marriage. I hope that, unlike your first, this one is legal and you have stopped collecting counterfeit relatives. I have seen Mr Berryman of Berryman's Cereals on television advertisements; he looks a lot older than you … and honest. Let us hope he can keep you on the straight and narrow. Admittedly, you were young and foolish when you almost married Stefan Vincent, but that doesn't excuse the fact you lied when you altered the date on your birth certificate. If the registrar had bothered to look beyond all the make-up you were wearing, he'd have realized you were under-age. Stefan was, and still is, spineless. He eventually slunk home with his tail between his legs and, last I heard, he'd married a girl in Wellington. His father, Ivan, is causing havoc in the valley buying up smaller orchards to expand the family business. He's a fool if he thought I didn't know he had his eye on Aurora.*

*Before Grant passed away, he told me what really happened the night of your seventeenth birthday. I'd never been able to get to the bottom of things; Grant was too bitter to talk and Heather wasn't interested. Everybody assumed that you rebelled and ran away because your parents finally meted out some long-overdue discipline after the car crash. I now know that was wrong.*

*I've thought about you a lot since Grant's funeral. You were a very spoiled child, but you didn't deserve to be treated so unfairly and should have been included in Grant's will. Heather attended the funeral and the reading of the will and was surprised to be left out. (She was also nearly run out of town by the locals.) You always loved my antique diamond and emerald peacock brooch and matching bracelet by John Smith. He died young, and the pieces he designed are in great demand. After the funeral, I put the brooch and bracelet behind the panel in the wardrobe in the master bedroom at Aurora. Heather doesn't know I'm giving them to you, and won't until my will is read. If you want the jewellery, you'll have to go and get it. I placed it in the house because I'm too old to put up with the drama of having it thrown back in my face. You were always adept at getting what you wanted, April; I'm sure you'll think of a way to get the jewellery.*

*Ever since you left, there has been speculation in Pisa about your parentage. I don't know who started the rumours, but I thought you should know. Perhaps while you're there, you could shine a light on some misconceptions and redeem some reputations — including your own. Keeping secrets has a way of rebounding on the person who keeps them.*

*Yours sincerely,*
*Rosamund Dreyfuss*

April was irritated by Rosamund's parting shot about secrets. It was easy to preach about right and wrong when you were living out your twilight years in an expensive nursing home in Nelson; not so easy when you were fourteen and have caught your mother in bed with a hotel waiter on a shopping trip to Wellington, or seventeen and discovered her having sex in the orchard packing house. Sometimes telling the truth wasn't an option; sometimes it was easier to bend it — *especially* when your mother responded to teenage tears and half-baked threats to tell your father about the hotel waiter with some weird threats of her own. 'You're not going to tell anybody. You'll keep my secrets — and I'll keep yours.'

What secrets? At fourteen, April didn't understand. Staying out all night and sneaking in the bedroom window wasn't the same as cheating on your husband. April stopped accompanying Heather on her shopping trips and stayed with her father at Aurora. Grant liked having his daughter choose his company over her mother's.

Heather laughed scornfully and continued shopping, but April was aware that something fundamental had changed in her relationship with her mother. She was too young to understand that she'd failed an important test. So far as Heather was concerned, you were either on Team Heather or a member of the opposition — and April had chosen the wrong team. Three years later, Heather paid her back in the worst possible way.

A year after she had received Rosamund's letter, April's marriage to Ralph Berryman went the same way as her almost-marriage to Stefan Vincent. Ralph was thirty years older than April. She'd been nineteen when they married, and was honest enough to admit that Ralph's main attraction was that he represented safety and stability. She had told him she was alone, but wouldn't give details about why she was estranged from her parents.

For most of the four years of their marriage, April had loved Ralph; and for most of those four years, Ralph had seemed to love her. Or at least he had until April couldn't get pregnant. And then he'd bumped into his mother-in-law for the first time at a fundraiser and she'd tearfully dripped poison into his ear about why his wife was estranged from her parents, about her wildness and the sleepless nights she'd caused them when she'd stayed out drinking and sleeping around. Heather had touched Ralph's sleeve and said softly, *earnestly*, 'I'm *so* glad April has finally stopped abusing her body and found a good man.'

Ralph had been incandescent with rage. His lovely young wife was not only infertile — she was a slut, too.

This time the relationship didn't peter out because two spoilt, immature teenagers didn't know how to cope without their parents picking up the bills. This time April had run for her life. She'd been so desperate to get away from Ralph that she'd run away from their marriage empty-handed rather than negotiate a divorce settlement. She'd also learnt an important lesson: when it came to choosing men, she was a dud.

A set of traffic lights suddenly appeared in the middle of Aurora Street. April slammed on the brakes and got hit in the back of the head by a red pitchfork and a black police truncheon. Fortunately, the pitchfork and truncheon were only made of plastic and the red wig provided plenty of padding. Hayley, and the third occupant of the car, Susie, clutched their seat belts and fell backwards. Nine years ago, Pisa hadn't had traffic lights. April gazed at them in surprise through the fat red curls grazing her brows.

Susie snatched her policewoman's hat off the passenger-seat floor. 'I thought you said you knew your way around!'

April squinted at the lights. 'There weren't any traffic lights when I left.'

She should be wearing her glasses: without them she was as blind as a ninety-year-old granny. Unfortunately, she had accidentally sat on her handbag when they'd stopped for a snack in Queenstown and had broken one of the lenses. The glasses were three years old and the lenses were too weak, but they were the only pair April owned, and the last expensive thing she'd bought herself. Breaking the glasses upset her more than owing rent or owning a clapped-out Laser. Being kicked out of her flat and not having a car would only make her homeless and fitter, whereas breaking her glasses meant having to buy a cheap pair from a chain store and looking like Ozzy Osbourne. The lights changed. April put the Toyota in gear and continued down the street.

The Velcro tape holding the sides of Susie's skintight black mini-skirt together had separated. She yanked the skirt apart with a vicious *Zzzzippp!* and stuck the sides together again. 'How long ago?' she demanded sulkily.

'What?' April was busy cataloguing the changes in Pisa so that she didn't have to think about how she was going to slip away from Hayley and Susie and creep into the wardrobe in Aurora's master bedroom.

When she'd left, the only things open in Pisa on a Friday night had been the fish and chip shop and the pub, but now there were wine bars and cafés with tables and chairs spilling onto the pavement outside. April found it hard to believe that the people sitting at the tables enjoying the spring evening were locals. The way she remembered it, only people in the Ritchies' social circle drank wine and ate antipasto platters; everybody else went to the pub and visited the fish and chip shop when they wanted to eat out.

'How long is it since you were last here?' Susie persisted.

'A while,' April replied vaguely.

Hayley didn't always have all four paws on the mouse, but Susie was different. She was using the extra money she earned doing strip-o-grams to pay for her university tuition and books. Susie didn't like April. She thought April looked down on stripping and earned too many tips doing kiss-o-grams and waitressing at promotional events. She plonked her police hat on her knee and glared at April. Aurora's new owner wasn't the only person April had to worry about.

'If I didn't know better, I'd think you were trying to disguise yourself, April,' Susie said nastily.

'And if *I* didn't know better, I'd say you were being stupid, Susie,' April replied sweetly.

She was taking a big risk coming back — the kind of risk that brazen, self-centred seventeen-year-old April Ritchie had taken all the time. *That* April hadn't just thumbed her nose at the rules, she'd also raised her middle finger, safe in the knowledge that few people would complain about the behaviour of Grant and Heather Ritchie's pampered only child, or at least not to their faces.

April drove quickly past the wine bars and Pisa's most famous landmark: a giant sculpture of a pear, apricot, apple and cherry. On two separate occasions, some boys from the high school had managed overnight to build a replica of the leaning tower that'd made the other Pisa so famous, but both times it had fallen over. There was no sign of any building in progress or collapsing, so either Pisa's current youth lacked carpentry skills or the town cop, Roger Prescott, had routed them.

Hayley was enchanted by the fruit sculpture. 'Can we stop so I can take a photo? Cliff loves art!'

*Huh!* thought April. *The only kind of art Cliff appreciates is shaped like hearts, clubs, diamonds and spades, and found on a deck of cards.* 'No,' she said, as she stepped on the accelerator, 'we'll be late.' In the rear-view mirror she saw the corners of Hayley's mouth collapse. 'I promise we'll stop on the way home.'

'It'll be dark!'

'Use a flash.'

Pulling over to let Wonder Woman take photos of the sculpture was a sure-fire way of drawing attention to themselves. It'd be just April's luck that one of her old schoolteachers, or Roger Prescott, had developed a taste for pinot gris and was sitting outside one of the wine bars. She'd been bratty and disrespectful at school, and her teachers definitely held grudges against her.

As for Roger, he'd have worked out who was responsible for some patient files going missing from the hospital the night April left, so he would definitely be after her head. She'd heard that Emma Murfitt, the receptionist on duty that night, had lost her job. At the time April hadn't cared, but nine years on she knew what it was like to be broke, unskilled and in need of employment, and she felt bad about Emma.

If she had to, April could finesse her way out of a confrontation with Emma, her teachers, or even Roger — but not the man her lies had harmed the most. Tarn Elliott wasn't a local. His connection to Pisa had been through his parents, Carole and Murdoch Elliott, the housekeeper and orchard manager at Aurora. Nine years ago, Tarn had been a lieutenant in the New Zealand Army and on leave after returning from Timor. Remembering the look on Tarn's face when April had said it was him she'd seen Heather wrapped around, half-naked, could still make her break out in goose bumps. Murdoch was dead, Carole had left the area, and Tarn was probably a general now and knocking insurgents into shape somewhere in the world. But April would bet that he hadn't forgotten that night and the damage she'd done to his reputation.

# Chapter 2

*Birthdays are good for you. The more you have, the longer you live.*

ANON

## *Sweet Seventeen ...*

Carole Elliott slammed the breakfast tray onto the butcher's block in the centre of Aurora's vast kitchen. 'Madam sent it back. It was hard-boiled instead of soft the way she likes it.'

Tarn leaned against the big wooden dresser that almost filled one wall of the kitchen and cast an eye over the local paper, the *Pisa Press.* He was twenty-six years old and had just returned from Timor. Usually he avoided the Ritchies' imposing residence in favour of the modest three-bedroom house that came with his father's job, but this morning he'd been press-ganged by his mother into shifting furniture for the Ritchie kid's party. Carole insisted Tarn let her cook him breakfast and he gave in; his mother loved to cook, and she loved cooking for him and his father most of all. He flipped over a page and heard a dull thud from the hallway followed by the front door slamming.

'The princess has landed. Little brat.' Carole scraped the contents of the princess/little brat's breakfast into the scrap bucket for the chickens.

Grant's nickname for his daughter was 'Angel', but whenever

April's name was mentioned Carole hummed Elvis Presley's 'Looks Like An Angel', in particular the part about the angel being a devil in disguise. Heather and Grant were notoriously difficult employers, but they knew what they had in Carole and her husband. When April complained, they told Carole to stop humming Elvis, but she only switched to Linda Ronstadt's 'You're No Good' instead.

'I bet she has that car wrapped around a tree or lamppost before the week is out.'

Tarn detected a hopeful note in his mother's voice. Earlier on they'd observed Grant Ritchie buffing the chrome on a brand-new yellow convertible parked in the driveway and heard his daughter's shriek of excitement when she'd presumably spotted it from her bedroom window. Grant was a hard-nosed, inconsiderate bastard who paid other people to polish his vehicles, but Tarn figured the Honda 2000 deserved special attention because it was the equivalent of the princess/brat's magic coach.

Tarn thought back to when he'd first met April, six years ago. She'd been a precocious, demanding eleven-year-old with a deceptively waif-like appearance, and he was an officer cadet. His mother and father had just moved to Aurora, and he'd used his leave to come and visit them.

April stared at Tarn's uniform. 'You're a soldier?'

'In training.' Tarn was surprised the blue-green eyes and platinum hair didn't come with a Swedish accent.

'Cool. I got a new pair of camouflage jeans last week. I wanted a hat to go with them, but the lady in the shop said they didn't do them. I bet they have them in the army. Can you get me one?'

'No.'

April wrinkled her brow. It wasn't a word she heard very often. She stared at the scars on Tarn's cheeks. 'What happened to your face? Did somebody shoot you?'

'Don't be so rude!' Carole snapped.

Tarn was long past caring about his old acne scars, but still thought the Ritchie kid was a brat. 'Acne.'

'Acne?' Her eyes widened. 'I didn't think old people got zits.'

He almost smiled. Twenty had seemed old to him, too, when he was eleven.

Carole opened her mouth to shout, but Heather had one of her rare moments of maternal responsibility; plus, she liked the look of Tarn. 'April! Apologize to Tarn!'

April shrugged. 'Sorry.'

Since that first meeting, their paths had crossed about every two years, and Tarn had seen enough to know that April had matured physically but still seemed to be playing catch-up emotionally. She ignored him — he'd obviously been written off as a lost cause. Instead, to get what she wanted she batted her big eyes at Murdoch or her father, and later at an assortment of gangly, sullen-looking boys who still thought shaving was a novelty.

Murdo Elliott finished washing up in the utility room next door and came into the kitchen, drying his hands on a towel. He was upset at his wife's comment about April and the car. 'Don't say things like that, Carole. Imagine how you'd feel if April did have an accident.'

Carole jammed the lid on the scrap bucket and pulled two plates filled with sausage, bacon, eggs, tomatoes and mushrooms from the oven. She dumped the plates on the heavy wooden table in the centre of the room. 'Nothing bad ever happens to that one — she's Teflon-coated.'

Murdo sat down and reached for the salt shaker. 'April's not all bad. She loves working in the orchards. She qualified as a quality controller in the packing shed last season,' he told Tarn proudly.

Carole was jealous of any attention Murdo gave to another female. 'Stop putting so much salt on your food! You know what Dr Giles said about your blood pressure.'

Tarn took the chair opposite his father. 'What's wrong with your blood pressure?'

Murdo shook his head impatiently. 'Nothing.'

He looked at his mother, but she avoided his gaze and turned away to hang the dishcloth over the rail on the oven.

When he was young, Tarn had spent nights lying in bed listening to his mother accusing his father of having affairs with women working in the orchards. It was how he'd found out that his parents had had to get married because his mother was pregnant, and answered the question people often asked: why a man as handsome and kind as Murdoch Elliott had married a woman as plain and sour as Carole. She loved Murdo obsessively, and he was fond of her. So far as Tarn knew, his father never looked at another woman and denied Carole's accusations of infidelity. Their arguments always ended in the same way: she cried and begged Murdo not to leave her, and Murdo packed up his family and left for a job at another orchard.

The close relationship that Tarn had shared with his father when he was growing up changed when he joined the army. Murdo had wanted Tarn to follow him into the stone-fruit industry, but Tarn had set his heart on joining the infantry; he'd left for Officer Cadet School just before his parents moved to Aurora. Three months later, on leave from Waiouru, Tarn paid his first visit to the orchard. Whilst he appreciated the fairytale pink, white and green of the cherry orchard in springtime, he also appreciated the dangers posed by Heather Ritchie's 'come hither' looks. Aside from the fact she was married to the man who employed his parents, he wasn't interested in older women and kept his visits short.

Murdo usually fell silent or changed the subject when Carole got agitated about a woman, so Tarn was surprised when he defended April Ritchie. 'It would help if Grant took her interest in the orchard seriously instead of trying to marry her off to Stefan Vincent. She's only just turned seventeen.'

Tarn hadn't met the Vincents. The big orchard owners were a select bunch who socialized with each other, not their managers and their families, but he knew from his parents' conversations that Stefan Vincent would one day inherit Mount Pisa Cherries.

Carole snatched the salt shaker from her husband. 'They deserve each other. Stefan is a lazy, spoilt little brat, too.'

Murdo glowered at his wife. 'Give me the salt, Carole.'

'No. It's bad for you.'

His expression indicated salt wasn't the only thing that was bad for him.

'*Mum,*' Tarn murmured.

She turned troubled brown eyes on him.

He held out his hand. 'Give me the salt.'

Carole seemed surprised she was still holding it. She stared at the salt shaker and handed it over to Tarn. Murdo shoved his hands against the table, got to his feet and stalked from the room. Carole jumped up and made to follow him, but Tarn caught her wrist. 'Let him go.' She tried to twist free, but Tarn straddled his chair and stood. He set his hands on Carole's shoulders and she reluctantly subsided into Murdo's chair.

'I should go after him and apologize.'

'You'll only fight.'

She looked at the egg yolks congealing on Murdo's plate and said fretfully, 'His breakfast is getting cold.'

'Forget about it,' Tarn insisted brusquely. 'What's wrong?'

She twisted her fingers together in her lap. 'He's having an affair.'

Tarn didn't answer.

'He is! I'm not imagining it!'

'You don't seriously think he's having an affair with a seventeen-year-old girl?'

Carole drew back in shock. 'Not April! *Heather!*'

Tarn considered telling her that Heather Ritchie had a reputation for liking younger men and he was fairly sure the only Elliott she was sniffing around was him, but changed his mind. If his mother knew Heather had designs on either of the men in her life, she'd probably steal the princess's new convertible and run Heather over.

Shit. He'd take a tour of duty over a family argument any day.

April was puzzled how a woman as miserable as Carole Elliott had managed to snag a man as nice as Murdo. Heather laughed and said Murdo probably got Carole pregnant and had to marry her. Even their son stayed away. Carole said it was because he kept getting posted to international hot spots, but April bet Tarn Elliott asked to be sent abroad so he didn't have to spend too much time with his mother.

She showered and dressed in record time to get downstairs to her father and her new car. If she hadn't known that Grant would disapprove, she'd have run down in her skimpy PJs, but instead she left them and two wet towels on the bathroom floor. Halfway down the stairs she did an arabesque, landing with a thud in the middle of the antique rug before hurrying outside. Grant stood beside the convertible, dangling a set of keys. April flew down the steps and stood on tiptoe to throw her arms around his neck.

He set her on her feet and jingled the keys. 'Who's the best father in the world?'

'You are!'

They'd been arguing a lot lately, mainly about April's recent behaviour with her boyfriend, Stefan Vincent. The Vincents owned the second biggest orchard in Pisa. When Stefan's father, Ivan, and Grant had first talked about April marrying Stefan, she'd thought they were joking — but they were serious. It would unite the two most influential families in the valley, and would also mean that Grant could hand over the reins to Ivan, who was ten years younger than him. Grant hadn't been feeling well lately and had already handed over most of the day-to-day running of the orchard to Murdoch. He didn't know that Murdo was training April, and had dismissed her assertions that she could take over the business, rather than Ivan.

April resented being passed over because she was a girl. Sometimes it seemed like her father was stuck in a time warp. Stefan was nineteen, spoilt and an only child like her. He was constantly in trouble with his parents for staying out all night with his drinking buddies. April had hit back at her father's high-handedness by hooking up with Stefan — after all, it was what he wanted — and staying out all night and losing her virginity in his car.

Grant had yelled and grounded her, but April had climbed out her bedroom window and stayed out even longer. So Grant had been forced to resort to Plan B — there was always a Plan B — and bribe her into submission instead with the yellow convertible. When it came to April, Grant's anger was always short-lived; he liked to think she was a chip off the old block and got her rebellious streak from him.

Even so, April knew the car came with conditions. She reached for the keys, but Grant raised his arm so they were out of reach. 'Tell me again.'

'You're the best father in the world.'

He relinquished the keys. 'And don't you forget it.'

April focused on the car instead of his words. She wished the convertible wasn't yellow, but was confident she could talk her father into a paint job.

Heather Ritchie drifted out of the house, trailing perfume and trouble. At forty-two she was blonder, more toned and even more dangerous than she'd been at twenty-five. She admitted to being thirty-seven and relished the shock on people's faces when she told them she had a sixteen-year-old daughter. 'You can't be April's mother! You look too young!' Heather smiled and thanked the women and looked through her lashes at the men and murmured, 'I feel young, too.' Flirting came to her as naturally as blinking. April had been the same until she grew old enough to understand the subtext of her mother's body language.

Grant, however, was fifty-seven years old and hunched and bald. He reminded Heather of a tortoise without its shell. He'd never been handsome, but his refusal to wear a hat or sun block had left him prematurely wrinkled. He looked more like April's grandfather than her father. Heather's lips curved in a tiny smile of satisfaction as she watched April flit about the car, firing questions at Grant. She'd definitely done the right thing by bringing this one home from the hospital. Grant's belief that he was responsible for April's blonde prettiness amused Heather. April's only physical flaw was her short-sightedness. It was the reason her eyes sometimes appeared cloudy and vague. Heather hated seeing April wearing glasses, but April couldn't tolerate contact lenses. She'd hidden April's glasses when she was small and told her, 'Don't hide your eyes behind those ugly things.'

'But, Mummy, I can't see the board at school.'

'Then sit at the front of the class,' Heather had retorted.

April had until she'd realized that only nerds and kids with problems sat at the front, then she'd gradually drifted to the back of the room where the cool kids and troublemakers sat. Her grades had suffered, but she was smart enough to always move up the following year.

Whilst Grant didn't want his daughter to pursue a career, he didn't want her to be dumb either. He'd bribed April to do better at school with promises of jet skis, music centres and holidays abroad, while Heather had murmured in her ear that getting a good report wasn't nearly as important as marrying the right man. Pisa High School was the place where April had held court and socialized with her friends. She'd ignored her teachers and read novels under the desk, prompting one teacher to write in her school report: 'If April paid as much attention to reading school texts as she does to reading novels, she would be a star.' Grant had used his position as chairman of the board of trustees to make life so uncomfortable for that teacher that she'd resigned.

Grant showed April how to lower the roof on the Honda.

Heather wandered across to the driver's door and looked in

at April. 'You're not going to school on your birthday, are you?' she asked. 'Stay home and we'll drive into Queenstown and go shopping. You said you wanted to get your hair beaded for your party.'

Grant frowned at his wife over April's head as the roof folded neatly away. 'Of course she's going to school.'

Heather rolled her eyes. 'Oh for God's sakes, Grant, let her have the day off. Nobody but us will know.' *Or at least, nobody who matters.*

Besides being the chairman of the school's board of trustees, Grant was also the president of the business round table. He had a lot of influence in the community. Heather watched his grizzled brows draw together, and marvelled yet again that he could grow eyebrows like tumbleweeds and have a scalp like a pink bowling ball.

'She's going to school,' Grant insisted.

April tuned her parents' bickering out and put a Nelly Furtado disk in the CD player. Her plans didn't include going to school *or* shopping with her mother. She drove away with 'Hot In Here' blasting from the speakers. Grant failed to notice that April didn't have the black canvas tote she usually took to school. And Heather didn't care. Her mind had already turned to far more interesting subjects, like what she was going to wear to the party, and how enticing Tarn Elliott had looked in his camouflage gear when he'd arrived the day before. He was lean and fit, with ridiculously short, light brown hair and distant brown eyes. There was a lot going on behind that quiet gaze. The scars on his face and his elusiveness only added to his appeal.

Whenever Heather Ritchie looked at him, Tarn imagined a female praying mantis just before it mated and bit the male's head off. He'd rather do back-to-back Battle Fitness tests than be somewhere dark and secluded with Mrs Ritchie.

On the last two occasions Tarn had visited his parents, he'd set tongues wagging by taking Emma Murfitt to dinner and the movies in Queenstown. He was unaware that Mrs Murfitt had panicked at the thought of Emma marrying a soldier and having to set up house in an international hot spot, while Emma entertained romantic thoughts about the quiet, dark-eyed lieutenant.

Tarn was driving into town to take Emma to lunch, and congratulating himself on getting in and out of the big house without Heather grabbing hold of his leg and humping it like a dog, when he saw April's brand-new convertible coming towards him on the wrong side of Ritchie Road. He spun the wheel of Murdo's truck to avoid the Honda and left twin trails of black rubber on the tarmac behind him as he hit the brakes. The Honda wasn't so lucky: it veered across the road and slammed into a tree. Tarn jumped from the truck and ran across the road.

Shakira's 'Whenever, Whatever' blared from the sound system. There were four teenagers inside the car; two boys and two girls. One of the girls was Emma's younger sister, Courtney, and the other was April Ritchie. She wasn't the driver. A pimply-faced youth, with gelled hair and wearing a *South Park* T-shirt, was in the driver's seat. He yelled when Tarn appeared at the window. April and Courtney screamed, too. Tarn figured they were OK and turned his attention to the boy sitting beside Courtney in the back seat; he was staring straight ahead.

'Are you OK?' he shouted over the music. 'Can you speak?'

The boy opened his mouth and mouthed '*Fuck …*'

Tarn reached over and switched off Shakira.

Courtney cradled her wrist and burst into tears. 'My … my wrist hurts!'

April turned quickly to look at her friend, gasped and grabbed the back of her neck.

'Stay still!' Tarn barked. 'You've probably got whiplash.'

She cradled her neck. 'Muppy?' she called. 'Are you OK?'

Courtney sniffled. 'I think my wrist is broken.'

April glared at the driver from the corner of her eye. '*Stefan, you idiot!*'

'It was an accident,' he said sullenly. 'Nobody died.'

'So that makes it alright?' Tarn pulled his cellphone from his pocket.

'Who are you calling?' April asked warily.

She'd had her hair plaited and beaded since he'd seen her that morning. School obviously hadn't been on the agenda today. 'An ambulance, and the police.'

'Don't!'

Tarn gave her a look.

April swallowed — she was in *big* trouble. 'At least, not the police,' she pleaded. It was bad enough that her new car was wrecked only hours after she'd got it, but her father would go ballistic if he found out she'd let Stefan drive it. She'd told him not to play chicken, but Stefan had ignored her and done it anyway. Tarn's contemptuous expression made April want to slide down in the seat, but her neck hurt too much.

Tarn finished the call and slipped his cellphone into his jeans. He gripped the top of the door and glared at the pimply youth in the driver's seat who he guessed must be Stefan Vincent. The kid drew back in alarm. 'You were driving on the wrong side of the road, you stupid little prick. You're lucky nobody was killed.'

'You mustn't tell my parents I was driving! Or April's father!' Stefan looked at April and fumbled with his seat belt. 'Swap seats with me: you've got to say you were driving. I've already got demerit points — this time I'll lose my licence,' he said urgently.

Tarn shoved him back in the seat. 'Stay where you are.' He signalled to the others. 'None of you move until the ambulance and cops get here.'

He let go of Stefan and went to check on Courtney's wrist. She leaned against his chest sobbing while he made a sling out of her headscarf. 'My mother is going to kill me …'

Tarn was fond of Emma's little sister. 'Probably — after she's spent a few days fussing over you.'

When the sound of sirens drew near, April tried one last time to get Tarn to change his mind. '*Please,* Tarn.'

He didn't even bother to look at her. 'Save it for the cops.'

'I'll give you five thousand dollars if you'll say April or Kyle was driving,' Stefan said quickly.

Kyle made a sound of protest. April squirmed.

Tarn itched to do some damage to the Vincent kid's spotty face. 'Tell you what,' he replied thoughtfully, 'I'll take your five thousand dollars …'

April and Courtney gasped. Stefan looked relieved.

'… and donate it to charity. Now shut up.'

Courtney's wrist was sprained, April had whiplash, and Stefan and Kyle got off with a few bruises.

April had never seen her father so angry. She suspected he would have hit her if Dr Giles hadn't made her wear a soft collar because of the whiplash, and if she hadn't made a swift exit from the study.

As sunset approached, she wandered around the orchard feeling hard done by, eventually settling down in the gooseberry bushes near the packing house. She hated Tarn Elliott for being so pig-headed and perfect, but hated herself even more for being stupid enough to let Stefan drive. He was reckless and irresponsible. Courtney was her best friend; but Stefan understood her better because his home life was just as messed up as hers.

The white foam collar supporting her neck felt hot and itchy. She took it off and dropped it on the ground. Tarn ran past her hiding place. April watched him cut through the orchards and jog up the hill behind the main house. She'd seen him do it before. The view on the hill was spectacular in autumn, when the leaves on the trees were gold, orange, pink and red. April shredded pieces of grass and continued to sulk in the bushes as Murdo drove past in his truck and disappeared up the road towards Pisa.

She was puzzled when her mother strolled by and went inside the packing house. Heather wasn't interested in the orchards and never went near the packing house. April was considering following her mother to see what she was doing when Murdo reappeared on foot and slipped inside the packing house.

She sat up and stared at the green corrugated-iron building. Not Murdo and her mother! Murdo was decent and nice. He took her interest in the orchard seriously. They needed Murdo. Grant had lost interest; without Murdo, Aurora would be in trouble.

April got to her feet and brushed off the seat of her jeans. Tarn jogged past on his way back to Carole and Murdo's house. She waited until he was gone before slowly crossing the driveway to the packing house. She rested her hand against the office door. It still felt warm from the sun. Maybe she was wrong; maybe there was a reason why her mother and Murdo were meeting. Maybe they needed to talk about something. Maybe …

The door opened soundlessly. April crept through the office and into the main building. Heather was sitting on one of the tables used to sort the cherries with her head thrown back. She was naked from the waist up and her skirt was bunched around her thighs. Murdo stood between her legs with his face buried in her breasts.

April sucked in a breath and they looked up. Murdo's face went slack with shock.

Heather rearranged her skirt and reached for her bra on the table beside her. 'You really are a pest at times, April.'

'April! Are you in there? Why aren't you wearing this collar?'

They froze at the sound of Grant's voice outside. April remembered the foam collar she'd dropped beside the driveway, and clapped a hand over her mouth.

Heather smiled. She pushed Murdo away and slid the straps of her bra up her arms. She looked remarkably calm for a woman about to be caught in the act by her husband. It was April who told Murdo to get a move on. He ran to the other side of the building and out the side door as Grant stormed in clutching the white collar. Grant wasn't expecting to see his wife. He stumbled and crashed into a stack of buckets used by the pickers. They toppled over and bounced hollowly around his feet on the concrete floor.

Heather sat on the table watching him, and slowly eased her white camisole over her bra. April saw that she was smiling. She hugged herself.

Grant's mouth worked. He crushed the collar in his hand. '*Who were you in here with?*'

Heather jumped lightly off the table. 'April.'

'You're lying!' He turned to April. His face was white except for a red patch on each cheek, and his eyes looked glassy. April was terrified. He looked like he was going to die. 'Tell me who it was, April!'

April rubbed her sore neck. She was used to her parents fighting, but never like this. Her gaze slid to her mother. Heather watched her intently, daring her to answer, warning her not to.

Grant bared his teeth. 'Don't look at her! *I'm* the one you have to worry about. You're already in enough trouble, girl — don't buy yourself more! Tell me the truth. Was it one of the workers?'

She tried to shake her head, but her neck was too sore. Her mother liked younger men, but the male workers were mere boys. Heather liked masculine men who were a challenge — men like Tarn Elliott. The thought popped unbidden into her head as Grant advanced on her. April backed into another stack of buckets and almost fell. She couldn't tell the truth: Murdo was only a few years younger than Grant, and he wasn't well either; they might hurt one another.

'Tarn,' April whispered. 'It was Tarn.'

Tarn had just got out of the shower after his run when Grant stormed into Carole and Murdo's house. To Grant, it looked like Tarn was washing off the evidence of his tryst with Heather. He would have dragged April into the bathroom if she hadn't fought him and Carole hadn't screamed for her son.

Tarn arrived in the hallway with his jeans half-zipped and water dripping into his eyes to find a white-faced, collarless April clutching her neck and trying to twist out of her father's hold while Carole clung determinedly to his other arm. Tarn plucked his mother away and caught Grant's arm and twisted it behind his back. 'Let her go!' Tarn was used to giving orders. His voice cracked like a whip.

The older man was incensed. He tried to resist. 'Let go of me, you bastard!'

Tarn applied pressure to his arm and Grant dropped April's wrist.

She backed away and pressed against the wall. Next to Tarn's fit, brown body, Grant looked like a dry, brittle twig. 'Please don't hurt him!' she whispered. 'He isn't well!'

Grant didn't appreciate having his physical weakness pointed out. The look he gave April made her cower.

'If he keeps his hands to himself, I won't have to.' Tarn released Grant.

He staggered upright, gasping. '*Keep my hands to myself*? Tell him!' His hand shook as he pointed at his daughter. 'Tell him what you saw!'

April cupped her neck and stared at the carpet. Why hadn't she said it was one of the guys Murdo hired to clean up around the orchard? They were young backpackers and only here for a few weeks — the ramifications would be far less serious. Her voice shook. 'Tarn ... and ... Mum.'

'*Where?*' Grant rasped.

'In the packing house.' She peeped at Tarn through her lashes, and recoiled when his eyes whipped towards her and she saw his response — shock, fury and, worst of all, *contempt*. April dropped her eyes. He probably thought she was paying him back for telling the truth about who was driving her car.

Carole finally found her voice. 'That's rubbish!'

'Ritchie,' Tarn said coldly, 'I'd rather put my dick in a swarm of bees than in your wife.'

April's eyes widened. Grant spluttered.

Then Murdo walked in, carrying a container of milk and a newspaper. April was both relieved and scared at his arrival: Murdo would tell the truth, which would get Tarn off the hook but expose her lie. But, given a choice, April would rather be in Grant's bad books than Heather's.

Murdo stood in the doorway. 'Hello, Grant.' Then he saw Grant's face. 'Something wrong?'

Grant found his voice. 'Your son has been fooling around with *my* wife!'

'What!' April had to admit that Murdo was very good at pretending to be shocked.

'April *saw* them!'

April's eyes slid to Murdo. 'I … think.'

Grant whipped around. 'What do you mean, *you think?*'

She silently begged Murdo to speak up. But he didn't. He said he'd been to Pisa to get milk for Carole, and let Tarn take the blame.

Grant looked old and ill. April was changing her story, and Tarn had made him look like a fool. He pointed at the younger man. 'Don't ever show your face around here again.'

Tarn ignored him. He walked away, and somehow managed to have the last word.

Carole had been uncharacteristically silent, but suddenly spoke up. 'If Tarn isn't welcome at Aurora, then neither are we.' She stared at Murdo. 'Are we, Murdo?'

He didn't answer.

Grant didn't understand how Tarn Elliott had got the upper hand. He hadn't considered the possibility he might lose his manager and housekeeper if he kicked their son off the property, but he couldn't back down without looking an even bigger fool than he did already.

'There's plenty more where you came from.' He grabbed his daughter and went to find his wife.

Heather didn't seem to care that she'd lost her housekeeper, which should have alerted April that she'd been planning to leave. Her mother liked her home to run smoothly with the minimum of input from her. If she'd been staying, she would have been furious to lose Carole; instead, she merely shrugged. Finding out that Tarn Elliott had said he'd rather have sex with a swarm of bees than her had sent Heather into orbit, which was the reason Grant told her. Heather retaliated by dropping the bombshell she'd been concealing for seventeen years.

'If you don't believe it's true, ask Dr Giles. He knew April wasn't yours when she hurt her leg when she was nine and needed a transfusion. We're both blood group A; April's group B.' Heather smiled mockingly. 'Her real surname is Gutsell.'

April stood like a statue. 'That isn't funny, Mum.' She appealed to her father, 'Tell her it isn't funny!'

He called Dr Giles instead. The doctor wanted to talk to him in person, but Grant refused. When he hung up, he seemed dazed. April was curled up in the burgundy wing chair beside the fireplace, shaking.

Grant gripped the edge of the desk. 'Where's ... what about ...?'

Heather was enjoying herself. 'The other one? She wasn't yours either — too dark and foreign-looking. That's why I brought April home.' She studied April's white face. 'I did warn you, April.'

Grant stared at April accusingly. 'You knew about this?'

She looked dazed. 'She must be lying. It's … it's illegal to … steal babies.'

Heather wasn't worried about Grant reporting her to the police. He wouldn't want the scandal. An unfaithful wife was an embarrassment, but a criminal one was a calamity.

She shrugged when he told her to get out. 'I left years ago.' She felt better now that she'd found a way to vent her fury at Tarn Elliott, and delivered a parting shot as she left the study: 'You'd better remember that Aurora is half mine when it comes to arranging the divorce settlement.'

Grant slumped into the big leather chair behind the desk and stared at nothing. His wife and daughter had made him look a fool — only April wasn't his daughter. It made him feel better, less of a failure. She wasn't his. She was nothing to him.

'Daddy?' April whispered.

He lifted his head. 'You're a liar, too,' he said tonelessly. 'Get out. You don't belong here.'

Stefan picked up April at the bottom of the driveway and distracted Emma Murfitt while April snuck into the room where the hospital records were kept and stole her and Nola Gutsell's files. He was in trouble with the police and his parents, and wanted to run away and get married. Stefan didn't really believe April wasn't a Ritchie. He wanted to assert his independence without actually having to take responsibility for his actions; in other words, have his cake and eat it. His father wanted him to marry April. *He* wanted to marry April. If they stayed away long enough to make his parents understand they couldn't boss him around, and long enough for Grant to realize that Heather was talking bullshit, Stefan felt certain he and April could return to Pisa and have a great life. Marrying April would put him in his father's good books.

April was numb. Finding out there really was a file for somebody named Gutsell had dashed her hope that Heather had been lying.

'But it won't be legal if we get married,' she said woodenly. 'I'm not eighteen.'

Stefan draped an arm around her shoulders as they sped out of Pisa in his car. 'Don't worry about that; I know some people who can fix your birth certificate. We'll do it again next year when you are.'

# Chapter 3

*If a woman tells you her real age, she'll tell you anything. Don't trust her.*

Anon

April headed the Toyota out of town. 'It gets dark quickly this far south. I want to make sure we get to the house before the light goes.'

As April turned off the main highway and headed across the valley into the gathering night, Hayley peered at the dark outline of the mountain range that gave the town its name, and at the trees planted either side of the road protecting the orchards. If it had been daytime, Hayley would have seen that the road they'd just turned into was Ritchie's Road and the signpost below pointed the way to Aurora Valley. 'It's just as well you came, April. I would never have found it.'

'Yes, it was really nice of you to give up your day off when you're not even getting paid,' Susie said sarcastically.

April ignored her. The last time she had driven this road she'd been behind the wheel of her brand-new Honda 2000 convertible. She turned left into a wide driveway with curved, wooden gates bordered by shelter-belts of tall poplars.

She regretted it wasn't a month later when the cherry trees would be in blossom. Hayley loved pretty things, and there were few things prettier than a cherry orchard in springtime.

The Toyota bumped over first one pothole and then another. April frowned — the drive had never had potholes when she'd lived at Aurora. As she drove on, the drive rose gently and curved to the left to reveal the white two-storey Georgian-style house built by Rosamund's grandfather. The upstairs windows each had six panes; the ones on the main floor, twelve. A portico supported by paired Ionic white columns protected the centred, single-leaf, black wooden door with its ornate fanlight. Three deep steps led up to it from the gravelled driveway. There were two chimneys and, inside, seven fireplaces. On the eastern side, hidden in the darkness, was another larger portico, supported by four more columns, which shaded an outdoor seating area. Heather had never cared for the house, but Grant had loved it. So did April.

She stopped the car a short distance away and drank it in. A lump rose in her throat, and her eyes stung as she was bombarded with memories.

Light spilled from the downstairs windows and sudden bursts of male laughter could be heard. Cars, trucks and SUVs were parked next to the trees edging the driveway. Beneath her Wonder Woman wig, Hayley's eyes were the size of a juggernaut's wheels. 'Wow …' she breathed.

Even Susie was impressed. 'Bloody hell! This place is a mansion!'

The front door opened and a man wearing jeans and a bulky sweater emerged. He walked to the top of the first step and peered at the Toyota. 'Are you the strippers?' he bellowed.

Hayley wound down the window. 'We're from Wild Women Do,' she called.

April parked the car in front of the house. The man descended the steps as the women got out.

'I'm Sled.' He had close-set eyes, a receding hairline, and big muscles which could be put to good use helping them carry their things inside. 'Why are there three of you? The bet I won off Cliff was for two strippers.'

Hayley bridled at the mention of the bet.

April smiled and waggled her fingers. 'We've got a special offer of a free kiss-o-gram this month.'

Hayley hissed like a goose.

Sled took in April's red rubber dress, spiked heels and fishnet stockings. The dress looked as if it had been sprayed on. April was small but curvy. The dress clung lovingly to her waist and hips, and the tab of the silver zipper nestled in the valley created by her Wonderbra. His face fell. 'You're not a stripper?'

'No,' Susie said acidly. 'She's the apprentice.'

She was sick of being upstaged by April — *who didn't even take her clothes off*. Men were such dicks. April looked fragile, but she was tough as old boot leather and smart. If she had an Achilles heel, it was her friend Latoya, WWD's receptionist. Latoya was the same age as April but her opposite in looks and personality. She was tall, skinny, dark and sweet, and had epilepsy which was well controlled unless she forgot to take her medication or was tired or stressed.

April was very protective of her. Once Susie saw her whack a guy on the back of the head with her serving tray for groping Latoya when she was filling in for a sick waitress. The guy dropped like a stone and believed April when she told him she'd tripped and accidentally hit him in the head with the tray. Susie was convinced April's angel costume and blonde hair were the reasons she got away with so much bullshit. She hoped April's luck changed when she was dressed as a devil.

From inside the drawing room, Tarn Elliott heard Sled yell a welcome to the strippers he'd organized for Tarn's supposed thirty-fifth birthday. Sled had got his former OC's age right, but not the date of his birthday, which was in May, not September.

'Is that right?' Sled had said. 'Aw well, we're only a couple of months late.'

Staff Sergeant Frank Jepson prised the caps off four beers. 'Or eight months too early for his thirty-sixth.'

Twenty members of the New Zealand Infantry were gathered in Aurora's shabby drawing room to celebrate Major Tarn Elliott's non-birthday. There was a mix of soldiers and officers, mostly from Bravo Company, but some from Alpha and Charlie companies as well. The high turnout demonstrated the respect they all had for Tarn, who'd retired from the army six months earlier, following a tour of duty in Afghanistan. It was also their way of acknowledging the three men from Bravo Company who had died or been injured in the final week of the tour.

Wylie, aka 'Coyote', slid a hand between the antique lace curtains covering one of the drawing-room windows to get a better look at the evening's entertainment. 'There's three of them, sir.'

'Stop calling me "sir", Wylie,' Tarn said. 'I'm not your OC anymore.'

The young lance corporal disagreed. The quiet, dark-eyed man sitting in a burgundy wing chair on the other side of the room nursing a Scotch would always be his OC. Even out of uniform, the major still looked like the major.

Wylie peered at the strippers in growing surprise. 'They're really nice, sir.'

Tarn grimaced.

Sled was responsible for organizing the evening's entertainment. The downstairs powder room had been set aside as a changing room for the strippers and was out of bounds to the men. When it came to choosing women, Sled's track record wasn't great. He'd earned his nickname because he was pulled by dogs, so nobody expected the girls to be attractive. They'd felt even more dubious when Sled revealed he'd won them in a poker game.

Frank joined Wylie at the window. 'They can't be.' He stuck his shaven head through the gap in the curtains. 'Shit! They are!' He ducked back under the curtain and looked at Tarn. 'Wonder Woman, a cop, and I think the little one's a devil.'

'Great,' Tarn responded evenly. 'If the devil gives any trouble, the cop and the superhero can sort things out.'

He knew that his 'birthday party' was just an excuse for the men to get together. They were all still trying to get over what had happened on the tour in Afghanistan. What had started out as a routine patrol had ended with two men dead, and Warrant Officer Aaron Kinsella getting the bottom of his leg blown off by a land mine.

The dead soldiers were flown home and given military funerals; Tarn still kept in touch with their families. Aaron was patched up, and given a prosthetic limb and rehab to learn how to walk again. The patrol survivors were given counselling, but the best 'therapy' was being together and getting on with their work. Healing came from not having to explain why certain jokes or situations left a sour taste in their mouths, or why they laughed at things civilians found objectionable.

Frank came to sit beside Tarn. 'Have you seen Aaron lately, Boss?'

Tarn poured two fingers of whisky into a glass and handed it to him. Like him, Frank shared an appreciation of a fine single-malt whisky. 'I visited him last week; spoke to him yesterday. You?'

Frank rolled the whisky on his tongue. 'Called last week, but nobody could find him. I've arranged to meet him for a drink when I leave here, that way he can't avoid me.'

Aaron was avoiding calls and visits from the Bravo lads. When they did manage to track him down, he was his usual insouciant self. Their former warrant officer's mental toughness was what had saved him when he was first injured, and his high level of fitness had speeded his recovery and got him walking again. But they all knew that Aaron wasn't OK — he just pretended to be.

Frank shook his head. 'I don't get how he manages to keep disappearing, Boss. He's only got one leg.'

'One and a half,' Tarn corrected. 'And for crissakes, call me Tarn.'

'OK, one and a half. It's not like he can run away, *Tarn*.'

'Last time I spoke to him, he said he'd ordered one of those prosthetic blades that runners use.'

Frank choked on the Scotch.

Away from work, Aaron had had the busiest and most colourful private life of any member of Bravo. For this reason, Tarn hadn't shared the startling news that Aaron had a wife tucked away at home. The self-contained, pleasant-looking young woman Tarn had met on one of his visits to Aaron was nothing like the high-maintenance, exotic creatures Aaron favoured. His love life had always been complicated, so Tarn was intrigued but not surprised when Aaron brushed aside his matrimonial status by saying, 'It's more of a business arrangement.'

Frank gestured with his glass to the window seat where Private Lincoln 'Missing' Dwyer was applying himself to the task of getting drunk. Dwyer had already bent Tarn's ear about his suspicions that his girlfriend was sleeping around while he was away. 'Did Missing tell you about his girlfriend?'

'Yes, and the great deal Sled got him on the engagement ring he never got round to giving her.'

Sled's ability to acquire things cheaply or for free had caused Tarn a few problems over the years, which explained why he was dubious about letting Sled arrange some strippers.

Despite the fact he wasn't married, Tarn had done his fair share of relationship counselling over the years. It was part and parcel of being the company OC. The men brought their problems to him. Like Wylie, Linc couldn't get his head around the fact that Tarn was no longer in charge. He was worried that his girlfriend had been sleeping around while he'd been away. When Linc wouldn't shut up about her, Sled and Wylie had sent him to Tarn. He could have done without that vote of confidence. Aaron usually dealt with any girlfriend problems — 'Get another one' — leaving Tarn with the tricky stuff: problems with wives. When he'd half-heartedly pointed this out, Wylie had shrugged and replied, 'Aaron's not here.'

'What makes you think she's playing up?' Tarn asked Dwyer.

'I didn't let her know I was coming home, sir. Knocked on the front door, went round the back, and the toilet seat was up.'

A raised toilet seat was a red flag to an absentee soldier.

Wylie nodded emphatically. 'She's screwing around on you.' And Sled threw in his ten cents' worth: 'A couple of beers and that one is anybody's unit.'

Tarn reflected that it was little wonder Sled had never risen above the rank of sergeant.

'Never mind,' Sled continued, 'there's plenty more where she came from.'

'Why don't you go and help Frank with the kegs?' Tarn suggested before Linc forgot Sled was a higher rank, and punched him.

Sled and Wylie took the hint and disappeared.

Linc sat down and explained to Tarn that he'd been planning to dump his girlfriend anyway. Tarn listened patiently. He had heard it all before: young, horny soldiers parted from girlfriends they'd known a month before they were posted abroad. When they got home they had only one thing on their minds: dumping their kit and diving into bed.

'Are you sure you're not just upset she dumped you first?' he asked.

'I guess so. Maybe,' Linc admitted.

'Oy! Missing!' Sled called. 'Keg's open! Those who can't smell or navigate to the watering hole don't drink!'

Linc excused himself and hurried to the kitchen.

Tarn reflected on how things were much simpler when you were twenty. That was how old he had been when he joined the army. He had served in Bosnia, Timor and the Solomon Islands, and had had UN postings to Africa and the Middle East. He'd seen men injured and killed; he knew the risks of the job and accepted them. He had considered himself a career soldier, but even before the deaths of his men and Aaron's injury he had started to wonder if he wanted to spend the rest of his life in the army. He was over watching good men get injured. Sometimes death was cleaner and better for all concerned. He'd had enough of the field, and of cleaning up after damaged people in damaged countries.

Even so, buying the Ritchies' historically listed house and cherry orchard in Central Otago three months ago had been madness. He'd then topped things off by purchasing a helicopter: a second-hand Robinson 44 was now in a hangar behind the house. Flying choppers was one of Tarn's few hobbies. His justification for buying one was that they were used to combat rain and frost, and so he could earn extra money hiring out his services.

He couldn't really afford the Robinson. The house needed work, and the orchard was neglected. He knew nothing about restoring historical houses, and not a lot more about looking after cherry trees. His father had been the orchardist. Buying the orchard and the helicopter were reckless acts for a man not known for impulsive, self-indulgent behaviour. Tarn figured he was having his mid-life crisis a decade early. He'd bought Aurora because his father had loved it, his mother needed a home, and he needed somewhere quiet where the spring thaw didn't wash land mines down from the mountains, and the only things 'sown' were seeds, not butterfly mines thrown from helicopters.

Right now, he didn't much care if the house fell down and not a single cherry grew, but he was also aware that if he didn't change his attitude his mother would be homeless, he'd be broke, and the only winners would be the bank and Ivan Vincent, who'd swoop down and buy the place for a song. So far, Tarn's dealings with Vincent had been brief, but enough for him to know that the man was just like Grant Ritchie — a pompous, opinionated pain in the arse. Vincent had wanted to buy Aurora when Grant died, and hadn't been pleased when he'd found out that Rosamund Dreyfuss had beaten him to it.

Rosamund was too old to manage the place herself, and scathing about the efforts of the managers she'd employed to do it for her. She was also adamant she didn't want the Vincents to get their hands on Aurora. When Tarn had called her, she'd let him have the place for a good price provided she retained a share. After the way the Ritchies had treated his parents, Tarn felt a measure of satisfaction in acquiring Aurora, even if it did mean sharing ownership with the bank and Rosamund, and having to put up with her interference. She might be an impatient, autocratic old bitch, but she was an invaluable source of information on the best way to run a cherry orchard. It was Rosamund who had told Tarn he needed to offer a service grading and packing the crops of other orchards to help offset the reduced crop Aurora would produce this season.

'Ivan Vincent does the grading and packing for the whole valley and makes everybody pay through the nose for it. It was different before Grant died: Aurora offered the same service and kept the Vincents honest — or as close to it as they're ever going to get,' Rosamund had said contemptuously. 'Offer a lower price and the other growers will come — but you'll need to find a quality controller to oversee the packers, grade the fruit, and do the export paperwork for the auditor.'

So far, Tarn hadn't been able to find a quality controller; everybody he approached had said no. He had a feeling Ivan Vincent had something to do with that. The petty fights and snobbishness of the Vincents and the Ritchies irritated him. *Civilians* irritated him — throwing tantrums about the price of petrol or the supermarket running out of their favourite brand of bread. He'd worked in places where the only food was what the aid agencies managed to ship in, and petrol was available only on the black market.

Unlike his mother, Tarn had put behind him the damage done by April Ritchie's lie. He'd eventually worked out who had been in the packing house with Heather, and the realization that his father had let him take the blame for his own sordid affair did irreparable harm to their relationship. It would have helped if Murdo had admitted what he'd done, and not waited until a couple of months before he died from prostate cancer to tell the truth and apologize. By then it was too late to put things right between them. Tarn felt betrayed and disappointed with his father, and guilty because he hadn't believed his mother when she'd said Murdo was having an affair with Heather.

Since his return to Aurora, Tarn had thought a lot about that night, and his father, and April Ritchie. He doubted she had any idea of the damage her lie had done to his relationship with his parents, and was convinced she'd been motivated by spite because he'd refused to lie about who was driving when her car crashed. He knew that Grant's fury at Heather had overflowed to his daughter: Grant had finally meted out some long-overdue discipline.

Tarn also knew that April had run away with Stefan Vincent, and that, for some strange reason, on their way out of town they'd stopped at the district hospital. He'd heard how Stefan had struck up a conversation with Emma Murfitt on the reception desk while April had used the toilet, and that later Emma had realized some files had been stolen. She hadn't been able to prove April was the culprit and so had lost her job because she was responsible for the medical records.

It was a strange act of defiance. For a while April and Stefan became Pisa's equivalent of Bonnie and Clyde — they'd followed up the medical-record heist by getting married illegally — until being cut off from his parents' bank account had doused the flames of Stefan's rebellion and he'd crept home. April was either made of sterner stuff, or too scared to front up to Roger Prescott. Nobody had heard anything about her until she'd made the six o'clock news a few years later for marrying and divorcing a millionaire more than twice her age. There hadn't been a scandal to equal it in Pisa since. And ridiculous rumours continued to abound, including one that April wasn't really Grant and Heather's daughter.

Tarn had better things to do with his time than speculate about the whereabouts and motivations of the spoiled princess of a rural town. Nine years earlier, he and his parents had been powerless against the Ritchies. Nine years earlier, Heather and Grant, and to a lesser extent April, had ruled the town.

Things had changed since then.

Sled wasn't sure how the major would feel about a naked woman ripping off his shirt and rubbing herself against his chest while a bunch of liquored-up, heckling soldiers looked on. Tarn wasn't a prude, but he wasn't 'one of the boys' either, and didn't mince his words when he was pissed off.

Frank snorted. 'Don't be an idiot. He'll cope fine.'

'If it makes you feel better, she can body-glide me,' Wylie offered.

Sled thought the kiss-o-gram girl was a welcome bonus. She could test the waters. He turned to the girl in the red wig and rubber dress. She had the pale complexion of a natural blonde and looked tense. Sled was a sucker for blue-eyed blondes with small waists and nice breasts. He paused with a hand on the drawing-room doorknob. 'Are you nervous?'

April plastered a smile on her face. 'Not at all.' She wasn't nervous about dancing around in a devil's outfit and singing 'Happy Birthday' to the major. It was being back at Aurora and the thought of playing cat burglar that was giving her butterflies.

She kept telling herself the jewellery was hers, so technically she wasn't stealing. 'I'm an old pro at this.'

Sled's brows shot up.

'What I mean is, I've been doing kiss-o-grams for a long time,' April explained hastily.

He left the drawing-room door ajar behind him like they'd agreed. April grasped the brass doorknob, extended a black stiletto heel and fishnet stocking through the gap, and slithered into the room to loud cheers. She twirled to face Major Tom sitting in a chair opposite the door, pointed her pitchfork, dipped her knees and opened her mouth to sing 'Happy Birthday'.

April froze mid-dip. The words to 'Happy Birthday' dissolved in her brain.

Major Tom stared at April. And April stared at Major Tom.

His name wasn't Major Tom. It was Tarn Elliott.

# Chapter 4

*Smile! It irritates people.*

Anon

Sled stared at the empty doorway in disbelief as catcalls and loud boos erupted around him.

'Are you sure they're real strippers, Sled?'

He snatched the pitchfork from the floor. 'She's an apprentice.'

'That explains why she forgot the words to "Happy Birthday".'

'Never mind, Sled: she looked good.'

'I'd risk going to hell for a night with her.'

Wylie laughed. 'She's left her weapon. We should charge her.'

'If you don't shut up, Coyote, I'll stick this pitchfork up your arse,' Sled warned.

Tarn topped up his whisky. 'I'd keep quiet if I were you, Coyote. You spent so much time in front of my desk you wore a hole in the carpet.'

The other men laughed. Sled disappeared to get the strippers.

'You might want to run through the words to "Happy Birthday" first this time,' Frank called after him.

'Fuck off, Jepson!'

While they waited for the strippers, Tarn stared at the empty doorway. Something about the little devil's big, startled eyes bothered him.

Wonder Woman and the policewoman appeared. Amidst the whistles and applause, brows rose as Village People's 'In The Navy' erupted from the CD player. Frank rolled his eyes at Sled and mouthed 'wing nut'. Tarn grinned and forgot about the devil's cloudy blue eyes. He watched Wonder Woman and the policewoman strip, and let Wonder Woman take off his sweater and shirt, rub baby oil on his chest and tie him to the chair with her lariat. When she reached for the metal button on his jeans, he stopped her with a look; being stripped of his clothes didn't bother him, but Wylie and some of the younger soldiers wouldn't be comfortable. The looks on their faces when the policewoman climbed onto Tarn's lap and rubbed herself all over his chest were priceless.

Upstairs in the master bedroom, April was on her knees shoving a pair of nail scissors in the old-fashioned lock of the wardrobe door. What kind of idiot locked the door to their wardrobe? An idiot like Tarn Elliott, *that's who.* Judging by the noise coming from downstairs, he was probably being given a body-glide by Susie. Rather Susie than her. At twenty-six he'd been unapproachable; at thirty-five he was downright intimidating. April thought she was unshockable, but she'd almost had a heart attack when she saw Tarn sitting in the chair. If he found out she was in the house, let alone trying to pick the lock to his wardrobe, she was dead meat. Damn Rosamund! Why couldn't she put the jewellery in a bank deposit box and send the key like normal people?

April's heart thumped in time to the sound of Village People. Her palms were sweating. The scissors slipped from her hand. She banged her fist on the door, and sucked in a breath while she waited to see if anybody downstairs had heard, but nobody came. She grabbed the scissors, and set to work again.

Susie hooked one arm around the major's shoulders, pressed her knees against his hips, and did a little shimmy against his zipper. She ignored the catcalls and cheers from behind her as Village People faded. While Hayley worked the room, handing out business cards for Wild Women Do, Susie smiled into the birthday boy's shrewd brown eyes. He wasn't handsome, his face was too hard-bitten for that, but he certainly wasn't ugly either. Susie surveyed his naked chest approvingly and gave another little wriggle. He felt pretty good, too.

'Happy birthday, Major Tom.'

'Thank you.'

He had an elbow on the arm of the chair, and his jaw propped on his thumb and index finger. His other hand was shackled to Susie's wrist by a pair of handcuffs. Her bare breasts were inches from his face. He wasn't indifferent to the view — Susie could feel his appreciation pressing against her thong — but he didn't try to cop a feel like most guys would have done. She touched the scars on his right cheek with the tip of her index finger. 'How did you get these? Were you shot?'

Tarn didn't know why women always hoped the scars on his face were battle wounds. 'Teenage acne.'

'Oh.' Susie looked disappointed.

Aaron said he was a fool for telling the truth. 'If it makes 'em happy, tell 'em what they want to hear.' Aaron had nearly always found a woman to keep *him* happy. Or at least he had until he stepped on the mine.

'You don't feel thirty-five,' Susie cooed.

Tarn stretched sideways and scooped his shirt off the floor. Lately he'd felt as old as Methuselah. 'Looks can be deceptive.'

Susie tightened her knees as his hips rose and fell. Muscles *and* brains. She was about to give him her phone number when Hayley barged up and said, 'I want to apologize for April's anxiety attack. She said it's the first one she's had in years.'

The major went still. Susie checked his face: it looked like rigor mortis had set in.

'April?' he said abruptly. 'Her name is *April?*'

'Yes,' Hayley nodded. 'Why?'

A muscle began to tic in his jaw. He lifted the wrist handcuffed to Susie. 'Take these off.'

Susie exchanged glances with Hayley and silently removed the cuffs. She didn't know what was eating the major. Upon hearing April's name, he'd gone from faintly amused and horny to scary and forbidding.

'Do you … um … know April?' Hayley asked.

Tarn scooped Susie off his lap, sat her in the chair, and stalked from the room minus his shirt.

Hayley and Susie stared after him.

'What was all *that* about?' Susie asked.

'He's had a lot on his mind lately,' Sled replied. 'Would either of you ladies like a drink?'

The downstairs powder room was empty. Tarn checked the kitchen and utility room, the study, the formal dining room and the games room, but there was no sign of her. He ran lightly upstairs, and stopped to listen on the landing. A faint scratching noise was coming from his bedroom. He walked quietly down the hallway.

April was on her knees working on the lock of the wardrobe door. From the back, she looked like she'd been dipped in red latex. Long, fat red curls jostled the cello curve of her waist and hips, and the spiked heels of her stilettos pointed upwards like daggers. The scissors slipped from her hands. She made a sound of frustration, sank onto her heels and felt around on the carpet.

Whatever she was doing, it was illegal.

Tarn savoured the moment.

The scissors had fallen behind her. He watched her twist awkwardly in the tight rubber dress and pat the worn carpet. The red wig fell forward, obscuring her view of the floor — and his feet. She held it back with one hand and swept the carpet with the other in a vain attempt to find the scissors. Her shoulders dipped and her bottom rose as she widened her search. Above the rollercoaster curve of her spine, her red latex bottom swayed and her cleavage threatened to breach the zipper of the dress. On any other woman it would have looked enticing, but Tarn was unmoved. He knew the exact moment she spotted his white trainers. He waited.

She remained crouched on the floor with the ridiculous red curls spread around her and stared at his shoes. 'This probably looks really bad.'

Her voice had lost the youthful notes of girlhood. It was pitched an octave lower and was as wary as hell. Tarn didn't answer.

April kept her eyes on his trainers. 'I can explain.' *I wanted to collect a pair of pantyhose I left behind nine years ago.*

The trainers strolled closer and stopped in front of her. 'Take the wig off.' His voice was just the way she remembered it: flat and unfriendly.

As April hesitated, the wig was suddenly lifted from her head. She sank back on her heels as cool air rushed around her ears. She raised her eyes and looked through her false lashes into Tarn Elliott's chilly brown eyes. He was bare-chested. The part of April's brain that wasn't gridlocked with fear noted that it was an extremely nice chest. There were smears of baby oil on his pectorals from the body-glide Susie had given him, and he had goose bumps, but he didn't seem to notice the temperature. His eyes were colder than the room. Alongside the scars on his cheeks, there were deep grooves etched between his nose and mouth and hollows beneath his cheekbones. His light-brown hair wasn't army-short and he wasn't clean-shaven. He was bigger, older and tougher than April remembered. She gulped.

Tarn smiled thinly. 'April Ritchie.'

The way he said it made her shiver. If lions could talk, she imagined they would say 'wildebeest' or 'zebra' exactly the same way … right before they hunted them down and ate them. April wasn't easily rattled, but Tarn had managed it. April tried to read his face, but it was a closed book. She gave him her best hostess smile. 'Tarn Elliott. How are you?'

Hayley and Susie burst into the room. Hayley stopped so suddenly she looked like she'd been shot. 'April! What are you doing up here?'

'And what are you doing down there?' Susie demanded.

Tarn smiled with satisfaction. 'Trying to pick the lock on my wardrobe.'

Hayley fired April. 'You've betrayed my trust and tarnished the good name of Wild Women Do!'

April was tempted to point out WWD's name was tarnished long before she'd signed on to its payroll, but she needed Hayley and her car to get back to Christchurch. Once she was home, she'd think up another way to get the jewellery; one that involved Rosamund explaining the situation to Tarn. Unfortunately, April had underestimated how keen Hayley was to distance herself from a lock-picking kiss-o-gram girl, or how appealing the idea of extracting some long-overdue justice was to Tarn.

Susie didn't help. 'I knew there was something fishy about her offering to drive all the way from Christchurch and do a freebie. You realize your car was going to be the getaway vehicle, don't you, Hayley?'

Hayley blanched. She waited around only long enough to get her costume back.

'Hayley, you can't leave me here!' April protested. 'How will I get back to Christchurch?'

She threw April's clothes at her. 'That's not my problem!'

'Buy a bus ticket,' Susie sneered. 'And don't worry: I'll make sure Latoya hears what happened.'

April whirled on her. 'Oh no, you won't! You know what happens if Latoya gets stressed!'

Tarn listened with interest. Apart from a few speed wobbles, April had been as cool as a cucumber since he'd found her in his bedroom. He put it down to a lack of conscience. But whoever Latoya was, she obviously meant a lot to April. He didn't recall anything being said about a child when the details of April's divorce were splashed over the tabloids.

April wished she still had her pitchfork handy so she could jab Susie in the bum with it. She had only seventeen dollars and forty cents and a maxed-out credit card in her purse — her EFTPOS card had been eaten by the ATM when she'd tried to squeeze some cash out of her overdrawn account earlier in the week. Dressing up as a devil had been a mistake: Old Beelzebub was riding on her shoulder.

She took it back: Beelzebub was driving a white pick-up truck and taking her to Pisa police station.

April clung to the dashboard of Tarn's truck as they bumped down the potholed driveway, and tried not to sound as desperate as she felt. 'This is ridiculous. Roger Prescott is going to laugh you out of the police station. I didn't *do* anything.'

'You were trying to break into my wardrobe,' Tarn replied impassively.

'I told you, I thought it was my old bedroom. I left something in there.'

'Like what? Your teddy bear?'

He steered around a big pothole near the bottom of the drive and April blurted out, 'What happened to this driveway? It never had potholes when we lived here.'

Impossibly, Tarn's face hardened even more. Bad mistake.

'You thought your bedroom would be exactly the way you left it nine years ago, did you?' he asked sarcastically. 'Except it'd been moved from the other end of the house and turned into a wardrobe?'

April folded her arms. 'I'm wasting my breath trying to talk to you.'

'That's the first sensible thing you've said.'

Appealing to Tarn's sense of chivalry obviously wouldn't work because he didn't have one. April had a niggling feeling that he wanted something from her, and that it wasn't her body. 'How could you walk out and leave your guests? You're supposed to be the guest of honour.'

He turned onto Ritchie Road. 'They don't need me there to enjoy themselves.'

'Now *that* I can believe.'

'Wylie thought you should be charged for leaving your weapon behind.'

Any conversation that didn't include her and the wardrobe was to be encouraged. 'Who's Wylie?'

'The young corp who nearly swallowed his tongue when you came slithering through the door.'

'I don't slither.'

'If you say so.'

She revised her opinion: Beelzebub was full of fire and brimstone; Tarn was more like the Rock of Gibraltar — immovable. April had visited the real thing when Ralph took her to Europe on their honeymoon. 'What's a corp?'

'A corporal,' Tarn replied flatly.

His indifference didn't bode well for April if she was going to have to contend with Tarn *and* Roger Prescott at the police station. Under normal circumstances, she could charm most birds out of any tree, but the only kind of bird Roger resembled was a vulture, and anybody hoping to soften up the major would need full body armour, an axe and crampons. April was adaptable. She tried persuasion instead. 'Don't you think you're overreacting just a little? I didn't take anything.'

'Only because you can't pick locks. Bad luck about losing your job, but I guess the writing was on the wall when you forgot the words to "Happy Birthday".'

There was no sign of remorse on Tarn's face. If Hayley hadn't insisted on getting her costume back, he would probably have enjoyed taking April to the police station in the red devil outfit instead of her old jeans and fake leather and fur jacket.

A big white moon hung in the night sky. April shivered and hugged herself. Spring nights were perilous for the cherry industry: the temperatures still dipped to freezing, damaging the tender blossoms and killing the fruit before it could grow. Her thin jeans and jacket were no protection against a chilly Otago night. She looked longingly at the heavy, sheepskin-lined jacket Tarn was wearing. His confident attitude irritated April. As far as he was concerned, she was already breaking rocks with the rest of the chain gang.

'What were you looking for in the wardrobe?' he asked.

April met his eyes defiantly. 'I used to sleep in there when I was a baby.'

'What did you think you'd find? Lost innocence?'

*That's long gone*, she thought bleakly.

'Let's hope the officer on duty is touched by your story and those big blue eyes.'

April splayed her fingers on her chest. 'Why, Major, I didn't think you'd noticed the colour of my eyes.'

'They're hard to miss,' he countered. 'Just like those lies you've been spinning.'

His calm certainty did unpleasant things to her insides. If Roger Prescott was still in charge at the station, she was toast. He had a memory like an elephant. Even if she wriggled out of being charged for trying to break into the wardrobe, there was still the little matter of the missing hospital files. April wasn't going to let Tarn see he'd rattled her. 'Tell me, what *is* the penalty for damaging a door with a pair of nail scissors?'

He turned the truck into Pisa's main street. 'We'll find out soon enough.'

She swallowed. 'What do you want from me, Tarn?'

'What makes you think I want something?'

'I know when a man wants something.' She stared at him in the dimly lit cab. 'What do you want?'

He snorted softly. 'Not that.'

April wasn't offended — you needed self-esteem to feel insulted. 'I know you don't want *that*. What *do* you want from me?'

Tarn ignored her.

As they walked towards the police station steps, they were stopped by Clarence Negus, an old crony of Rosamund's. April didn't see Clarence, but he saw her on account of having had his cataracts removed the previous month, and crossed the street to get a closer look.

'April Ritchie?' he rasped. 'Is that you under all that face-paint?'

April squinted at the wizened figure standing beneath one of the reproduction street lamps that hadn't been there when she'd left. In the dark, and without her glasses, she couldn't see who it was, but the accordion wheeze of Clarence's voice identified him. April was grateful for anything that kept her outside the police station, and resisted when Tarn tried to usher her up the steps. 'Yes, it's me, Mr Negus. How are you?'

'Better since I got my cataracts done.' Clarence studied her disapprovingly. 'I can see all sorts of things I used to miss — like how you look.'

April wasn't surprised when Tarn removed his hand from the small of her back. Why pass up the opportunity to let somebody else insult her?

'I hope you're not a hooker now, April. Your grandmother

wouldn't be at all happy about it,' Clarence remarked.

'I haven't seen her in years. I don't think she'd be too bothered.'

'You're just splitting hairs.'

Her shoulder lifted in a shrug. 'I'm not a hooker, I'm a kiss-o-gram girl.'

'Is that another name for a hooker?' Clarence asked suspiciously.

'No.' April started up the steps to the station. 'Nice seeing you again, Mr Negus.'

Clarence wasn't finished. He pointed at Tarn. 'Is he another husband?'

She stopped at the top of the steps and looked down at Tarn. 'Him? No: too young, not enough money, and no sense of humour.' She waved to Clarence and disappeared into the station.

Tarn couldn't decide if April was very smart, very dumb, or just didn't give a shit. He climbed the steps and opened the glass door before remembering Clarence Negus standing beneath the street lamp, looking like a wizened gnome in his heavy coat and brown felt hat. It wouldn't hurt to introduce himself. 'I'm Tarn Elliott, Carole and Murdoch Elliott's son.'

'The one who bought Aurora?'

'Yes.'

'The one who got caught in the packing house diddling Heather?'

Tarn scowled. 'The one who was *wrongly accused* of being in the packing house with Heather.' He banged the glass door shut behind him.

Roger Prescott wasn't on duty, but his son, Lionel, was.

April was genuinely pleased to see him. They shared the same birthday, and had gone to the same kindergarten and schools. Apart from getting taller and filling out, Lionel hadn't changed all that much — he still looked perpetually worried, and had big ears that stuck out like car doors which had been left open, just like Roger's. She wasn't surprised he'd become a police officer. While everybody else kept changing their mind about what they wanted to be when they grew up, Lionel's answer had always stayed the same: he wanted to be a policeman just like his father. And every birthday and Christmas he'd got the same presents: police paraphernalia.

Lionel didn't recognize April when she walked up to the front desk wearing false eyelashes and her devil make-up. He glanced at her curiously and nodded at Tarn over her head. 'Evening, Tarn. What can I do for you?'

Seeing Lionel reminded April of happier, simpler times. She dropped her guard and cried, 'Lying Hell! How are you?'

Lionel's brows slammed together and harpooned the bridge of his nose. 'April Ritchie,' he said flatly. 'Is that you?'

Too late she remembered how much he'd hated the nickname he'd been given in school because he was such a goody two-shoes.

'I want to report an attempted robbery,' Tarn said calmly.

'I *was not* trying to rob him,' April insisted. 'I just wanted to look at my old room.'

'You know damned well that wasn't your old bedroom.'

She spoke to Lionel. 'I didn't take anything.'

Tarn placed a hand — large and brown, and covered in cuts and scratches from pruning trees — on the reception desk. 'What about the damage to my wardrobe door?'

April looked down her nose. 'A few scratches on the woodwork from a pair of nail scissors.'

Lionel thought Tarn was remarkably composed for a person who'd just foiled a robbery; he began to suspect that Tarn had an ulterior motive for bringing April to the station. And she hadn't changed — she was as impossible as ever. Lionel doubted the charge would stick, but took their statements anyway.

'Once the paperwork is done you can go,' he told them. 'We'll review things in the morning and decide if there's enough evidence to proceed to court.'

'Thank you, Lionel.' April shot Tarn a look. 'I'm sorry we've taken up so much of your time.'

Tarn didn't respond. 'Let me know what's happening in the morning, Lionel.'

'Will do,' he replied. 'You can go, too, April.'

'I've got nowhere to go.' She glowered at Tarn. 'I *lost* my ride back to Christchurch.'

His smile lacked warmth. 'She got sacked from her job as a kiss-o-gram girl. She forgot the words to "Happy Birthday".'

Lionel stared at April. She'd said she worked in the hospitality industry. 'You're a *kiss-o-gram girl?*'

'It was temporary,' April insisted.

'She was working her way up to becoming a strip-o-gram,' Tarn explained.

She glared at him. 'Why don't you shut up?'

It had been a long day; Lionel was tired and wanted to hand over to the next shift. He also needed to decide if he was going to tell his wife that April was back. 'Book into a motel,' he said. 'The Pisa Palm is new; the owners won't know you.'

It was humiliating to admit that the motel owners who remembered her probably wouldn't rent her a unit. 'I don't have enough money to rent a room,' April muttered.

'Perhaps Pisa police station has an empty cell you can use for the night?' Tarn suggested. He didn't want her going anywhere without him.

Lionel sighed and stacked the paperwork into a neat pile. 'Go home, Tarn.' He looked at April and blew out an irritated breath. 'I suppose you'll have to spend the night here.'

Clarence was still outside when Tarn left the station, but had taken refuge in his car, a late-model Volvo which he'd parked facing the wrong way across two marked parking spaces. As Tarn descended the steps, the car window lowered and Clarence's sharp pixie face appeared. 'Did Lionel throw the book at her?' His breath fogged in the cold night air.

Tarn tucked his hands in the pockets of his jacket and crossed the pavement to the car. 'He's thinking about it.'

'About what?'

'Charging her with attempted robbery.'

'Is that all?'

'Being obnoxious isn't illegal.'

Clarence gave a wheezy laugh. 'She's still the same, then?'

'Pretty much.'

'Did Lionel mention the missing hospital files?'

Tarn had forgotten about the hospital files. He knew the attempted-robbery charge wouldn't stick, but doubted April would be so lucky when it came to the missing files, especially if he jogged Lionel's memory about it. The possibility of extracting some revenge was appealing. 'No.'

Clarence pressed his thin lips together, which made the upward curve of his chin even more prominent. 'I suppose that's something, but it's only a matter of time before Roger reminds Lionel about it. Did he lock her up?'

'She's staying the night.'

The point of Clarence's chin almost collided with the end of his beaky nose. 'Rosamund won't be pleased.'

Tarn had his own agenda; he wasn't interested in Rosamund's. He raised a hand in farewell. 'I'm going. I've got a houseful of guests.'

'Have you had any luck finding a quality controller for the packing house yet?' Clarence called.

He stopped and looked over his shoulder. 'How do you know I'm looking?'

'Everybody does. Did you know that April qualified when she was sixteen? Trained her myself.'

Tarn stood absolutely still. It was the perfect solution to an annoying problem. And making April work for him while thwarting her attempts to get to whatever it was she wanted in the wardrobe only added to the fun. 'It must have been a pleasure teaching her,' he remarked. 'April always took instructions so well.'

Clarence wheezed again, and started the Volvo. 'I can't feel my toes anymore. I'm going home, too.'

He pulled away from the kerb, muttering, 'I should be in front of the fire watching *Glee* and having a whisky.' He'd only come into town to buy more because he'd dropped the bottle when he'd tried to pour out the tiny amount he allowed himself each night. Thanks to April Ritchie's shenanigans, he'd missed *Glee* and would spend the rest of the night on the phone breaking the news to Rosamund that her long-lost granddaughter was in jail.

# Chapter 5

*A compromise is an agreement whereby both parties get what neither of them wanted.*

ANON

Although Lionel didn't lock the cell door, April still felt like a criminal. There was no window in the cell, and the bed was narrow and uncomfortable. When she did manage to doze off during the night, the constable who took over from Lionel woke her up by crashing the sliding panel in the door back and forth each time he checked on her. He hadn't introduced himself, but April guessed he must be a local. 'Can you do that a little louder?' she called out. 'I don't think they heard you in Queenstown.'

April knew all about humiliation. It was humility she still struggled with.

She'd run out of tears a long time ago; they'd disappeared to the same place her pride and self-esteem had gone. She comforted herself that staying at the police station had saved her money and that Lionel thought she'd probably get a fine because it was her first offence. But that raised the issue of how she was going to pay it, and how she was going to get the jewellery stashed in Tarn Elliott's wardrobe. April knew he'd search the wardrobe when he got home, but doubted he'd find the jewellery's hiding place — only the family knew where the hidey-hole was.

Trying to charm him clearly wasn't an option: he was a cold, unforgiving man. If April had thought that offering him her body would work, she'd have gritted her teeth and made the sacrifice, but the major obviously didn't go for small, opinionated blondes. Anyway, April was allergic to men with hard eyes and stern mouths.

Lionel brought her a tray with cereal and a mug of tea when he came back on duty the following morning. She was starving; the last thing she'd eaten was a sandwich at lunchtime the previous day when she'd stopped at a café with Hayley and Susie. Her face was itching because she hadn't been able to remove her make-up, and she desperately wanted a shower and to change her clothes but she only had the ones she was wearing.

'What happened?' Lionel asked when he saw April's face. 'Have you got some sort of skin disease?'

'I've got sensitive skin. I couldn't take off my make-up.'

'Do you want me to call Dr Giles?'

Dr Giles had been old when she was little. Surely he'd been called to the big hospital in the sky by now? 'He's still alive?'

'He's semi-retired. He's got partners who do most of the work.'

'Pisa has got more than one doctor?'

'It's got a lot bigger since you left, April.' Lionel made it sound like the increase in population was a direct result of her leaving. 'Do you want me to call Doc Giles or not?'

'No!' He was bound to bring up the missing files. When Lionel bristled at her tone, April smiled and softened her voice. He'd been nice to her even though April knew he had plenty of reason not to be — Lionel had often been the butt of her and Courtney's jokes. 'I just need to cleanse my face. I don't suppose you'd have any make-up remover?'

It was the first time Lionel had ever been asked for make-up remover. Usually, it was for a cigarette break or to see a lawyer. 'I'll see what I can do.'

He returned with a bag of cotton-wool balls, a bottle of cleanser and another of moisturiser.

April sighed blissfully as she removed her eye make-up. 'Lionel, you are the best. Where did you get this?'

'I got it from my wife. I live in the police house behind the station.'

The eye she wasn't cleansing widened. *'You're married?'*

He glowered. 'Yes. Don't look so surprised.'

'I'm … I'm … not!' April felt awful. 'Lionel, I'm sorry.' He gave her a disbelieving look. '*Truly* — I appreciate all the trouble you've gone to for me.'

Lionel grunted, and picked up the tray and walked to the cell door. From the back, his elbows and ears both stuck out at ninety-degree angles to the rest of his body. 'There's a toilet with a sink down the hallway if you want to wash up. You need to make another statement.'

She fished another cotton-wool ball from the plastic bag. 'Why? I already gave you a statement. You said the charge would probably be dismissed.'

'We need to take a statement about what you were doing at the hospital the night some medical files went missing.'

April froze. 'Have you been talking to your father?'

'Of course I have; he's just come on duty.'

April sat at the table in the interview room where Lionel had taken her statement the previous night. The only difference was that this time it was Lionel's father, Sergeant Roger Prescott, she faced, and

Tarn Elliott was sitting next to her.

'Normally I'd speak to you separately, but the front desk has had more visitors this morning than the information bureau gets in a month.' Roger's faded blue eyes bored into April. 'I think we all know the reason for that.'

Instead of blaming her, April thought Roger should look a little closer to home and speak to the officer on the night shift — he'd obviously wasted no time in broadcasting that she was in one of the cells. But she kept quiet; Roger had never been her number one fan. He'd never managed to catch her doing something illegal, though. April had always been one step ahead of him, thanks to a reliable network of friends who'd tip her off — she'd been long gone when Roger had responded to reports of somebody doing doughnuts on Ritchie Road or that it had been April's idea to build a wooden tower next to the fruit sculpture.

Roger's hair was grey, he had jowls, his shoulders were stooped, and he had the beginnings of a paunch, but his gaze was exactly the way April remembered it — like something from the Spanish Inquisition. April lifted her hair over her shoulders, crossed her legs, folded her hands in her lap and stared back at him. She knew she looked a mess. Tarn had stopped in the doorway and raised his brows when he first saw her, but April would have liked to see how good *he* looked after a night spent on a cell bed in full devil make-up.

'We considered charging you with attempted theft or wilful damage,' Roger began.

'With a pair of nail scissors?'

His grizzled brows met over his nose. 'I'd keep quiet if I were you.' Then he added, reluctantly, 'We're not going to charge you.'

April thought Tarn must have had a change of heart — or

discovered he had a heart. Either way she was grateful. She smiled at him. 'Thank you.'

'I wanted you charged,' he replied.

'It was a police decision not to proceed,' Roger said sourly. 'We don't waste our time pursuing cases where a conviction is unlikely.'

April had stood up to bigger bullies than Roger and Tarn. 'I'm not a criminal,' she insisted. 'If I'd been wearing my glasses I'd have realized Major Elliott's wardrobe wasn't my old bedroom.'

'Why weren't you?' Roger asked.

'Because somebody sat on them.' No need to mention it'd been her. 'And I'm only allowed to wear them with certain costumes.' Schoolgirl, schoolteacher and saucy secretary.

'Devils don't wear glasses?' Tarn enquired.

'No,' April smiled sweetly. 'If you'd ordered a schoolteacher to sing you "Happy Birthday" it would have been different.'

His eyes cut into her. 'I didn't order anything.'

'Oh, that's right: it was your soldier buddy who arranged everything.' Baiting Tarn wasn't sensible, but that rigid self-control wasn't normal. He seemed to plan everything — April bet he knew what colour underwear he'd be wearing this time next week. She was more the act-first-and-patch-up-mistakes-later type.

'I need to talk to Miss Ritchie about some patient files removed from the local hospital the night she left town,' Roger said. 'I'll have to ask you to leave, Major.'

'I'm retired from the army now; Tarn will do.' And Tarn wasn't going anywhere. If he left, April would probably drop herself into more shit and get banged up in prison, and then he'd lose his quality controller.

April cleared her throat uneasily. She did *not* want to talk about the missing hospital files or the reason she'd taken them.

'I feel badly about last night.' *A night on that cell bed would make anybody feel bad.* 'I haven't seen my home in nine years. I let sentiment overrule my common sense and I invaded Major Elliott's privacy.' *There was more chance of invading India.* 'I want to make amends, but I've lost my job and I'll struggle to pay a fine, and the job market for unskilled workers isn't exactly buoyant.'

Roger moved one set of papers aside and reached for another file. 'I already explained to you, that charge has been dropped.'

During the long hours in the cell, April had come up with a plan. She'd promised Latoya she'd sort out their financial problems. She *had* to get back to Aurora.

'Major Elliott — Tarn — is new to the orchard industry. I know a lot about growing and harvesting cherries. I believe in restorative justice.' April was annoyed when Tarn snorted.

*This is too damned easy*, Tarn thought. 'I believe in restorative justice, too. I've had no luck finding a quality controller for the packing house. You're qualified, aren't you, April?'

She had a horrible feeling she'd just walked into a trap. The picking season didn't start until the beginning of December. Her version of restorative justice involved a week. Tarn was thinking months. 'I can't stay that long; I've got commitments.'

'You said you'd lost your job and would have trouble getting another one because you're unskilled, but that isn't the case here. The magistrate will probably look more favourably on you if you've been doing community service,' Roger pointed out reluctantly.

'I lost my accreditation,' April said quickly.

'Clarence Negus can spend a few days training you again — I checked this morning.' Tarn stared into her furious blue eyes. 'I know what happened last night isn't the only thing weighing on your mind,' he said, in a not-too-subtle reference to the missing hospital files. 'Who knows? If things work out, it might even lead to a permanent job.'

'That's between you two.' Roger checked the time. 'I need to take April's statement about where she was the night the files were stolen from the hospital.'

'One of them was mine,' April pointed out. 'How can I be accused of stealing my own hospital file?'

Tarn shook his head. She'd just admitted she'd stolen the files. Her stupid schoolgirl prank was coming back to haunt her.

'Nola Gutsell's file wasn't yours.' Roger had never forgotten the name on the other file.

April flinched when Tarn suddenly clamped a hand around her elbow and rose. 'She'll be back to make a statement after she's seen a lawyer,' he said firmly. 'Ready, April?'

Word had spread that April Ritchie was back in town, had spent the night at the police station, and was being released that morning. Brad Tecklenberg took time off from his job as a petrol-pump attendant to book a doctor's appointment and get his ears syringed, which upset his girlfriend because she'd been trying to get him to do it for months.

'You'd better not be going to the doctor via the police station!' she shouted as he left her house. 'I know you had a crush on April Ritchie all through high school!'

'That was years ago,' he replied. 'She probably looks like a hag now.'

As he watched April saunter down the steps outside the police station, Brad knew nobody would ever accuse her of looking like a hag. Her face was thinner, her shoulder-length blonde hair was a shade darker, and the big blue-green eyes that once dared the world to say 'no' looked weary and disillusioned; but to Brad, April was exactly the way he remembered her — a new-millenium Marilyn Monroe. She wore cheap, chain-store clothing the same way she'd worn designer labels in high school, and carried herself with the careless grace of a catwalk model, shoulders back and hips tilting from side to side as she swung her legs down the steps.

'How am I going to afford a lawyer?' she demanded, and Brad belatedly noticed she was accompanied by the stony-faced major who'd bought Aurora.

'Paying for a lawyer isn't your biggest problem,' the major replied. 'Finding one is.'

The Cupid's bow in her upper lip dipped as she hauled on the straps of the bulky green bag hanging from her shoulder. Couldn't the major see it was too heavy for her? 'What does that mean? Pisa has lawyers.'

'At the moment, it has *a* lawyer. She's an old friend of yours: Emma Murfitt.'

She stumbled on the last step. Brad leapt forward to catch her, and take the bag. 'Are you OK, April?'

April heard a man's voice and felt his hands on her. Ralph had left her with an aversion to men she didn't know touching her. She jumped away and blinked up at him. 'Yes … thanks!' April was unprepared for the concern on Brad's face. She relaxed and smiled.

Her smile was like a neon sign, Tarn thought irritably: it lit up whenever a susceptible male was in the vicinity. He recognized the guy from one of the local petrol stations. April recognized the distinctive buck teeth of the Tecklenbergs.

'It's Brad — Brad Tecklenberg,' her rescuer prompted. 'Remember me?'

She did. He'd been a cute little kid who'd spent all his time in the sandpit at primary school. Her smile grew. 'Of course I do. You're Billy's little brother.'

Brad beamed. 'That's right.'

'How's Billy?'

'In prison.'

'Oh.' Billy had been one of April's accomplices in the tower-building project. 'I'm sorry to hear that.'

'If you need a lawyer, I can give you the name of Billy's.'

April's response was lukewarm. 'Thanks, I'll keep it in mind.'

Entertaining though it was listening to Brad's offers of help, Tarn didn't have time for idle chitchat; a mountain of work awaited him back at the orchard. He took April's bag from Brad and slung it over his shoulder. When he reached for April's elbow, she stepped away. Tarn dropped his hand. 'We need to go.'

Brad looked between them. Like everybody else in Pisa, he knew about the bad blood between April and the major. 'You're staying at *Aurora?*'

'The major has offered me a job,' she replied smoothly.

'That's one way of putting it.' Tarn nodded sideways to indicate they were leaving. 'Come on.'

As they walked away, April waved. 'Bye, Brad.'

Brad pointed to his ear. 'I've got to get my ears syringed. See you around, April.'

Tarn strode down the street. 'Stop practising your beauty-queen wave, and hurry up. I've got a chain saw to pick up and trees to prune.'

It was impossible for April to keep up with him, so she didn't even try. 'If you don't slow down, soldier, this beauty queen is going to fall flat on her tiara.'

His lips thinned. He slowed, and was surprised when April slid her hand into the crook of his arm and sauntered along as if they were on the red carpet. Apparently, the 'no touching' rule only applied one way. There was a name for women who played those games, and Tarn had zero tolerance for them. He shook off her hand.

April was unperturbed. 'Why are you still pruning? You should have finished that in winter.' Pruning in winter increased the vigour of a tree and made it more robust.

'Because there are thousands of cherry trees, and only one of me,' he replied curtly, as he entered the Mighty Mower and Cycle Repair Shop.

She followed. 'You don't have any help?' April looked around the shop. On one side, there were racks of bicycles, and on the other, rows of ride-on mowers. 'What's the matter, Major? Did everybody desert?'

'I need *experienced* help.'

Big orchards could afford to employ experienced, full-time staff — Aurora used to — but smaller orchards relied on seasonal workers who followed the harvests, or temporary workers from abroad. Unfortunately, the overseas workers were allowed to stay in New Zealand for only a year, which meant that as soon as they were trained up they left and the orchard owners had to start all over again.

As Tarn walked ahead of April to the counter, he reached beneath his sheepskin jacket and pulled a battered wallet from the back pocket of his jeans. She noticed with detachment that he filled out a pair of jeans nicely, far better than Ralph ever had — but then Ralph had twenty years on the major. She had avoided physical intimacy since she'd run away from Ralph. Any flirting she did was restricted to public places and never went further than smiles and occasionally patting a guy on the arm. Taking Tarn's arm and snuggling up to him had surprised April as much as it had him. He was too stern-looking and taciturn to qualify as handsome, but April admitted that in the days before her inner slut died and she'd been single she would have noticed him. She was glad that Tarn had shaken her off; if she had to spend time with him, she needed to feel safe. April waited while he handed over a ticket to the young shop assistant behind the counter, and the assistant disappeared out the back.

A young woman wearing a too-tight, plum velour tracksuit and carrying a toddler on her hip came into the shop. April recognized Jacinta Evans. In school she'd been a sanctimonious little tattletale, full of unwelcome advice. Jacinta had big lips and a fondness for bright lipstick, which was why April had nicknamed her Fish Lips. She'd been a bitch, too — only less creative. She was one of the few people from school April didn't feel she owed an apology.

Jacinta stopped when she saw April, and wrinkled her nose as though she'd smelled something bad. April stared back, but Jacinta looked right through her and spoke to Tarn instead. 'Hello, Major. We haven't met: I'm Jacinta Woodall.'

She was wasting her time trying to get friendly with Tarn. So far as April could tell, Tarn wasn't only immune to blue-eyed blondes — he didn't like anybody. She didn't recall any Woodalls in Pisa and concluded Jacinta's husband must come from out of town.

Tarn nodded briefly at Jacinta. 'Call me Tarn.'

He really had a bee in his bonnet about being called 'Major'.

Jacinta frowned. 'I wouldn't feel comfortable calling you by your first name, Major.'

April pulled faces at the toddler, who giggled and ducked his head into his mother's neck. 'It's that upright, military bearing. It'd be a lot easier if you didn't look like you had a broomstick strapped to your back all the time.'

'You finished?' he enquired coolly.

The shop assistant returned to the counter. 'I can't find anything out there for Major.' Tarn scowled at him: 'It's under the name *Elliott.*' The assistant flinched and scuttled away.

Jacinta moved the baby to her other hip so that he couldn't see April. 'I'd have thought you'd have learnt some manners by now, April.'

Tarn watched April prepare to do battle. If she did anything that landed her in jail again, Roger and Lionel were welcome to her.

April sighed, 'What can I say? I'm a work in progress. And how have you been, Jacinta?'

'I'm married,' Jacinta replied smugly. '*Once.*'

'I guessed that. You had a reputation for never putting out.'

Her complexion darkened. 'Unlike some people!' she snapped.

'Work in progress, Jacinta — work in progress,' April murmured. 'What's your little boy's name?'

The baby leaned out to get another look at April. 'Samuel, stop that!' Jacinta dragged him back, before turning again to April and asking nastily, 'How was jail?'

April pondered. 'They could do with a few more choices on the breakfast menu, and I had to remind them to turn down my bed and put out chocolates last night, but apart from that I've no complaints.'

Tarn kept his back turned so they couldn't see his smile.

Jacinta was furious. It was happening all over again: April Ritchie was getting the better of her. 'Perhaps if you got a respectable job instead of working as a *kiss-o-gram girl*, you wouldn't end up in jail.'

'Hey! I was damned good at it until I retired.'

Tarn stared at an advertisement for a triathlon on the wall behind the counter. That was one way of putting it.

'What happened to all the money you got from your divorce?'

He turned. Now *that*, he was interested in.

April was used to people thinking they could ask her personal questions because they'd seen her divorce from Ralph played out in the newspapers. She'd become adept at replying without actually answering them. 'You know how it is, Jacinta: shoes, clothes and fast men. Before I knew it I was down to my last million. The fast men were cheap — it was the shoes and clothes that ruined me.'

'You haven't changed one bit!'

'That's not true. I haven't been with a fast man or bought a new pair of shoes in weeks.' *Three years, in fact.*

'There was a rumour you got kicked out of Aurora because you weren't the Ritchies' real daughter. If I'd been them, I'd have prayed it was true!' Jacinta spat.

Tarn frowned; it was a low blow. He waited for April to come back with some wisecrack, and looked over his shoulder when she didn't. Her face had paled. Jacinta looked triumphant, until April rallied and smiled, 'If you were my mother, Jacinta, I'd have prayed it was true, too.'

It lacked her usual high-calibre smart-aleckness but was enough to send Jacinta storming off between the racks of bikes with Samuel.

The assistant returned with the chain saw. Tarn paid for the repairs, picked up April's bag and the saw, and walked out. April stared after him uncertainly until it occurred to her that he might throw her bag in the gutter and leave without her. She rushed from the shop and looked up and down the street. Tarn was already some distance away; she had to run to catch him up by the truck.

'Are you set permanently on self-destruct?' he asked when April reached him.

She clutched her side and panted, 'No — stun.'

He put the chain saw in the back of the truck next to an upturned wheelbarrow, and threw April's bag between them.

'Careful with that! It's all I've got!'

Tarn couldn't believe that the Princess of Pisa's wardrobe was reduced to what she carried in the green bag. 'What happened to all the clothes and shoes you bought with your divorce settlement?'

'It's mostly make-up. By the way, we haven't discussed my wages.'

He opened the passenger door. 'Rescuing you from Roger and another night in the cell is reward enough.'

Her blue eyes shot sparks. 'I need some clothes. How much are you going to pay me?'

Tarn didn't even pretend to think about it. 'Ten dollars an hour.'

'Ten dollars! The minimum hourly rate is twelve seventy-five, you tight-arse! Ordinary packers get fourteen dollars; a good quality controller gets eighteen. And I'm bloody good!'

'You're trying to impress the magistrate by doing community service, remember? And calling the boss a tight-arse just ruined your chances of an end-of-season bonus.'

Her hands curled into fists. 'You can stick your end-of-season bonus in the same place as your minimum hourly rate!'

Across the road, four women pushing babies in strollers had stopped and were staring at April. Tarn sensed an ambush.

April had noticed them, too. Her face lit up when she recognized Courtney. She jumped up on the side of the truck and balanced on her hands with one foot bent behind her. 'Courtney! It's me — April!'

With her back arched, breasts thrust forward and that platinum hair tumbling around her shoulders, she looked like a Playboy bunny with too many clothes on. Tarn's groin stirred. His mood got even darker.

Courtney put her head down and hurried away, pushing the baby stroller.

April watched her disappear and slowly dropped to her feet. 'That *was* Courtney Murfitt, wasn't it?' she asked in a subdued tone.

'Yes.' He wasn't going to feel sorry for her. Courtney hadn't heard from April since the night she'd left town, so it wasn't too surprising that she didn't want to talk to her. When the remaining women showed signs of crossing the road, Tarn's cold stare stopped them.

'She's got a baby,' April said.

She liked children. That hadn't been an act. 'A little boy called Kieran. And her name's not Courtney Murfitt anymore, it's Courtney Prescott.'

Her eyes widened. 'Courtney is married to *Lionel?*'

Tarn nodded.

'Oh.' She shrugged a shoulder. 'I guess it was her cleanser and moisturiser I used this morning.'

Tarn always treated those under his command with respect. He was clear about what he expected from them and quick to acknowledge a job well done. Bullshit artists were given short shrift — and April was a bullshit artist. She needed to learn a few basic truths — like who was in charge. He took her shopping at the cheapest store in town.

April surveyed the inside of the shop; it sold everything from outdoor furniture and kindling to underwear and pencil sharpeners. 'Major, you don't seem to understand that I'm an investment.'

'I see a nuisance, not an investment.' He glanced at his watch, a complicated-looking affair with a thick black strap. 'You've got ten minutes.'

Nobody could accuse him of wasting words, which was a shame, because, if talking was an Olympic event, April would have won a gold medal.

'Clearly you've dipped out in the imagination department. Personally, I blame it on all that army training.' She selected four bra-and-panty sets and dropped them in the shopping basket on her arm. 'I suppose I should be grateful Pisa doesn't have an army-surplus store.'

'You've read the situation well.' Tarn plucked the bra-and-panty sets from the basket and hooked them on a rack of rugby shirts.

'They're on sale! I'm not working bare-arsed and bra-less!'

The Playboy bunny cavorted in his brain. His lips barely moved: 'Nine minutes.'

It wasn't until he'd arrived at the police station that morning and seen her without the ridiculous wig and make-up that Tarn had realized how much April had and hadn't changed. She was far too thin — he could have circled her wrist with his thumb and forefinger, and her face was all angles and big eyes. Tarn knew, however, that although April looked fragile, she wasn't. The Brads of the world might be bewitched by her delicate face and dazzling smile — they were too stupid to realize April would still be standing when the bell rang and they hit the canvas — but Tarn wasn't.

Before she'd married Ralph, April hadn't thought twice about showcasing her assets to get what she wanted, but she'd been leery of doing it since leaving him. However, Tarn Elliott was proving to be a hard nut to crack. She hooked back one side of her fake fur jacket and splayed a hand on her hip. She was no Dolly Parton, but she wasn't Olive Oyl either. Beneath the jacket, she was wearing a stretchy teal-blue top with a scoop neck that showcased 'the girls' to perfection. 'I need another bra.'

Tarn had already noticed that she'd filled out in the last nine years. 'Save the Lolita act for one of your admirers. One bra and a pack of that underwear in the sales bin over there — take it or leave it.'

She banged him in the thigh with the basket as she pushed past to go to the bin. She'd been aiming higher. 'Cheap bastard!'

'I'm pleased we're clear about that.'

Everything in the children's section was fifty per cent off. Tarn found a navy-blue waterproof jacket with a hood and held it up for April to see. 'It's an investment.'

April left the shop with a pair of fleecy tracksuit pants, two sweatshirts and T-shirts, a pair of red gumboots, one bra, an economy pack of six panties in shades of turquoise, orange and fuchsia, an economy pack of five pairs of thermal socks in purple, pink and lime, two pairs of boy's pyjamas in a camouflage print, the jacket, and a blue tartan hat with earflaps that reminded her of the one Clarence had worn the previous night.

She had learnt that going head to head with Tarn was futile. It was better to inflict lots of small wounds than go straight for his jugular. She twirled the hat on the end of her finger as he paid for the clothes. 'I asked you to get me a hat the first time I met you. Do you remember?'

'No.' The only thing Tarn remembered about their first meeting was that April had been a pubescent pain.

'I wanted a hat made out of camouflage material, but you said no.'

'I probably didn't understand you,' he replied insincerely. 'We don't call it camouflage material, we call it DPM — short for "disruptive pattern material".'

She widened her eyes. 'Gosh, Major! That is so interesting!'

Tarn slid his wallet into his back pocket. 'That hat is much better. You'll be the envy of the valley when we're out fighting frosts.'

There was more than a little frost in April's eyes. She knew that. *She* was a local; *he* was the interloper.

On the drive back to Aurora, Tarn resisted her attempts at conversation. April chattered non-stop about anything and everything just to bug him. She pulled a pair of the camouflage pyjamas from the bag and held them under her chin. 'Do they suit me?'

'Not as much as the ones marked with black arrows that Roger Prescott has lined up for you.'

'That's not very nice, Major.' She put the pyjamas back in the plastic bag. 'Maybe I should join the army.'

'Try the navy or air force instead.'

April was looking forward to seeing Aurora in the daylight. She peered out the window at a paddock filled with strange-looking sheep. 'What's wrong with those sheep?'

Tarn thought she was joking until he saw that she was frowning and her eyes were almost crossed. 'They're goats.' Discovering his quality controller couldn't tell the difference between Lamb Chop and Billy Goat Gruff was a concern. 'Are you really that blind? What are you going to be like checking the fruit?'

'I'm short-sighted; I have trouble seeing things in the distance, not close up.' April arched a brow. 'If you're that bothered, buy me some new glasses.'

So that was what she was after. 'I'd rather buy a gag to shut you up.'

'That's employee harrassment.'

Tarn was done with the chitchat. He looked at April and said coldly, 'One more thing: my mother got back from visiting her sister in Christchurch today.' He paused. 'You *will* be nice to her.'

# Chapter 6

*Love your enemies. It makes them so damned mad.*

P. D. East

April didn't want to see Carole Elliott almost as much as she did want to see Aurora. She hid her nervousness behind a show of outrage at the state of the big, curved wooden gates at the entrance of the driveway. The white gates were a landmark on Ritchie Road; it was how people found the orchard. Last night the darkness had concealed their scruffy, unpainted appearance. When Tarn turned the truck into the driveway, April gasped and cried, 'What happened to the gates? They're a disgrace!'

He knew that. When he'd moved in, the gates were a scabby, peeling mess because some idiot had used the wrong kind of paint. In the army, equipment was well cared for and tasks were completed to a high standard. The appearance of the gates offended Tarn as much as being behind schedule with the pruning. He'd rubbed off the blistered paint with the intention of repainting them as soon as he had a spare moment. He hadn't found any spare moments, and didn't appreciate April pointing out the obvious.

'Making things look pretty isn't at the top of my priority list at the moment,' he said shortly.

She replied tartly, 'I can tell that by the state of your hair and that stubble.'

His hand was halfway to his jaw before Tarn realized what he was doing. The gag was becoming more appealing by the second.

He made April wait outside in the truck while he went in and spoke to his mother. He had parked on the side of the house opposite to the kitchen — April guessed this was why she didn't hear Carole's screams of protest. Tarn returned ten minutes later, looking his usual stony-faced self. Clearly, he'd won the argument — as if the result had ever been in doubt.

'Come into the kitchen,' Count Charisma said.

April picked up the two lightest shopping bags.

'Leave your stuff in the truck.'

She frowned. 'Why?'

'I'll explain later.'

Carole Elliott's response when April entered the kitchen was predictably hostile. 'Look what the cat's dragged in.'

'Hello, Carole.'

April was shocked at the change in her: Carole's hair was completely grey, she'd piled on weight, grown extra chins, and her mouth drooped bitterly. And the Carole whom April remembered wouldn't have stopped at name calling — she'd have grabbed her rolling pin and chased April around her kitchen. Even so, April didn't trust her. She noticed the wooden knife block an arm's length from Carole, and made sure she kept Tarn between her and his mother as she studied the interior of the old kitchen.

Some idiot had changed the blue-and-white wall tiles to a garish lime green, and had hung gaudy café-style curtains on the window over the sink, but apart from that everything looked the same. The big old dresser still stood against the wall, and the massive wooden table still held centre-stage on the quarry-tiled floor. April searched for, and found, the marks left by her Magic Marker pens when she'd been four and had drawn a picture of herself on the skirting board. Her throat closed and her eyes stung. People had let her down, but never this house. For that reason, April had far deeper attachments to places than to people. When she'd run away from Ralph she'd missed having a home, but the place she'd always missed most was Aurora.

'What idiot changed the wall tiles?' she demanded.

Tarn let his breath out slowly through his nose. He might have known April would start throwing her weight around as soon as she walked in. Ironically, his mother had reacted the same way when she'd first returned and seen the kitchen. He gave April a long look. 'You're forgetting who owns the place.'

Her pale cheeks reddened. She looked away from Tarn's flat, brown stare and Carole's satisfied smile. A gentle curl of steam rose from a pot on the stove, and a light glowed in the oven. April sensed Tarn was still watching her and was grateful when something beeped and Carole turned away and picked up a soup ladle. Her stomach recognized the smell of Carole's home-made chicken soup and garlic bread, and growled in response. She swallowed the lump in her throat, and said more forcefully than she intended: 'If you're paying me slave wages, the meals had better be free.'

Carole slammed down the soup ladle and whirled around. 'Listen here, madam!'

Tarn shoved back the sleeves of his sweatshirt, and spoke over her. 'Is lunch ready?'

'When you called and said you were bringing somebody back, I thought you meant Emma.' She jabbed a finger at April. 'Not *her!*'

April listened with interest: so things were back on with Emma and Tarn. She guessed Emma was quite a catch now she was a lawyer, and — April regarded Tarn critically — she supposed he would be, too, if you liked men who had all the charm of two-day-old road kill.

Tarn seemed perplexed. 'I never said I was bringing Emma home.'

Inside her head, April rubbed her hands together and skipped. *Finally*, a chink in the major's armour.

'How long is she staying?' Carole demanded.

April laid a hand on her chest. 'Do you mean *moi?*'

Tarn's eyes skewered her. 'I told you, Mum: until the end of the picking season. She's our new quality controller.'

*In your dreams.* As soon as she got into the wardrobe and collected the jewellery, April would be leaving, even if she had to walk all the way to Queenstown.

He grabbed a loaf of bread from the pantry and a tub of butter from the fridge and dumped them on the beautifully set table. The beautifully-set-for-Emma table.

'I made garlic bread,' Carole said petulantly.

Tarn threw the loaf on the kitchen counter and returned the butter to the fridge. He sat down at the table and rested his forearms either side of his placemat. His face darkened when he noticed April's smirk. 'Sit down!'

'Why, thank you.' She drew out a chair, shook out her napkin and placed it on her lap. 'Perhaps Emma can make it next time,' she murmured.

Carole sucked in an angry breath.

Tarn waited for the soup to be served. April was like a jack-in-the-box: slap her down and she popped right back up again. She needed to be taken down a peg or two again.

Carole addressed her soup. 'Where's she staying?'

April took dainty sips of the delicious soup, and looked up at the ceiling in the direction of her old bedroom. She wondered if it had changed much.

Tarn reached for some more garlic bread. 'In one of the workers' caravans.'

She almost dropped her spoon. He couldn't be serious. There were *six* bedrooms. April laid down the spoon. 'Why can't I sleep in my old room?'

He took a bite of garlic bread, chewed and swallowed. 'Family members sleep in the house — workers sleep in the staff quarters.'

Their eyes clashed. Being relegated to sleeping in one of the caravans was far more humiliating than sleeping in the police cell. April could tell that Tarn knew it, and had planned it that way.

'You'll eat with us in the kitchen,' he added graciously. 'You could do with gaining a few kilos. I don't want you passing out on me.'

Carole's spoon crashed against her soup dish.

'And you can use the shower in the downstairs powder room.' He smiled humourlessly: 'Everything you need is downstairs.'

In other words, she was banned from going upstairs. April's lip curled — as if that was going to stop her.

'Do you remember how to work?' Carole asked. 'Or did you forget while you were with that millionaire husband?'

April's insides oozed with pain and anger. 'Of course not: who do you think supervised the staff?'

She didn't have any credit on her cellphone, so after lunch April took another bite of humble pie and asked Tarn if she could make some calls.

'If they aren't local calls, keep them short.'

He was either incredibly poor, or incredibly mean.

She intended to phone Rosamund in Nelson to complain, and Latoya in Christchurch for comfort, and stay on the line until either Carole or Tarn kicked her off or she ran out of things to say. Tarn wouldn't know until he got the phone bill, and by then she'd be long gone.

Unfortunately, he had her measure. 'I meant it when I said keep them short. I brought you here to work. There's still plenty of daylight left.'

April clenched her teeth. She would be polite — or die trying. 'But I haven't even had a chance to move into my accommodation yet.'

'It'll only take a couple of seconds to throw your bags inside and acquaint yourself with the caravan — it's the smallest one.'

The humble pie threatened to choke her. 'I'm not happy about the meal arrangements.'

Tarn's expression didn't alter. 'Are you complaining?'

'Your mother hates me. How do I know she won't poison me?'

'How do you know I won't?' He pulled a pair of work gloves from his pocket. 'Use the phone in the drawing room. You've got ten minutes to make your calls. Meet me outside the packing house when you're done.'

She clicked her heels and saluted. 'Yes, sir!'

The first thing April noticed when she walked into the drawing room was the burgundy wing chair she'd been sitting in the night she found out she wasn't Grant's daughter. She turned her back on it.

Rosamund spent the first two minutes of their conversation berating her for sneaking into Aurora dressed as a kiss-o-gram girl, and spending the night at the police station. April hated speaking to Rosamund, because she didn't know what to call her: 'Rosamund' seemed disrespectful, 'Mrs Dreyfuss' was ridiculous, and 'Grandma' wasn't right.

'How did you find all that out? Crystal ball? Or Clarence Negus?'

'I never tolerated your insolence when you were a child, April,' Rosamund said, 'and I'm not about to start now. I'm assuming you called me because you want something, in which case you will listen to whatever I have to say first. Is that clear?'

'As a crystal ball.'

'I'm quite happy to hang up. My mah-jong group is waiting.'

Rosamund was just an older, female version of Tarn. April saluted and clicked her heels. 'Sorry. Do go on.'

Unaware of the little pantomime occurring on the other end of the line, Rosamund continued, 'I was relieved to hear that you'd been released from jail.'

'I wasn't in jail.'

'Semantics,' she replied frostily. 'I was also relieved to hear you'd given up taking your clothes off and have a respectable job at Aurora.'

'I never took my clothes off, and I got fired.'

'Will you stop interrupting me?'

It was time Rosamund realized April was past the age of being seen and not heard. 'I'm afraid I can't do that. You've put me in an impossible position. By rights, Tarn owns the jewellery because it's in his house. Why couldn't you have just put it in a safety deposit box and sent me the key? I'm banned from going upstairs. How am I supposed to get into the wardrobe?'

'For goodness' sakes, April, you're twenty-six years old and reasonably pretty—'

'Thank you.'

'It wasn't a compliment.'

'I realize that,' April said flatly.

Rosamund swept on. 'You have one, almost two, marriages behind you. Ever since you were six weeks old and learnt how to smile, you've been winding men around your little finger. Tarn Elliott is definitely a man. Surely you can find a way to gain his trust?'

'Are you suggesting I seduce Tarn Elliott?'

'Certainly not! If you gained his trust, you could offer to do some housework.'

'Good,' April replied tartly, 'because the major's got about as much warmth as a glacier. In fact, I seriously doubt he's *capable* of red-hot passion.'

'He strikes me as being far more capable of it than Stefan Vincent or the cereal baron,' Rosamund added reminiscently, 'My brother Edwin was a captain in the infantry.'

April couldn't believe she was having a conversation about Tarn Elliott's virility with Heather's eighty-four-year-old mother. Rosamund had never made a secret of how much she'd disliked her husband, Donald. And what did her brother Edwin have to do with anything? The old girl must be going senile.

'I'm not losing my marbles,' Rosamund said crisply, as if reading April's mind.

'I get it: I offer to dust and vacuum his room and then sneak into his wardrobe. There's just one problem — the door is locked and there's no key.'

'A flippant attitude will get you nowhere.'

April was tired of taking the blame for everything. She wasn't responsible for everything that went wrong — including Tarn's bad mood. It would be nice if somebody bothered to try to gain *her* trust for a change. She said as much to Rosamund and was surprised by her response.

'I admit you do have a point, but ...'

April rolled her eyes. She might have known it was too good to be true.

'... did you hear about what happened on Tarn's last tour of duty?'

They'd been talking for twelve minutes; April expected the major to bang on the window at any moment. She settled onto the faded cushions on the window seat just in case he couldn't see her. 'No. Did somebody forget to wind up the key in his back and he missed reveille one morning?'

'To have any chance of success, you need to change your attitude.'

'Sorry, but my attitude is pretty much stuck on flippant.'

Rosamund sighed impatiently. 'Do you recall seeing the reports about the soldiers killed in Afghanistan last year when a patrol came under attack?'

'Yes.'

'Tarn was in charge of that patrol. Two men were killed and a third was badly injured. Edwin always said the men he fought with knew him better than his own family, and losing any of them was like losing a family member.'

April stared out the Georgian window at the rows of cherry trees stretching into the distance beneath a canopy of nets to keep the birds out. She remembered the reports on the news and the photos in the papers of the military funerals, and how she'd felt saddened that such young men had died and so far away from their homes and family.

She didn't want to feel sorry for Tarn, though, and was certain that he wouldn't appreciate it anyway. Hearing about other people's pain stripped the scabs off her own wounds. She expended a lot of energy keeping them covered, and resented it deeply when anybody or anything picked at them. April tucked a foot beneath her bottom and turned to face the room. 'Perhaps you're right. Perhaps I should offer the major tea and sympathy.'

'I refuse to participate in this conversation anymore,' Rosamund snapped. 'Call me again when you've grown up.'

The line clicked.

April was glad she'd left her call to Latoya until last. The answer machine clicked on at the flat they shared — Latoya must have got the money to pay the phone bill. April bet her fiancé, Tim, had loaned it to her.

Latoya's voice said, 'Hello. You've reached Latoya and April. Leave a message and we'll call you back.'

A bang on the window accompanied the *beep* of the answer machine. April jumped and gasped. *'Shit!'*

Tarn stood on the other side of the glass, glowering. He jerked his thumb over his shoulder. 'Move it!'

She gave him a glorious smile and mouthed, 'I'm coming, you pig.'

He went still. April's smile froze — apparently, he could read lips. She licked hers nervously. 'Latoya, I'm OK. I'm at Aurora. Don't believe Hayley or Susie: I didn't steal anything.' Tarn flattened his palm on one of the windowpanes. He narrowed his eyes and leaned closer. Her eyes darted to his hand. It looked huge. *'Call me!'*

April dropped the phone on the window seat. She skedaddled out of the drawing room and through the kitchen, startling Carole who dropped the potato she was peeling on to the floor. Halfway to the packing house, her pride reasserted itself. She forced herself to saunter the rest of the way. Tarn wouldn't murder her — he needed her.

It proved to be a costly mistake.

Tarn found her waiting inside the packing house. He looked calm enough, but April had the feeling she'd stepped over an invisible line. She pointed over her shoulder in the direction of the house. 'I think you may have misunderstood what I said back there.'

'Did I?' he replied.

'Yes. I said "*You're big*".'

'You're full of bullshit.'

April's hand hung above her shoulder. 'That's a very literal interpretation.'

Tarn gestured to her jeans and jacket with his work gloves. 'You need to get changed. I put your bags in the caravan. Let me show it to you,' his voice deepened with anticipation, 'and what I want you to do this afternoon.'

She regarded him warily. 'I thought I was going to help you with the pruning?'

Her alarm grew when he almost smiled. 'No, I'll do that. I've got something else for you to do.'

There were three caravans next to the packing house. Tarn had towed the smallest one to the area behind the house where the garages and sheds were.

April stood on the top step of the caravan and looked through the door at the cramped interior. To the left there was a minuscule kitchen with a hotplate with two elements, a small sink bench and a tiny fridge. To the right was the sleeping and sitting area — the bed doubled as both. April refused to give Tarn the satisfaction of seeing how upset she was. She braced her hands against the sides of the doorway and cooed, 'It's lovely.'

'Roomy enough for you?'

'Oh, absolutely. A cat could swing itself in there.'

'Glad you like it.'

When April had lived at Aurora, the garages had housed cars, a tractor and machinery needed for the orchard. Since she'd left, a bigger, taller shed with a wide opening had been added. There was a blue helicopter inside. She pointed to it. 'Is that yours?'

'Yes.'

The major was full of surprises. April knew very little about helicopters, but guessed they weren't cheap to buy or run. 'Why have you got a helicopter?' Tarn didn't seem the type to have boys' toys — but then what did she know? He might have a model engine railway and a train-driver's hat tucked away in that locked wardrobe.

'Because I like them, and because orchard owners will pay six hundred dollars an hour to have one hover over their trees when it rains or the temperature suddenly drops overnight.'

April was reluctantly impressed. 'Unless things have changed, Ivan Vincent likes people to hire *his* helicopters.'

'I've only got one.'

'He doesn't like competition.' Her mouth curled as she pictured Ivan's reaction. 'And I'm guessing you'll be cheaper.'

'Probably,' Tarn deadpanned. 'I'll meet you at the packing house in ten minutes.' He started to walk away.

Something occurred to April. 'Hey, Tarn!'

He stopped and looked over his shoulder.

'Who's supposed to look after Aurora when the frost alarms go off at one o'clock in the morning if you're out playing chopper hero?'

He gave her one of his smiles that wasn't a smile at all, and carried on walking.

April went inside the caravan. She'd known what his answer was going to be, but still had to ask. How on earth did he expect her to light all the salamander heaters in the rows between the trees, check the temperature of each row and adjust the heaters accordingly all by herself? *And* keep doing it until the sun came up? It was Hayley who'd come to his party dressed as Wonder Woman, not her. April counted to fifty, and when that didn't help, she counted backwards to one. Eventually, there was nothing left to do but get changed into some of the clothes Tarn had bought her and return to the packing house.

She had picked out the smallest pair of track pants she could find on the sale rack, but the fleecy blue pants were still too big around the waist and too long in the leg. April rolled the hems of the legs into cuffs, but couldn't do anything to stop the elasticated waist slipping around her hips and had to keep hauling the pants up on the walk to the packing house.

Inside the shed, Tarn pointed to rows and rows of the white buckets used by the pickers, stacked in towers on the concrete floor. 'They all need to be washed.'

There had to be at least a thousand buckets, which all should have been cleaned at the end of last season. 'You're joking!'

Tarn watched the track pants slide down her hips and the rolled-up hems pool around her gumboots. She looked like she was ten and had dressed up in her mother's clothes. 'No.'

'Why weren't they cleaned at the end of the picking season? All sorts of mould and gunk will have grown in them!'

'Best get started then.' He headed for the door.

April kicked the bottom of a bucket and one of the towers toppled over. Buckets bounced on the concrete. 'You *are* a pig!' she shouted.

'Yes,' Tarn agreed. 'A *big* one.'

The day after April's release from the police station, Courtney Prescott and Emma Murfitt met for lunch at their favourite café. As the only lawyer in town, Emma's practice was very busy. Courtney didn't get to see her as much as she'd like to, and Emma felt like she was missing out on her two-year-old nephew, Kieran.

They had just placed their order and were sitting at a table outside sipping coffee when Jacinta Woodall appeared, pushing Samuel in his stroller. Courtney swallowed a groan; she wasn't in the mood for Jacinta. Her nerves were still jangling from seeing April. A combination of guilt and anger at her so-called best friend had kept her awake last night. Her tossing and sighs had eventually driven Lionel from bed.

Courtney had leaned up on an elbow and peered at him in the shadowy darkness of the bedroom. 'Where are you going?'

'To sleep in Kieran's room. I won't be able to get up in the morning if I don't get some shut-eye. For God's sake, go and see her, Muppy,' Lionel had grumbled before disappearing up the hallway towards the baby's room.

Her eyes had filled with tears: 'Muppy' was a shortened version of 'Muppet'. April had begun calling Courtney 'Muppet' in kindergarten because she was obsessed with the television show. Long after Courtney had outgrown the phase, April had still included a muppet in her birthday present. There were thirteen of them sitting on the windowsill in Kieran's bedroom. Courtney blamed Lionel for her confusion. If he hadn't said that April seemed different, she could have gone on condemning her for getting Emma fired and never bothering to call.

'What do you mean, she's different?' Courtney had asked.

Lionel had shrugged in that maddening way men had. 'I don't know — just different.'

'Give me an example,' she'd insisted. He'd looked at her helplessly, and Courtney had wondered how a man so good at solving crimes could be so dense.

'She thanked me for getting the cotton wool and make-up stuff, and apologized for being surprised when I told her I was married. Do you remember April Ritchie ever thanking anybody or apologizing?'

Only the people she cared about. Courtney could imagine April's surprise that Lionel was married: they'd teased him horribly about his ears, and run around pointing pretend guns and calling themselves Lionel's Angels when he was around. By now, April would know Courtney was married to him. She'd probably laughed herself sick when she found out. But Courtney didn't care. She loved Lionel. He was kind and honest, and had more integrity than any person she knew — certainly more than April Ritchie. Courtney just wished Lionel didn't think she was as good a person as he was and expect her to confront her feelings and ask for explanations.

Emma and Courtney exchanged resigned looks as Jacinta

parked Samuel's stroller next to Kieran's and dragged a chair from a nearby table. Samuel was sweet and was Kieran's best friend, which was why Courtney tolerated his mother. Like the rest of them, Jacinta had mellowed since high school, but she still had a tendency to regress to her old bossy, spiteful ways when she was angry. And she was definitely angry now; her plump, scarlet lips were tightly pursed. Courtney knew why. She'd been avoiding Jacinta's calls, but couldn't avoid the messages she'd left on the answering machine.

'You won't believe what that woman said to me after she got out of jail,' Jacinta began as soon as she had parked her butt.

No prizes for guessing who *that woman* was.

'Staying overnight at the police station isn't the same as being in jail,' Emma pointed out. 'She wasn't under arrest.'

Jacinta was perplexed. Emma Murfitt was the last person she expected to champion April's cause. 'It is in my book. She wasn't the slightest bit embarrassed about spending the night in a cell or about working as a kiss-o-gram girl.' She made 'kiss-o-gram girl' sound like 'mass murderer'.

Courtney glanced at Emma, but her expression remained cool. She tried to lighten the atmosphere with a joke. 'If I could lose the belly roll I got from having Kieran, I'd sign up as a kiss-o-gram girl. The extra money would come in handy.'

'I can't believe you're defending her!' Jacinta exclaimed crossly.

'I'm not!'

If anybody had reason to be upset, it was Emma. When April had stolen the medical files and said Tarn Elliott was with Heather in the packing house, Emma had lost not only her job but her boyfriend, too. Courtney had always thought that her sister was more taken with Tarn than he was with her. His return and subsequent purchase of Aurora had set tongues wagging again. People were split fifty-fifty on whether Emma could pick up where she'd left off with Tarn Elliott nine years ago. So far Emma had played it cool, but it didn't seem to be having any effect. Tarn seldom ventured into town, and, while he'd always been self-contained, now he was offhand to the point of rudeness.

At thirty-three, Emma bore little resemblance to the hospital receptionist she'd once been. Her dark hair was parted on the side and fell sleekly to her jaw. She wore a narrow, dark skirt and matching jacket, a pale-pink blouse, silky black hose and a pair of killer black heels. A slim black briefcase rested against the slender calves tucked demurely beneath the table. Emma was attractive, sophisticated and successful. But Courtney knew her sister envied her for having Lionel and Kieran.

Jacinta dug around in her bag and pulled out a plastic container of apple slices. She handed one to Samuel. 'I asked her where all the money from her divorce settlement went.'

Courtney gasped. Even Emma looked shocked. The April Courtney remembered would have wiped the floor with Jacinta and left footprints on her back as she departed. 'Jacinta! You *didn't!*'

Jacinta picked up the piece of apple Samuel had thrown beneath the table. 'I did. She made me so damned mad! I went into the shop to ask if our lawn mower was ready, and there was April with the major.' She frowned. 'It's the first time I've met him. He looked more like a mercenary than a major to me. He's quite intimidating — not very chatty.'

Courtney leapt to Tarn's defence. 'He never used to be like that. Something happened on his last tour.' She knew Tarn needed workers and that Ivan Vincent kept snapping up anybody with experience, but she still couldn't believe the rumours that he was employing April. Was he *that* desperate? Emma said it was Tarn's way of getting revenge. 'Did he say why he gave April a job?'

Jacinta shook her head and passed Samuel another piece of apple. 'We started arguing and he ignored us.'

'So, did April say what she spent her divorce settlement on?'

Emma rolled her eyes, but Courtney didn't care. There wasn't a person in town who knew April who hadn't followed her marriage to Ralph Berryman when she was nineteen and he was forty-nine — or been surprised when they'd got divorced.

'She said she spent it on shoes, clothes and fast men. She's still the same: you can't believe a word she says,' Jacinta muttered.

Courtney bit her lip. Emma sipped her coffee. Samuel threw the apple at Kieran and woke him up. He rubbed his eye and began to grizzle.

'You know what else she said when I told her I was married? She looked at Samuel and said she thought I must be because I never put out in school. God, I hate her!'

Kieran threw the apple back at Samuel. It missed and went under the table. Courtney dived down to retrieve it and stifled her giggles in her lap.

Emma soothed Kieran and checked her watch. 'Have you finished yet, Jacinta? I have to go back to the office soon, and I was hoping to have a quiet lunch with Courtney and Kieran,' she said pointedly.

Jacinta leaned closer. 'The major was seen buying her underwear.'

Emma stopped tapping her foot and Courtney stopped giggling. She sat up and glared at Jacinta. As usual, she was reading way too much into something. 'So what? Perhaps he gave her an advance on her wages.'

Jacinta was angry that Courtney was defending April after

everything she'd done to her and Emma. In high school, Jacinta had longed to be part of April and Courtney's crowd but had never been invited to join. Since they'd both had their sons, she'd worked hard to establish a friendship with Courtney, but it seemed that her efforts had been a waste of time — as soon as April returned, Courtney started making excuses for her. She turned to Emma, 'I thought you should know.'

Courtney wished Jacinta would keep her fish lips closed. She waited for Emma to give Jacinta one of her chilly put-downs, but she picked up her briefcase and stood up instead.

'We'll try it again another day shall we, Courtney?' Emma pecked Kieran on the cheek and walked away, the rapid click of her high heels telegraphing her annoyance.

Jacinta stared after her. 'She really has it bad for the major, doesn't she?'

Courtney's bad mood escalated. 'Oh, shut up, Jacinta!'

She stuck her chin out and cried angrily, 'This is just like it was in high school! You always stuck up for April then, too!'

'Of course I did — she was my best friend! We stuck up for each other.'

Jacinta snatched up the container of apple and jammed it in the pocket on the back of Samuel's stroller. 'April Ritchie is nothing special. Without her designer clothes and hair extensions, she looks just like everybody else. And at least *I* know who my parents are!' she snapped, and marched away, buttocks jiggling beneath her red tracksuit.

'That was just a rumour!' Courtney yelled at her departing back.

'Says you!' Jacinta yelled back.

# Chapter 7

*Beware of the half-truth. You may have got hold of the wrong half.*

ANON

Central Otago has the distinction of being the hottest, driest and coldest place in New Zealand, and of having the fewest permanent residents. The terrain is rugged and peaceful; a semi-desert fragmented by a schist plateau filled with mountains, rivers, rocks and tussock, and presided over by a vast, star-studded sky at night.

Into this Eden, Tarn reintroduced a serpent named April Ritchie. All he required of her was that she worked hard, and understood that he called the shots around the place; he didn't have the time or the interest to deal with her theatrics. April's theatrics, however, were her stock-in-trade. She'd stumbled through most of the past nine years on half-truths and evasions, exploited her angelic looks, and pretended to be what she wasn't — a frothy blonde airhead. April had never had 'a place'. Tarn had more chance of teaching a dolphin to drive a tractor than of getting her to toe the line.

Scrubbing the buckets left April feeling tired and dirty. Being in the packing house alone was depressing; it reminded her of Heather and Murdo and the stupid lie she'd told. She wondered why Tarn hadn't brought it up, or asked who she'd really seen with Heather, but he didn't seem interested in the past. It was her recent misdeeds that he was punishing her for. She was reluctant to return to the house, and would have continued scouring out the buckets if her stomach hadn't started to rumble and the phone hadn't rung in the office attached to the packing house.

It was Tarn. 'Where have you been?'

April hadn't spoken to him since he'd left the packing house, but when she'd gone outside to empty the buckets she'd seen him pruning trees in the distance with a man she didn't know. She wanted food, a shower, and to fall asleep in the cramped little caravan. 'Where you left me, Bwana, in the packing house cleaning buckets.'

'You weren't there when I looked in half an hour ago.' Tarn had gone to the house to check whether April had sneaked back out and was in his bedroom trying to get at whatever it was she wanted in the wardrobe.

'It must have been when I took a toilet break. Don't worry, it won't happen again. If you get me one of those catheter bags I could strap to my leg, I'd save a whole five minutes — ten if I have to go twice.'

April was surprised when he chuckled. She'd begun to think that if she peeled back his skin he'd have a futuristic steel skeleton like Arnold Schwarzenegger in *The Terminator*. Did he do ordinary things like sweat or pee or, even more mind-boggling, have sex? Susie had certainly liked him — April could tell by the amount of baby oil she'd seen left on Tarn's chest when he'd surprised her by the wardrobe. She was mildly alarmed that she was thinking about sex at all. Her sex life had been on hold for the past three years. April wasn't in any hurry to resurrect it, and, in the event she was, it was unlikely that Tarn Elliott would volunteer to help her.

'Time to shut up shop,' he said. 'Dinner will be on the table in ten minutes.'

'I'm filthy.' April clasped her forehead. Freud would have a field day.

'I thought that was just your mood. It's dark. Do you want me to come down and walk you back?'

'Er ... no, I can find my way. Why are you being so nice?'

'I'm hungry, and Mum won't serve dinner until everybody is here.'

April only had time to wash her hands and face in the powder room before she entered the kitchen. She felt self-conscious about how bad she looked.

Tarn was already at the table, sorting through mail and adding it to a growing pile at his elbow. He'd showered and changed into a clean sweatshirt and jeans. His hair was wet and he looked like he'd shaved. He certainly looked and smelled a lot better than April. She didn't know that she was responsible for Tarn's improved mood. She'd surprised him by working hard today, and he'd had a call from the owner of one of the smaller orchards asking about bringing this season's crop to Aurora for grading and packing. Clarence must have put the word out; he'd been responsible for finding Smitty, the guy who'd helped Tarn with the pruning.

Carole looked April up and down. 'You look a mess.'

She sat down at the table. 'It's your precious son's fault — he's a slave driver.'

'Don't you dare criticize Tarn! I still can't believe you had the cheek to turn up here.'

'You know what they say about bad pennies, Carole.'

Tarn looked up from the bank statement he was reading. 'Will you two give it up?' It was normal for orchard owners to have an overdraft in the early spring, until they got paid for the next crop, but it was a new experience for Tarn. Listening to them bicker wasn't doing his appetite any favours. He looked at his mother: 'Leave her alone, she's worked hard.' He raised his brows at April: 'If you'd rather eat in the caravan, it can be arranged.'

She shrugged but held her tongue, and Tarn returned to his bank statement.

Carole was upset that he seemed to be taking April's side. It brought back memories of Heather twisting Murdo around her little finger. She snatched up a dishcloth to take the plates of food from the oven, and muttered under her breath about daughters being like mothers.

April stiffened. 'Keep your opinions about my parents to yourself, Carole.'

Tarn looked up curiously. She was very touchy about her parents, but then Heather and Grant's style of parenting had been piss-poor.

'Are you going to let her speak to me like that?' Carole demanded.

It was at times like these that he really missed the army. 'And deprive you both of a good bitch session?' He looked at the plates of roast chicken and vegetables in his mother's hands. 'Is there any chance of eating that before it goes cold?'

Carole dumped the plates on the table and turned back to the big kitchen range. She was taking out her bitterness at Heather and Murdo on April. Tarn had given up trying to reason with her. He loved the mother he remembered from his childhood, and felt guilty because he'd never believed her when she'd said his father was unfaithful.

Suddenly Tarn's plate disappeared from in front of him and was replaced by April's. He braced his hands on the table and looked at the smaller plate of food. Apparently April hadn't been joking when she'd said that she was worried Carole might poison her.

Carole brought her plate and the gravy jug to the table and frowned at the trail of vegetables that stretched between Tarn and April and her son's reduced dinner. She put down the jug and looked at April accusingly. 'What are you playing at now?'

April poured gravy over the towering pile of food in front of her. 'You heard what Tarn said: I need fattening up.' She speared a potato and popped it in her mouth.

Tarn's expression indicated that he was rapidly coming to the end of his tether. If they didn't shut up, *he'd* eat in the caravan. He waited until Carole sat down, then picked up his knife and fork and started to eat.

Across the table, April attacked her plate enthusiastically. She was usually a picky eater, and lived on junk food and processed meals that could be reheated in the microwave. Carole and Tarn watched in mounting disbelief as she made inroads into his dinner. Eventually, April admitted defeat and sat back. She couldn't remember the last time she'd enjoyed a meal so much.

'Carole,' she sighed, 'that was wonderful.'

Carole regarded April suspiciously over her glass of water. She loved cooking for people, especially the ones who appreciated her talents, but feeding a Ritchie was different.

Tarn had polished off his meal and helped himself to seconds. He surveyed what was left on the plate in front of her. She *was* too thin, but the air of fragility that clung to her was deceptive. Beneath that flippant attitude and prima donna act, there was pure grit.

'You're sure you don't want us to pack what's left in a doggy bag so you can take it back to the caravan in case you get hungry in the night?' he asked drily. 'Just throw the bones out the window when you've finished gnawing on them.'

April was imagining what Tarn would look like with a decent haircut to go with his stubble-free jaw. Mention of the caravan punctured her bubble of almost-happiness. She didn't want to leave the cosy, familiar warmth of the kitchen for the cold little caravan when she could be sleeping in her old bed upstairs. She gave Tarn a big smile and deliberately set the cat among the pigeons. 'It's sweet of you to offer, but I'll pass. If I get too fat I won't be able to fit into all those lovely new clothes you bought me.'

Carole gasped. 'You bought her *clothes?*'

'Yes. Wasn't that nice of him?' April still had one more bullet to fire. 'I notice you've shaved,' she said innocently. 'Are you meeting Emma in town tonight?'

When April exited the powder room after her shower, Tarn was sitting in the burgundy wing chair in the hallway with one ankle balanced on the opposite knee and the daily newspaper spread across his lap. April's wet hair hung down the back of her camouflage pyjamas and a pair of lime-coloured socks covered her small feet.

Tarn turned a page. 'Very fetching.'

'The sad thing is you probably mean that.' April knew he was making sure she left the premises without taking a detour to his bedroom. 'You know there's a name for men who hang around women's rest-rooms — perverts.'

He continued reading the newspaper. 'That's assuming I'm tempted, which I'm not.'

*Only because I haven't been trying. If I had, you'd be plenty tempted.*

'The bromide is working, then?' April asked.

That got old Arnie's attention. 'The what?'

'The bromide.' She repeated it slowly as if his hearing was impaired. 'I thought they handed it out by the truckload so you soldier boys could keep your mind on the job — or off *it*.'

Tarn dropped the paper in his lap and leaned his head against the back of the chair.

April squinted. Was that a smile hovering around his mouth?

'They stopped handing out bromide a long time ago, April.'

It occurred to her that she'd never seen him smile properly, and that his grim exterior might be a sign of unhappiness instead of a miserable disposition.

'We don't stay away for years at a time, and besides,' his dark eyes regarded her steadily, 'there's always women available if you're looking.'

The hallway was lit by an ornate gold and burgundy lamp on the oak console table beside the front door. It felt quiet and intimate — like Tarn's gaze. The blonde Lolita who'd been wrapping men around her finger since she learnt how to smile shifted nervously from one lime-coloured foot to the other and blurted, 'You know Mrs Murfitt was worried that if Emma married you she'd have to set up house in an international hot spot.'

Tarn stared. His brown eyes crinkled and the scars in his cheeks became dimples. He started to laugh.

Warmth trickled through April as she watched the transformation. 'If I'd known being called a pervert would make you so happy, I'd have done it a lot sooner.'

He stopped laughing and rubbed his eyes with his thumb and forefinger. 'April?'

'Yes?'

He gave her his Terminator look: 'Don't mention Emma around my mother.'

'OK.' She raised her arms and finger-combed her damp hair. 'Why?'

'Because it gets her hopes up.' His gaze drifted from her tousled blonde hair to the outline of her breasts beneath the pyjama jacket. 'You know there's a name for women who flaunt themselves with no intention of delivering the goods?'

April felt like she'd been slapped. She dropped her arms. She'd been using her looks to get what she wanted for so long that she did it without even thinking. She wasn't proud of it.

Tarn picked up the newspaper again. 'Go to bed, April,' he said coolly. 'Your caravan is calling.'

One of April's biggest failings was not knowing when she was beaten. Her pride and dignity might be in shreds, but she refused to slink away with her tail between her legs. On the rare occasions when fluttering her eyelashes and other parts of her anatomy failed, she fell back on the other weapon in her arsenal — her ability to make people laugh. She stepped into the red gumboots she'd left at the bottom of the stairs and lifted her new jacket off the newel post.

'I'm sorry.' She threaded her arms into the sleeves. 'I thought you liked Emma.'

Tarn didn't look up. 'Go to bed.'

She freed her hair from the collar of the jacket and gazed at the top of Tarn's head. In the summer, April bet his light-brown hair had the kind of natural blond highlights women had to pay for. 'I was thinking …'

He ignored her.

'… you're obviously too busy to get a haircut. I spent a year working in a hair salon and got pretty good at cutting men's hair. I could cut yours if you want.'

Tarn sighed and raised his eyes. Didn't she know when to give up? He looked at her kiddie jacket and the boy's pyjamas tucked into red gumboots and wanted to laugh again. 'You think I'm going to let a woman who's too blind to tell the difference between a sheep and a goat loose on me with a pair of scissors?'

April waved her hand languidly. 'Don't be boring.'

'Better boring than missing an ear.' He eyed her keenly. 'What are you really after, April?'

Damn, he was annoying. She had been going to suggest doing his hair in his bedroom; he must have the key to the wardrobe hidden in there somewhere. 'That haystack on your head offends me, and I don't even like you. Imagine what Miss Sword of Justice will think if the bromide wears off and you change your mind and ask her out.'

Tarn snapped the newspaper. 'Good night, April.'

She sauntered to the door. 'Seeing as you're my boss, I was only going to charge you forty bucks.' She ignored his snort. 'I'm a Libran. We do our best work in harmonious, beautiful surroundings. That haystack is *not* beautiful.'

'You're not a Libran. I know because Mum is, and her birthday is in October. You were born on April Fool's Day.' He smiled grimly: 'I remember.'

Steering the conversation in that direction probably wasn't the smartest move. 'What time is reveille?' she asked irritably.

'When I bang on the door of your caravan.'

Tarn was turning out the downstairs lights and trying to put the poisonous, provocative Ms Ritchie out of his mind when the telephone rang. It was too late for a social call. Fearing something had happened to Aaron, he raced into the drawing room to answer it. 'Hello?'

'Hello, I'm sorry to call so late,' a young woman's voice said diffidently. 'I wondered if I could speak to April Ritchie.'

'She's in bed.'

'Oh.' She seemed disappointed. 'Who am I talking to?'

Tarn replied with little pleasure. 'Tarn Elliott, her boss.'

'You're the major!'

'That's right.'

The girl cried, 'Whatever April did, she didn't mean it!'

*She knew that April had tried to break into the wardrobe?*

'Who are you?' Tarn demanded.

'The receptionist at Wild Women Do,' she said. 'And April's flatmate. People tend to misunderstand her — she's a *really* good person.'

He laughed explosively. 'You must know a different April Ritchie to the one I do.'

'Yes, I do. I know the real April,' she said firmly.

Tarn rolled his eyes. From what he'd seen so far, there were many Aprils. He was damned if he knew which was the real one.

'She's had some bad things happen to her,' the girl continued.

'What bad things?' he asked sharply.

'That's her business,' she replied hastily.

Tarn wasn't prepared to let her off the hook so easily. 'Do you know what April came here for?'

'She used to holiday in Pisa when she was a kid. She felt like visiting again. I'm sorry about the mix-up over your name.'

*Why had April lied about living here?*

‘Sorry, I missed that. What did you say?’ Tarn asked.

‘Your name: we thought it was Tom, but Susie said it’s Tarn.’

‘Don’t worry about it. It’s not the first time I’ve been called Tom.’

If Wild Women Do hadn’t got his name wrong, April would never have set foot in Aurora and he wouldn’t have found his quality controller. Although Tarn was beginning to wonder if hiring her was worth the aggravation.

‘And the music.’

He frowned. ‘What about the music?’

‘We played “In The Navy” by Village People. We didn’t know you were in the army; the information we received was a bit garbled.’

That was probably because Sled was drunk when he gave the details at the poker game. ‘Don’t worry about it. How long have you known April?’

‘Almost three years,’ she replied warily. ‘After my sisters, she’s my closest friend. Look at the time! April said the day starts early on a cherry orchard and I’m keeping you up. Would you give her a message please, Major?’

Tarn couldn’t believe that April had such a sweet, polite friend, and he was happy to take a message if it helped solve some of the mystery that surrounded Ms Ritchie. ‘Sure. What’s your name?’

‘Latoya.’

‘Latoya who?’

‘Latoya Gutsell.’

Gutsell.

*Gutsell.*

Tarn had an excellent memory. He knew he’d heard the surname Gutsell somewhere. He lay in bed and racked his brains and eventually made the connection: the other hospital file April had stolen had belonged to Nola Gutsell.

As promised, he woke April by knocking on the door of her caravan at six.

There was a long pause followed by a muffled 'Grrr awah!'

The wind had picked up overnight and there were snow flurries. It was colder than an orca's nuts. 'Breakfast will be on the table in five minutes. Get dressed and wear your hat — it's freezing.'

'I think I'm getting a cold.'

'Starve a fever, feed a cold.'

'What are you? A hundred years old?'

Tarn couldn't discern any movement from inside the caravan. He rapped on the door again.

'I'm *sick!*'

'No you're not. You've just remembered how cold the mornings are down here. There was a phone call for you last night,' he added silkily. 'From Latoya.'

There was a thud. 'Shit!'

Tarn guessed April had either fallen out of bed or crashed into the edge of the table. He stepped back quickly as the caravan door was flung open. She stood above him with a blanket wrapped around her shoulders and her fluffy, lime-green toes curled around the top step. There were pink marks on her cheek from the pillow, and her hair was snarled in a knot on one side. He remembered how soft she'd looked underneath those horrible pyjamas and said the opposite of what he was thinking: 'You're a real picture in the morning.'

'Why didn't you tell me?' April screeched.

‘Because you were asleep, and I’m considerate.’ He gazed at her speculatively. ‘She said her name was Latoya Gutsell.’

Her lips clamped together. She grabbed the handle of the door and yanked it closed. The talkative Ms Ritchie wasn’t talking.

‘I wrote down her message.’ Tarn flipped up the collar of his jacket. ‘There’s bacon, eggs, sausages and mushrooms waiting for you in the kitchen. Get it while it’s still hot and before Mum poisons it.’

# Chapter 8

*Best friends are the siblings God chose not to give us.*

**Anon**

After she'd run away from Ralph, April had gone looking for Nola Gutsell. She knew from Nola's medical file that her husband's name was Barry. Gutsell was an unusual surname, so it wasn't hard to track them down to a small town on the remote West Coast of the South Island. Barry and Nola managed a takeaway bar with occasional help from their seven children: Christobel, Toni, Jayson, Lateesha, Farrah, Shontell and Latoya.

The sign above the takeaway bar read *The Flying Dragon, Chinese Takeaways, Fish 'n Chips.* Nola was taking orders. She wore a short blue-and-white checked polyester smock with a name badge pinned to the front, and towering wedge heels so that she could see over the service counter. A triangle of blue material that had been all the rage in the 1970s held back her faded platinum hair. April looked past mascara-clogged lashes into turquoise-blue eyes and knew she was looking at the woman who'd given birth to her. She felt like she'd been jolted with a cattle prod. The hair on her neck lifted, and goose bumps dimpled her arms. She guessed she looked as strange as she felt because the blonde woman was staring at her.

'What can I get for you, love?' Nola asked in a throaty smoker's voice.

'A …' April tore her eyes away and looked at the menu on the wall behind Nola. 'A beefburger, please.'

Nola cleared her throat. 'Cheese?'

April stared at her and nodded.

'Beetroot?'

She nodded again. If Nola had said radioactive waste, she'd have agreed to that, too.

Nola took April's money and looked over her shoulder at the big, bald guy standing in front of the deep fryer shaking baskets of chips. A grizzled, greying blond beard covered the lower half of his face and brushed his chest. Beads of sweat clung to his forehead and scalp. Beneath his apron, he wore a brown singlet and faded black shorts, and he had jandals on his feet. Health and Safety regulations seemed to have somehow bypassed his notice.

Nola turned towards him.

*Please!* April prayed. *Let him be a friend. An employee.*

'Barry?'

She sucked in a breath and let it out. It ended in a tiny whimper.

Barry gave one of the baskets a shake. 'Yeah?'

'A beefburger with the works.'

Nola studied her intently. 'You don't look too well, love. You look like you could do with a good feed. Are you sure you don't want some chips to go with that burger?'

April shifted nervously and flinched when a scab on one of the cuts left by Ralph's belt buckle caught on her shirt. Some of the cuts were deep. She hadn't stuck around long when Ralph had come home bellowing like a mad bull after meeting Heather. April had been at home in bed. She'd had an appointment with the gynaecologist that day, and had broken out in hives and started sneezing following one of the treatments to desensitize her to Ralph's sperm.

Things had become tense between them when April hadn't been able to get pregnant. One of the reasons Ralph had chosen such a young wife was because he wanted a big family. He'd taken the news that April was allergic to his sperm personally. April hadn't been too thrilled either: breaking out in hives and curling up in pain every time you made love with your husband wasn't very romantic.

It had never been a problem before, because she'd never had unprotected sex. Fortunately there were treatments, and she'd been happy to put up with any amount of discomfort to have a baby because she'd loved Ralph, and been grateful that he loved her. He'd always treated her like a queen. That had changed after he'd read somewhere that women who had multiple sex partners were more likely to develop allergies to sperm. There were a few times in the year between when Stefan had left and she'd met Ralph that April had woken up with men whose names she couldn't remember, but generally she married the men she slept with. After Ralph had bumped into his mother-in-law for the first time, and Heather had dripped her poison into his ear, he'd been convinced his wife's promiscuity was the reason for her allergy. She was definitely a liar.

April sat in bed and watched Ralph tear off his clothes and fling them around the room. She listened to him rant and was reminded of Grant. His behaviour was out of character. April argued back. That was out of character, too.

'Heather's the liar and slut, Ralph! She deliberately swapped me with her baby at the hospital because she'd had an affair and her baby was too dark. You mustn't listen to her!'

'Do you think I'm going to believe a story like that? The poor woman was in tears when she was telling me.'

'Don't be an idiot!' April shouted. 'Do you really think I'd make something like that up?'

Incensed, Ralph picked up his belt and swung the buckle at her. April deflected the first blow with her hands. The second caught her across her shoulder before she scrambled off the bed and ran. Ralph hit her another six or seven times on the back before she escaped. April heard things breaking as she ran downstairs and grabbed the key to her Mercedes.

Weeks later, April still felt dazed. The red-faced ogre swinging a belt over his head wasn't the man she had married. The Mercedes belonged to one of Ralph's companies; April had dropped it off at a police station, giving the key and Ralph's name to the cop at the desk. She couldn't face seeing or talking to him, and had avoided visiting a doctor or a hospital to get treatment for her back in case Ralph came up as her next-of-kin and they contacted him. April had taken the precaution of photographing her wounds by standing in front of a mirror with her digital camera. She had little money and only a vague idea of what she was going to do next. The only thing she knew for sure was that she wouldn't be returning to Wellington and her husband.

Now, as she waited for her takeaway, April watched Nola and Barry and wondered what Ralph would think if he could see his real in-laws.

Nola called out: 'A portion of chips too, Barry.'

Barry winked at April, threw chips into a basket and lowered them into the deep fryer. As Nola walked past, he pinched her on the bottom. Her boobs sagged and she needed to lose twenty pounds, but Barry still seemed to think she was hot. Nola paid no attention, just carried on walking, but April noticed that her hips swung a little more beneath the polyester smock. Barry noticed too and grinned.

The theme from *Deliverance* started playing in April's head.

She was curious about Nola and Barry and their daughter who was the same age as her, in that order. It was easy to pick out Latoya when she entered the takeaway bar through the back door with her oldest sister. Christobel was a younger version of Nola. Latoya was taller and darker than her parents and sibling. She stood out like a brown sheep in a paddock full of white ones.

Latoya wasn't allowed to drive because her epilepsy wasn't well controlled. Nola insisted that Christobel show April a good motel to stay in while she was in town. On the way, Christobel smoked. April stuck her head out the car window and pretended to admire the scenery.

'Don't smoke, huh?' Christobel asked. 'Jayson, Shontell and Latoya are the only ones who don't in our family. Every now and then we try to give up. We reckon we keep the drug companies that make the smoking patches in business.' She flicked the cigarette out the window and mentioned that Latoya was moving to Christchurch to train as a florist.

On impulse, April gave Christobel her new mobile number. 'I'm moving to Christchurch too. If Latoya's looking for a place to stay or wants to catch up, she can give me a call.'

Latoya moved into the flat April was sharing with another girl, and when the other girl left they shared the rent between the two of them. Latoya saw April's back, knew she'd run away from Ralph Berryman, and supported her during the divorce. April took care of Latoya when she had a seizure, and, when the job with the florist didn't work out, April got her a job as the receptionist at WWD. Latoya met her boyfriend, Tim, when he booked a strip-o-gram for his best friend's birthday.

Nola wasn't too enthused when Latoya and Tim got engaged. 'That girl might be rough around the edges, but she isn't stupid,' Nola grumbled to April. 'She's always been the brainbox in the family. Lateesha was the same until she discovered boys and swapped school for the games arcade. I don't want Latoya to end up like her sister.'

However, Nola changed her mind about Tim, who was an electrician, when he decided to set up his own business.

Because Latoya and April shared the same birthday, Nola always sent April a card and present too. If April was sick, Nola called to check on her and treated her like one of the family. The irony didn't escape April.

It was Latoya who brought up how much more April looked like the Gutsells than she did. 'Mum and Dad think they were given the wrong baby at the hospital.'

April went hot and cold. She imagined telling Latoya the truth, but knew she couldn't do it. Latoya was part of a family, but April's upbringing had been much more privileged. She felt like she'd stolen something from Latoya; she couldn't muscle in on her family, too. 'Of course they weren't!'

'I don't look anything like Mum and Dad, or my brother and sisters. But they've never treated me any different to the others,' Latoya said. 'I was born in a little place in Otago called Pisa. Do you know it?'

Lies tripped people up. If you couldn't tell the truth, it was better to tell a version of it. 'I had a couple of holidays there when I was a kid.'

'Where were you born?'

'Christchurch,' April said firmly. 'I was born in Christchurch.'

It was early afternoon. April had finished washing the buckets in the packing house. She sat on an upturned bucket and looked at the yellow slip of paper Tarn had given her with Latoya's message. It was like the major: brief and to the point. *OK. Don't worry. Moved in with Tim. Car towed. Books back to library. R u OK?*

Outside, the wind whistled around the cherry trees and the white net canopies shook. At that time of year orchardists welcomed the wind because it kept the frosts away. Frost was the biggest enemy of the buds emerging on the trees. The night before, the little caravan had shuddered against the elements, but inside it had been quite cosy.

The packing house was cold. April wore her jacket and the blue hat with the earflaps, and shivered whenever she stopped moving for any length of time. Her despair grew as she looked at Latoya's message. Being back at Aurora and around Tarn Elliott wasn't good for her. She had to get her hands on Rosamund's jewellery and make some long-overdue apologies in town, but she needed Tarn to be away for her to do one, and provide transport for her to do the other.

The outside door opened and banged shut. Tarn emerged from the office into the packing house, rubbing his hands together and blowing on them. He was wearing a black knit hat pulled over his ears; it accentuated his austere features and the scars on his cheeks.

His face was unrelentingly masculine, or rugged if you wanted to be nice about it. The doctor who'd delivered him must have looked at his face and known he was a boy long before the rest of him arrived. April could see why the major rang Emma's and Jacinta's bells — which made the episode outside the powder room last night all the more embarrassing.

Tarn stopped when he saw that April was reading the message he'd given her. He'd seen the despair on her face before she saw him and her expression soured. He'd take sour over those fake smiles any day.

'What are you doing here?' she demanded. 'I'll ring if I need you.' She waved a hand in dismissal. 'Go and finish the pruning with your new friend Smitty.'

Nobody could accuse the princess of being short on gall. 'We have finished.' Tarn sat down on another upturned bucket and leaned against the leg of one of the packing tables. He stretched out his legs as if he was settling in for a long chat. 'Are you upset about your car being towed?'

April didn't want to talk to him; he asked too many awkward questions. 'My car was a piece of junk; whoever towed it did me a favour. I'm more upset about my books going back to the library. I hadn't finished one of them.'

He crossed his heavy, black lace-up boots. They looked suspiciously like they were army issue. 'What was it called?'

'I don't name my cars, but I try to be open-minded about that kind of thing. What do you call your truck?'

The princess was in a really shitty mood. 'The book,' Tarn said patiently. 'What was the name of the book?'

She was tempted to say the *Kama Sutra*. '*The Seven Daughters of Eve*. It's about mitochondrial DNA. It only gets passed down the female line. Most Europeans can trace their ancestry back to seven women who lived thousands and thousands of years ago.' April could tell that Tarn thought she was making it up. Her anger at him, and the world in general, grew.

'Who's Tim?'

'My pimp,' she snapped. 'Latoya does the books for him.'

'No, she doesn't. She told me she's the receptionist at Wild Women Do. Don't lie about things like that.'

'Why not? Plenty of people have thought it. *You* did last night.'

Tarn looked at her sitting on a bucket with the ugly blue hat pulled down around her ears. 'I don't think you're a prostitute, April.' She *was* a flirt, though.

'Then you're stupid,' April said cuttingly. 'If I thought screwing you would get me what I want, I'd be naked and have my tongue down your throat right now.'

He studied her intently for a few moments, then taunted softly, 'Go on then.'

She felt the same way she had the day of the accident when it seemed like Tarn was going to take Stefan's bribe — let down. She hunched her shoulders and dropped her eyes to the toes of his boots, and followed the length of his jean-clad legs upwards to the juncture of his thighs. April flushed. The major was definitely interested.

'That's why it's called cock-teasing, April,' Tarn said flatly. 'What's in that wardrobe that you want so badly?' When she wouldn't answer him, he slapped his hands against his thighs in frustration and stood up. 'I'm going into town.'

April sat up and pleaded, 'Can I come with you?' There were things she needed to do before she chickened out, like apologize to Emma Murfitt, and Courtney.

'No, you can't. There's white paint for the gates in the garage next to your caravan. Sort out how many cans there are and some paintbrushes. If you need more, tell me.'

She pointed her thumb at her chest and cried, 'You want *me* to paint the gates?'

Tarn merely raised his brows in answer.

One of the things April most disliked about him was that he was unmoved by wheedling, pleading or flirting. She should know by now that being blunt was more likely to get a result. 'But I need some things!' She held out her hands. 'Look what cleaning those buckets has done to my hands!'

He barely glanced at them. 'I'll buy you some gloves. Write me a list of what you need.'

She lowered her eyes and said demurely, 'They're personal things; I'd rather not.'

'Like what? Tampons?'

She scowled. *See? Blunt.*

April forced a smile. 'I'll write a list.'

Tarn wasn't a moody person, but being around April was turning him into one. It was her fault that he had to go to town in the first place. He'd promised to take her to see a lawyer before she gave her statement, but the only lawyer Tarn knew was Emma and she definitely wouldn't represent April — so it had to be somebody out of town. And even if she'd wanted to, Emma couldn't because she was a witness. He felt uncomfortable approaching Emma to ask her to recommend another lawyer, but he didn't have much choice. His bad mood abated as he read April's list, which Tarn knew was the exact opposite of what she'd intended.

Regular tampons with short — not *long* — strings. Hair removal shower gel. Evening primrose oil capsules for PMS — two bottles (*It gets really bad*, she'd written next to it). Licorice-flavoured dental floss. Aubergine and Nasturtium Hair Shampoo and Conditioner. A fifty-dollar top-up for her cellphone.

Tarn crossed off the dental floss and fifty-dollar top-up, drew circles around the tampons, primrose oil capsules and shampoo and conditioner, and knocked on Courtney and Lionel's front door.

Courtney confirmed that there was no such thing as tampons with different-length strings. She'd never heard of Aubergine and Nasturtium Shampoo and Conditioner, so Tarn crossed that off, too. She started to giggle. 'April was always one of the naughty kids in class.'

'She still is.' Tarn recalled his response to April last night and again today. She wasn't the only one thinking of misbehaving.

'April never had PMS when I knew her, but maybe that's changed. You can get the primrose oil at the health shop.' Courtney's brow creased. 'Maybe it'd be better if I got all this for you.' People were still talking about Tarn buying April clothes. They'd lay an egg if they heard he'd bought her tampons. She hesitated. 'How is she?'

'Painful, deceitful, useful — take your pick.'

Tarn took the ball Kieran offered him and rolled it across the kitchen floor. Kieran chuckled and set off after it again, and Tarn realized he was being trained by a two-year-old. 'I think she'd like to see you.'

He was a fool. April didn't want his help. She wanted a pair of gloves and access to his wardrobe. It'd help if her tough, smart-aleck exterior didn't sometimes slip and reveal a wistful, yearning woman. He took the ball from Kieran.

Courtney watched pensively as her son toddled after it. 'I'm still really angry with her, Tarn. We were best friends right from kindergarten; she should have been a bridesmaid at my wedding. But she just dropped me, not even a phone call – nothing.'

'You don't need to tell *me* how infuriating April is.' He stood up and unhooked his jacket from the back of the chair. 'I need to get going; I want to see Emma.'

Courtney grabbed Kieran by the back of his trousers as he barrelled past to throw his ball to his new friend. Kieran protested loudly. 'Emma?' Courtney asked above the noise. 'What do you want to see Emma for?'

Sometimes women were so damned transparent, Tarn thought. Or at least the ones that weren't called April Ritchie were. 'I want her to recommend a lawyer from out of town.'

'For you?'

Tarn shook his head and grinned. 'Who do you think?'

Courtney's stomach did a little drum-roll of appreciation at the grin. Tarn always did have a wonderful smile. If Emma didn't get a move on, some smart woman was going to snap him up. When she was younger, Courtney had really wanted Tarn for a brother-in-law, and had been almost as upset as Emma when he'd stopped visiting. Growing up and getting married to Lionel had made Courtney revise her opinion. While it was important to have things in common with your partner, Emma and Tarn were *too* alike. They both liked being in control too much. Courtney suspected that if they ever got married their lives would be so organized they'd end up dying of boredom. They needed partners who could appreciate their strong natures and organizational skills, but were able to throw a spanner in the works every now and then and keep them on their toes.

Courtney thought about April's list again. April was certainly doing her best to throw a spanner in Tarn's works.

'There's a good lawyer at the practice I used to work for in Queenstown. His name is Rob Sturmley.' Emma paused. 'Or did you want somebody more local?'

'The Ritchies are so well known in these parts — especially April — I think somebody in Queenstown might be better.' Tarn smiled apologetically. 'Thanks, Emma; I appreciate the help. I apologize for asking, but I didn't have much choice.'

Emma toyed with the fine black-and-white merino scarf knotted at her neck. It matched her slim, knee-length black-and-white-checked wool skirt. She wore a long-sleeved red knit top with a scoop neck, sheer black pantyhose and shiny, black high-heeled pumps. Her chunky silver-and-black earrings matched the bracelet on her wrist. Emma looked the way she always did: attractive and professional. 'That's alright.' She saw Tarn hesitate. 'What is it?'

'Emma, do you remember the name on the other medical file April took?'

She remembered every detail of that night. And how she'd felt when this man had walked away. April Ritchie's selfishness had wrecked Emma's dreams for the future, and now Tarn was helping her. 'Nola Gutsell.' Her expression remained smooth as she wrote down the other lawyer's details.

Tarn took the paper she held out. 'Thanks. I'd better make a move: I left April painting the front gates, but she won't stay there.'

'Where will she be?'

'Where she shouldn't be.'

Before April sorted out the cans of paint and brushes in the garage, she took a quick detour upstairs to Tarn's bedroom. Carole was feeding Smitty coffee and cake in the kitchen. It didn't escape April's notice that she hadn't been invited.

The big bed in Tarn's room was made, and the room was tidy. There was a book on the nightstand, and a pair of new-looking black dress shoes in a shoebox on the floor at the end of the bed. April paused briefly when she saw the shoes. There was something very personal about a person's discarded shoes. Tarn's were like him: good quality and attractive without being fussy.

April made a beeline for the wardrobe. Her feet faltered when she saw the envelope propped against the foot of the door with her name on it. Thanks to the note he'd given her from Latoya, April recognized Tarn's handwriting. She gazed at the envelope and fumed. Tarn had eyes in the back of his head, his knees, his bum and everywhere in between. He was always one step ahead of her. April knew the door was locked but she tried it anyway. She didn't open the envelope, or trash the room like she would have done when she was a teenager. If she had, Tarn would have proof she'd been in his room and April wasn't about to give him the satisfaction of knowing he'd outsmarted her again. She could guess what he'd written in the note: a pithy comment about mending her ways and getting back to work.

Angry and frustrated, she ran down the stairs and automatically jumped the last six. She wobbled on landing and winced. She wasn't seventeen anymore, plus she was out of practice.

'That had better not be you, April!' Carole shouted from the kitchen. 'You're supposed to be painting the gates!'

April tiptoed quickly to the front door and let herself out quietly. She slipped around the side of the house, past the rhododendron bushes and their gorgeous pink display, and stomped to the garages. She stopped to take a closer look at the blue helicopter. The chances of Tarn taking her for a ride in it were non-existent. April went into the garage where the paint was stored. There were some new-looking cans of white paint, a couple of bottles of turpentine and some paintbrushes. There were also some old cans of green, brown and mustard yellow. She wrinkled her nose. They'd probably been bought by whoever had butchered the kitchen décor.

The cans of paint reminded her of her disruptive-pattern pyjamas. The letter on the door had only reinforced what April already knew: that going head to head with Tarn wouldn't work; to beat him, she needed to be creative. Fortunately, April was *very* creative. She stepped daintily over the cans of white paint and hooked her fingers through a can of green paint and a can of mustard paint. It might take a little while to wear the Rock of Gibraltar down, but she was up for the job.

When Tarn returned, he was pleased to see that April had made a start on painting the gates, but was critical of her slow progress. He brought it up at dinner after they'd gone through the ritual of swapping meals and Carole had bitten April's head off about it.

'I'm not going to ruin good food trying to poison you! And don't think I didn't hear you in the hallway this afternoon. Tarn told you you're not allowed upstairs.'

'I don't know what you heard, Carole, but it couldn't have been me. I was painting the front gates.'

Tarn had to hide a smile — he'd known April wouldn't be able to resist paying a visit to the wardrobe while he was out. 'About the gates,' he began.

She forked up some more of the fragrant chicken curry and fluffy white rice. 'Yes?'

'You only managed to paint one of the pillars and part of one gate.'

The gates were always left open, so that the front of them was the only part visible. Nobody ever bothered to look at the sides folded back against the fence, and April was relying on Tarn being too busy to check. If he did, he would soon realize she'd done a lot of painting — only it wasn't white.

'That's because I'm meticulous about my work,' she told him. 'I had to cut back the camellia trees either side of the pillars before I could begin painting.'

His gaze didn't waver. More like she'd wasted time trying to get the wardrobe door open. 'Is that all you got up to today?'

April stared back. 'Absolutely, Major. How did the shopping go?'

'Fine.' He applied himself to his curry. 'I'll give you your things later.'

He was sitting in the burgundy chair again reading the paper when April emerged from her shower, wearing her disruptive-pattern pyjamas. Tarn leaned over, hooked a finger in a plastic supermarket bag on the floor beside the chair and held it out. 'Here you go. I couldn't get the short strings or the shampoo, but Courtney gave me the name of a brand that was just as good.'

April reached for the bag and stopped. 'You saw Courtney?'

'She was a big help — especially about the strings.'

She didn't answer, but took the bag, put on her gumboots and jacket and let herself out.

Tarn watched her go, and felt mean.

# Chapter 9

*A closed mouth gathers no foot.*

Anon

Being around Tarn unnerved April. He had a way of looking at her that made her want to blurt out all her secrets. She was terrified that he'd ask who'd really been in the packing house with Heather. At first, when she had to work alongside him, she talked non-stop so that Tarn didn't have an opportunity to ask any difficult questions. The major's pained expression indicated that he couldn't believe anybody could talk so much crap for so long. It took April a while to understand he was a man who was comfortable with silence. She gradually calmed down as the days passed, and he didn't bring up the night of her birthday.

Once she got used to it, April liked the seclusion and cosiness of the caravan. She didn't have to worry about paying rent and had a place to escape to at the end of the day. She'd forgotten how cold and physical the work was, and how much she'd missed Aurora. For the first couple of weeks, she barely had the energy to eat dinner and shower before she fell into bed.

The big thing April had in her favour was that she knew more about running a cherry orchard than Tarn did, but he was a quick learner. He sat outside the downstairs powder room every night in the hated burgundy chair, and read the paper. April got used to seeing him there when she exited the powder room in her pyjamas. She elicited more information from Tarn in their brief nightly chats than she did all day working alongside him in the orchard. For instance, she found out there were seasonal workers arriving from Taiwan soon, and that that was one of the reasons he'd given her the smallest caravan. Until then, Tarn, April and the new worker, Smitty, were it.

Smitty was a quiet, balding man in his late fifties who'd been 'found' by Clarence. April didn't know where, and at first thought it would be better if Smitty got lost again. He was a good worker, but depressing to be around. Smitty smiled and talked even less than Tarn, and he liked the boss. Tarn was surprisingly patient with Smitty, and got the best out of him. He even put up with Smitty calling him 'Major'.

April revised her opinion of Smitty when he came across her putting the finishing touches to the gates one day while Tarn was working on the helicopter behind the house. Smitty was supposed to be doing some maintenance work on the pump used to bring water down the hill from Aurora's dam to irrigate the orchard. April was crouched down adding mustard-coloured daubs of paint when she heard Smitty remark, 'Don't think that's what the major had in mind when he asked you to paint 'em.'

She started and fell backwards, landing on her butt in the gravel. Mustard paint flew into the air and landed in her hair and on her face. 'Don't *do* that!' April shrieked.

Smitty was large and thickset. He caught her beneath the arms and lifted her easily to her feet. 'He's not going to be happy when he sees that. He told you to paint 'em white.'

April swatted dirt from the seat of her track pants. 'They are white — on the outside.' She watched him look between the gates and the pyjama jacket she'd hooked on a nearby bush for artistic inspiration. He either grunted or laughed — April wasn't sure which.

'You've done a good job,' Smitty conceded, 'if you wanted your gates camouflaged.'

'Are you going to tell Tarn?'

Gerald Smit was aware of the tension between the major and April. The major was a shrewd but fair boss, who was clear about his expectations and wouldn't accept any corner-cutting. His style of management was perfect for Gerald, but not so perfect for April who didn't appreciate anybody telling her what to do, especially around the orchard. Gerald suspected the major's retribution would be swift when he saw the gates. He put his hands in the pockets of his dark-green vest and shook his head. 'It's between you and the major.'

'Thanks, Smitty.'

'Don't thank me. The major likes things done properly.' He nodded at the gates, 'He ain't goin' to be too happy when he sees that, and I ain't comin' to your rescue when he does.'

'I don't need to be rescued; I can look after myself.'

'Not what I heard. I was told you got banged up in jail the night you arrived.'

April imagined Carole relating the tale over one of their coffee-and-cake sessions in the kitchen. 'I *stayed* the night at the jail because I couldn't afford to pay for a motel room.'

Smitty looked unconvinced. 'Paint 'em white,' he advised, and walked away.

A single knock on the back door heralded Gerald Smit's arrival for coffee and cake. Carole kept him waiting while she dried her hands and hung the towel on the rail beside the kitchen sink. She'd never kept Murdo waiting; she'd always rushed to him like an over-eager puppy to its master.

Carole tugged her rose-pink, hand-knitted jumper over her bottom. She wished she hadn't let herself get so fat since Murdo died, but food had always been her solace when she was sad and depressed. Tarn enjoyed her cooking, but he was too busy to linger over meals and treated them like pit stops to refuel his body. In the months before Murdo had died, Carole had lost so much weight that Tarn and the doctor had started to worry about her more than Murdo. Even Murdo had noticed how thin she was, and complimented her, which had been a rare thing. 'You're the same size you were when I met you that night at the dance,' he'd said. She remembered blushing with pleasure — Murdo had always been able to make her blush — while her stomach had clenched with the old feelings of shame and guilt when she remembered the night of the dance and lying about being on the pill.

Now, jumper in place, Carole turned and opened the door. Gerald was standing with a hand braced against the wall of the house, toeing off his gumboots. He smiled at her and she nodded back. Her stomach didn't leap and her face didn't flame. Gerald wasn't a looker like Murdo had been. Apart from the silver semi-circle at the back of his head, he'd lost all his hair; he also had the knobbly 'cauliflower' ears of a former rugby forward. Gerald didn't look at her with resignation and regret; his gaze held kindness, sadness and loneliness. It was the sadness that had prompted Carole to offer him coffee and cake the first time, that and the 'starved wolf' air of a man struggling to make the transition to being a widower. She continued the daily ritual because feeding Gerald and listening to him talk about his wife comforted her. It confirmed that long, happy marriages did exist. When he talked about Bronwyn, Gerald's lugubrious expression lifted and the dam burst on his tongue.

Carole took a saucepan of hot milk from the stove and made milky coffee for both of them. Gerald sat down and cut two slices of the cake on the table, a big one for him and a smaller piece for her.

'Madeira; my favourite,' he said.

The corners of her mouth lifted fractionally. He said the same thing, or a variation of it, every time he ate some of her cake. Carole put the mugs of coffee on the table and joined him while Gerald added sugar to his coffee and sweetener to hers and stirred them. He reached into his green vest and pulled out an old yellow-and-white envelope. 'I brought some photos.'

She retrieved her glasses from the kitchen dresser and opened the envelope. Brown celluloid strips of negatives fell onto the table, a reminder of the days before the digital camera. Gerald scooped them up carefully. 'They were taken on our wedding day.'

Carole cradled the precious photos in her hands and studied Gerald thirty years younger, with thick, black hair and wearing a smart black suit. He had his arm around the shoulders of a pretty young woman wearing a crinoline wedding dress and a veil on her long, brown, curly hair. Carole had wanted to wear a dress just like it when she'd married Murdo, but by the time they'd finally agreed on a date she was five months pregnant and wasp-waisted crinoline wedding dresses were off-limits.

Gerald touched a finger to a photo. 'We had a great day.'

'I can tell.' Carole swallowed the knot of sorrow lodged in her throat. She picked up the next photo in the pile and tried not to feel jealous. Bronwyn Smit wasn't beautiful, but Gerald had adored her. 'Bronwyn looked lovely.'

He sensed he'd upset her. The time he spent with Carole in the kitchen was the highlight of his day. Her way of dealing with her grief was different to his. She didn't volunteer much information about her husband or her marriage, but seemed content to let him talk about his. Gerald wanted to return the favour. He knew she'd nursed Murdo while he was dying, and didn't know if it was worse watching somebody you loved slip away bit by bit, or have them die suddenly and without warning, like Bronwyn had.

'Guess your wedding was the same,' Gerald ventured.

Carole took her time returning the photos to the envelope. Her wedding album was hidden away in a drawer in her bedroom. She'd never put her wedding photos on the mantelpiece or wall, the way Bronwyn Smit probably had, because they portrayed a mockery of what should have been a happy event. Carole wasn't sure if Tarn had ever even seen them. 'My wedding wasn't like yours,' she said briefly.

Gerald raised his brows. 'No?'

'No.'

Lying to Murdo had been wrong, but she couldn't regret it because it had given her Tarn. He was the best son a mother could wish for. She'd been shocked when he'd announced he was leaving the army, but he'd said it was time. Although he never discussed it, Tarn was weighed down, too, by what had happened on the patrol and the deaths of his men.

In a couple of weeks it would be her sixtieth birthday. Listening to Gerald and looking at his wedding photos wasn't going to change the way things had been between her and Murdo any more than the pink jumper was going to make her slim and beautiful.

Carole's gaze swept the front of the faded grey sweater Gerald wore beneath his green vest. It was machine-knitted and had holes in the elbows. Perhaps she should offer to make him one; it would give her something to do at night besides staring at the television and eating biscuits. She handed him the cake knife. 'You cut yourself some more cake and I'll heat another lot of milk for coffee.'

The weather was still unpredictable. Frost was the biggest concern. Tarn and April studied the MetService weather reports each day like students swotting for end-of-year exams, and tended the trees as though they were newborn infants.

April worked her way along a row of trees, gently touching the swollen buds for signs of sticky bud. If they had it, it meant the buds would be burned by frost and a frost was expected that night. She was wrapped up like a mummy in layers of clothing, which she gradually removed throughout the day. One of the first things she put on each morning was the blue hat.

The salamander heaters that stood between the rows of trees had been filled with diesel in readiness for lighting when the temperature fell at night. In spring the temperature could still drop as low as minus four or five degrees Celsius during the night. Bringing in helicopters could raise the temperature by as much as four degrees and save thousands of dollars' worth of fruit being ruined. One of the orchard owners had hired Tarn to take the helicopter up tonight, so he'd asked Smitty to stay the night and help April and Carole. Smitty had returned from eating cake with

Carole, looking even more miserable than usual, and gone to fill the last of the salamander heaters on the other side of the orchard.

Tarn was checking trees in the row beside April. Her eyes kept straying to his blunt-tipped fingers. Somebody had taught him that the correct way to check a bud was to fondle it. She didn't think the stony-faced major knew how to be so gentle. 'Why are you so nice to a miserable coot like Smitty and so horrible to me?' she asked irritably.

'Smitty doesn't ask me to buy tampons with short strings or primrose oil for his PMS.'

'Maybe you should. If ever a man looked like he had PMS, it's Smitty.'

The cold didn't bother Tarn and Smitty nearly as much as it did April. By midday, if the sun was out, they were usually stripped down to T-shirts. Her gaze lingered on Tarn's face and arms. They were already turning brown.

Tarn didn't notice; as usual he was focused on the job at hand. 'Without Smitty, I'd never have got the pruning done.'

'And without me, the raspberries and boysenberries would never have got pruned.' Until April had told him, Tarn hadn't known there were any raspberries and boysenberries, or that they were sold to restaurants in town and at the orchard gate during the summer. 'I can see why you and Smitty hit it off. He's about as chatty and smiley as you.'

He finally looked across the stretch of ground separating the rows of trees. 'You do know Smitty's wife had a heart attack and died very suddenly last year?'

April's face fell. 'No. He never talks.'

'He does to Mum.' Tarn suspected sharing the recent loss of their partners and Carole's cooking had loosened Smitty's tongue.

‘Has he got any children?’ April asked.

‘He never talks about any.’

She touched a swollen bud and murmured, ‘That’s sad. Having children makes all the difference.’

Tarn continued to study her. He didn’t know why he was so curious about April, just that he was. ‘What about you? Didn’t Berryman want kids?’

She checked another bud. ‘I was allergic to his sperm.’

He stared. ‘What?’

‘You heard me. Lots of people have allergies.’

‘To bees and penicillin but not to …’ Tarn ground to a halt. He wasn’t talking to a soldier.

April laughed hollowly. ‘Don’t worry; I’ve heard all the things it’s called, and all the jokes.’ She was surprised she’d told him. ‘I’m not the only woman who’s allergic to it, but, as you can imagine, Ralph took it a little personally. What’s the point of having a child bride if she can’t help you found a dynasty?’

Her self-deprecating little joke bothered him. Tarn chose his words carefully. ‘You can’t have children?’

‘Ah.’ She wagged an index finger and walked to the next tree in the row. ‘Now that’s where things get interesting. I don’t know if it was just Ralph’s that was the problem, or any man’s. I thought about getting a MedicAlert bracelet, but instead I decided it was better to go cold turkey and swear off the hard stuff,’ she joked.

The annoying thing about April was that it was impossible to know if she was telling the truth.

By four that afternoon they knew they were definitely in for a frost. Tarn checked the box that housed the frost alarm, and the frost lights attached to the tops of posts in the orchard. When the temperature dropped to minus five degrees Celsius, the frost alarm would be activated and his cellphone rung. The frost lights changed colour depending on the temperature, from a 'happy' flashing white light to solid green, to solid white, to red and then finally, if the temperature dipped too low, to a red flashing 'we're in the shit' light.

After he'd finished checking the alarm and lights, Tarn went inside the house and discovered April trying to drag the La-Z-boy armchair from the study into the drawing room.

'What are you doing?'

'Putting this by the window so I can see the mirror on the post outside that reflects the frost lights.' She tried to shove the armchair closer, but it got caught on the rug.

He moved her aside and lifted it free. 'Why didn't you get the red chair in the hallway? It's closer.'

'I don't like it.'

*How could you not like a chair?* Tarn carried the La-Z-boy to the window.

April sat down and squinted out the window at the post. 'More to the right.' Tarn shifted the chair. 'Back a bit.' He did as she asked. 'Perfect.' She tipped her head back and looked up at him standing behind her. 'Now all I need is a pillow and a blanket.'

He looked down at her. 'Why should I let you sleep in here tonight?'

'Somebody has to. It's the best place to watch the lights change colour.'

'That'd make perfect sense if you weren't as blind as a bat and barred from the house.'

'I can see colours and I'm only barred from the upstairs.' She smiled smugly. 'I'll know the temperature has dropped before your cellphone goes off.'

'Tarn! Wake up!'

Tarn jerked awake as his cellphone began to ring on his bedside table. The bedroom light was on and April was standing beside his bed fully dressed with her blonde hair loose on her shoulders and that awful blue hat pulled down around her ears. He grabbed the phone and got out of bed. Downstairs, he could hear Carole and Smitty moving about. He grabbed his underwear from the pile of clothes he'd left in readiness on the floor beside the bed and rasped, 'What's the temperature?'

April didn't answer. She was too busy staring — the major slept in the buff.

Tarn dragged his underwear up his legs and covered the part of him she was staring at. He snatched up his pants, shoved in a leg and barked, 'April! What's the temperature?'

Colour bloomed in her pale cheeks. 'Zero,' she mumbled, and ran downstairs.

April's breath fogged in the air. Her cheeks stung with a mixture of embarrassment and cold as she worked her way between the rows of trees, lighting the salamander heaters. Smitty was at the other end of the orchard doing the same thing, while Carole took the middle. They all wore headlamps so they could see, and carried gauges to check the temperature in each row and then adjust the heaters accordingly. It took about twenty seconds to light each heater. Once they were all lit, the rest of the night was spent tending them until the sun rose and Nature took over the job.

All over the valley, orchard owners hurried to protect the

season's yet-to-be-born cherries. Lights glowed in the darkness as salamander heaters were lit. Windmills stirred. Overhead sprinklers hissed into life. The water would form ice around the buds which would protect them from the frost. The distant, rhythmic beat of helicopter blades provided background music.

Tarn had flown overhead in the Robinson as April lit the first salamander heater. She was glad he'd gone so that she didn't have to face him in the orchard. He'd caught her looking; *staring*, to be precise. April shouldn't have been surprised that Tarn slept naked — most men his age did.

Her experience with Ralph's sperm and belt had dealt her libido a severe blow, and working at Wild Women Do had lowered it even further: seeing inebriated men in various stages of undress wasn't sexy. But watching Tarn Elliott climb out of bed was. He was in a lot better shape than April's clients. She felt like a pickaxe had struck deep into the arid desert of her womanhood and a geyser had spouted forth — not good for a woman who'd sworn off the hard stuff, or whose mother had thrown herself at the man responsible for the eruption. If the old argument of nurture prevailing over Nature was true, April had been on the fast track to slut-hood the day Heather brought her home from the hospital.

She tugged on the earflaps of the blue hat and went to check the next row of trees. Tarn Elliott should buy himself a pair of disruptive-pattern pyjamas, and keep his penis and the rest of himself covered up.

Tarn checked the temperature probes in the chopper. Sometimes the warm inversion layer of air couldn't be found, but tonight it had been easy. He kept the chopper twenty-five feet above the tops of the trees and flew back and forth along the rows, pushing the warmer air down towards them. The orchard he was working on was next to Aurora. Tarn looked across at the glow from the heaters in the rows between his trees and saw an occasional moving light from the headlamps worn by his mother, Smitty and April. Thinking about her reminded him of how she'd looked at him when he'd climbed out of bed. Tarn frowned and rearranged the front of his jeans. He didn't believe her story about swearing off sex, and wouldn't put it past her to have planned the little charade at the bedside.

He turned the helicopter away from Aurora. He needed to concentrate on what he'd been paid to do, not think about April Ritchie and what he might like to do to her instead.

It had long been a habit for people to congregate in Aurora's driveway on frosty nights. A collection of trucks and four-wheeled farm bikes clustered around the gates as people took turns taking a break from tending the salamander heaters and checking temperatures to have a hot drink. Carole's home-made carrot and chocolate cakes were also a big drawcard. April noticed Smitty got a much bigger piece than she did.

April was unsure what kind of welcome she'd get from her old neighbours, and so only stayed long enough to gulp down a coffee and some cake. But, apart from a few nosy questions and some ribbing about her night in jail, the talk was all about the weather and the crop; that was far more important than the return of the town pariah. She even received some compliments on the paint job she'd given the gates, especially the camouflage pattern which somebody sitting on the fence noticed as the sky began to lighten. April got nervous when one of the gates was closed to give everybody a better view of her artwork, and kept squinting nervously at the helicopters.

April clutched her mug of tea and sidled up to Smitty. 'Is that Tarn's helicopter?' she whispered.

He tipped back his head. 'Don't think so.'

'Do you take commissions, April?' one of the neighbours quipped.

She smiled at the neighbour, and hissed at Smitty: 'Make them put the gate back the way it was!'

He scratched one cauliflower ear. 'He's goin' to find out sooner or later. Might as well get it over with.'

'Later would be better. I'd like to see my twenty-seventh birthday — *please* make them open the gate!'

The birds were twittering as Carole arrived on the quad bike with a fresh supply of cake and hot thermos flasks. The lights of her quad bike lit up the inside of the gates. She stopped the bike and frowned so deeply that her brow reminded April of the furrows in a paddy field, minus the rice.

Carole searched for April amongst the people coming and going by the gates. But she'd gone.

Tarn folded his arms and studied the closed gates in the early morning sunshine. The helicopter was back behind the house. The orchard owner who'd hired him was pleased with Tarn's work, but had said he wouldn't be hiring him again.

'Why not?' Tarn knew the answer, but had asked anyway.

The neighbour had looked uncomfortable. 'Ivan Vincent gave

me a call. If I want him to pack my fruit he expects me to use his helicopter service, too. Sorry, Tarn.'

Tarn had been angry and elated at the same time: Vincent was worried. He'd nodded sympathetically. 'I understand your position, but don't forget that Aurora has a packing house, too. We can pack your cherries.'

His neighbour had looked confused. 'I thought April wasn't staying.'

'Who told you that?'

The neighbour had raised his brows and smiled faintly.

'She's staying,' Tarn had replied firmly. 'Right until the end of the season.'

Now he was scowling as he studied the gates. He didn't want any reminders of the army. He didn't need any — he carried the faces of the men who'd died on the patrol inside his head.

Ms Ritchie was trouble, but she wasn't going anywhere.

April was catching up on some much-needed sleep in her caravan when Tarn banged on the door and called out her name. The clock on the table read *8:17*. She'd been asleep for an hour. She pulled the covers over her head and played dead.

He banged on the door again. 'If you don't open this door in ten seconds, I'm coming in!'

There was a fine line between playing dead and courting it. She rolled out of bed and opened the door.

Hands on hips, Tarn glared up at her. His eyes were bloodshot, and stubble covered his jaw. 'Get dressed. We're going to Queenstown.'

April hugged herself and hopped from one foot to the other as cold air invaded her cosy nest. 'I don't want to go to Queenstown.'

His expression indicated that her wishes were immaterial.

'What for?' she demanded.

'To see a lawyer.'

Her heart rate kicked into double-time. 'We've both been up all night. Let's do it another day.'

'Let's not.' Tarn checked his watch. 'We're leaving in forty minutes. Look presentable.'

# Chapter 10

*All people have the right to stupidity, but some abuse the privilege.*

**Anon**

P – I – G.

*Pig!*

April said it over and over again in her head as she sat beside Tarn in the pick-up truck. He hadn't spoken to her since they'd left Aurora.

'What did you say?'

She hadn't realized she'd been mumbling. '*Pig*,' April replied. 'I've been calling you a pig.'

'That's really adult of you.'

'A girl has to work with what she's given. You're too big to beat up. Are you sure you're only nine years older than me? I swear it feels more like fifty at times,' she said sourly.

April was far more world-weary than any twenty-six-year-old Tarn knew. Her appointment to see the lawyer wasn't until two o'clock that afternoon, but he had to meet his bank manager at ten which was why he'd dragged April out of bed and gone without sleep himself.

The winding road followed the path of the Kawarau River as it pushed its way past pale grey and white Otago schist. Steep hills dotted with trees, and brown tussock rose on each side of the river and road. Latoya had sent a small parcel of April's things. She was dressed for summer in a frivolous turquoise dress with straps made from satin ribbon. A longer strand of the ribbon tied beneath her breasts. It matched her high-heeled mules. Her fake leather and fur jacket was her only concession to the weather. She looked like she was going to a garden party, not to visit a lawyer on a cold, windy spring day. Knowing how badly she felt the cold, Tarn felt compelled to point this out as April emerged from the caravan, to which she retorted it was this or her baggy track pants and kiddy jacket.

'You're going to freeze,' he warned.

'Your balmy personality will keep me warm,' she said grumpily.

April tapped her fingers on the passenger door and toyed with the end of the platinum braid hanging over her shoulder. It wasn't a schoolgirl braid; April's version was loose and tousled, like she'd just fallen out of bed — which she had. She gazed at Tarn critically. 'You look terrible.'

'Good.'

His black polo shirt and chinos were nice enough, and his tobacco-coloured sports jacket matched his eyes, but his hair was a disaster. April itched to cut it. He had great hair, thick with a slight wave. Already, it was sun-streaked. By summer, he'd look like a surfer. She pictured Tarn poised on a surfboard in drenched board shorts, zigzagging across waves, and wasn't too pleased when her nerves hummed like tuning forks. Lack of sleep must be responsible; the major was not the kind of guy she went for.

Unaware his alter-ego was balanced on a surfboard, Tarn muttered, 'Maybe I'll scare the bank manager into extending my overdraft.' As soon as the words were out of his mouth, he wanted to kick himself: it was exactly the kind of information April could use to her advantage. She shrugged. 'All the orchard owners have overdrafts at the moment. They're broke until they get paid in February. I don't know what you're worried about. Da—, I mean Grant, always said you weren't a real orchard owner if you weren't a couple of hundred thousand dollars in the red by the end of the season.'

Her cavalier attitude to money annoyed Tarn. It highlighted the fact that April had spent the first seventeen years of her life cocooned in luxury. He turned on the CD player, hoping she'd take the hint and shut up. April was surprised to hear one of her favourite bands. 'You like Matchbox Twenty?'

'No, I hate them. That's why I listen to them.'

'Were you this disagreeable when you spoke to your men or soldiers, or whatever it was you called them?'

She had no idea how disagreeable he could be. If she had been one of his men, Tarn would have tossed her out of the truck and made her work off her attitude with some strenuous, painful exercise. 'I'm only disagreeable when people piss me off, which you do on a regular basis.'

April dredged up a pale replica of her Hollywood beam. 'Flatterer.'

Tarn turned up the volume on the CD player.

She turned it back down. He wasn't the only one feeling tired and irritable. 'Tell me the name of the first movie you remember seeing.'

*What is she up to now?* 'What?'

'This is obviously a little challenging for you, so I'll go first to help you out,' April said kindly. 'The first movie I ever saw was *The Little Mermaid*. It made me cry.'

He sighed. She wouldn't give up until he answered. '*Herbie Goes Bananas*.'

Her face lit up. 'I saw that! How old were you?'

'I don't know. Four or five.'

'I was about ten.'

'I'll tuck the information away for future reference.'

'You're being disagreeable.'

'I'm giving it my best shot.'

'What's the first movie that you cried at?' April raised her brows. 'Or were you a hard-nosed, aloof child, too?'

He was only hard-nosed when the situation demanded it. '*The Fox and The Hound*.'

She opened her mouth.

'I was six,' Tarn said wearily.

'Courtney and I *loved* that movie. We cried buckets.'

*Why bother with star ratings? Why not award empty tissue-boxes instead?* 'My favourite movie was *Gremlins*.'

'Don't tell me: you loved the part where the gremlin was put in the blender.'

'I liked watching Phoebe Cates best of all.'

April gasped. 'You were having unclean thoughts about Phoebe Cates? How old were you? Ten?'

'Nine.' Tarn smiled reminiscently. 'That dark hair and those big brown eyes pushed all the right buttons.'

*The major likes brunettes. So what?*

'Phoebe Cates was in the best kid's movie of all time — and it wasn't *Gremlins*.'

'Enlighten me,' Tarn said in a bored voice.

'*Drop Dead Fred*. Do you know it?'

'Of course I know it; I'm a Phoebe follower.'

'That's very disturbing.'

April made Tarn name his favourite movies and songs through pre-teens to teens and onwards, and told him hers. Not too surprisingly, their tastes were poles apart. Growing up, she'd loved The Backstreet Boys, The Spice Girls, Shania Twain and *NSYNC; Tarn had favoured INXS, Tom Petty, Aerosmith and Poison. April was particularly offended when she heard he'd liked Poison. 'I hate "Every Rose Has Its Thorn". Stefan used to sing it to me all the time.'

'Can't think why.'

They got into an argument when April said *Titanic* was the best movie ever made — or at least Tarn shook his head while she argued.

'How dare you say it was one of the worst movies ever made? Kate and Leonardo were incredible. What about that scene where they stand together on the front of the boat?'

'It's called a prow, and it was incredible alright — if you've got ovaries.'

April sniggered.

'Sean Connery and Alex Baldwin were superb in *The Hunt For Red October*, but did you see them perched on the front of the sub pretending to fly?'

She laughed and yawned at the same time.

'Go to sleep, April.'

'You just want me to stop talking.'

'Smart girl.'

She rested her cheek against the passenger window and blinked sleepily at the pale jade and frothy white water of the river. 'It looks like a jade-coloured cappuccino. I'd forgotten how beautiful it was.' Her eyelids drooped. 'Turn the music up a little.'

Tarn adjusted the volume on the CD player. The haunting wail of the guitar at the beginning of Matchbox Twenty's 'Hand Me Down' spilled softly from the speakers. The song was a favourite of Tarn's. He'd heard it a hundred times, but for some reason this time he was reminded of April — which was stupid: April was a survivor, not a victim.

He kept glancing at her as she slept. At seventeen, she'd been a wild, pretty, spoiled child of no interest to a twenty-six-year-old infantry lieutenant. Nine years on, she was still high-maintenance, but the spoiled child was gone, and the prettiness had tarnished and matured into something much better. Her face had character and strength. She poked fun at herself now; not other people. It had been easy to ignore April the girl; it was not so easy to ignore April the woman.

She shivered in her sleep. Tarn turned on the heater and resigned himself to sweating for the remainder of the journey to Queenstown. He leaned forward and looked out the windscreen at the clear blue sky. There was a heavy rain warning in place for the region tonight. Provided they didn't hang around after April had seen Rob Sturmley, they should easily make it back to Aurora before the weather closed in.

The bank manager's name was Phillip Northcott, but April called him Uncle Phil. Tarn found that out at the bank after he'd refused to give April an advance on her wages so she could go shopping. 'Ten dollars won't go far, unless you're planning on buying a big ice cream.'

Her chin rose with her temper. 'I've earned more than ten dollars, you cheapskate! I worked right through the night, which in my book means I get double my hourly rate.'

Tarn smiled and said, 'In my book there's no such thing as double your hourly rate.'

She spluttered indignantly. She had only seventeen dollars.

'Major Elliott?'

Tarn turned his attention from April's flustered, pink face to the hand his bank manager was holding out to him. 'Mr Northcott.'

Phillip Northcott gripped Tarn's wrist as they shook hands. 'It's a pleasure to see you again, Major.' He spotted April, and his face went slack with surprise. '*April? April Ritchie?*'

Her pout blossomed into one of her trademark smiles. Tarn barely had time to step back as April flew past him, flung her arms around Phillip Northcott's neck and morphed into the frothy blonde she wasn't. '*Uncle Phil!*'

There was a rapid exchange of information as April and Phillip brought each other up to date. Tarn cooled his heels while April admired photos of grandchildren and Phillip commiserated on her divorce. Clearly, he was deeply curious about her failed marriage, but April managed to chatter away without saying a damned thing. When it seemed Phillip wasn't going to let the subject drop, and Tarn was about to step in, she pressed Phillip's arm and murmured, 'The divorce was for the best. I know you'll understand, Uncle Phil.'

Northcott was powerless against her big blue-green eyes, even though his wife would be furious if she ever found out that he'd missed an opportunity to dig the dirt on the Ritchies and find out whether the rumour that Heather and Grant had been given the wrong baby at the hospital was true. How Grant and Heather had discovered they'd been given the wrong baby — and April's sudden disappearance, only to resurface as Ralph Berryman's wife — had kept the gossips busy for months. The reason for the Berrymans' divorce and the financial settlement were kept hush-hush, too, but the consensus was that April had received plenty of money for the four years she'd spent with Berryman. History repeated itself when she dropped out of sight again. Phillip was astounded when he now saw her with Aurora's new owner. The plain-spoken, stern-faced major was nothing like her husbands. It was another mystery.

April knew what Phillip Northcott was thinking and what a vicious gossip his wife was. It sparked her mischievous streak. She decided to give Phillip, his wife and their cronies something to talk about. She clasped Tarn's arm and rested her cheek against the sleeve of his jacket. 'I'm working with Tarn at Aurora.' She sighed happily. 'It's so lovely to be home again.'

Phillip looked sharply from one to the other, and connected the dots. The picture he came up with was all out of whack.

Tarn had warned April about playing games like this, but she wouldn't listen. 'April's going to be in charge of quality control in the packing house,' he said firmly.

The bank manager's 'Haw, haw, you lucky dog' smile faded. 'Is she?'

It was about then that Tarn guessed he must be Ivan Vincent's bank manager, too.

April wanted to sock Tarn in the eye. Was he too dense to see she was trying to help him? She let go of his arm. 'I'll let you two get on with your meeting.' She smiled sweetly. 'Can I have the hundred dollars you promised me?'

Tarn smiled grimly and opened his wallet. He handed April fifty dollars. 'Don't spend it all at once.'

She stared at the bills in her hand. In the past, she'd spend that much on a lipstick. 'I'll try not to go mad in the outlet store.'

Phillip's hawk-like expression made her decide to have one more try at making sure Tarn knew which way the wind blew. She hooked a hand around his neck and dragged his face down to kiss his cheek and whisper furiously in his ear, 'He's Ivan Vincent's bank manager, too, you cheapskate!' April stepped back and said, for Phillip's benefit, 'I promise I'll be back in time for you to take me to lunch like you planned.'

Tarn had had enough of being played by Ms Ritchie. He scooped her up and kissed her hard on the lips. It was the most intimate physical contact April had had with a man in three years — sitting on strange men's knees in a crotch-skimming angel's outfit and fishnet stockings didn't count.

He set her down. 'Good. There's a McDonald's not far from here.' He followed up the kiss with an insulting pat on her bottom, and pointed her in the direction of the glass doors at the front of the bank. 'Have fun.'

April seethed as she left the bank. How *dare* he manhandle her like she was a … a trollop.

Outside in the precinct, she spotted a table with two women behind it collecting for Breast Cancer Awareness. April always supported the Pink Ribbon appeal held in October. She walked to the table and pushed the fifty dollars through the slot in the lid of the collection bucket.

'Thank you *so* much!' one of the women cried.

April accepted the tiny pink ribbon she held out and pinned it to her dress. 'You're welcome,' she said, and joined the throngs of tourists strolling through town.

'A girl has to work with what she's given.'

*Does that mean batting her lashes and climbing all over any man with a pulse? Can't she put that scheming brain of hers to better use?* Tarn thought with disgust.

When April hadn't returned to the bank by noon, he was forced to go looking for her. Her tip confirming that Northcott was Ivan

Vincent's bank manager had been useful. Tarn had secured an extension to his overdraft on the strength of the extra income the packing house would bring in now that he'd found a quality controller. Until now, Northcott had baulked at an extension, which infuriated Tarn when he knew that other orchard owners owed as much as he did yet still had the support of the bank. Without saying outright that he suspected Northcott had a conflict of interests, Tarn conveyed his suspicions; and the bank manager had no choice but to let him have an extension.

April was a valuable asset, but Tarn still didn't trust her. He'd searched the wardrobe from top to bottom but was no closer to discovering what she was after. To get into the wardrobe, she needed access to his bedroom. Sleeping with him was one way of getting it. How far was she willing to go to get what she wanted? The thought left a sour taste in his mouth.

Tarn found April on the shores of Lake Wakatipu, shivering and feeding the ducks the sandwich she'd bought for lunch. She was in a strange mood, distant and unsmiling. It matched his. The wind had picked up even more. It ruffled the surface of the lake, tipping it with white. Overhead, dark clouds gathered, blocking the sun and swaddling the top of the Remarkables mountain range in a dirty grey. In April's book fifty bucks wasn't much, but Tarn was surprised that she didn't appear to have bought anything apart from the sandwich. According to his mother, spending money had been Heather and April's religion.

'Didn't you go shopping?'

'Of course I did.' She threw the last of the bread to the squabbling ducks and hugged herself against the cold.

'You haven't got anything to show for it.'

The wind whipped April's platinum hair into her face and

caught her breath. 'Darling, the aim of the exercise isn't to have anything to show for it, but to spend the money.'

Tarn wanted to shake her.

She knew, and smiled. 'I got this.' She turned back the edge of her jacket and pointed to the tiny pink ribbon on her dress. 'Fifty dollars — it was a bargain.'

His eyes glittered furiously. He was reminded of April the spoiled brat.

She rose from the seat and demanded, 'Give me the name and address of the lawyer.'

Without a word, Tarn handed over the paper with the information Emma had given him.

April smiled when she saw Emma's name and business logo.

'What's so funny?' he demanded.

'You, you're so predictable,' she lied, and walked away.

Rob Sturmley's office had a superb view of the lake, but today the weather was ruining it. As April entered the room, the clouds parted and rain poured down as if a huge bucket of water were being emptied into the lake. Rob Sturmley was the epitome of a well-heeled, successful lawyer in his late fifties. April had grown up watching Grant deal with lawyers, and had sat in on some of Ralph's business meetings at the beginning of their marriage when he'd wanted to show her off. She'd met a few Rob Sturmleys in her time. What set him apart from the others was the quiet charm of his smile, the kindness in his eyes, and his utter refusal to accept the abbreviated version of events April gave him of the night she stole the hospital files.

'You're leaving things out.'

April smiled tightly and crossed her legs. She did not want to be entombed in this room talking about things she tried hard not to think about. 'No, I'm not.'

'I don't think you're telling me the whole story. Parents don't cut their seventeen-year-old daughter off because her boyfriend wrote off her birthday present.'

Or at least, Rob wouldn't.

Rain sluiced down the window, further distorting the shape of the trees being tossed like streamers by the howling wind. The weather mirrored the maelstrom happening inside April. Her chest felt like it might crack open from the pressure of trying to keep everything in. 'Mine did,' she quipped weakly.

'Miss Ritchie, I don't want to waste your money or my time,' Rob insisted quietly.

April told herself she could do this; it was only words. 'OK!' She leaned forward and joked, 'Are you listening carefully? Then I'll begin.'

It was like ripping a scab off a wound and letting the pus drain away. It took longer than the hour Rob had allocated for her. Outside, thunder drum-rolled and lightning cracked. Rain poured and rushed along the pavement and streets and gurgled in the drains.

April told him everything, about finding Heather with Murdo, about hearing her tell Grant she'd swapped babies at the hospital and how Grant had kicked her out.

By the time she'd finished, Rob was sitting in the chair beside April and the room was dark. He poured her a glass of water. 'So you went to the hospital to retrieve your medical records and those of the woman you believed was your birth mother?'

She gulped at the water and clutched her belly when her empty stomach rebelled at the cold fluid. 'I went to the hospital because

I hoped Heather was lying and there *wouldn't be* a medical record for Nola Gutsell.' April put the glass on the desk. 'But there was, so I took it; and my file, too.'

'Emma Murfitt was the hospital receptionist?' Rob asked gently.

'Yes. She got the sack because of what I did.'

It explained why Emma had called and asked him to see April Ritchie as a favour. Emma did not discuss her personal life; she would be relying on Rob's discretion to keep her youthful mistake quiet. The woman sitting opposite him wanted to keep her past at arm's length, too. Her story was one of the saddest Rob had ever heard.

'You're not alone, are you? There's somebody with you?'

'I'm here with my boss. He used to be a major in the New Zealand Infantry.' April smiled weakly at the concern on Rob's face. 'Don't worry, Tarn wouldn't let me do something stupid like throw myself in Lake Wakatipu, and I wouldn't anyway because I hate the cold.' She was exhausted. 'If this ever gets out it could hurt a lot of people.'

'Who? Heather?'

She made a gesture of irritation. 'No, not Heather — I don't care about her. Her daughter, Latoya.'

'You *know* her?'

'She's my closest friend.'

'Does Latoya know?'

April shook her head.

'You mean you've carried this secret alone all this time? You didn't even tell your husband when you were married?'

'He wouldn't have understood.' April hadn't mentioned the beating Ralph had given her, just that they'd split up because she couldn't have children.

'April,' Rob said firmly, 'the judge needs to know all the details.'

'*No.*'

'I need you to trust me. Please think about it.'

Before she left, April washed her face in the ladies' room. She felt like a half-empty bottle with the stopper missing. Once she'd started, it had been hard to stick to telling Rob just about the night of her seventeenth birthday. She patted her face dry with a paper towel and dug around in her handbag for some blusher and lipstick. A check in the mirror confirmed that she looked ghastly. Missing lunch hadn't helped, but the thought of food made her want to throw up.

It was time to put the genie back in the bottle and jam in the cork. April composed herself, and went to find Tarn.

He was waiting by the downstairs entrance. His hair and the shoulders of his jacket and the bottom of his trousers were soaked. 'What took you so long?'

April held her handbag above her head and peered at the rain bouncing off the concrete. 'Time flies in the company of a charming, intelligent man.'

Tarn replied impatiently, 'There's been a slip on the road between Queenstown and Pisa. We're going to have to find a place to stay for the night, which isn't going to be easy because there are a couple of conferences in town.'

She was light-headed and crabby from fatigue and hunger. 'I'll have to insist on a minimum of four stars. The Millenium is nice.'

'So is backpacker accommodation. The truck is parked around the corner; we'll have to make a run for it.'

April felt so weak that she couldn't have run if her life depended on it, but she wasn't going to admit to Tarn how awful she felt. She pointed at her feet instead: 'In these shoes?'

'Oh, for crissakes!'

Tarn lifted her over his shoulder and ran down the street in the direction of the truck. By the time they had reached it, April was soaked and would have thrown up if she'd had anything in her stomach. She looked so ghastly, Tarn dug around in the glove compartment and found some barley sugar left behind by Carole. He force-fed April two pieces and watched her suck on them lethargically while he made calls on his cellphone to find a room for the night.

'*Rooms*,' April insisted weakly, as Tarn jotted down details on an old envelope.

'We'll be lucky to get anything. Don't worry, you're safe with me.'

She crunched on the barley sugar. 'It's nothing personal; I have to think of my allergy.'

Tarn wished she'd shut up about her allergy. He'd almost given up hope of finding them somewhere when there was a late cancellation at one of the hotels on the waterfront. As he'd predicted, it was for only one room.

The barley sugar had revived April enough for her to cause trouble when they reached the hotel. She was still upset from the meeting with Rob Sturmley — and when she was upset, she was reckless.

'Name?' the desk clerk enquired politely.

'Mr and Mrs Smith.' April made a show of checking Tarn's wedding finger. 'Good, you remembered to take it off this time.'

Tarn handed the desk clerk his credit card. 'Tarn Elliott. And no, she isn't the old ball and chain. Thank God.'

The clerk allowed himself a small smile and entered Tarn's

credit card details into the computer. 'Do you have any luggage, Mr Elliott?'

'Just the attitude,' April replied. 'He left his medals at home.'

Tarn was unamused. She belatedly remembered what Rosamund had told her about his men dying on the patrol, and felt even more wretched.

They were walking towards the lifts when a well-preserved man of medium height, in his fifties, emerged from the hotel restaurant. He had greying dark hair, clothes that fell into the smart/casual category, and he was holding the hand of a blonde woman in her twenties. She was heavily pregnant.

Tarn was tired and hungry. He barely noticed them, and would have continued walking to the elevators if April hadn't stopped in her tracks and stared at the couple with a stricken expression. 'What is it now?' he snapped.

The man spotted her. His steps faltered, and his face sagged. His lips moved soundlessly: 'April …'

Tarn recognized the face he'd seen on cereal boxes.

April pivoted. He made a grab for her, but was a moment too late. She fled across the foyer and bumped into a tall flower arrangement by the entrance. The ornate urn holding the flowers toppled to the floor. April clapped her hands over her ears and ran out into the rain.

He found her down by the lake dry-retching into a rubbish bin. Tarn prised her arms from around the metal and picked her up. She was a shivering, pathetic wreck. Her teeth chattered. 'Don't … don't … take me back … there.'

The freezing rain pounded them. Tarn put his mouth against April's ear. 'It's OK. It'll be OK.'

She buried her face in his neck, and let him carry her in.

# Chapter 11

*Teach people how to treat you.*

ANON

Tarn adjusted the temperature on the shower and looked at April standing huddled in the middle of the bathroom. He was cold, but she was colder. Her skin had a blue tinge, and her eyes had the dazed look of somebody in shock. She needed to get warm and eat something.

He raised his voice above the hum of the extractor fan and spoke firmly to get her attention. 'April, take off your clothes and get in the shower. I'll be in the bedroom if you need me. Can you do that?'

She slowly raised her hands to the front of her jacket.

Tarn stepped from the bathroom, but left the door open a few inches in case she needed him. He'd seen men react the same way after they saw combat for the first time, but didn't expect it from a woman because she'd seen her ex-husband. What had Berryman done to make her so scared?

He ordered room service, and then removed his waterlogged new shoes and stripped off his socks and jacket. His shoes and jacket were ruined. He couldn't afford to replace them, just like he couldn't really afford the hotel room. Tarn bundled everything into a plastic housekeeping bag, yanked his shirt from his trousers and unbuttoned it. He reached for the button on his cuff and paused. From within the bathroom, the shower water flowed steadily — it wasn't splashing the way it did when a person was under it.

Tarn crossed the room and tapped on the open door. 'April?'

No answer.

He pushed the door open.

She was standing exactly where he'd left her, staring at the mirror and clutching the edges of her jacket. Her eyes looked empty. Water dripped from the ends of her hair onto the tiled floor. Tarn was no longer sure whether her shudders were from cold or fear. He moved behind her and touched her gently on the shoulders. 'April, take your jacket off.'

She blinked at him in the mirror. Her empty expression worried him. *What the hell had Berryman done to her?*

This wasn't the time to observe the social niceties. 'I'll get you started. You take over whenever you're ready.' Tarn eased April's jacket down her arms to reveal the pretty turquoise dress held up by scraps of ribbon.

And stopped.

Small, pink ridges were scattered across her white shoulders and between her shoulder blades. Some were the size of a nail head; some were a few inches long. All were testimony to her having been beaten with something sharp. Tarn stared. He couldn't believe what he was seeing, and brushed his fingers across one of the biggest scars. Fury expanded inside him like a mushroom cloud as a large piece of the puzzle that was April Ritchie fell into place. He didn't need to ask who'd done it.

April cringed when she felt Tarn touch her scars. *'Don't!'* She tried to twist away, but her wrists were trapped in the sleeves of her jacket.

He badly wanted to go looking for Berryman, but couldn't leave April. Tarn freed her hands from the jacket and dropped it on the floor. She spun to face him, while at the same time trying to cover her shoulders with her hands. His eyes were drawn to the reflection of her back in the mirror.

*'Don't look!'*

He snatched his gaze from the mirror. 'Alright.'

April felt sick with shame. Now he knew she was one of *them* — a woman valued so little by her husband that he thought it was OK to beat her up. Her face contorted with pain. She jumped when Tarn wrapped an arm around her waist, lifted her and carried her into the shower cubicle.

Water poured over them. He stood behind her and placed his palms on the tiles above her head. Instead of feeling trapped, April felt safe. Only later would it occur to her to wonder why.

'What are we doing?' she asked in a reedy voice.

'Getting warm.' Tarn stared at the marks on her shoulders. The tips of his fingers turned white as he dug them into the wall tiles.

The warm water and the heat radiating from his body felt comforting. April didn't want to think about Ralph or the pregnant woman with him. She looked up at Tarn's large, capable hands pressed against the tile wall, and down at his bare, brown feet planted either side of hers. His trousers were plastered against his legs. 'Your trousers will be ruined,' she said weakly.

'I'll cope.'

He would. He always did. Unlike her.

April touched her fingers to her eyes. They came away black with mascara. 'I haven't got any make-up remover,' she said forlornly.

Tarn recalled the damage her make-up had done to her skin after the night at the police station. Obviously, it was important to her. He turned April to face him, lathered his hands with soap and washed her face.

It was one of the kindest things a man had ever done for her. April knew she'd have red, blotchy skin in the morning from the soap, but she didn't care. She closed her eyes and rested her palms against his chest. If Tarn felt the hot sting of her tears amidst the soap suds, he didn't say. His hands were calloused but gentle. His chest felt warm and solid.

April lifted her face and leaned into him. 'I've got sensitive skin. I bet I break out in spots in the morning.'

'Probably.' Her face was as delicate as a kitten's. Tarn rinsed it, shut off the water and opened the cubicle door. 'Dinner is on its way. Time to get out.'

The water had revived her. She followed him from the shower. 'You're going to feed me, too?' She smiled wanly when Tarn replied, 'Do I have a choice?'

He grabbed a couple of towels and handed one to April. 'Don't take this the wrong way, but you need to get out of those clothes.'

She unzipped her sodden dress and wriggled it down her hips. It plopped onto the floor. Beneath it, she wore a pale pink see-through thong and matching bra. The phrase 'small but beautifully made' described her perfectly. The see-through underwear revealed the tender pink tips of her breasts and the pale blonde hair between her legs. Her blue eyes were guileless and trusting. Tarn found it infinitely more arousing than her *femme fatale* act.

April reached back to unclip her bra. She didn't see the point in being modest. He'd already seen the part of her she kept hidden.

'Stop right there!'

She froze, elbows bent, chin on chest and peeped up at him.

A knock on the door signalled the arrival of room service. Relief poured through Tarn. 'I'll get that.' He went to answer the door.

April didn't think she'd be able to eat, but Tarn made her. When they were finished, they lounged opposite one another at the small table in the corner of the room, wearing matching white robes with the hotel emblem on the breast pocket. April kept expecting Tarn to ask her about Ralph, but he didn't. At first she was relieved, but then it occurred to her that maybe he just wasn't interested, and her feminine self-esteem took another dive. Her bathroom strip hadn't raised his interest — or anything else for that matter. April reminded herself that she had enough problems to deal with without adding a randy boss to the mix: she'd had experience dealing with them and it wasn't good. It would help, though, if Tarn wasn't sprawled opposite her with his chest and most of one thigh exposed.

'Can you make yourself decent?' she asked petulantly. 'I've already seen Big Boy or Tiger or whatever it is you call your penis — we don't need to get reacquainted.'

Tarn had deliberately kept quiet in case she wanted to talk about Berryman. He rearranged his robe as Big Boy/Tiger — *How the fuck did she come up with these names?* — twitched to life.

April tucked her fists beneath her elbows and hunched her shoulders. 'What are we going to do about the bed? Both sleep in it and build a wall of pillows down the middle? Or flip a coin for the sofa?' She was smaller. She should take the sofa, really.

'You can have the bed.'

His kindness made her weak. She got up and walked to the sofa. 'I'll take the sofa. You'd better not snore.'

Tarn understood why April was picking a fight. He decided to give her what she wanted. 'You'd better not talk in your sleep. I've already had to listen to you all day long.'

She changed route and headed for the bed. 'I've changed my mind: I'm taking the bed.'

'Suit yourself. I can sleep any— *Put that back on!*' Tarn barked as April dropped her robe on the floor.

She climbed between the sheets. 'I can't. I'm a restless sleeper. If I wear it, I'll be tied in knots by morning. Don't worry, Major, you're safe from me,' she said sarcastically, and switched off the bedside lamp.

Tarn lay on his back with an arm tucked under his head and listened to April rolling around the bed. Seeing her naked, and hearing her sighing and the sheets rustling, was making it impossible for him to sleep. Only another man would understand that Big Boy/Tiger had its own agenda and that it in no way reflected Tarn's opinion of what had happened to her.

Thanks to her ex, April didn't have a very high opinion of men. Until today, Tarn didn't have a very high opinion of her, either, but that was changing. Seeing Berryman had turned her into a quivering wreck. She'd bounced back because she was resilient. Life kept dealing her shitty hands, and April kept thumbing her nose at it and cheating her way out of what she'd been dealt. But if something didn't change, the time would inevitably come when she wouldn't be able to pick herself up again.

April wasn't lying when she said she was a restless sleeper, although he suspected that Ralph Berryman was responsible for all her tossing and turning. She had already been in a strange mood when he'd met her outside the lawyer's; seeing Berryman had sent her over the edge. Old demons were the worst. Tarn didn't dream about the men who'd died on the patrol; he didn't have to fall asleep to see them — their faces were emblazoned on the insides of his eyelids. In summer, when the rocky, hilly terrain of Centrral Otago turned brown and dusty he'd probably be reminded again of Afghanistan. Memories were inescapable.

April woke and sat up.

Tarn's eyes were attuned well enough to the dark to see her clutch the bedcovers to herself and look around wildly.

'You're at the hotel—' he began.

She yelped and scuttled back against the headboard.

'—with me.'

She sighed.

'What did Berryman hit you with?'

April peered at his outline on the cramped sofa. Confessions were much easier in the dark. 'His belt.'

Tarn pictured a belt wrapped around the cereal baron's hand and the tender white skin on April's back, and went cold.

'He only did it once.'

There was no 'only' about it.

'I ran out and took one of the cars from the garage,' she continued, matter-of-factly. 'I gave it back so Ralph wouldn't find me. I took photos of my back in a mirror in a public toilet the night it happened. I've still got them … somewhere,' she ended vaguely.

For a few moments, Tarn couldn't speak as he imagined her standing before a mirror in a public toilet holding a camera above her head to take shots of her torn and bleeding back. 'You didn't get anything in the divorce settlement, did you?'

'There was no divorce settlement, just an agreement that Ralph would stay away from me or I'd show everybody the photos. Pretty stupid, I know, but it suited me at the time. Can we swap?'

Tarn was trying to process the brickbats April kept throwing his way. 'What?'

She got out of the bed and groped around on the floor for her robe. 'I want to sleep on the sofa.'

'Why?'

'I was in bed when Ralph came home and started hitting me. I'll sleep better on the sofa.'

They kept on coming.

Tarn got up and felt for his own robe. 'Why did he hit you?'

April gave up trying to find hers. What the hell — it was dark and they'd both seen what each other had. 'He met Heather at a fund-raising event. I couldn't go because I wasn't feeling well. By the time Heather had finished, Ralph was convinced I was the biggest slut ever born and Heather was a poor wounded, grieving mother who'd tried against all odds to do her best for her delinquent daughter. I told him she wasn't my mother, but he didn't believe m—'

'What did you say?'

'Oh.' She paused. 'Didn't you know about that? I'm not Heather and Grant's child. Heather had an affair and produced a daughter a few shades too dark to pass off as Grant's, so she swapped her for me at the hospital.'

Confessions really *were* easier in the dark.

Tarn sank onto the sofa and put his elbows on his knees. His mind reeled with the implications of what April had just said.

'If you don't believe me, ask Dr Giles.'

He could hear the hurt in her voice. 'Oh, I believe you.' He lifted his head and peered at her outline by the bed. 'When did you find out?'

'The night of my birthday, after …' she trailed off.

Tarn grunted.

'I'm sorry, Tarn,' April said softly.

'Apology accepted. Is that why you ran away?'

She laughed hollowly. 'It was a *fait accompli.* Grant kicked me out, or I ran away — take your pick.'

'You were only seventeen!' Tarn sensed her shrug. 'Is that why you stole the medical files?'

April was done talking. 'I can't find my robe, Major. It's dark, which should spare your blushes. Stand aside, I'm coming through.'

He got up and she slipped past him and into the warm nest he'd left behind on the sofa.

Tarn saw the pale shape of her body and blonde hair float by, smelled the soft, floral scent of the hotel soap, and felt the silken brush of her leg against the back of his calf as she slid beneath the covers. He looked down at the indistinct shape on the sofa.

April's leg tingled from the contact with his hair-roughened calf. She adored the difference between her body and a man's — or at least, she used to before Ralph. Her libido took a few more cautious steps out of the nunnery. She looked up at Tarn and held her breath. He turned and walked to the bed, and she released it. *Keep talking, April, before you do something* really *stupid — like try and climb into bed with Tarn Elliott.*

She listened to his robe hit the floor and said nervously, 'Speaking of movies I've cried at ...'

The sheets rustled as he got in. 'We weren't.'

April had never realized how erotic the rustle of sheets could be. She cleared her throat. 'I cried at *E.T.* too, especially the part when E.T. holds out his hand and says "Mama". Heart-rending.'

Tarn knew he wasn't going to get any more confessions from her tonight. 'E.T. had a head shaped like a rugby ball and long, bony fingers. He was ugly.'

'He was *cute*.'

He pressed his thumbs against his eyelids and sighed. There were much better things he could think of doing with a naked blonde at two-thirty in the morning than argue about E.T.'s cuteness, or lack of. 'Go to sleep, April.'

There was a pause. 'I can't.'

He linked his fingers, cupped his head and played along. 'One of the last movies you cried at was *Titanic*, wasn't it?'

'How did you know?'

'Just about every woman I've ever dated has cried at that movie.'

April sat up. 'Were they soldiers?'

'One or two.'

'What did you talk about? Battle tactics? Did you meet on the parade ground?'

Tarn heard the mischief in her voice. 'You know, the French don't have a word for date. They think the whole concept is ridiculous.'

April turned on her side and propped her head on her hand. 'How do you know?'

'I spent some time with a French woman.' First in Africa, and later at her apartment in Paris. 'Or, I should say, a *Parisienne*.'

She leaned forward, entranced by the way Tarn rolled the word off his tongue. 'What did she do?'

'She was a war correspondent — a journalist.'

'I know what a war correspondent is, Tarn. How nice,' she mocked. 'Can you speak French?'

'Enough to get by.'

'What was her name?'

'Delphine.'

His accent was so perfect April nearly fell off the sofa. 'Did she teach you how to French-kiss?' she teased.

'I already knew.'

The air crackled.

*This is madness,* April thought.

*Heading for a fall,* Tarn thought.

He broke the spell. 'Why did Heather choose you?'

April debated not answering him, but decided that Tarn was entitled to some answers because of what he'd done for her today. 'It was me or Lionel Prescott.'

Tarn didn't laugh. He'd spent months in places ravaged by war where life wasn't just cheap, it was considered worthless. Heather was right down there with the terrorists, war lords and megalomaniac leaders.

'Latoya Gutsell is Heather's daughter, isn't she?'

April lay down and rolled to face the back of the sofa.

Some things couldn't be said. Even in the dark.

## Chapter 12

*One rock cannot start a fire alone.*

ANON

The trip to Queenstown changed things between them. Many of their long-held misconceptions had been proven wrong: the major wasn't cold and aloof; the Princess of Pisa wasn't grasping and selfish.

They didn't talk about it in the morning when they woke up and took turns using the bathroom, or in the truck on the drive home. It was too much to take in. At the hotel, Tarn growled at April for staying in the shower too long. She retaliated by dawdling over breakfast.

He watched her gaze out the window and trail her spoon through the contents of her cereal bowl, and demanded, 'You want to walk home?'

She propped her chin on her hand and flashed him her Hollywood smile. 'Only if I take your credit card shopping first.'

His credit card was so maxed-out she'd be lucky to buy a packet of chewing gum with it. Tarn scowled at his ruined shoes and wriggled his foot inside the hard leather. His fringe flopped into his eyes and he shoved it back irritably. 'You've got five minutes to eat your breakfast and get your stuff.'

She saluted with the spoon. 'Yes, sir!'

Tarn looked at the spoon, the flimsy turquoise dress and frivolous turquoise mules and at the sorry state of her fake leather and fur jacket. He wanted to shake her for being such a smart-aleck, and to wrap her in his arms to try to make up for the horror story on her back, and for what Heather had stolen from her. He picked up the keys to the truck and headed for the door instead.

'*Five* minutes.'

Carole paid a visit to April's caravan that night.

April was preoccupied. Tarn hadn't been sitting in the burgundy chair when she'd come out of the powder room after her shower. She wanted to know why he wasn't there, and why it didn't occur to her that his absence gave her a perfect opportunity to creep upstairs and search his room for the key to the wardrobe.

When Carole knocked, April was in bed reading. Latoya had included some books from April's 'to be read' pile in the things she'd sent. Tarn's comment about Delphine, the Parisian war correspondent, had made her reach for *What French Women Know,* a book about French women's attitudes to love and sex, amongst other things. Images of Tarn entertaining and being entertained by 'Delphine, la Parisienne' had filled her mind all day.

The lighting in the caravan wasn't good for late-night reading so April had resorted to wearing the headlamp she used at night in the orchard. She knew right away that it wasn't Tarn from the polite *rat-a-tat-tat* on the door. Tarn's knock was brief and barked *Pay attention!* April sighed, switched off the headlamp, and opened the door.

She looked down at Tarn's mother and grimaced. 'Carole. What a nice surprise.'

Carole frowned when she saw April wearing her headlamp and pyjamas. 'Why are you wearing your headlamp?'

'To read. What can I do for you, Carole?'

'About last night,' Carole began.

Tarn had told her what happened? April was bitterly disappointed. 'What about last night?' she asked coldly.

'Don't go getting any ideas about Tarn just because you spent the night together in Queenstown.'

She almost laughed. Carole seemed to forget that Tarn was thirty-five years old, and the man least likely to be manipulated by any woman. At the same time, she envied Tarn for having a mother who'd fight to protect him.

April cocked her hip and splayed her fingers on it. She wished her nails were long and scarlet, instead of chipped and ragged. If Carole insisted on painting her as Pisa's reigning scarlet woman, April thought she deserved to look the part.

'Too late, Carole, I had my wicked way with him at least seven times last night.' She pointed a thumb at the book on the bed behind her. 'I'm reading a sex manual to brush up my technique. Imagine my surprise when I found a whole chapter devoted to headlamps.'

Carole made out the word *French* on the dust jacket. She narrowed her eyes and spluttered. 'He's got too much taste to be attracted to a woman like you.'

April wasn't going to let her see how much her words stung, or that she agreed. 'So why are you here?'

'I want to make sure you realize Tarn is too good for you, and too smart. If you think you're going to make him husband number three, you're dreaming.'

'Husband number *two*, Carole. My marriage to Stefan wasn't legal, remember?'

'Stay away from him!' Carole shouted, and stormed back to the house.

Tarn was in the study doing paperwork. Carole hurried past the door and into the kitchen to make tea. She could imagine what his reaction would be if he found out what she'd said to April, but Carole didn't care — she wasn't letting April Ritchie get her hooks into him the way Heather had with Murdo. Tarn didn't discuss his private life, but Carole knew him well enough to know he wasn't a womanizer like his father.

Her hands shook as she placed cups, saucers and a milk jug on a tray, and warmed the teapot. The run-in with April wasn't the only reason for her agitation. Last night, when Tarn had called to say they weren't going to make it home, Gerald Smit had volunteered to stay in case the storm caused any damage. It was the first time they'd truly been alone together …

Carole was grateful for Gerald's offer of help. The last time there'd been a strong southerly, one of the high-tensile wires securing the overhead canopies had snapped and the net had ended up in a neighbouring orchard, causing damage to the trees on both properties. Usually Tarn or April were somewhere in the orchard, or coming and going to get a drink or something to eat or to check on the weather report.

After dinner, they'd stayed sitting at the kitchen table, sipping tea and eating cake and listening to the wind howl and the window-panes rattle. Carole was wearing her pink jumper again. She felt tongue-tied and shy, which was ridiculous for a woman nearing sixty. 'I've made up the bed in the downstairs guest room and put out towels,' she told Gerald. 'You can shower in the powder room.'

'Thanks.'

She pushed the plate containing the remains of a banana cake towards him. 'Have another piece of cake.'

'Better not; I won't be able to fit my clothes if I keep eating your cookin'.'

'You're not fat. I'm the one who should be worrying about weight.'

Gerald studied her over the rim of his cup. He shook his head. 'No, you shouldn't.'

Carole was mortified when she blushed, and turned even redder as a result. She gestured hastily to the threadbare blue sweater he wore beneath his green vest. 'I've been meaning to say that if you want a couple of things knitted, I could do them for you. I've run out of knitting.'

'Really?' he said wonderingly. 'You'd do that for me?'

She shrugged. 'I like to keep busy at night. Of course, you'd have to buy the wool.'

'Of course.' Gerald stood up and unzipped his vest. ''Spect you want to measure me.'

She blinked up at him. 'Pardon?'

'Bronwyn always did.'

'Oh — yes! I'll just get my tape measure.' She escaped from the kitchen to get her sewing box.

They discussed patterns and colours while she measured him.

'Did you make the pink one you've got on?' Gerald asked.

Carole enjoyed the sensation of touching a man again as she ran the tape measure down his arm. 'Yes. Why, do you want a pink one, too?' she joked.

He grinned and her heart did a little pirouette in her chest.

'You don't have any wedding photos around.'

Carole knew Gerald wondered why she didn't talk about her marriage. She slowly folded the tape measure and debated what to say. The truth seemed the best. The words came out in a rush, like a burst water main.

'My marriage wasn't like yours. You loved Bronwyn and she loved you; I loved Murdo, but he didn't love me.' She drew a deep breath and forced out her shameful secret: 'He only married me because I got pregnant. His family were strict Catholics. I lied and told him I was on the pill; it was the only way a plain girl like me could get a bloke like Murdoch Elliott. It was only once … I honestly didn't think I'd get pregnant.'

Gerald looked stunned. His Adam's apple bobbed. 'Oh.'

She gazed at him defiantly. 'I don't regret it, because I got Tarn.'

He said quickly, 'Anybody'd be proud to have a son like that.'

'I *am*. Murdo was the one who was disappointed, because Tarn didn't want to work in an orchard. He didn't understand why he wanted to join the army and travel.'

Gerald frowned. *He* didn't understand Murdoch Elliott. 'Carole?'

She busied herself putting the tape measure away in her sewing box. 'What?'

'You're not plain.'

She stiffened. 'Don't patronize me.'

'I'm not. You're unhappy, not ugly.'

It was the most backhanded compliment Carole had ever received. She looked at Gerald and smiled. 'Is that how you used to compliment Bronwyn?'

He flushed. 'I'm more of a doer than a talker.'

'That's one way of putting it.'

'I didn't mean any offence.'

'I'm not offended.'

'I thought when I saw you the other day, and again tonight, that you look nice in that pink jumper,' he continued doggedly.

'It's nice of you to say that,' Carole said politely.

Gerald looked into her eyes. His Adam's apple bobbed again. 'I'm not being nice, Carole.'

As she carried the tea tray to the study, Carole remembered how she'd stuttered goodnight and gone to bed, even though it had only been half past seven. Her thoughts then turned to April: had she really been reading a sex manual? Carole had never seen one, let alone read one. Women like April Ritchie read sex manuals, not women like Carole Elliott. April could have been lying, but Carole would've liked to know for sure.

Tarn discreetly exited the page he'd been looking at on the Internet as she set the tray on one end of the desk. Apparently, April wasn't lying about women being allergic to sperm.

Carole poured the tea and handed him a cup. Tarn preferred a mug, but put up with a cup because he knew she enjoyed using the china tea set each night. He ignored the handle and wrapped his palm around the dainty china. 'Thanks.'

She carried her cup and saucer around the room, tweaking curtains and cushions that didn't need tweaking, and dusting tabletops and the mantelpiece with her hand. When she turned around, Tarn was watching her.

'What's wrong?' he asked.

*I keep thinking about sleeping with a man, and he's not your father. I'm worried that you are sleeping with April.*

'April said she had you seven times last night.'

He coughed into his cup. '*What?*' The word cracked out like a rifle shot. 'What did *you* say to *her?*'

Carole looked defensive. 'She was wearing her headlamp. She *said* she was reading a sex manual. That girl always had the ability to push my buttons.' She paused and stared at him. 'Has she been pushing yours, too?'

Tarn started to laugh.

'It's not funny! I'm not going to let her do to you what her mother did to ...' She ground to a halt.

They'd never spoken of the night that April had accused Tarn of being in the packing house with Heather. Carole suspected that Tarn knew it was Murdo who'd been with Heather, and that she'd stayed quiet and let Tarn take the blame instead of sticking up for him like she should have. Every time she thought about it, her sense of self-loathing grew.

Tarn's laughter dissolved and his expression closed.

Carole put down her teacup. 'Tarn, please let me explain about that night—'

'Save it — I care about here and now, not something that happened nine years ago.' He stalked around the desk.

'Where are you going?' she said warily.

'To sort out the mess you made.'

*Bang! Bang! Bang!*

April jackknifed into a sitting position and clutched her book to her disruptive-pattern pyjama jacket. She knew that knock; any moment now, it would be followed up by a demand to open the door.

The door opened. A booted foot landed on the floor of the caravan, followed by a denim-clad leg, then the rest of Tarn. He closed the door, propped his hands on his hips and glared at her. 'Where do you get off telling my mother you '*had*' me seven times last night?'

Her disappointment grew. April threw her book at him, but even at a short distance and wearing a headlamp, she still managed to miss him.

'Jesus, you really do need those glasses.'

'Get out of my caravan!'

'I'm flattered you think I can do it seven times in one night, but I doubt I could have managed that even when I was battle-fit.'

Tarn looked around the shadowy interior of the caravan and frowned. He hadn't been inside it since April moved in and hadn't known the lighting was so poor. She kept the small space very tidy; everything had a place. A pile of books was stacked neatly on the table beside a cut-down cupboard box which held her hairbrush, a folded scarf, hair ties and grips, and a small silver pair of hairdresser's scissors. A box of tea bags, a small jar of coffee and a red mug with a teaspoon inside it were lined up on top of the tiny refrigerator.

April's headlamp sent light arcing across the floor and walls as she bounced out of bed and pointed at the door. 'Get out! First your mother, and now you! I'm entitled to some privacy!'

'I didn't say anything to her about last night,' he said quietly.

Hurt and confusion clouded her eyes. She looked away and shrugged. 'I don't care what you do. Just do it outside my caravan.'

'It's *my* caravan.'

Her gaze snapped back. 'Fine!'

She tried to push past him to the door, but Tarn caught her around the waist. April panicked and lashed out at him. Her pathetic punch and the fragile feel of her bones beneath his hands made his heart squeeze. *Berryman. You bastard.* He sat her on the bed. 'I'm not going to hurt you.'

April batted his hands away. Tarn stepped back and studied her averted face. In different circumstances the headlamp would have made him smile, but not tonight. Thanks to his mother's insecurities and interference, the fragile trust between him and April had been broken. April wasn't going to listen to him — but Tarn wasn't going to back down. 'I'm taking you to Pisa tomorrow to buy you some glasses.'

'No, thank you.'

'I wasn't offering: I was telling.'

She said coldly, 'You can't afford them, remember?'

'I can't afford a half-blind quality controller, either.'

'I'll buy my own glasses.'

'You haven't got any money. I make sure of that so you can't escape.' Tarn nudged the book on the floor with the toe of his boot. 'Besides, how else will you be able to read sex manuals?'

April gritted her teeth. 'I already told you, I'm short-sighted. I need glasses to drive, not to read.'

'I forgot.'

Her lips tightened. He didn't forget anything.

'I need you to be able to drive so you can take the truck and run errands into town when I'm busy. I don't want it smashed up because you're too blind to see where you're going.'

Her eyes gleamed at the possibilities. 'Aren't you worried I'll steal the truck and escape?'

Tarn shrugged. 'You wouldn't get far. Roger Prescott is dying to arrest you again.'

April bristled. 'You're going to buy me a cheap pair of glasses so I'll look like Ozzy Osbourne.'

'Have a little faith, April. I was thinking more of Thelma out of *Scooby Doo*.'

They had four nights of frost in a row, so Tarn didn't take her to Pisa the next day as he'd planned. He picked up work in the helicopter on two of the nights, so Smitty stayed and slept in the guest bedroom the next day. The frosty nights were followed by bright, sunny days.

The orchard had one dam which held 600,000 litres of water, not enough to irrigate all of the trees. In the dry, arid conditions of Central Otago, water was as precious as the gold the miners had panned from the rivers over a hundred years ago. The orchard owners took turns taking water from the Kawarau River, but a dam was better because it was high-pressure and, if it was big enough, could irrigate an entire orchard.

Tarn and Smitty got to work putting in another dam. They stripped off their outer layer of clothes to cut down trees and prepare the area for the digger, and organized for rocks to be delivered by truck to line the hole.

It was hot. Even April shed her kiddy jacket and sweatshirt. Carole fussed over Tarn and Smitty, bringing them cold drinks and food and bucket-loads of sunblock. In the space of just a couple of days, Tarn turned as brown as a nut, and his hair became streaked with gold.

Watching him was causing April problems. He'd pull his dirty, sweat-soaked T-shirt over his head and swipe his face and chest with it, and she'd imagine him naked. He'd heft a rock from the ground, and she'd stare at his bare shoulders and the long, lean sweep of his back, and imagine him naked. She prayed for cloudy days.

Tarn was having similar problems. He knew what lay beneath April's clothes. He knew that her porcelain skin felt even softer than it looked, and that her curves were real, not manufactured. He'd stop to take a drink from his water bottle and catch her looking at him across the dam site, and a vision of her removing the hotel robe and dropping it on the floor would replay slowly in his mind. Unlike April, Tarn didn't back away from his thoughts.

The buds began opening on the trees, smothering them in white blossoms and turning the orchard into a fairyland. April arranged for beehives to be delivered. The bees would stay for about three weeks after the trees flowered, and needed warm days with no rain or wind to go about their business. Without the bees, there would be no cherries. Pollen had a use-by date, a limited amount of time to touch the stamen of the blossom and fertilize it. Some varieties of cherry grown at Aurora were self-pollinating, but they still needed good weather for the pollen to drop down onto the stamen. Each year was different, but the rule of thumb was the earlier the flower, the later the fruit and vice versa.

While Tarn and Smitty worked on the dam, April checked that the packing house and big chiller unit were in order, and that the new trees Tarn had planted were flourishing. Tarn arranged for Clarence to come and work alongside her when the picking season commenced, so that she could get her accreditation renewed. The first variety of cherry Aurora produced was a big, sweet, glossy red cherry called 'Celeste'. It would be ready for picking in early December, in time for the Christmas market. The most lucrative cherry crop, however, was the delicate, white 'Rainier'. It was a big favourite with the Asian market, but was extremely tender and required careful handling. If she was still here, April planned to help pick it. *If* she was still here.

For days, Tarn saw April only at the dinner table. They were both busy, but he suspected she was avoiding him because she was still angry. During a break from dam-building, he went looking for her and found her painting the front gates.

He watched her erase her DPM artwork for a few moments. 'I've changed my mind. Paint the inside of the other one to match.'

April gripped the handle of the paintbrush so tightly that her knuckles turned as white as the paint splashed on her hands. Sweat had made Tarn's hair stick to his forehead and neck, and his T-shirt to his chest. She wished he'd go back to digging holes with Smitty. April turned her back and resumed painting. 'If you want them painted that way, you do it.'

'They're my gates.'

'My hard labour.'

Tarn observed the indignant quiver of her bottom as she plied the brush. 'You seem to forget I'm the boss.'

'You were serious about that? I thought it was a joke — like the wages you're paying me.'

'I prefer the DPM look.'

She straightened and clicked her heels. 'I beg to differ — *sir!*'

Warm brown eyes slid over her. 'I wouldn't try saluting with that paintbrush if I were you.'

Three long years of celibacy ganged up on her. April wanted to throw down the paintbrush, lean into him and slide her hands up the length of his back. She wanted to pull down the neck of his sweaty T-shirt, bury her nose in that brown neck and inhale the salty scent of him.

Tarn eyed the paintbrush clutched tightly in her hand and warned, 'You'd better not be thinking about throwing that.'

It was herself, not the paintbrush, she was thinking of throwing at him.

'You'll probably miss anyway.'

Not if she was the missile.

He started walking back towards the house. 'You need to get cleaned up. We're going to town to buy you some glasses.'

# Chapter 13

*The nice part about living in a small town is that when you don't know what you're doing, someone else does.*

ANON, 'THE JOYS OF WOMANHOOD'

He didn't buy her a pair of glasses that made her look like Ozzy Osbourne, or Thelma from *Scooby Doo*. He took her to an optometrist, paid for her eyes to be tested, and let her choose from the frames in the back-lit recesses lining the walls. Tarn was sure she tried on every pair.

The shop was new. None of the staff knew April.

'I'm afraid April can't have lenses from our library,' the woman helping them explained. 'We'll have to send away to get them specially made for her.'

'Figures,' Tarn remarked drily.

April was ecstatic. 'Can I have a new case for them, too? My old one is really shabby. It would be wrong to put something so nice into something so—'

He raised his hands to stop the flood. 'Choose one!' He knew he'd just been scammed into buying the case, but didn't care because she looked so happy.

Outside, April said earnestly, 'Are you sure you can afford them?'

'I'm already up to my ears in debt. What's a few hundred dollars more?'

'I *will* pay you back.' She squinted across the road. 'Is that who I think it is?'

Ivan Vincent was walking past the shops on the opposite side of the road. He was small and neat, with a head of gleaming white hair and brilliant blue eyes that had made him look handsome when he was young, and like a slimline, beardless version of Santa Claus now he was older. Stefan got his height and darker colouring from his mother — Charmaine Vincent topped Ivan by a full head. However, there was never any question about who wore the pants in the Vincent house: Ivan's word was law there, and, increasingly, in the valley.

'It's your ex-almost-father-in-law.' Hearing himself, Tarn grimaced — he was starting to sound like her.

April continued to squint. 'Is he giving me the evil eye?'

Ivan nodded at Tarn and looked straight through April.

'He's pretending he can't see you.'

Her hand rose. She waved and called, 'Uncle Ivan! How are you?'

Ivan stiffened, and walked on.

'Why do you go looking for touble?' Tarn asked.

April shrugged. 'It finds me anyway. Wrong parents, wrong husbands, allergic to sperm …'

Tarn still wasn't convinced it wasn't one of her stories. A woman passing by overheard them, glared, and walked on.

April was unruffled. 'That's Mrs Thorburn, my old Economics teacher. Our relationship was always a little strained. I could never bring myself to care too much about the difference between Gross Domestic Product and Gross National Product, and Mrs Thorburn had a problem with me listening to The Backstreet Boys on my headset in class. She won't be surprised to hear I'm too broke to buy myself a pair of glasses.'

Tarn felt for Mrs Thorburn. April was the most infuriating creature he'd come across. Delphine would like her, though, because she lived in the moment and didn't ask for explanations about everything. The French understood about secrets.

'You Anglos always need to know *everything!* Where is the mystery in that? Where is the fun when everything is all so … so *out there?*'

April had plenty of secrets. Having her around was like standing too close to a fireworks display. It was impossible to know when a sky rocket might go off and where it would land.

Tarn spied Brad, the petrol-pump attendant and head of April's fan club, speeding towards them. He reeled April in and walked briskly in the opposite direction. He needed to get rid of her. He had something to do.

Meanwhile, April was trying to decide the best way to get rid of Tarn. His presence distracted her from the things *she* needed to do. She was relieved when he let her go.

'I need to see my accountant.' His accountant was on holiday.

'I want to go to the library and see if they've got a copy of *The Seven Daughters of Eve*.' She didn't have a library card.

They agreed to meet outside the library building in an hour.

'Try not to get into any trouble while I'm gone.'

'As if.'

Tarn walked in the direction of where he'd parked the truck.

April hurried towards Emma Murfitt's office.

Her apology was unwelcome and unwanted, but April made it anyway. She was surprised that Emma agreed to see her, but when she saw her sitting behind her desk immaculately dressed and beautifully groomed, April understood that Emma wanted her to see how much better she'd done than the spoiled Ritchie heiress.

'I'm sorry you got fired because I took the hospital records.'

Emma stared at April. She hadn't expected an apology — the Ritchies never apologized for anything. April's turquoise dress and shoes were cheap and tired-looking, and her blonde hair wasn't styled, but she still managed to look pretty and desirable. Emma spent an hour each morning washing and blow-drying her hair, applying her make-up, and making sure her shoes, jewellery and clothes matched. Looking good wasn't effortless for her the way it was for April Ritchie.

'As you can see, it hasn't held me back,' she said coolly.

'No.' April looked around Emma's large, sunny office. 'You've done really well for yourself.'

There was an uncomfortable silence.

'And thanks for giving Rob Sturmley's details to Tarn.'

Emma didn't want to ask, but couldn't help herself. 'How is Tarn?'

'He's somewhere in town seeing his accountant.'

'Is he?' She looked puzzled. 'I thought John was on holiday.'

April blinked. Why had Tarn lied to her? He was overbearing and inflexible, but he was reliable and honest, too, and she'd begun to trust him. So the major told lies; it was no biggie, and who was she to point a finger? She told little white lies to the people she cared about, great honking black ones to the people she didn't.

April picked up her bag. 'Thank you for seeing me.'

'I'll let you see yourself out.'

It was done. It hadn't been pleasant, but she'd done it.

Somewhere along the way, she'd forgotten the reason she'd come to Aurora in the first place: to get the jewellery. What she thought of Tarn Elliott, and her relationship with him, was irrelevant. Now she needed to see Courtney. April knew saying sorry to her former best friend was going to be a lot harder than apologizing to Courtney's big sister. Courtney wasn't cool and calm like Emma. On the rare occasions April and Courtney had fought as children, bad things had been said and blood drawn.

When Courtney saw who was on her doorstep, she tried to shut the door, but April wedged her foot in the gap.

'Get your foot out of my door!'

'No. If you want me to go, you'll have to call the police.'

'They're *next door*, April!'

'You think I don't know that? I spent the night in the cells, remember?'

Courtney gave up and let her in. 'I'm only letting you in because Kieran's having his afternoon nap and I don't want you banging on the door and waking him up.'

Mention of Courtney's son made April smile. 'He's gorgeous, Muppy. Or at least, what I saw of him in the stroller looked gorgeous.'

She led the way to the living room. 'Don't call me that.'

April looked around curiously. It was a typical, modest house, exactly what she'd expect a young couple with a baby and only one income to own, and nowhere near as grand as Aurora or the homes April had shared with Ralph. This was much nicer. There was a highchair in the kitchen and baby toys on the hallway floor.

'Don't call you what? Muppy? What do you want me to call you? Mrs Prescott?

Courtney spun to face her. 'If you're here to apologize for *deserting* your best friend and not bothering to call *once* in nine years, you're doing a lousy job of it!'

There was a faint wail from further down the hallway.

'Shut up!' April hissed. 'You'll wake Kieran!'

Courtney shoved her into the living room and shut the door. 'Lionel will be home for something to eat soon. Say what you came to say.'

April sat down in the nearest chair, hoping that this would make it harder for Courtney to throw her out. 'I'm sorry you didn't hear from me. I tried to call, but every time I did your mother or Emma answered.'

Courtney stood over her with her arms folded. 'You couldn't write a letter instead? Were your hands in plaster or something?'

April replied, 'First, I was ashamed, and then I was angry.' *At Stefan for refusing to get a job and spending what she earned on CDs and cigarettes instead of food and the electricity bill.* 'Then I was … sad.' *And beaten up, and scared.* 'I know you don't believe me, but I really missed you.' Her eyes stung as she remembered how much. She dropped her chin and finger-combed her hair to hide her reaction. 'I'm sorry I missed out on your wedding and Kieran being born.'

Courtney saw April's eyes turn glassy before she ducked her head, and some of her anger dissolved. She knew the difference between April's crocodile tears and the real thing. 'We were going to be bridesmaids at each other's weddings.'

'I know. I'm sorry.'

'You had two chances to ask me.'

'One,' April corrected. 'My marriage to Stefan wasn't legal.'

'Yeah, we heard.' Courtney sniffed. 'I s'pose I wasn't grand enough to be a bridesmaid at your wedding to the rice-bubble millionaire. I saw it on the six o'clock news.'

'Courtney, *I* wasn't grand enough to be at my wedding to Ralph Berryman, and I was the bride.'

Courtney refused to laugh. 'There was a rumour that you aren't Heather and Grant's daughter.'

'I'm not.'

'You're … *not?*'

April shook her head. 'I wrote to all The Rolling Stones hoping they'd misplaced a love child, but they never got back, which was a shame because I'd have made a really good rocker-chick.'

Courtney giggled, even though it wasn't really funny. But that was the way it had always been when she and April got together: they spent most of their time laughing.

'Why'd you run away?'

'I didn't run away. Grant kicked me out.'

Courtney sank onto the arm of the sofa. Hearing April call her father Grant made her story more convincing. 'If you needed help, why didn't you come to me? I was your best friend.'

'You'd hurt your wrist in the car crash, remember? Your mother was hardly going to roll out the red carpet if I knocked on the door.'

That was true. 'How'd he find out?'

'Heather told him.'

*Heather*, not *Mum*.

Courtney slid off the sofa arm and onto the seat. 'How did she know?'

'She guessed.' April resented lying for Heather. 'Remember when I needed the blood transfusion when I cut my leg? I'm the wrong blood type.'

Courtney remembered how April had milked the injury for all she was worth and gotten out of games for months, even though she still spent most lunchtimes dangling upside down in the adventure playground. The rest of the kids had played lookout and alerted her when a teacher was coming.

'How did it happen? Was there a mix-up at the hospital?'

April picked at her cuticles. 'Yeah.'

'That's why you stole the files from the hospital!'

'One of them was mine. The other belonged to my birth mother.'

Courtney's eyes rounded. 'You *met* her?'

'And Heather's daughter.'

When they were young, they used to tell each other everything, but now April had said as much as she wanted to. There was a long silence.

'So why'd you come back, April?'

'Rosamund left something at the house for me. I'm having trouble locating it.'

'People think you're after Tarn. Are you?'

'Only for the wages he owes me. He isn't my number one fan either.' That was probably overstating things a little. *So he lied. Big deal.*

'I don't hate you.' The sound of the back door opening interrupted their conversation. 'But if you say anything nasty about Lionel, I will,' Courtney warned.

Lionel walked into the living room from the kitchen, wearing his police uniform. He stopped when he saw April. She waited tensely to see if he'd kick her out, but he only nodded and said, 'Hi, April.'

She smiled tentatively. 'Hi, Lionel.'

'I hope you two've made up. Courtney's been a real pain to live with for weeks.'

Courtney glowered at him. April knew she still wasn't completely forgiven and perhaps never would be.

She stayed for lunch and helped Kieran feed himself in his highchair when he woke up. He returned the favour by rubbing banana custard through his hair and April's.

Courtney grabbed his hand and wiped it with a dishcloth. 'Kieran! No! You don't rub banana in your hair or April's.' She handed the dishcloth to April. 'Here.'

April dabbed at the sticky, brown mess. 'He's so funny. He reminds me of you, Lionel.'

Courtney gave her a look.

'I didn't mean it that way,' April said quickly. 'I meant he *looks* like his father.'

Lionel lifted Kieran from the highchair. 'I hated you two at school. I used to pray you weren't in any of my classes.'

'April was worse than me,' Courtney insisted.

'I was not.'

'It was you who thought up Lionel's Angels.'

'It was you who started singing "It's Hip To Be Square" every time he came into the room.'

Lionel looked at his wife accusingly. 'You said that was April's idea.'

She busied herself scooping brown gunk off the highchair. 'It was a long time ago. We always said it was April who thought up stuff because we knew she wouldn't get in trouble.'

*Because her parents let her get away with murder, and the teachers were too scared to complain.*

Lionel and Courtney's eyes met. They used to envy April when they were kids, but now they were adults and parents themselves, they realized how awful it had been.

Tarn knocked loudly on the back door of Dr Tom Giles's house. The house was an old wooden villa, painted white and trimmed in dark green, and almost hidden from the street by the pittosporums growing inside the front fence. It wasn't until a person ventured beyond them that the full beauty of the garden was revealed.

Tom was well into his seventies, retired and partially deaf without his hearing aid, but he could still be lured from his garden to fill in if one of the local GPs were sick or wanted a vacation. He knew everybody in Pisa and the surrounding area. He knew everybody's secrets, and how important it was to guard those secrets — especially in a small town.

A vegetable patch took up most of the back garden, and an old and ugly bulldog with protruding lower canines snored on the back step. It snuffled and opened rheumy eyes when Tarn's knock disturbed it, before going back to sleep again. He heard a muffled 'Coming!' from within the house and saw a long, lanky shape through the pink, green and white stained-glass panels in the top half of the back door.

Tom stared in surprise when he saw who it was. The doctor had contacted Carole when he'd heard Murdo was sick, and had attended the funeral. 'Tarn Elliott!' He reached for his hand. 'How are you? How's your mother?'

He ushered Tarn into the cramped charm of his living room, settled him into an armchair and poured them both a generous amount of whisky. The doctor saluted him with his glass. 'To a good Scottish single-malt.'

Tarn raised his. 'To a good Scottish single-malt.'

They savoured their first sips.

Tom adjusted the volume on his hearing aid. 'What can I do for you, Major?'

Tarn wasn't looking forward to having this conversation. His reply was brisk. 'You know April Ritchie is back? And she's working for me at Aurora?'

'Everybody knows. The Ritchies were Pisa's equivalent of the Kennedys: money, glamour and scandal. Ivan Vincent keeps trying to take their place — I'm damned if I know why. They've got the money, and Stefan to provide the scandal, but Ivan and Charmaine don't have the glamour Grant and Heather did. They don't have the *cojones.*' Tom leaned forward and chuckled. 'Great word that, "cojones" — heard it on an American television show the other day.'

Tarn had forgotten how much he enjoyed Tom's ability to send himself and everybody else up.

'You delivered all the babies around here until a few years ago, didn't you?'

'All of 'em. Would've delivered you, too, if Carole and Murdo had been living here.'

'Do you remember the night April was born?'

Tom nodded cautiously. 'You want to know how Heather and Grant got the wrong baby?'

Tarn was startled by the question. 'April definitely isn't their daughter?'

'No.' He cocked his head. 'How much has April told you?'

'I'd like to say everything, but with April you can never be sure.'

'You've come to check out her story because you can't believe it's true?'

'Yes.'

Tom set his glass aside and linked his fingers over his belt buckle.

'I knew she wasn't Grant's, but I didn't know that she wasn't Heather's either until Grant kicked April out.' His chin sank onto his chest while he thought, and Tarn waited.

'There were three babies born that night — April, Lionel Prescott, and another baby girl to a woman from out of town. Three babies in one night was the equivalent of a population explosion in a town the size of Pisa. I was on my own with one nurse. The two girls were straightforward, easy births, but Joy Prescott had trouble with Lionel. The nurse wasn't a local, but she knew what she was doing. She kept an eye on the two women who'd delivered and their babies, in between helping me with Joy. In the morning, the mother from out of town left early with one baby girl. It was her seventh; she didn't want to stay.' Tom looked up at Tarn. 'And later in the morning, Heather Ritchie left with the other baby.'

Tarn watched him. 'Do you think Heather swapped the babies?'

Tom smiled faintly. 'What I know and what I suspect are two different things.'

'April said she did it because she wanted a blonde baby.'

'I can't comment on that. What I do know is Heather Ritchie has no morals. If she'd been born poor, she'd probably be in jail by now.' Tom raised his shoulders in a helpless gesture. 'I blame myself for April finding out the way she did.'

'How did you know she wasn't the Ritchies' daughter?'

'Some things didn't add up.'

Tarn could tell the doctor wasn't prepared to expand on that.

'I shouldn't have answered Grant's questions over the phone, but I was busy that night. As soon as I could, I went out to Aurora, but Grant had already thrown April out. Seventeen years old and he kicked her out!' Tom cried. 'It doesn't say much for a family when a teenage girl has only her boyfriend to run to. Rosamund has been beating herself up about it ever since, and so she should. She stood back and let Donald Dreyfuss ruin Heather, and then watched as Grant and Heather did the same thing to April.'

*Rosamund has regrets about April? Does April know that?*

Tom raised his hands in a helpless gesture and let them fall back onto the arms of the chair. 'In hindsight, getting away from here probably saved April: if she'd stayed, she might have ended up just like Heather.'

*No, she wouldn't have; April is too tender. It's a miracle that she hasn't broken.*

'I've got one more thing I need your help with.' Tarn explained about April's allergy.

The doctor listened intently. 'She's allergic to sperm?'

'That's what she says.'

'You don't believe her?'

Tarn didn't know what to believe. April spun so many tales it was hard to sort out the truth from the lies. 'I don't know,' he said honestly. 'I looked it up on the Web, but …'

'You couldn't believe that either,' Tom finished. 'Oh, it's real alright. Hell for the woman, and damned unpleasant for the man, too. It's a marriage-wrecker. I've come across it only once.' He tugged irritably on one droopy earlobe. 'That girl just doesn't have much luck, does she?'

It was good to speak to somebody who didn't screw up their face and wish April to hell.

'You thinking of sharing some of yours with her?'

If Tom had asked Tarn the same question last month when he'd found April dressed in a red rubber dress and picking the lock on his wardrobe door, his reply would have been an unequivocal 'no' —

but a lot had happened since then. The night in Queenstown had changed things dramatically. Tarn wasn't planning anything, but he wasn't going to deny that he wanted to take April to bed, either.

Tom thrust himself to his feet. 'Either way, you'll be needing condoms, and you won't want to buy them in town in case it gets reported in the *Pisa Press*. People are still talking about you buying April tampons.'

Tarn grimaced.

'The medical reps still drop by occasionally to say hello and show me anything they think might interest or amuse me …' Tom rummaged in a cupboard in the sideboard and emerged with a box of condoms in each hand. 'They're flavoured.' He checked the boxes: 'Chocolate and strawberry. How many do you want?'

Tarn was late reaching the library because he made a detour to the truck to hide Tom Giles's gift. The doctor wanted him to take half a dozen boxes and was disappointed when Tarn accepted only two. Tarn wedged them under the driver's seat and hoped like hell they wouldn't fall out on the drive home: if April saw them she'd think he was planning a fuck-fest. He wasn't … but he wasn't ruling out the possibility either.

April wasn't waiting outside the library when he got there. She wasn't inside the library, either. Which, as usual, meant she was somewhere she shouldn't be. Sometimes Tarn felt like he'd employed The Scarlet Pimpernel. He went inside and asked the librarian if April had checked out any books.

She reacted to the notion as if she was a bank teller and he was a thief demanding she empty the till. 'She can't! She hasn't got a library card.'

Tarn was getting heartily sick of small-town prejudice. 'What about me? Can I get a library card?'

'Of course, Major: *you're* a resident.'

He gave the librarian a stony look. 'So is April.'

She licked her lips nervously. 'A *permanent* resident. All we require is a letter showing your address and some form of ID.'

'Have you got a book called *The Seven Daughters of Eve?*' he asked brusquely.

'I'll ... just take a look.'

She located the book on the database. Tarn showed her his driver's licence, but he didn't have a letter with his address.

'Seeing as it's you, Major Elliott, I think just this once we can waive the formalities,' the librarian whispered across the desk, even though the library was empty except for her and Tarn. 'If you promise to bring the letter next time you're in town, I'll issue you with a card.'

April was waiting on a wooden bench in the sunshine when Tarn emerged from the library with the book tucked under his arm. 'Where *were* you?' he demanded.

She glanced at the book, lifted her face to the sun and twirled one foot. 'Here and there. How did the meeting with your accountant go?' she asked airily.

Something in her manner, and the fact she didn't ask to see the book, alerted Tarn that all was not well. 'Fine,' he replied cautiously.

'Good.' April smiled distantly. 'I'd better start working off what I owe you for the glasses. Let's go home.'

# Chapter 14

*I think I could fall madly in bed with you.*

**Anon**

That night, Tarn started reading *The Seven Daughters of Eve* and got hooked on the story of how Professor Bryan Sykes and his team of helpers discovered that seven women were the maternal ancestors of all Europeans, and that those seven women were in turn descended from one woman in Africa: the original Eve.

The professor had given the women names — Ursula, Xenia, Helena, Velda, Tara, Katrine and Jasmine — and built profiles for them. Each woman had left a unique calling card in her descendants' DNA that could be identified from a simple mouth swab. Thousands of years after their deaths, those descendants were able to say: 'I am descended from Ursula; she lived 45,000 years ago', or 'I am descended from Katrine …'

Tarn understood the significance of the book for April. She belonged to nobody. But her DNA couldn't lie; it would tell her where she'd come from.

She'd been different since Tarn had taken her to town to buy her glasses. There was nothing specific that he could put his finger on, but he knew now not to take her at face value. He couldn't fault her work: she was up at sparrow's fart and put in long days at the orchard with the rest of them. She ate, showered and retreated to her caravan, where, judging by the glow through the curtains, she read by headlamp until, presumably, she fell asleep.

Tarn put stronger light bulbs in the caravan so it was easier for her to read. She thanked him and made a smart remark about company bonuses. He introduced her to the exporters who took Aurora's crop. April asked whether she got a wardrobe allowance now that she was networking. She was her usual contrary, insolent self, but at the same time distant.

Tarn wanted some answers; April wanted to get into the wardrobe. He decided to let her, but on his terms.

The sunny weather ended the day Tarn and Smitty finished the dam. It was also Carole's sixtieth birthday. They celebrated both occasions by opening a bottle of champagne and drinking a toast down by the dam. When April wished Carole a happy birthday, Carole looked wary.

'Don't worry, Carole, I haven't put a hex on you.'

She unbent enough to thank April.

Carole was feeling nervous and happy: tonight she was going to Queenstown with Gerald to have dinner and see a movie. Tarn had given her a six-place dinner service that matched her beloved china tea set. The pattern was hard to get and expensive, and Carole knew Tarn didn't have spare cash to throw around. She burst into tears when she opened his present.

'I'm hoping they're happy tears,' he said drily.

She hugged him and sobbed against his neck. 'How did you find it? How can you *afford* it?'

He hugged her back. 'We're not destitute yet, but whatever you do, don't break it.'

She blew her nose and laughed.

Tarn wanted to take her to dinner to celebrate, but Carole declined. 'You're tired, and broke, and I don't want a fuss.'

Then Gerald told her a movie they both wanted to see was on in Queenstown and asked if she'd like to go with him. How could she accept Gerald's invitation after she'd turned down Tarn? And why did she want to go so much when Murdo had been dead less than a year?

Gerald saw her expression and backed off. 'It was just an idea. I only asked because I feel stupid sitting there on my own and I knew you wanted to see— '

'I *want* to come! It's just …' Carole explained about turning down Tarn's invitation, but not about feeling guilty about Murdo. Gerald guessed anyway; he felt the same way — it was the first time he'd asked a woman out since Bronwyn had died.

He had noticed the tension between Tarn and April. If they didn't sort out their problems soon, they'd spontaneously combust. They needed some time alone to do it. He told Tarn about the movie he and Carole wanted to see.

Tarn was surprised his mother wanted to go to the movies with Smitty instead of have dinner with him, until he thought about what they had in common. It made sense that they would be friends. He didn't want to become the centre of her universe the way his father had been.

'She doesn't need my permission, Smitty.'

'She didn't want to hurt your feelings.'

'She won't. What movie are you going to see?'

When Smitty answered, Tarn knew a lot more than his feelings would be hurt if he had to sit through it. 'Enjoy yourself.'

Carole was anxious to let him know that she was only friends with Gerald. 'We both like going to the movies, but feel stupid sitting there alone. It's just for company.'

'Of course,' Tarn replied. 'I never thought anything else.'

She felt slightly miffed.

'You're over the age of consent — we both are.'

She wasn't sure what to make of that.

Tarn sat at the bottom of the stairs with a foot on the floor and an elbow braced on his knee, reading the newspaper. He was waiting for April to emerge from the powder room. Smitty and his mother had left for Queenstown and wouldn't be back for hours, which gave him plenty of time to have things out with her.

April finally materialized in her pyjamas, pulling a hairbrush through her wet hair. She stopped when she saw Tarn on the stairs and raised her brows imperiously. 'Yes? Can I help you?'

'I need a haircut.'

Her hand stilled. 'What? Now?'

'What's wrong with now?'

'I have things to do.'

'Like what? Reading sex manuals by headlamp?' Tarn pointed to his fringe: 'I can't see what I'm doing.'

'Maybe you need glasses.'

She was starting to piss him off. 'And maybe *your* eyesight is bad because you've been reading too many sex manuals.'

'And maybe the reason you're thirty-five and have never even been engaged is because you haven't read enough of them.'

Tarn folded the newspaper. 'I've been engaged.'

April's jaw fell. '*You have?* Who to?'

'Delphine.'

'War correspondent Delphine?'

He nodded.

'Why did you—'

'If you want answers, you'll have to cut my hair.'

April sped towards the front door. 'I'll get my scissors and meet you in the kitchen.'

'Upstairs.'

She stopped with her hand on the doorknob and looked over her shoulder at him. She wanted to get into his bedroom — but without him. 'Think of the mess. The kitchen will be much better.'

Tarn put one booted foot on the bottom stair. 'I like mess.' He began to climb.

'You do not. You run this place like an army camp.'

'Upstairs.' He kept on going. 'Five minutes.'

April watched him disappear from view. He'd thrown out a lure no woman could resist: information about the past relationships of a man she was attracted to.

'Wash your hair!' she shouted after him. 'It has to be wet for me to cut it!'

Sometimes people keep secrets to protect others. Sometimes they keep them to protect themselves. April knew that better than anybody.

She also knew that people were flawed and not to expect too much from them, but when it came to Tarn she seemed to have a blind spot. She thought he was different, that he was reliable and honest — painfully so — and that he wouldn't shy away from telling the truth. Thankfully, he wasn't also a student of the 'I always speak my mind' school, which in April's experience was filled with a lot of idiots bent on airing their views when they were of no interest to anybody else and achieved nothing positive.

Considering the whoppers Stefan used to tell her about why the grocery money had disappeared or why he hadn't got a job, Tarn's lie about seeing his accountant wasn't even a blip on April's personal radar; it was more a timely reminder that the major was like everybody else — *flawed.* She was a big girl, she could handle it.

What April couldn't — *wouldn't* — accept was being manipulated, and she realized that Tarn was doing exactly that when she walked into his bedroom and saw the wardrobe door open. *Wide open.*

Judging by the noises coming from the en suite, Tarn was washing his hair in the basin. Only the Dreyfuss and Ritchie families knew about the secret compartment. Provided the spring on the catch was still in good order, it would only take a couple of seconds to liberate the jewellery from its hiding place. He wouldn't know anything was missing.

Her temper began to simmer. April wasn't about to let Tarn Elliott dictate terms. Letting him know that was suddenly far more important than obtaining Rosamund's brooch and bracelet.

The major had great hair. April couldn't wait to get her hands on it.

She'd spread an old sheet on the carpet beside the bed and was picking up the wooden chair she'd brought up from the kitchen when Tarn walked in drying his hair on the towel draped around his neck. He'd taken his shirt off to wash his hair, and put it back on without buttoning it. April got a first-class view of what she'd ogled across the dam. She itched to take a marker pen and write *FAKE* across his pectorals.

His gaze didn't even flicker in the direction of the wardrobe. 'Where do you want me?'

'Let me think.' She put a finger to her chin. 'Dangling over a yawning chasm would be good.' A small vee appeared between Tarn's brows; April laughed lightly. She put the chair in the middle of the sheet, and patted the seat. 'Here will do.'

Tarn gave her a long look before he sat down. He tucked his feet beneath the chair, and rested his hands on his thighs as April drew the comb through his hair. People raved about the colour of April's hair, but she would have swapped it for Tarn's in a flash. His was all the shades of brown, from caramel through to gold; hers was boring old platinum. His was thick and wavy; hers was baby-fine and as straight as a ruler. Any wave or curl was tortured into it courtesy of curling tongs or heated rollers, and frozen into place with a can of hairspray.

April tilted his head back against her breasts and began to lightly massage his scalp. 'How do you want it?'

Tarn was wise to her games. He caught her wrists and lifted her hands away. 'Shorter.'

'How short?'

'You're the hairdresser — you decide.'

'OK.'

April set to work butchering his hair.

As she snipped, she glanced at the wardrobe, especially the door, and got madder. Some jeans, the pants and jacket Tarn had worn to Queenstown, and a few shirts hung on one of the racks. There were a couple of army kit bags on the floor, and an officer's cap and some T-shirts on the shelves. April remembered having seen

Tarn in DPMs when he'd visited Aurora, but she'd never seen him in uniform and wearing the cap. Once upon a time she'd been as susceptible as any other woman to a man in uniform, but meeting male strippers in dress whites stuck together with Velcro had cured her of that.

Gold-tipped brown hair fell onto the sheet. April's breast jostled Tarn's right ear. He tilted his head away, but otherwise sat like a statue. She moved closer and ran her fingers through his hair. She couldn't decide whether to go for a mullet or a mohawk.

Tarn knew she was up to no good. He tried to touch the hair above his ear and got a slap for his trouble. 'April …' he muttered warningly.

She patted his bare shoulder reassuringly. 'Just relax and leave it all to me.' Her hand stayed on his shoulder as she lifted her leg, slipped it between his knees and turned to face him.

All the patting and breast-jostling was getting to him. 'What are you doing?' he asked suspiciously.

'Cutting your fringe. So why didn't you marry Delphine?'

Tarn was forced to close his eyes to avoid injury. 'Aaron asked me the same question.'

'If you think I'll get sidetracked and ask who Aaron is, you're wrong. Tell me why you didn't marry Delphine.'

He shrugged. 'She was a war correspondent; I was a soldier. We didn't think our occupations boded well for a long marriage. I met her while I was doing a UN posting. When I came back to New Zealand, things cooled off between us.'

April suddenly noticed the shape of him beneath the zipper of his jeans. She paused. There was something about an aroused man with strong thighs wearing faded blue jeans. Her eyes drifted upwards — and a deep chest. They moved higher, and encountered

Tarn's interested brown stare. April began hacking away at his fringe and his eyes closed again.

'Does Carole know?' she asked briskly.

'No. And I don't want her to.'

Tarn relaxed his knee so his thigh touched the inside of April's. She didn't appreciate that the balance of power had shifted. To hell with it, she'd give him a mullet *and* a mohawk.

'Why not?' she asked.

'Because it happened years ago, and she'll be hurt that I didn't tell her. In hindsight, it was just as well I didn't.'

'Why?'

'Because I wasn't really serious about getting married.' He cracked open one eye and squinted at her. His eyelashes were gold-tipped like his hair. 'We spent most of our time in bed.'

April felt aroused, disappointed and angry all at the same time. She focused on the disappointment. 'You were stringing Delphine along?'

'I didn't say that. We loved our careers more than the idea of getting married, so we made the decision to call it off.' She wasn't the only one who was disappointed. 'What's in the wardrobe, April?'

'Why did you lie about visiting your accountant?'

Tarn stared. 'How did you know I didn't visit my accountant?'

'Emma Murfitt told me he was on holiday,' April said spikily.

'You went to see *Emma?*'

'I went to make my apologies to her and Courtney. Nine years too late, I admit, but time management was never my strong suit.'

Tarn glanced warily at the sharp silver scissors in her hand. 'How'd that go?'

April gripped his shoulders and unhooked her leg from between his. 'We bonded like Superglue.'

He wished for once she'd give him a straight answer. 'I went to see Dr Giles.'

'Sure you did.' She returned the scissors to their case. 'You're done.'

'No,' Tarn said firmly, 'I'm not.'

'Alright, *I'm* done.' She walked towards the door.

'April! Get back here!'

'Go screw yourself, Major.'

Tarn let her go, because he knew that if he didn't he might strangle her.

The memory of the embarrassing conversation he'd had with Tom Giles and the boxes of condoms in his bedside cabinet made his blood boil. He dragged a hand through his hair and frowned when he encountered a small hillock on the top of his head. He stalked into the bathroom, checked in the mirror and swore like a soldier. He looked like a cross between Sonic the Hedgehog and Frankenfurter.

Tarn made a quick trip back to the bedroom to snatch a box of condoms and a key ring from the bedside cabinet, and strode out.

A light rain was falling as April opened the door of the caravan and ducked inside. The thud of boots coming closer indicated the major was on the warpath. She wasn't surprised — the haircut she'd given him wasn't exactly army issue.

April closed the door and locked it.

Tarn unlocked it and barged in.

April sat on the bed and sighed, 'Major, we've been through this before.' She splayed her fingers across her chest. 'Me — caravan.' She pointed to him: 'You — house.'

He pointed to his hair. 'What did I do to earn this?'

'Left your stupid wardrobe door open.'

'You want to get in there!' Tarn snapped.

'Without you!' April snapped back.

He jammed his hands on his hips. In all his years in the army, he'd never come across anybody as obstinate, headstrong and fucking *deluded* as April.

'*First,*' Tarn began ominously, 'you're going to listen to what I have to say without interrupting. *Then* you're going to fix my hair.' He tossed a small box onto April's lap. It burst open, spilling condoms across her knees, the bed and the floor. 'I got those from Dr Giles when I went to see him. Is that proof enough for you?'

She surveyed the foil packages scattered across her lap and bed and littering the floor. 'Most men bring flowers.'

His face contorted. 'Can we dispense with the bullshit?' He jabbed a finger at April when it looked like she was going to answer him. 'No! I did not go to see Tom to get condoms — he gave them to me.'

She raised a brow. 'When I lived here, he gave away cabbages from his vegetable garden, not condoms.'

His eyes shot thunderbolts. 'You asked me why I lied and I'm telling you, so do me the favour of *shutting the hell up!* I went there to talk about you!'

'Why did you do that? Everybody else just stands in the street.'

'So help me, April, I am *that* close,' Tarn held up his thumb and index finger, 'to strangling you and burying you in the fucking orchard! I wanted to find out what happened the night you were born.'

Her disdainful expression cracked. 'Why would you want to do that?'

'Because it's impossible to get a straight answer out of you. Because I don't like injustice. Because even if you were a brat, you didn't deserve what happened to you!'

She stared at him. Her throat worked.

Tarn raked a hand through his hair and scowled when he hit the hillock. 'Tom doesn't have proof Heather switched you with the other baby girl born that night, but he suspects that's what happened. He also said that he felt bad about answering Grant's questions over the phone the night of your birthday. He came to Aurora as soon as he could to check you were alright, but you'd already gone.'

April's chest felt tight. 'That was nice.'

'I think he'd like to see you.'

'He's the only person in Pisa who does.'

'You're forgetting Brad Tecklenberg.'

A bubble of laughter rose in her throat and escaped. 'Dr Giles knew I wasn't Grant's when I was nine and had to have a blood transfusion. Parents who are blood group A don't produce children who are blood group B. I know because I got a book out of the library and read up about it. That's how Heather convinced Grant that night. I'm sure Dr Giles didn't know I wasn't Heather's either.'

The unfairness of what had been done to her filled Tarn with helpless rage. He sat down on the bed beside her, spilling condoms onto the floor, leaned his elbows on his knees and clasped his hands.

April patted his arm. 'Don't let it get to you. How did you like your hair?'

He looked sideways at her, amazed by her ability to shrug, move on and shit-stir all at the same time. 'What do you think?'

'That a mullet doesn't look right on somebody with a big neck.'

'A mullet doesn't look right on anybody, and my neck isn't big.'

'I beg to differ, Major.'

'You need to do more of that.'

'More of what?'

'Beg.'

April chewed her lip to keep from smiling.

Outside, the light was beginning to fade. The bed was a perfect size for April, but not big enough to accommodate a large, surly infantry major as well. Tarn was pressed against her from hip to knee. Heat spread through her and began a slow burn in the pit of her stomach. April nudged one of the condoms on the floor with her toe. Her nails were painted turquoise blue. Tarn couldn't recall ever seeing turquoise nail polish teamed with DPMs before.

She picked up a condom. 'Chocolate flavoured — nice.'

'I've got a box of strawberry-flavoured ones, too.'

'I prefer chocolate.'

Silence stretched. The air grew heavy with possibilities.

She'd been in a sexual wilderness for too long. April wanted the major to lead her out of it. Beside her, Tarn was strung as tight as a bowstring. She prayed she hadn't misconstrued the reason for it. 'So, Major, d'you wanna have sex?'

Tarn replayed her words in his head. No, he hadn't imagined them — April had just asked him to have sex. Big Boy/Tiger jumped up and beat his chest until Tarn remembered her so-called allergy. 'What about your allergy?'

She held up the condom. 'Wear this, and it won't be a problem.'

'I've never slept with a woman who might turn blue and stop breathing when I deliver the goods.'

'I don't turn blue and stop breathing. It hurts and I break out in hives.'

'Great, I feel a lot better.'

April stood up and unbuttoned her pyjama jacket. 'It's been three years since I did this.'

'Feeling better all the time.'

She grasped the edges of her jacket and spread them apart. 'I don't want your pity.'

Tarn gazed at the soft, round, pink-tipped beauty of her breasts and her narrow ribcage and waist below. 'Believe me, April,' he said hoarsely, 'it's not my pity I want to give you.'

He pulled her between his knees, framed her left breast with his right hand and kissed the tip. April shivered. '*Definitely not my pity ...*' His lips closed around her.

She clutched Tarn's shoulders when he slid his hand beneath the elastic waistband of her pyjamas and cupped her bottom. He had big hands. April thought vaguely that it was probably the first time she felt confident that her bum didn't look too big in something.

Tarn made short work of her pyjama bottoms and top. April's feminine insecurities reared their head as he tossed them aside. 'I'm not in the same shape as you.'

'Thank God for that.'

He was an equal-opportunities lover: he divided his time between her breasts, her ribs, her navel, her arms, her knees — and everywhere in between — gently nipping, kissing and sucking in all the right places while his fingers worked their magic below. He was also an innovator; and the more Tarn tinkered, the more frantic April became. Eventually, she clambered onto his lap and wrapped her legs around him. 'Take your clothes off!'

Their lips clung as April dragged his shirt down his arms and threw it over her shoulder. Tarn was right when he'd said he knew how to French-kiss. He was throwing off more heat than a nuclear reactor, scorching the sensitive area between April's thighs. She tightened her legs and grabbed his wrist. 'Enough tinkering!' she panted. 'Take off your jeans!'

Tarn flipped the tab on his jeans. 'Bossy little thing, aren't you?'

April crawled off him and onto the bed. 'I know what I want.' She watched him strip off his jeans and underwear and pointed: 'I want that.'

He took a long time putting on a condom. He still wasn't convinced about her so-called allergy, but wasn't taking any chances.

'Can you get a move on?' she demanded.

Tarn refused to be rushed. 'I don't want to have to phone for an ambulance.'

The condom was getting more attention than her. April leaned back against the pillows, put an arm behind her head, tucked up her knees and pressed them to one side. She pointed her toes and gave Tarn a campy, smouldering look and pout worthy of the centrefold in a men's magazine. 'I've got three years to make up for, Major. You might be the one needing that ambulance.'

Tarn laughed. He braced his hands and a knee on the mattress. 'Part those knees.'

She did. A little.

'Wider.'

The Hollywood-style pout deepened.

'*Wider.*'

She obliged, and Tarn's heart nearly seized. He dived across the bed and knocked April onto her back. She lunged for him and winced as she paid the price of three years of sexual inactivity.

April wriggled frantically, but it didn't help. She felt like bursting into tears.

Tarn brushed the hair from her eyes. 'We'll take it slow,' he soothed, and prayed he could. He pushed one of her knees high against the pillow, while his other hand got busy doing the kinky things she liked so much, but it was still a tight fit. He braced his weight on his arms. 'Are you OK?'

Her blue eyes were luminous. 'Stop talking, Tarn.'

It didn't take long. April won first prize, but Tarn was a close second. He searched her face. 'Are you OK?'

'No,' she stretched her arms above her head and linked her fingers together and turned them over, 'I'm perfect. Can you do that again, Major?'

# Chapter 15

*Men are from Earth. Women are from Earth. Deal with it.*

**Anon**

'Nice socks.'

April lifted a leg above the covers and surveyed her pink thermal sock in the low light cast by the lamp on the table. A post-coital trip to the powder room had necessitated getting dressed and putting on her gumboots. 'My cheapskate boss bought them for me. He's making me sleep with him to pay them off.'

'Sounds reasonable to me.'

Tarn grunted when she lowered her leg and jabbed him in the thigh with her heel. The only way they could share the bed was for him to lie crosswise with her on top of him. Unfortunately, April rested the way she did everything else — in perpetual motion. If he hadn't seen her fall asleep in the truck on the journey to Queenstown, he wouldn't have believed she slept at all.

His eyes drifted shut as she snuggled against him and traced the scars on his cheeks with the tip of her finger. 'You talked to Dr Giles about my allergy, didn't you? That's why he gave you the condoms.'

He kept his eyes closed and an arm around April's shoulders. 'What did you expect me to do? We've been generating enough heat to set the orchard on fire. I needed his advice.'

'Which was?'

'Use a condom, but don't get carried away and double-bag.'

April lifted her head. 'What on earth is double-bagging?'

'Wearing two condoms. It's a bad idea because the latex can tear.'

She peeled off her socks and tucked her feet under his calves.

Tarn jerked. 'Jesus! Your feet are freezing!'

April wriggled them deeper into their warm nest. 'My feet are always cold at night. You're better than a hot water bottle.'

He frowned. 'You're cold in here?'

'It's Central Otago in spring; of course it's cold in here.' The top of her head brushed against Tarn's jaw as she shook her head. 'Two boxes of condoms … you've ruined my reputation in Pisa.'

'You've had two husbands, April; your reputation was ruined a long time ago.'

'I was born again after Ralph. It hurt almost as much tonight as it did the first time I did it with Stefan in his car.'

Tarn kissed the top of her head. 'Sorry about that.' He traced the marks on her back, but stopped when April stiffened. 'How did you meet him?'

'Who? Ralph?'

'Yes.'

'After Stefan left, I went off the rails for a while. I stayed in a squat until we all got evicted, then I slept rough or on strangers' couches,' she explained dispassionately. 'Then one morning I woke up naked, and with a really bad hangover, in the bed of a stranger and I decided it was time to make some changes. I had a tiny emergency fund which I spent on the nicest outfit I could afford. I went to the casino in Christchurch every night for a week and sat at the bar drinking lemonade and spurning the advances of sleaze-balls until I found a rich man I liked and thought I could trust. And then I married him,' she finished simply. 'Heather didn't teach me much, but she did teach me how to showcase my assets.'

April rolled onto her stomach and rested her chin on his chest. Tarn looked down at her. 'How old were you?'

'Eighteen. I turned nineteen just before I married Ralph.'

'How much older was he?'

'Thirty years.' April saw the disgust on his face and smiled cynically. 'I might have been nineteen, but inside I was ancient. For the first couple of years Ralph treated me like a queen. Or at least he did until I couldn't get pregnant.' She shrugged. 'I loved him; he took care of me and I was grateful. You saw that woman with him. If I could've had a baby, we'd probably still be together.'

Tarn didn't answer, and April didn't want his opinion anyway — she was just reciting the facts. She was so incredibly honest in some ways, and so damned elusive in others.

She fiddled with the hair on his chest. 'Is Aaron the soldier who got his leg blown off?'

'Yes,' he replied cautiously.

Her blue-green eyes didn't waver. 'And you were in charge?'

Tarn nodded.

'What happened?'

Just like her, he recited the facts.

'Aaron is — was — the warrant officer. It was his job to keep an eye on the NCOs and let me know if there were any problems. He had concerns about a young looie—'

'A lieutenant.'

'Yes — not being up to scratch. I decided to accompany the patrol and took Aaron and a signalman along, too. The intel that day was that there were no problems expected in the area. The intel was wrong. We came across a village with a couple of vehicles parked nearby, which wasn't normal — villagers are too poor to own vehicles.' Tarn rubbed a strand of April's pale hair between his thumb and forefinger. 'I sent Aaron to higher ground to get a better view. He stepped on a mine. The lead scout came under small-arms fire from the village and was killed. I gave orders to hold positions, but two of the men had already gone to check on Aaron and the scout, and one of them was shot.'

April stared at him. 'How old were the men that died?'

'Twenty-three. The scout was twenty-four.'

Only a few years younger than her.

'And Aaron?'

'He's about my age. He should be a higher rank than warrant officer, but whenever he was offered promotion he turned it down. I've known him since I joined the army. I've known a lot of the guys in Bravo a long time; they know *me* better than my family do.'

April regarded him sombrely. 'That's the thing about disasters: you can't see them coming, but always think you should have.'

Tarn stroked her hair. He'd gone over and over the events of that day, thinking about the 'if onlys': if only they'd had better intelligence; if only he hadn't sent Aaron off the track to get a better view; if only he'd ordered a withdrawal when they spotted the vehicles. He'd made the right decisions at the time, but that didn't stop him bitterly regretting what had happened.

He was about to ask about Latoya Gutsell when the sound of a car coming up the driveway in front of the house reached them. The air whooshed from his lungs as April used his chest as a springboard to sit up.

'It's your mother!'

Tarn rubbed his chest. 'Probably.'

She tried unsuccessfully to shove him out of the bed. 'Get out of here! She might see you!'

'She'll definitely see me if I leave now. Why are you whispering?'

April clutched his bicep. 'Did you clean up the hair on your bedroom floor?'

'No, I had other things on my mind.' Tarn hastily cupped his testicles as she scrambled over him. 'April, will you calm down? My mother gave up tucking me into bed a long time ago. She won't know I'm not there.'

'Carole loves you and hates me. Who do you think will get the blame if she finds out what we've been doing?' Still naked, April searched for her hairdressing scissors.

Tarn leaned up on an elbow to watch. 'Come back to bed.'

'Get up. I'm going to fix your hair.'

'Now?'

'Yes, *now.* I still have some pride left. I'm not sleeping with a man with a mullet.'

She was serious. Tarn sighed and swung his legs slowly over the side of the bed.

April advanced on him brandishing the scissors and a comb. The white sheet hung over one of his thighs. His waist and chest rose above it enticingly. Even his rumpled mullet looked sexy.

'I thought my hair needed to be wet.'

'I ran the comb under the tap.' She attacked his hair with it.

Tarn clasped her waist and watched the agitated bounce of her breasts. 'I've done some unusual things over the years, but this is the first time I've had my hair cut by a naked woman — not that I'm complaining.'

The silver scissors flew. 'What kinds of unusual things?'

He stroked her buttock and kissed the underside of one breast.

'Come back to bed and I'll show you.'

She flinched at the feel of his stubble against her ribs. 'Stop that. My hand might slip.'

Tarn's hand slipped instead. April jumped, but soldiered on.

The instant she was finished, he plucked the scissors from her hand, closed his arms around her and fell backwards onto the bed. Nose to nose, they looked at each other.

'You're not going to go, are you?' April asked.

'Nope.'

Tarn's hand slipped again.

Her breath caught. 'What kinds of unusual things?'

Carole didn't have much to say about the mess in Tarn's bedroom or his haircut except 'She could have cleaned up afterwards.'

'I said I'd clean up. Guess I didn't do a good enough job.'

Tarn thought it was odd that his house-proud mother's response was so muted, but didn't say anything. He wasn't going to sneak around and hide his relationship with April from his mother, but he wasn't going to rub it in her face either.

If Carole hadn't been so distracted, she'd have known something was different. Tarn's army training meant he was thorough when he did something. If he'd been supposed to clean up after April, his bedroom would have been spotless. But her mind was elsewhere.

Gerald had called her 'Caro' tonight. He'd kissed her. Or she'd kissed him. Or maybe they both did it at the same time.

Carole wasn't sure how it had happened. They'd both made a special effort with their appearance. She'd worn her navy linen slacks and a pink and navy striped shirt with flared sleeves, and carried a soft, navy mohair shawl. Gerald had looked smart in a hunter-green checked blazer, a beige shirt and trousers, and a green paisley tie. They'd had a wonderful evening together, and when Gerald had stopped his old truck by the gates and leaned hesitantly towards her, it had seemed right to meet him halfway and put her lips against his.

It was nice, *very* nice. Her heart thumped like a mad thing in her chest, and thumped even harder when Gerald cupped her breast. It was full and no longer firm, but the warm pressure of his tongue on hers and his hand against her breast made her feel like a teenager again. Carole made a strangled sound of surprise and pleasure in her throat and Gerald let go and backed off.

'Sorry! I shouldn't have—'

She flapped a hand. 'It's OK! I'm not ang—'

'When I asked you out, I wasn't thinking about …'

*You weren't?* Carole felt deflated.

'I had a good time, Carole. I didn't mean to spoil it.'

*What happened to Caro?*

'You didn't,' she said miserably.

'I haven't touched another woman since Bronwyn.'

'I've only ever been with Murdo, and it wasn't much good.'

'It … wasn't?'

Her face burned with embarrassment. Carole was glad the interior of the truck was dark. 'No. I never did it for him.' She pretended to search for her handbag even though she could feel it resting against her leg.

'The bloke was an idiot.'

Her head shot up. 'What?'

'Murdo was a bloody idiot,' Gerald said gruffly. 'You do it for me.'

Her lips shaped the word 'oh', but only a puff of sound emerged.

'I don't want you to take that the wrong way.'

*What way am I supposed to take it?*

Gerald put the truck in gear and drove the rest of the way to the house. The house was in darkness. Tarn hadn't even left the porch light on.

'Tarn must have decided to turn in,' Carole said.

'Yes.'

She waited to see if Gerald would kiss her again. 'He's up early, and then he stays up late working in the study,' she said inanely.

'You did a good job raisin' him.'

Her, Murdoch and the army. Tarn had done most of his growing up once he'd left home.

Carole reached for the handle and opened the truck door. 'Thank you for a nice night.' She slipped to the ground.

'You're welcome. I'm sorry about—'

She slammed the car door. *Don't say it.*

'Good night, Gerald.' She hurried towards the porticoed entrance to the house.

He lowered the passenger window and called across the seat, 'I'm really sorry if I've upset you, Carole!'

She was upset because she was attracted to him, and he was too polite or stupid to do anything about it. It was probably just as well, Carole thought glumly, because sleeping with Gerald was bound to be the same embarrassing disappointment sleeping with Murdo had been.

'Happy birthday!'

She waved at him without looking, and closed the door.

The next morning, as she collected mint from the herb garden by the kitchen door, Carole wondered how a sixty-year-old woman with a history of a failed marriage and an indifferent sex life encouraged a shy, respectful fifty-eight-year-old man to disrespect her, without making a complete fool of herself.

April drove by on the quad bike, wearing a straw cowboy hat, big, dark sunglasses and the awful blue trackpants Tarn had bought her. Carole watched her glumly. Women like April were born knowing how to get a man's attention — she didn't need to read books about French women's attitudes to love and sex.

Carole snipped off some sprigs of rosemary to go with the mint. Her widowed sister Beverley was fifteen years older and glad she no longer had to worry about 'all that kind of rubbish' since her husband had died four years ago. Beverley assumed that her sister felt the same way. Until last night with Gerald, Carole would have agreed.

April drove the quad bike around the duck pond and up the hill behind the house. Carole took the mint and rosemary inside. She added the rosemary to the leg of lamb she was going to roast for dinner and set the mint aside to make a sauce to go with it.

She'd have to figure things out for herself.

Tarn wanted April to move back into her old bedroom. She was sorely tempted. The haircut she'd given him showed off that square jaw and those warm brown eyes. He looked like a soldier again, but not so unapproachable. She lay on top of him in the cramped caravan bed in a warm post-coital haze, and sleepily studied the contrast of her blonde hair caught in the darker hair on his chest. 'Why do you want me to move into my old bedroom?'

'Because you get cold in the caravan and your old room is closer to mine.' Tarn couldn't see her face because her hair was covering it. The only time April was still was when he managed to wear her out making love.

'On a scale of one to ten, what's more important: keeping me warm, or my old room being closer to yours?' she mumbled.

'Ten.'

'For which one?'

'Both. If you're just down the hallway it'll be much easier — and a lot more comfortable — to do this, and when we do this,' Tarn touched April's warm, toasty feet with one of his, 'you definitely warm up.'

'Moving down the hallway smacks of convenience sex.'

*What the … ?*

'I refuse to be drive-by sex.'

Tarn puffed out his lips. Her mind was like the Starship Enterprise: it went where nobody had ever gone before. 'April, what are you talking about?'

'I expect a man to work for the pleasure of pleasuring me. You might as well paint golden arches over the bedroom door.'

'Did you read this in a library book?'

'Don't be patronizing — it's lazy.' April rested her chin on his chest. 'You don't seriously think I'm going to sneak into your room and sleep with you?'

'I'll sneak into your room instead.'

They both knew he wouldn't sneak.

'I'm not having sex with you while your mother is asleep just down the hallway. People already know you've bought me clothes, glasses and tampons. If word gets out we're fornicating, I'll be run out of town for defiling Pisa's most famous son.'

'I wasn't born here, I'm not famous, and any fornicating I do is my business.'

April gave his shoulder a sympathetic pat. 'That's where you're wrong. Getting something published in the Helpful Hints section of a women's magazine turned Mrs Dunwoody into a local celebrity. You, Major, are a superstar.'

So Tarn had no choice but to keep visiting April in the caravan. He complained bitterly about the size of the bed and objected to providing 'convenience sex'.

'Convenient? You?' she said scornfully. 'You're a big *inconvenience* in my life. I like the cramped conditions; they make you more inventive. The thought of stern Major Elliott creeping out in the middle of the night to have illicit sex does things for me. I saw some strawberries in the fridge; why don't you steal some tonight and bring the strawberry-flavoured condoms?'

It was hard to turn down an invitation like that.

They had fun in the caravan. Inside the walls they were just April and Tarn. Occasionally, *very* occasionally, April would talk a little bit about her childhood and the years after she left Aurora. She'd made up for being such a poor student by borrowing books from the library on a mind-boggling array of subjects.

'Heather is a narcissist,' she announced one day.

'That's another way of putting it.'

'No really, Tarn, she is.'

He gave her one of his looks.

April waved a hand impatiently. 'Yes! I read it in a book! But it's true. It's a personality defect.'

'I know what it is, April. It still doesn't excuse what she did.'

'No, but it does explain a little of the unexplainable.'

Tarn didn't argue. It was April's way of dealing with the whole sordid mess of her childhood. She was slowly shedding her disguises to reveal a vulnerable, funny, brave woman, but with April there would always be a twist.

The house that Carole and Murdo used to live in was empty. Tarn was keeping it for the manager he hoped to employ next year. Increasingly, he thought he should offer April the job. She knew the cherry industry inside out and the best way to run Aurora. She was a hard worker, smart and enthusiastic, and she loved the place. But April made it clear she'd be gone when the season ended.

'And after you've got what you want from the wardrobe,' Tarn said, coolly. When she refused to comment, he added: 'The lure of the glamorous world of kiss-o-grams is obviously stronger than I thought.'

'Try not to be a bitch, Tarn.'

April locked the caravan door against him that night. He needed to know there was only so much interference she'd tolerate, and that she wasn't one of his men.

Tarn didn't use his key to unlock it. He left the wardrobe door unlocked, too, but had no way of knowing if April had taken anything — although if she suddenly disappeared, he'd know why. Another thing she wouldn't discuss was her relationship with Latoya Gutsell.

After speaking with Rob Sturmley and receiving her new glasses, she borrowed Tarn's truck and went into town to give her statement to Roger Prescott.

'How did it go?' Tarn asked when April returned.

'Roger thinks I should be locked up, but Rob's hoping for a fine and community service.'

She didn't add that Rob thought a letter from Nola Gutsell might help her case. 'It's important the magistrate understands the extenuating circumstances and what happened the night you took the files,' Rob had explained.

April wouldn't even consider it.

The same thing had occurred to Tarn.

The same night April locked the door against him, Carole went to town to visit a friend; this had made Tarn even surlier, because he could have made love to April in his own decent-sized bed. Instead, he spent a fruitless half-hour in his study trying to track down Aaron and find out how he was doing. He was just thinking about how exasperating and unpredictable both Aaron and April were when the phone rang.

The clock on his laptop read 22:11. Tarn guessed it was either Latoya or Aaron, or Carole calling to say she was going to be late. It wasn't any of them. It was Nola Gutsell.

# Chapter 16

*The most important thing about communication is to hear what is not being said.*

**Anon**

April's birth mother wasn't well-educated, but she was warm, unaffected and to the point.

'This is Nola Gutsell. I'm April's friend's mother. Sorry to ring so late, but I wanted to get a message to April. Who's this?'

'Tarn Elliott.'

'The major bloke?'

'That's right. If you wait a few minutes, I'll go outside and get April for you.'

'What's she doing outside at this time of night?'

'She lives in a caravan behind the house.'

'What? I've been to Pisa; it's bloody freezing at night!'

'The caravan is heated.' Tarn's attempt to defend his decision to put April in a caravan in an Otago spring fell on deaf ears.

Nola was outraged. 'There's not much of her! She feels the cold — like me.'

It was an odd thing to say.

'April told Latoya there's loads of room in the house. Couldn't you spare one lousy bedroom?'

Why was she taking this so personally?

'April won't move into the house.'

'Why not?'

Tarn couldn't tell her.

'How about I go and get her so you can speak to her yourself? The signal is too weak for me to take the phone to her.'

'And drag her out into the cold? What good will that do?'

He'd really blotted his copybook with Mrs Gutsell.

'Tell her Latoya had a seizure and they're keeping her in hospital for a couple of days to do some tests.'

'Is it serious?' Tarn asked sharply.

'It happens every now and then,' Nola replied grudgingly. 'Sometimes Latoya needs her medication adjusted, or she overdoes things. Tim, her fiancé, is a good sort, but he's still learning about Latoya's condition. He's not as good as April at knowing when she's going downhill.'

'Latoya has epilepsy?'

'No, she likes falling down and banging her head on the floor.'

No prizes for guessing where April got her smart mouth from — Nature had definitely won out over nurture in that department.

'She's had it since she was a baby. If we didn't know April was watching out for Latoya, we'd have worried ourselves sick when she moved to Christchurch. April's a lovely girl.' Nola paused. 'She's special.'

*April's a lovely girl. She's special.*

Tarn pressed the phone closer to his ear. 'How long have you known April?'

'I met her three years ago.' Nola began conducting her own fishing expedition: 'How long have you known her?'

'Since she was eleven.'

'Where did you meet her?'

He was stepping into territory he had no right to enter. 'Locally,' Tarn replied briefly. 'I'll make sure April gets the message. Please give my best wishes to Latoya.'

*She's special.*

April was special to Nola. So special that Nola yelled at a stranger for making April sleep in a caravan, and leapt at the chance to get information about her childhood.

Tarn rapped on the caravan door. He was getting heartily sick of doing it.

'If you don't go away,' April called, 'I'm going to call Lionel and report you as a stalker.'

'Your mother just phoned.' He stepped back from the door and waited.

It didn't crash against the side of the caravan, but opened by slow degrees to reveal April wearing her DPMs and headlamp, and a blanket draped around her shoulders. She regarded him warily. 'Heather called?'

Tarn had forgotten all about Heather. 'Not Heather,' he said gently. 'Nola.'

She pursed her lips and her eyes got big.

'Latoya's in hospital.'

Her grip tightened on the blanket. 'She's had a seizure?'

'Yes. Nola said they're keeping her for tests and to see if her medication needs adjusting. She says you know the drill.' Tarn stared at her intently. 'She told me off for making you sleep in a caravan because you feel the cold … like her.' He paused. 'Nola knows, April; or at the very least, she suspects.'

She sat down on the top step and muttered, 'No, she doesn't.

Nola collects waifs and strays. She and Barry are always broke. They've got seven kids who're usually unemployed, and their house is falling down, but they've always got people staying. They like me because I'm good to Latoya.'

The night sky was cloudless and glowing with stars. The leaves on the trees rattled as a thin wind blew through them. April shivered and wrapped the blanket more tightly around herself.

Tarn dug his hands into the pockets of his sheepskin jacket and sat down on the step two below April. He addressed his boots. 'You're worried the Gutsells are going to turn on Latoya the way Heather and Grant turned on you, aren't you?'

She put her chin on her knees and picked at a loose thread on her socks. 'No, Nola and Barry wouldn't do that. I'm worried about what will happen if Latoya goes looking for Heather and finds out what a bitch she is. Heather couldn't cope with me being short-sighted; how do you think she'll react to Latoya being epileptic?' April snapped off the thread and threw it in the grass. 'I'm the lucky one. Nola and Barry might not be the sharpest tools in the shed, but they're good people. At least I didn't get half my DNA from Heather.'

Who was or wasn't the lucky one was open to debate.

She looked at Tarn suspiciously: 'You didn't say anything to Nola, did you?'

Tarn thought it was long past time that April made her peace with the Gutsells. 'I keep hoping you'll grow up and do it yourself.'

Her head shot up, and her sock-covered foot shot out in an unsuccessful attempt to push him off the step. 'Get off my steps!'

He refused to budge.

'I'm not one of your bloody troops!' April jabbed Tarn with her heel to drive home the message. 'Having sex with me doesn't give you the right to poke your nose into my business.'

He grabbed her ankle and tipped her neatly backwards onto the caravan floor. 'You're right: you don't need anybody to help you screw up your life.'

April tried to scramble up, but he still had hold of her ankle.

Tarn picked her up, blanket and all, and dumped her on the bed. He loomed over her. 'Until you front up to Latoya and the Gutsells, you'll always be looking over your shoulder. You're an expert at picking fights: when are you going to start fighting for April?'

It was all very well for Tarn to talk about fighting for herself — he didn't understand what it was like to *be* her. Tarn was used to directing traffic; April was used to being the traffic. Her hatches were firmly battened down, and she didn't appreciate him trying to prise them open.

There were other things about Tarn that bothered April. Like how he did what he said he was going to do, and didn't play games with people's feelings. Her taste in men was lousy; she usually went for looks and no substance. Ralph had seemed like the total package, a handsome silver fox with morals and manners, but under pressure he'd turned out to be as much of a dud as Stefan. Tarn was a worrying combination of brains, brawn and a shoulder to lean on. He didn't have the face of a Hollywood heart-throb — he was the quiet, stern-faced character actor capable of stealing the leading man's thunder and his girl.

April had been around the block too many times to think they had a future together. They got along best when they were naked. The moment they put their clothes back on they started arguing — or at least April argued and Tarn ignored her until she 'made sense'.

'Are you calling me a nag?'

'If the cap fits,' Tarn replied, implacably.

She hated implacable. She didn't *do* implacable.

'Wives nag. I'm an employee.'

'You've had more experience as a wife than you have as an employee.'

During the day, when April was 'making sense', Tarn asked her opinion about the orchard. He paid close attention to what she said and frequently implemented her suggestions. At night, he paid just as much attention to the giving and taking of pleasure in April's cramped bed. Afterwards, he kept a wary eye on her for signs of an allergic reaction — an allergy that he still wasn't convinced she had. April noticed and pretended to thrash around the bed scratching and choking.

Tarn wasn't amused. 'Why'd you do that?'

She smiled sweetly. 'The build-up and main event is always so good, but then you have to go and ruin things by watching me from the corner of your eye like I'm about to explode.'

'Is that so?'

'*Yes — it is.* Can't you take up smoking and have a cigarette, instead?'

Tarn yanked her under him to repeat the build-up and main event, and this time he didn't ruin things afterwards.

April knew he now left the wardrobe door unlocked. She'd have taken the jewellery and left if it didn't mean leaving him high and dry in the packing house. So she decided to stay, for that, for the sex, for the pleasure of flipping the bird at Ivan Vincent, and … for the sex.

Ivan Vincent hit the 'End' button on his cellphone and replaced it in the holder clipped to his belt. He clamped his arms to his sides, curled his hands into fists, and paced between his desk and the window in the office of Mount Pisa Cherries.

Roger Prescott had asked Stefan to give a statement about what had happened the night April Ritchie stole the files from Pisa Hospital.

'Why couldn't she keep me out of it?' Stefan complained. 'I knew she'd cause trouble for me.'

Ivan knew she'd cause trouble for everyone. In that regard, she was just like Heather. If things had gone according to plan, Stefan would have married April, and, when Grant died, Aurora would have been absorbed into Mount Pisa Cherries like so many other orchards in the valley.

But things hadn't gone to plan. April wasn't a Ritchie and had no respect for authority, and Stefan was lazy and easily led. Ivan knew his son wouldn't last long without the comforts of home and his parents' money. Stefan didn't like hard work and wasn't interested in following in his father's footsteps, but Ivan didn't much care. He wasn't in any hurry to hand over the reins, and settled for financing Stefan and his wife Justine's lifestyle in Wellington. It kept Stefan out of Ivan's hair and left him doing what he did best — spending money and sleeping and arguing with his wife. Along the way, they'd produced two boys, so Ivan considered it money well spent. He didn't want April Ritchie upsetting things by dragging Stefan back to Pisa, or by making it easier for Tarn Elliott to make a success of Aurora and prevent Ivan from buying the oldest and most prestigious orchard in the area.

There were two nights of frost in November — hopefully the last for the year. Tarn picked up more work in the helicopter. April helped Carole clean and prepare the bunkhouse and the other two caravans in time for the arrival of the seasonal workers at the end of the month.

The trees shed their frills and decked themselves out in brilliant green. Tiny white balls began to appear amongst the foliage; they would soon grow and ripen to a dark, glossy red. It was still cold at night, but the daytime temperatures rose steadily. The sun beat down from a cloudless, deep-blue sky, bleaching the tussock-covered hills. While most people's thoughts turned to Christmas and the long summer break, the orchard owners geared up for their busiest period.

A week before the workers were due, Tarn received word that they'd got a better offer elsewhere and weren't coming. He suspected that if he went looking he'd find them working at one of the orchards belonging to Mount Pisa Cherries. Instead of punching Ivan Vincent, Tarn swallowed his fury and concentrated on finding a solution. He needed replacements, *fast.* He put the word out amongst his army buddies, and after careful consideration made one final call.

Tarn contacted Nola Gutsell to ask how Latoya was and to mention he was looking for casual workers for the coming season. April was right about him not forgetting important details: he remembered her comment about Nola and Barry's children being unemployed. If they were unemployable, he'd soon know about it and send them on their way. Hiring unskilled workers from abroad was just as much of a crap shoot.

'Latoya is fine. She only spent a couple of days in hospital. Didn't April tell you?' Nola asked.

She had, but Nola didn't need to know that. He moved on to the subject of seasonal work.

'Picking cherries?' Nola pretended to consider Tarn's question, but he could hear the excitement in her voice. 'My girls might be interested. How much are you paying?'

April found out from Courtney that their workers had deserted when she went to baby-sit one night. She subsided onto the sofa in Courtney's living room and said incredulously, 'Ivan Vincent hired *all* of them? How do you know?'

Courtney jiggled a grizzling Kieran on her hip. 'His manager was laughing about it in the pub. Jacinta's husband heard him. He told Jacinta, and Jacinta told—'

'I get *how* it happened. *When* did it happen?'

'A couple of days ago. Everybody is talking about it. Tarn knows.'

Why hadn't he told her? Losing the workers days before the start of the season was serious. They needed thirty people in the packing house, and at least another dozen out picking. Ivan had waited until he could do the maximum amount of damage. Tarn was relying on the money he would make grading and packing other orchards' crops.

April gritted her teeth. 'If I had a gun, I'd shoot Ivan Vincent and throw a party afterwards.'

'April, don't say things like that in front of me,' Lionel told her.

She waved a hand in his direction. 'Don't worry, Lionel, I wouldn't invite you — and you didn't hear that.'

Courtney transferred Kieran to the other hip. 'Go home if you want and talk to Tarn. We can go out another night.'

The only reason they'd asked April to baby-sit was because Roger and Joy had to go to a birthday party. The thought of April Ritchie baby-sitting their grandson probably had them choking on their entrées at the restaurant.

April stood up and reached for Kieran. 'No, you go out. Tarn didn't bother to tell me anything, so I'm assuming he doesn't want my input.' Instead of feeling hurt, she should look on the bright side: if the packing house wasn't staffed, there was no reason for her to stay.

'Are you sure?' Courtney let April peel Kieran away from her. 'He's really grizzly. I think he's getting another tooth.' She looked at Lionel. 'Maybe we should stay home.'

Lionel was desperate for some time alone with his wife. Kieran would only stay with his grandparents; it was time he got used to somebody else looking after him. 'The medicine will kick in soon, and he'll be out like a light.'

Kieran stuck his dribbly face in April's hair and yawned.

'There you go.'

Courtney hesitated. 'If you're sure …'

April stood like a statue. 'We'll be fine,' she whispered.

'I'll put him to bed,' Lionel said.

Kieran was quiet for the first twenty minutes after they'd gone. After that, nothing April did appeased him. Peekaboo was a washout, and when she gave him the ball to play fetch, he chucked it at the cat. She tried putting him back to bed with his favourite toy, but Kieran clutched the side of the cot and screamed blue murder.

'I know how you feel,' April said. 'I want to yell, too.'

An hour after Courtney and Lionel had gone, it was still light outside and Kieran still refused to go to sleep. April knew when she was beaten. She put him in the stroller with his toy and pushed him down the street to Dr Giles's house.

'You've got to fix him before Roger Prescott arrests me for grandchild abuse,' she said when Tom opened the door.

He grinned. 'April Ritchie.'

She jiggled the stroller. 'You're the first person to say my name and smile at the same time.'

Tom dosed Kieran with something and entertained them both by showing them around his vegetable garden. In true Pisa tradition, April left with a cabbage.

And a box of vanilla-flavoured condoms.

Tarn was at his desk when April walked into the study and tossed a cabbage and a box of condoms at him. The cabbage bounced onto the floor and the box hit his laptop and landed in his lap.

'To add to your collection. Vanilla.'

He took his time plucking condoms from his lap and returning them to the box. 'You've been to see Tom Giles.' He watched April stroll around the burgundy chair and slip into another opposite the desk. She really hated that chair.

April draped a leg over the arm and swung her foot back and forth. She was wearing a pair of black ankle boots and skinny-leg jeans which Latoya had sent her, and her fake leather and fur jacket. Her blonde hair was spread across her shoulders and her blue-green eyes sparkled with malice and mischief. Tarn knew that look. He folded his arms and braced himself.

'How did the baby-sitting go?'

'Kieran and I got on like a house on fire.' Thank God Tom Giles was handy and could put it out before they both spontaneously combusted. April cupped her chin in her hand and waggled her foot. 'He's a boy. I always get on with boys.'

'I forgot that. If he'd been a girl, it would've been a different story.'

Her lips curved in her Hollywood smile. 'That bitchy streak of yours is a lot wider than I thought, Major.' Her booted foot tapped the air irritably. 'Why didn't you tell me the seasonal workers had deserted?'

So that was what had got her worked up.

'I didn't tell you because it wasn't a problem.'

'Not a problem? Of course it's a problem. How are we going to pick the cherries and run the packing house without them?'

'It's all been sorted,' Tarn replied. 'I've arranged replacements and put ads on the Internet for more overseas workers.'

Her foot stopped tapping. 'You have?'

'I have.'

'How did you manage it so quickly?'

'I called in a few favours — put out the word to the right people.'

April regarded him warily. 'We're not going to be overrun by soldiers driving tanks, are we?'

'Tanks belong to the armoured division; I was in the infantry.'

She stared at him.

'We're not going to be overrun by soldiers,' Tarn assured her. *By Gutsells, but not by soldiers.* 'But you're going to have to move out of the caravan; I'll need it for the new workers.'

April felt a pang of disappointment; she loved the little caravan. 'This had better not be a ruse to get me into the house.'

'It is.'

'You admit you have an ulterior motive?'

'Yes, I do,' he replied in his maddeningly calm way. 'But I still need the caravan. Consider youself evicted.'

Carole was pleased when Tarn told her she'd be cooking for more people.

'I included lunch as part of the deal for the new workers. It's nothing you haven't handled before. I did a deal with one of the supermarkets for bread and discounted luncheon meat in exchange for April's raspberries and boysenberries.'

They didn't usually provide meals for the seasonal workers, but Carole assumed Tarn had done it to make it harder for Ivan to poach them. She didn't mind — if she was busy she would have less time to think about how awful she was being to Gerald. Since the night of her birthday she hadn't once invited him in for coffee and cake. Carole could tell he was hurt, which only made her more anxious about being alone with him in case he asked her what was wrong. How could she explain she was hurt because he didn't want to sleep with her?

Tarn continued, 'April's giving up her caravan and moving into her old room.'

Carole hoped she'd misheard him. '*Pardon?*'

'I need the caravan for the new workers. April will have to move into the house.'

'Have to? *Have to?*' she spluttered. 'She's been trying to get back in here ever since she arrived! She'll rob you blind!'

His gaze turned wintry. 'Has money gone missing from your purse?'

'No, but—'

'The family silver's disappeared?'

'You know we don't have any family silver!'

'So what do we have that's worth stealing? And why would April want to steal it?'

'There's obviously something valuable in your wardrobe that she wants!' Carole cried. 'Letting her move in is as good as giving her a key to the wardrobe door!'

Tarn's eyes drilled into her. 'It's been unlocked for weeks. April knows that.'

She stared back. Why was he championing April? And how did April know the door wasn't locked anymore?

April was glad the décor in her old bedroom had been butchered like the tiles in the kitchen. The black-and-white cityscape she'd painted on one wall was gone and a functional queen-size bed had replaced her lovely old half-tester. When she'd painted the cityscape on her wall, Grant had hit the roof but Heather had thought it was funny.

There was a lot more space here than in the caravan, as well as a bathroom right next door which meant she didn't have to put on her gumboots and coat to make the trip to the powder room if she wanted to use the toilet in the night. April should have been happy. But she wasn't. The room brought back memories of waking up and running down the hallway to her parents' room and jumping on the bed.

*Daddy, the blossoms look like they have eyelashes!*

*They're not eyelashes, silly, they're stamens.*

*Mummy, the blossoms make the trees look like brides. I'm going to dress up and be their bridesmaid.*

*You don't want to be the bridesmaid, April. Be the bride instead.*

She'd been too young to understand the barbs Heather and Grant had flung at each other, or that she was witnessing the disintegration of a marriage.

*Could you pretend to show some interest in what I'm telling you for once?*

*I'm not that good an actress.*

*There's not enough room in the wardrobe for my clothes and yours. I think I'll move to the big room down the hallway.*

*Husbands and wives should sleep together. I'll move my clothes out instead.*

*Your snoring is getting worse. I can't get to sleep at night.*

April's mouth quivered. It was a warm night, but she felt cold. Tarn was asleep down the hallway. She imagined him stretched out in bed, warm and naked. If she went to him, he'd make room for her. He'd take off her DPMs, and stroke and kiss the angle of her neck, the point of her shoulder, the inside of her elbow, wrist and thigh. He'd place his mouth against the most sensitive part of her, and only when she arched and tugged at his shoulders would he settle himself between her thighs and make love to her.

Afterwards he'd complain about her putting her cold feet on his legs, but let her wriggle them between his calves anyway. He'd try to make her stay the night, and if Carole saw them in the morning, he'd be prepared to deal with it.

April was tempted, but she wouldn't leave her bed. Carole might not be her favourite person, but she was a good mother and that was precious. She wouldn't come between Carole and her son.

Tarn waited to see if April would find her way down the hallway to him.

She didn't.

He missed more than the sex. He missed the surprise of getting to know her, and the pleasure of surprising her as she got to know him. He missed the intimacy.

Tarn understood that April's screwed-up relationship with Heather meant she would sacrifice her own happiness rather than risk coming between him and his mother. He also understood that his mother's hostility to April was wrapped up in her insecurities about how her own relationship had been with his father.

Carole mistook the tension between Tarn and April for dislike. Smitty, however, had to work with them all day in the orchard. He had guessed the real reason, and sympathized with Tarn because he was having similar problems communicating with Carole — although Smitty had a fair idea that things between the boss and April had progressed way beyond sharing coffee and cake, and a kiss.

Smitty envied them. He wished he'd been upfront and let Carole know that he wanted to do more than kiss her the night of her birthday. But the truth of the matter was he hadn't known he *did* want more until he'd kissed her, and then he'd somehow managed to botch things up so badly that now Carole was barely talking to him. His relationship with Bronwyn had been easy and comfortable. Carole wasn't like Bronwyn; she was spiky and challenging. Surprisingly, Smitty didn't mind that.

Tarn noticed Smitty's glum face and asked what was wrong.

Smitty took his time answering. 'Woman trouble,' he said at last.

Tarn raised his chin. 'Ah … *that.*'

'Yeah.' Smitty knew Tarn didn't have a clue he was referring to Carole.

Jayson and Lateesha had hair that was a darker shade of blond than Christobel's, Toni's, Farrah's and Shontell's, but their eyes were a similar shade of blue-green. Jayson and Farrah had been dark when they were born, which was why Nola hadn't looked too closely at Latoya. She was her seventh baby, and Nola figured she'd lighten up just like her brother and sister had. But Latoya never did. Her hair stayed dark, her eyes turned brown, she grew taller than her petite, blonde sisters, and she loved school and books more than boys and clothes.

Latoya wasn't even a year old when Nola read a magazine article about babies swapped at birth and showed it to Barry. He, too, had had doubts that Latoya was theirs, but they loved her just the same as their other children and knew they couldn't give her up. They decided not to try to find their other daughter, and naïvely assumed she'd be taken care of.

'We're doing alright by Latoya,' Barry had said. 'Chances are the other people are doing the same.'

Nola hoped he was right, but she still shed some private tears each year on Latoya's birthday and felt hollow when she thought about her other baby. And then Latoya had got sick and the whole family were kept busy with visits to doctors and hospitals and learning how to manage her epilepsy, and there was less time to think about the missing part of their family.

Until Nola had seen a small, pale-faced girl with platinum-blonde hair and haunted blue-green eyes staring at her across the counter of the takeaway, and had *known* she was looking at her daughter.

The girl was well-spoken and wore the kind of clothes found on the pages of glossy magazines. The shock of seeing her, of *knowing* her, was so profound that Nola thought she might faint from it.

She wanted to climb across the counter and grab her to make up for all the hugs she'd missed, for all the times she hadn't been able to hold her and rock her.

The Gutsells were not known for their self-restraint. They shouted when they were angry, laughed loudly when they were happy, and made a beeline for something if they wanted it. But something in the girl's manner alerted Nola that if she came on too strong, she'd bolt. She dug deep and managed to act and speak normally. She even fooled Barry: he didn't know anything unusual was happening until she told him to take a closer look at their customer. He almost dropped a basket of chips in the deep fat fryer.

'Don't say anything!' Nola urged. 'Let's just find a way to keep her talking.'

Luckily, Latoya and Christobel arrived, and the girl agreed to Nola's suggestion that Christobel take her to find a place to stay.

Barry wasn't happy. 'Get her to come stay with us.'

It wasn't what Nola wanted either, but she was being cautious: 'We can't. She'll do a runner. Don't ask me how I know; I just do. We've waited this long, we can wait a bit longer.'

When Christobel got back, she reported that the girl's name was April and that she'd said Latoya could look her up when she moved up to Christchurch. The information gave Nola hope: it meant that April was as curious about them as they were about her.

Nearly four years later, Nola was still waiting for an opportunity to make up for all the hugs she'd missed. April had become close friends with Latoya, but she held the rest of the Gutsells at arm's length. She always called to thank Nola for the birthday present she received with Latoya's, and always had an excuse to not come and stay when Latoya came home for a visit. Nola and Barry hadn't confided in Latoya, but she knew she was different from her brothers and sisters. When she was nine, she'd asked Nola if she was really her baby.

'If the doctors did one of those tests that can check out that kind of thing, maybe — and it's a *big* maybe — it'd say you're not,' Nola had replied. 'But it wouldn't matter, Toots.'

Latoya had accepted the explanation and appeared to be unaffected by it. But when April appeared in their lives, she was just as curious about her as Barry and Nola. The rest of the Gutsell kids were too busy with their own lives to pay much attention to Latoya's posh friend, April. Latoya kept trying to get April to come for a visit, and felt like she'd failed when April refused.

'I think it's the smoking, Mum,' she said. 'April doesn't like being around it.'

Nola swallowed her disappointment and took comfort from the deep friendship that had developed between the two girls.

'You've seen the way she looks at us. She's too flash for us,' Barry joked half-heartedly. 'She married that wanker that sells porridge on the TV.'

'She's getting a divorce. Latoya says the porridge-wanker knocked her about.'

His ruddy complexion turned purple. 'What'd her parents do about it?'

'She doesn't see them. Latoya doesn't know why.'

'Enough of this bullshit! Let's tell her we know who she is!'

Nola wrapped her arms around his waist and hugged his paunch. Barry's hand automatically dropped to her bottom.

'We *can't.* We gotta let her come to us.'

She was resigned that it wasn't ever going to happen, until she got the call from Tarn Elliott asking if anybody in the family was looking for work. Nola had a strong feeling the major knew about the link between April and them, which meant April must have told him. His invitation had gone some way towards reversing the low opinion Nola had formed of him when she'd heard April was living in a caravan. She rounded up her family members currently without jobs, including her two oldest grandchildren. Barry would have come, too, but somebody had to stay and run the takeaway.

'You can get off your bums and earn some money during the holidays instead of sitting around playing PlayStation,' Nola announced to her granddaughters.

Demi and Cushla stopped grumbling when they heard they'd be making money.

'Can we eat all the cherries we want?' Demi asked.

'You get paid by the bucket, stupid. The major doesn't sound like the type who'll put up with any mucking around.'

'Is he a real major?' Cushla wanted to know.

'Why don't you ask to see his gun?' Nola joked.

She looked intrigued. 'You reckon he's got a gun? Kewl!'

Nola hated the way her grandkids had hijacked sayings from her younger days and butchered them — 'cool' belonged to the 'seventies. 'I don't know. Maybe. We'll see when we get there.'

April was driving the quad bike towards the packing house when a couple of cars turned between the gates at the bottom of the driveway. She wasn't wearing her glasses so she couldn't see who was driving them, but guessed they must be the first of the seasonal workers.

She pulled the bike onto the grass verge and squinted. The cars were big and old. Their wheels sent up little roosters' tails of dust as they came towards her and stopped. As the dust settled, the driver of the burgundy car in front cranked the window down and slid her sunglasses onto the top of her head. April's smile of welcome faded when she saw Nola Gutsell. She gazed stupidly at Nola as the truth chipped a hole in her frozen brain: Tarn had set her up. Her heart whacked against her breastbone. She heard it in her head and felt it in the soles of her feet.

Nola studied her face. 'I guess the major didn't tell you we were coming.'

April scanned the faces of the other passengers in Nola's car, and the big gold one behind it. Three — no, *four* of Latoya's sisters and a couple of grandchildren were with Nola. She licked her lips and, in good Heather Ritchie style, lied through her teeth. 'Not at all. Follow me to the house.'

Carole heard the cars and came out of the kitchen to welcome the new arrivals. April introduced Nola, and let Nola do the honours for Latoya's sisters. April didn't know who was who: they all looked the same — younger versions of Nola. She could understand the puzzlement on Carole's face as she looked the group over and explained the accommodation arrangements.

April cornered her while the Gutsells were discussing who was going to sleep where. 'Where's Tarn?'

Carole seemed alarmed by the look in her eyes. 'At the old dam. Why? What's wrong?'

April jumped on the quad bike and sped off up the hill towards the dam.

Tarn was walking down the hill, talking to Smitty. He was hot and sweaty and carrying his work gloves in his hand. He saw the cars down by the house, and April coming towards him at a rate of knots, and stopped.

The quad bike skidded to a halt. April jumped off it and ran up to him. She drew back her hand and slapped him hard across his face, snapping his head back.

Smitty's jaw dropped.

April didn't notice. Her eyes looked stark against her white face and her lips barely moved. 'You meddling bastard! I put up with you making me stay and work for you, and forcing me to see a lawyer, but I won't put up with this!'

Down by the house, they had an interested audience.

Carole gasped and cupped her mouth. '*Tarn!*'

Nola shoved another piece of gum in her mouth. No doubt about it, there was definitely Gutsell blood in that girl.

'Not bad for a skinny girl,' Lateesha observed. 'Has he been screwing around?'

Carole rounded on her. 'My son does not "screw around"! He wouldn't touch April Ritchie with a barge pole!'

Nola gave her a malevolent look.

Up on the hill, April hauled back to hit Tarn again, but he caught her hand. She tried to shake him off, but he wouldn't let go.

He was shaken by her response, and furious with her for hitting him. 'That's enough!'

The air crackled with tension. Smitty looked at Tarn's big hand wrapped around April's fragile wrist, and murmured uneasily, '*Tarn …*'

He dropped her hand.

Smitty could see Carole amongst the group by the house. He knew the state she'd be in and hurried down the hill.

April spun away and scrubbed at her face with her hands. 'You did this on purpose.'

Tarn struggled for calm. 'I needed workers, and Latoya's

family needed work.' It wasn't the entire truth. What she called meddling, he called taking action about a long-standing problem she wouldn't deal with.

She looked over her shoulder. Tarn could see she was shaking. 'You're interfering! People have been doing it all my life: Heather, Grant, Rosamund — and *now you!*'

It dawned on Tarn that he'd forgotten something very important: it was April's problem, not his. Somewhere along the line the things that hurt and upset her had become personal. He didn't have time to think about that right now, he was too angry — beyond caution.

'Perhaps if you dealt with problems instead of running away all the time, people wouldn't feel the need to interfere!'

April recoiled. She'd been a fool to let him get so close. She hit back. 'You don't call resigning from a lifetime career because of a bad accident running away?'

'You bitch,' he said softly.

The silence between them grew dangerous. They were tearing holes in the delicate fabric of their relationship, taking big, ragged chunks out of something that had become precious to them.

'Yes, I am,' she retorted. 'You forgot that, and I let myself forget you had an axe to grind. We might not talk about it, but neither of us has forgotten the lie I told about you and Heather. If this is payback, you're quids in.'

His jaw clenched. 'It wasn't payback.'

April wanted to hurt him as much as he'd hurt her. She wanted to punish him for making her almost fall in love with him, and herself for letting it happen. She pinned on her Hollywood smile because she knew how much it infuriated him.

'You wanted somebody for the packing house, and you like

sleeping with me. Revenge, money and sex — it doesn't get much better than that.'

'I didn't hear any complaints from you when we were in bed together,' Tarn retorted, and had the satisfaction of seeing her flinch. 'You're right: when I saw you in the wardrobe in that stupid red wig the thought of getting some payback was very appealing. And when I found out you were exactly what I needed in the packing house, it was even better.' He paused and added, 'Sleeping with you wasn't part of my original plan — just a fringe benefit.'

April sucked in a breath. She didn't want to believe Tarn could be that cold and calculating, that he could have played her so well. He wasn't a hothead; he didn't shoot from the hip. If he'd wanted revenge, he'd done an excellent job of getting it.

Her smile hurt her face. 'You do like to follow a plan, don't you, Major? The night in the packing house, I lied and said it was you because—'

Christ. He was talking to Heather.

'Because it was Murdo you saw with Heather. I worked that out years ago. Mum knows too,' Tarn ground out. 'Satisfied?'

She was shocked into silence.

'What do you know?' he said coldly. 'I finally managed to put a stopper in that mouth.'

April gathered her scattered wits, and drove another nail into the coffin. 'You know, it would serve you right if I made you fall in love with me, married you and made your life miserable for the next fifty years.'

'You forget that I'm not Berryman or Tecklenberg.'

She gave the nail a vicious tap. 'Without your clothes on, you're *all* Ralph or Brad.'

'I forgot that's how you solve your problems: you get married.

It worked well with Berryman, didn't it?'

Her fingers curled. 'Some of us get married. Some of us get engaged and don't bother to tell our parents.'

Tarn stiffened, and administered the final blow. 'Just because I like fucking you doesn't mean I'd be stupid enough to marry you.'

April had seen it coming, but hadn't ducked fast enough. She turned and walked blindly down the hill. At the bottom, she asked Nola shakily: 'Nola, can I borrow your car?'

Nola hesitated. April looked like hell. 'You sure you're OK to drive?' When April nodded, she handed over the keys.

Shontell gaped. 'You're letting her drive the Valiant?'

'Put a sock in it, Shontell.'

Tarn arrived at the house in time to see the dust kicked up by the car's wheels as April sped away. His grim expression concealed the sick feeling in his gut. Carole was nowhere in sight. He was met by Nola and her daughters. They were like a set of platinum-haired, blue-eyed Russian dolls, with Nola the biggest, and April the smallest. Right now, the last thing Tarn needed was to talk to a lot of April lookalikes.

Nola was the leader; her daughters deferred to her. The deep wrinkles fanning out from her lips marked her as a heavy, lifetime smoker. She wore a short skirt and wedge heels to show off her legs, which were in good shape for a woman of her age, but she was let down by her long, girlish hair and the leathery skin displayed by the scooped neck of her white knit top. It was clear that the Gutsell sisters followed their mother's example when it came to showcasing their assets — skintight jeans, short dresses and high heels were *de rigueur*. Scrape off the make-up and swap the tacky clothes for something more up-market and their resemblance to April would be astonishing.

Tarn intercepted a flirtatious look from one of the daughters and a hostile one from their mother. He ignored the daughter and concentrated on Nola.

She didn't bother to introduce herself. 'I wanna talk to you, Major.'

He showed Nola to the study. April had just ripped his skin off; he might as well let her mother finish the job.

When Smitty reached the house, he said hello to the women and teenagers and shepherded a protesting Carole to the kitchen.

She was beside herself. 'She *hit* Tarn!'

'I know. I saw.'

'Why would she do that?'

He shrugged. 'Must've done something to upset her.'

Carole looked at him reproachfully. 'She's pulled the wool over your eyes, too.'

'April's not all bad, Carole.'

She twisted her wedding ring round and round her finger. 'Tarn didn't have to give her a job. He should fire her.'

Smitty didn't point out that Tarn needed April in the packing house, and that he'd been a little high-handed in his dealings with her to date, but let Carole vent instead.

She finally subsided onto one of the kitchen chairs. 'Where's Tarn?'

'I left him and April on the hill. Don't worry, he's more than a match for one skinny girl,' Smitty joked.

'April's *not* a girl, and she's not all that skinny either!'

He sighed. 'You really have got a bee in your bonnet about her, haven't you?'

She shook her head. 'You don't understand.'

'If she's filled out, it's because of your cooking. To me, she *is* a girl ...' their gazes locked, 'not a woman.'

The look they shared made Carole even more jittery. Thc sound of car tyres throwing up gravel on the driveway sent her hurrying to the back door to investigate. 'April's taken one of their cars and driven off!'

*Good*, Smitty thought. *Tarn and April need to put some distance between each other.*

The front door opened and closed. Carole shot into the hallway, leaving the kitchen door open.

Smitty leaned sideways and saw a grim-faced Tarn enter the hallway with the oldest of the women. Smitty was surprised that the look she was giving Tarn's back didn't draw blood. He looked like hell.

Carole tried to intercept him. 'Tarn!'

'Later.' He ushered the woman into the study and closed the door.

She looked hurt and bewildered. 'What on earth is going on?'

Smitty felt sorry for her, but was glad that she was talking to him again. 'I dunno, Carole.' He nodded towards the front of the house. 'D'you want a hand gettin' them settled in the bunkhouse and caravans?'

Nola perched on the edge of the burgundy chair and chomped her gum; she would have killed for a cigarette. 'Why didn't you tell April we were coming?'

Tarn leaned against the desk facing her. It took a supreme effort to dredge up an answer. 'Because she would have left.'

April might not even have bothered to visit his wardrobe before she went.

'You don't call taking off in my car leaving?' Nola demanded.

He thought a more accurate description would be 'fleeing the scene'. 'You seem more worried about April coming back than losing your car.'

Her eyes shot sparks and her jaw worked harder.

Nola's chomping was getting on Tarn's already frayed nerves. 'She'll come back when she calms down,' he said, with more assurance than he felt.

Her lip curled. She snorted.

His mood plunged even more as something new occurred to him.

'What?' Nola demanded.

'She needs her glasses to drive.' He was a fool to care.

'She can't see?'

Tarn walked to the window and looked down the driveway. 'Without them, she's as blind as a bat.'

Nola clutched her neck. 'Oh God …'

'She did drive all the way from Queenstown to Pisa without them once, but if she isn't back soon I'll call the local cop.'

If he went looking for April himself, she was likely to do something stupid. Maybe he should send Smitty.

'Yeah, getting her arrested will help,' Nola observed sourly.

'Lionel went to school with April,' Tarn replied curtly. 'And it's not like you'll be pressing charges.'

She came to stand beside him at the window, her brow creased with worry. 'The local cop was like a constipated old woman when I was here before.'

Tarn could imagine Nola and her attitude getting right up

Roger's nose. She'd probably be tickled pink if she knew April had taken up where she left off. 'He's still here.'

'I think I should go after her.'

'You saw the mood she's in. If you go after her, she's likely to turn into Daisy Duke and get arrested for speeding.'

'From what I saw, that'll only happen if *you* go after her.'

How right she was. 'April will come back once she's calmed down. There's something here that she wants.'

'What? You?'

'No,' he smiled mirthlessly. 'Not me.'

'The girls can get settled in. I'm going after April.'

His shoulders relaxed a fraction, and Tarn nodded.

It wasn't until she'd gone that it occurred to him they'd never talked about the real reason Nola was here.

April's stomach was churning with anger and despair when she got behind the wheel of the Valiant, but it was rapidly replaced by panic when she realized driving the Chrysler was like sailing an ocean liner down the road and that she'd forgotten her glasses. Nola's handbag was on the passenger seat. She'd let April drive away with her wallet and personal items.

April pulled over and bit hard on her lip to keep from crying. She'd said terrible things to Tarn, and he'd retaliated in kind.

That was how Lionel found her, hunched in the driver's seat of the Valiant, glassy-eyed with tears. April didn't even notice he'd pulled up in the squad car behind her until he tapped on the window. She sniffed a couple of times and wound it down. 'Did Tarn call you?'

'No.'

Her stomach sank.

'Why?' Lionel asked. 'What have you done now?'

'Nothing.' She could tell he didn't believe her. 'I didn't steal the car; I borrowed it from the owner. She's working at the orchard.'

'Where are your glasses?'

He'd always been a stickler for details. He'd been the only kid who'd kept a real logbook for his science project, not a made-up one like everybody else.

April was floundering for an answer when the big gold Chrysler Charger Christobel had been driving pulled up behind the Valiant. The door opened and a wedge heel hit the tarmac. The ankle wore a gold chain with two silver kiwis dangling from it. Lionel and April watched in bemusement as Nola emerged from the car, closed the door and walked towards them.

'Are you OK, April?' she called.

April stuck her head out the window. 'Uh ... yes.'

Nola looked Lionel up and down. There was something familiar about him, especially those ears. 'Is something wrong?'

April made the introductions. 'Lionel, this is Nola Gu*arrr* — the owner of the car.' They didn't seem to notice the way she'd stumbled over Nola's name. 'Nola, this is Lionel Prescott from Pisa police station.'

'Oh.' Nola lifted her chin in an unenthusiastic greeting, and chewed her gum. 'Why'd you pull her over?'

'Ms Ritchie was already pulled over when I drove up,' Lionel said frostily. 'I stopped to check if she was alright.'

'She's fine,' Nola replied. 'You can go now.'

April watched indifferently as Lionel and his uniform raised Nola's hackles, and her attitude and gum-chomping raised Lionel's.

'This has nothing to do with you,' Lionel said.

Nola tapped her nails on the roof of the car. 'Yeah, it does. April's my … my … She's driving my car.'

He turned to April. 'April, if you put your glasses on you can be on your way.'

'I saw them in your bag,' Nola said loudly.

April looked at Nola's handbag on the seat beside her. Right now, spending another night as a guest of the Pisa police didn't seem such a bad idea — at least that way she wouldn't have to see Tarn.

Nola and Lionel stared at her expectantly. She put her hand inside Nola's bag and rummaged around half-heartedly. A couple of boxes of nicotine gum fell out — the bag was jam-packed with them. Her fingers brushed against the smooth surface of a plastic case. She took it out and put on the glasses. They were a perfect fit. April looked up at Lionel and jumped. Unlike her, Nola was long-sighted.

His brow wrinkled. 'Are you sure you're OK? You look upset.'

She blinked owlishly. 'I forgot to bring the raspberries I'd promised Dr Giles — that's why I pulled over. I'll have to go back and get them.'

The holes in her story just kept on getting bigger. Fortunately, Lionel had better things to do than try to make sense of April Ritchie and her bolshie blonde friend. He got in the squad car and started the engine.

Nola gripped the bottom of the window and leaned in. 'How're the glasses?'

April leaned away. 'Scary. I'm short-sighted, not long-sighted.'

'Shit.'

Lionel was still waiting.

'Just take it real slow,' Nola ordered. 'I'll follow you in the Charger.'

She stuck another piece of gum in her mouth. If April damaged the Valiant, Barry would mince them both up and turn them into hamburgers.

April stirred enough to ask, 'Why did you let me take it in the first place?'

Nola chomped frantically. 'I've given up smoking. I'm not thinking straight.'

Neither was April. She did a three-point turn and drove slowly away. The unfamiliar car and Nola's glasses turned the simple manoeuvre into the equivalent of the Wright brothers' first flight. She slid the glasses down her nose so she could see over them and drove so slowly that a geriatric on a Zimmer frame could have beaten her.

She glanced in the rear-view mirror at Nola in the Charger. It seemed there was no getting away from the Gutsells, or Aurora.

Or Tarn.

Later that night, Tarn was lying on his bed trying to read the last chapter of *The Seven Daughters of Eve* when April walked in. He should have been downstairs in the study doing paperwork, but his concentration was shot to pieces. His overdraft had risen by another hundred grand. April might be able to cope with being in debt, but Tarn couldn't. It was a waste of time trying — just like it was a waste of time trying to read a book. Smitty had done him a favour when he'd asked Carole to the movies in Queenstown. Tarn had had enough of dealing with stroppy females.

At first, when April walked into the room he thought he must be imagining her. She was carrying a screwdriver and wore a look of determination. Tarn sat up, but she walked right past him and opened the wardrobe door. She crouched down and ran the tip of the screwdriver along the bottom of the door in the gap between the carpet and the wood, stopped and pressed upwards. The bottom left-hand panel on the inside of the door popped open. April reached inside and pulled out a black velvet bag with a gold drawstring. She closed the panel and walked out of the room, carrying the bag and without exchanging a single word or look with Tarn.

He stared at the wardrobe door. He'd just been robbed by Thumbelina wielding a screwdriver. A part of him was amused by April's audacity and by the way she'd let him think there was something *inside* the wardrobe.

She'd finally got what she came for. Tarn wondered how long it would be before April disappeared.

And he'd get over it.

# Chapter 18

*Accept that some days you're the pigeon, and some days you're the statue.*

ANON

April expected Tarn to demand the return of the jewellery, but she seemed to have fallen off his personal radar. He'd turned back into the Terminator. He was cool and distant. April was, by turns, cocky and combative. They were both angry and unhappy.

The only bright spot amongst the gloom was when April investigated the contents of the black velvet bag and discovered that, as well as the John Smith bracelet and brooch, Rosamund had included a silver locket set with a single fat emerald surrounded by marquisette diamonds. The locket was heavy and bore the initials *JS* on the back. April was no expert, but she was pretty sure the locket would be worth as much as the bracelet and brooch combined. She needed to get onto the Internet to do some research. The problem was, though, that Tarn's laptop was the only computer with a connection to the Web, and she wasn't going to ask to use it — or ask why he'd been reading *The Seven Daughters of Eve*.

April wrapped the bag and jewellery in her blue hat with the earflaps, and hid them under her bed. Not exactly the safest place to store valuable antique jewellery. She almost regretted liberating it from the wardrobe door. At least while it was in there, nobody but her could get to it.

Tarn tackled his mother before she could tackle April about hitting him.

'If you go after her, you'll come off worse.'

'What's that supposed to mean?'

'She's angry because you knew who was really in the packing house with Heather but never spoke up.'

The old shame consumed Carole. 'That doesn't make sense. *You've* got a right to be angry, not April Ritchie.'

Tarn said, 'Yes, she does.'

She gazed at him uncomprehendingly.

'April doesn't like you, but she thinks you're a good mother. Finding out you lied by omission popped her bubble.'

She pressed the tips of her fingers against her eyes and shook her head. 'I don't understand.'

'Yes, you do,' Tarn said in a low voice. 'You saw her grow up.'

Carole scattered chocolate sprinkles over the cake she'd made for Demi and Cushla, and remembered April the spoiled brat, the manipulative child looking for guidance somewhere, *anywhere*. 'Why did she hit you?'

'Because I went behind her back and did something.'

'She probably deserved it.'

Tarn lost his temper. 'April isn't to blame for Dad not being able to keep his pants zipped! She isn't the reason you're unhappy.'

'Tarn!' Carole was shaken, but didn't argue with him. She changed the subject: 'What did you do?' He was silent for so long, she thought he wasn't going to answer.

'The Gutsells,' he said at last.

She wrinkled her nose. 'Those women?'

'Before you turn your nose up, tell me who else you know with that colour hair and blue-green eyes?'

Her eyes widened. 'So the rumour is true? April really isn't Heather and Grant's?'

Tarn shook his head.

'Omigosh!' Carole had to put the container of sprinkles down. 'You asked them here, didn't you?'

'Yes.'

'Without April's permission?'

'Yes.'

'Tarn! You had no right to do that!'

'Don't worry, April has already pointed that out to me on the hill,' he said. He paused. 'I'm trusting you not to tell anybody about this.'

'Of course I won't! You know I won't. Carole hesitated. 'Tarn … why does it matter so much?'

'I don't know. I'm still trying to work out the answer to that.'

April wasn't in the mood to apologize to anybody, and definitely not anybody with the surname Elliott. She'd fooled herself into thinking Tarn respected her because he'd asked her opinion about running the orchard. He didn't. If he had, he wouldn't have gone behind her back and meddled in things that were so very personal and painful for her. He wouldn't have taken matters into his capable, interfering hands. And April wouldn't have turned cruel and attacked his Achilles heel.

Their relationship was based on lies and sex. For a while April had been in danger of forgetting that, and forgetting also that when it came to men she had a terrible track record. It was best that she ended whatever it was they'd started. April toyed with the idea of taking the jewellery and running, but there were things that held her back: Clarence was too old to take over from her full-time in the packing house, and if Tarn was ruined financially then Ivan Vincent would swoop down like a vulture and absorb Aurora into the Mount Pisa Cherries empire. Also, running away was exactly what Tarn expected her to do.

And, most important of all, now that she'd found her way back, April realized she didn't want to leave again.

She waited for Carole to come after her for hitting Tarn, and was surprised and perversely disappointed when she didn't. Tarn's revelation that Carole had known Murdo was the one in the packing house with Heather outraged April. Carole had a lot of faults, but she'd always seemed like a good mother, the kind that would put her child first, the kind of mother April would like to have. By keeping quiet, Carole had colluded with April's lie, and chosen her husband over her son. April had plenty she wanted to say to Tarn's mother about that, but Carole was oddly quiet. April suspected Tarn's influence; he was everywhere.

Tarn's army contacts paid off. Sons and daughters of his soldier friends, on break from university or high school, began to arrive. He also hired a smattering of Israeli, German and Taiwanese workers. Within a few days he had enough people to start picking and to run the packing house.

Brad Tecklenberg joined them. He'd split up with his girlfriend and thrown in his job at the petrol station, and thought he'd landed in heaven when he saw all the April doppelgängers wandering around Aurora. Brad accepted that April was out of reach and that Christobel was married and too old, but Lateesha, Farrah and Shontell Gutsell were a different matter. His hopes were dashed when he learned that Lateesha and Farrah had boyfriends, and Shontell had taken a shine to Tarn Elliott. It seemed grossly unfair that the major had triumphed yet again without any effort on his part; and even more unfair when he barely noticed Shontell's overtures. Even so, it didn't stop Brad dogging her heels in the orchard.

'That guy with the buck teeth won't take no for an answer,' Shontell complained to her mother.

'Seems to be the way they make 'em down here,' Nola replied. 'The local cop's ears stick out like car doors and he won't take no either.'

Tarn and Smitty were responsibile for training and overseeing the pickers. The overhead canopies were dropped, rolled up and put away. At six each morning, April, Tarn and Smitty walked the part of the orchard being picked and discussed what would happen that day. Smitty didn't have much to contribute — he was there to act as a buffer between April and Tarn. It was the time of day April both loved and hated the most. Tarn was crisp and businesslike. Some days April went out of her way to find non-existent problems, reasons she couldn't do what he asked, even though her plans almost always concurred with his.

Tarn was familiar with her self-destructive, perverse streak. His eyes would cool while he listened. 'I'm sure you'll manage.'

He didn't enquire how she was or make her laugh with one of his dry comments. She didn't make outrageous remarks just for the pleasure of seeing his wry grin. Before the Gutsells and the rest of the workers had arrived, they'd taken advantage of the seclusion and made love outside. Tarn had always carried condoms — he didn't anymore.

He was the boss. She was his employee.

Early in the season, the cherries don't all ripen at once. The first pick was known as 'colour picking' and was done in full daylight so that only the ripe fruit were chosen. The second pick took the rest. The pickers had to be fast and thorough. Without the barrier of the canopies, blackbirds, thrushes and starlings could strip a tree in minutes. At the start of the season the new pickers were slow, but they got faster as time went on.

Shontell, Cushla and Demi opted to be outside picking. Cushla and Demi thought Tarn was 'kewl' because he owned a helicopter, but soon changed their minds when he kept sending them back to pick more because their buckets weren't full enough.

'Eat less of what you pick and you won't have a problem.'

Demi batted her big blue-green eyes at him, and Cushla looked at him through her lashes as if somehow that would make their buckets look fuller. Tarn shook his head: the Gutsell women were born flirts. He bet they arrived in the world batting their lashes and smiling, and instead of slapping them the doctor smiled back. Heather wasn't to blame for April's flirtatious ways — it was in her DNA. The difference between Heather and the Gutsells was that the Gutsells did it for fun.

'We only ate a few,' Demi protested.

Tarn handed their buckets back and said sternly, 'Bring them back when they're full.'

'I dunno why Shontell fancies him. He's a real old misery-guts,' Cushla grumbled to her sister as they walked back to their row of trees.

'He's got a helicopter. Now *sssh!* He'll hear you.'

April managed the packing house with help from Clarence until she regained her accreditation. They spent two half-days packing a crop for a neighbour who grew a variety of cherry called 'Earlese', which produced at the very beginning to the season. Aurora's first crop was 'Celeste', followed by 'Sonnet', 'Samba', 'Stella' and the precious white 'Rainier', before ending with 'Cordia', 'Lapins' and 'Sweetheart'.

Nola, Christobel, Lateesha and Farrah worked with April in the packing house. It took a few days for April to realize why Shontell wanted to work in the orchard. If Tarn was picking, Shontell was usually in the row next to him; if he was driving the tractor, she took longer to unload her bucket than she did if Smitty was at the wheel.

Apart from her early-morning walk with Tarn, April stayed out of the orchard as much as she could. She communicated to Tarn and Smitty via walkie-talkie, or when they came into the packing house.

The Gutsells were hard workers and learned fast. However, the strict 'No Smoking' rule enforced by Tarn around the orchard almost caused Christobel, Lateesha and Farrah to walk out the very first day.

'We won't smoke in the packing house, but you can't stop us smoking outside,' Farrah insisted.

'Yeah, we'll be extra careful,' Lateesha chimed in.

Tarn wouldn't budge. 'You can smoke in the area outside your caravans. Everywhere else is a smoke-free zone.'

'We've got rights,' Christobel said.

'They don't include burning down our trees.' Tarn departed, thinking the matter was settled.

'Dictator!' Farrah fumed.

Shontell didn't smoke. 'I like him.'

'Yeah, we noticed.' Deprived of the opportunity to rail at the dictator, Christobel turned on April. 'Go and tell the brigadier we won't be treated like this.'

'Go and tell him yourself.'

Nola intervened. 'Leave April out of it, she's not the boss. It's about time you all gave up. I've already saved a heap of money.'

'Yeah, and put on two kilos,' Lateesha noted. 'I'm not getting fat.'

'You knew about this, didn't you?' Farrah accused her mother.

At that moment, April would cheerfully have killed the 'brigadier': she was the one having to work with the smokers and deal with the flak, not him.

Nola pulled her aside. 'Can you let me take an hour off? What I've got planned will only work if the girls don't know I'm doing it.'

April hoped it had something to do with ropes and gags. 'Is it illegal?'

'No.'

*Damn.*

'Take as long as you like.' If Tarn complained, she'd set the Gutsell girls on him.

Nola drove into Pisa and returned with boxes of nicotine gum. She replaced cigarettes with gum, and, as a precaution, removed the rotors from the engines of the Valiant and Charger and gave them to April. 'Put these somewhere safe, like in your knicker drawer.'

April wasn't sold on the idea of storing motor-parts amongst her underwear. 'What are they?'

'Rotors from the distributors. The cars won't go without them, so the girls can't drive into town and buy cigarettes. It'll make my life a lot easier not having to watch them doing what I want to.'

'You threw away their cigarettes?'

'Of course not; I sold them to the guy with the buck teeth.'

'Brad?'

Nola nodded. 'He said he can sell them back to the petrol station where he used to work. I'll give the girls back their cut when the time is right.'

April was impressed. Brad had been the weak link, the man most likely to be persuaded to provide a lift into town. Nola had in effect bribed him into joining the Anti-Smoking Lobby Group. April had visions of a starlit support group being held outside the caravans while Brad lurked behind them selling contraband.

'It wouldn't take much to turn Brad to the dark side again, and there are others who smoke,' she pointed out.

Nola shrugged. 'They'll always manage to bum a few cigarettes off the other workers — they're Gutsells — but not enough to support a packet-a-day habit. At the end of the season, I'm going to take them all to the Christchurch casino. They'll forgive me.'

Tempers were very short in the packing house. Nola the Nicotine Fairy flitted about in her wedge heels dispensing gum and encouragement. Tarn, Smitty and the pickers avoided the place. It was too scary.

Nola had taken over April's caravan. She was desperate to get closer to April, but April continued to keep her at arm's length. Nola had no choice but to go hunting for information.

It didn't take her long to discover that April was a popular topic with the gossips in Pisa, that nearly everybody had an opinion about her, and that few of those opinions were good. She put her thwarted maternal instincts to use by verbally slapping down anybody who bad-mouthed April.

Carole was frequently left with her mouth hanging open when she heard Nola in action. She tolerated Christobel and her daughters, Cushla and Demi, but thought the rest of the Gutsells were awful. This was reinforced when Barry paid a visit one weekend and the Gutsells ate lunch in the kitchen with Tarn, Carole, Smitty, Clarence and April. Barry kept a hand on one of Nola's thighs the entire time he ate. Carole and Smitty saw, because they sat either side of them. Carole didn't know where to look, but Smitty thought it was nice that a couple who'd been married as long as Barry and Nola, and had seven children and numerous grandchildren to show for it, still felt passion for each other.

When Barry heard that both Carole and Smitty had been recently widowed, his grip tightened on Nola's knee. 'It must be a bugger when they beat you to it.'

Smitty and Carole were astounded.

Tarn smiled for the first time in days.

April heard banjoes playing in her head.

Nola quickly deduced there was history between April and the major — April never looked directly at Tarn Elliott when she spoke to him, and when he answered, his voice became cold and clipped. After lunch, Nola took Barry for a walk around the orchard. They held hands, and when they weren't, Barry rested his palm on Nola's swaying bottom.

'Something's been going on between April and the major. Looks like it's finished but neither of them is happy about it,' she said.

Barry was surprised. 'The major? He's a bit of a dry stick, but I s'pose once you get past that he's alright.'

'The sterner and grumpier he gets, the more Shontell likes him. And he's got a helicopter.'

They turned and looked back at the lovely old Georgian-style house sitting beneath the hill, its arms spread in genteel welcome. Below it, rows of verdant trees studded with red stretched down the gentle slope towards them.

'Hard to believe one of our kids was brought up in a place like this,' Barry mused. 'Guess that's why she looks at us like she does.'

Nola's brows drew together. 'She doesn't.'

He took her hand. 'Yeah, Nola, she does.'

'She might've had a flash house, but her parents weren't so hot,' Nola insisted stubbornly. 'Heather Ritchie sounds like a real bitch.'

Barry gave her a comforting pat on the bottom. 'Let's go back to the caravan. I'll let you make me a cup of tea.'

They sat on the cramped bed drinking tea while Christobel and Shontell lounged outside in the sun. Nola wished they'd leave so she could continue talking to Barry about April. When they didn't, she turned her attention on Shontell.

'You're wasting your time with the major, Shontell.'

She didn't answer.

'He likes April.'

Shontell was lying on the grass. She slid her arms above her head and squinted at her mother. 'No, *you* like April; the major doesn't. He goes all "army" when she's around. All she cares about is cherry trees — stuck-up cow.'

Barry had never been much of a disciplinarian — he left all that to Nola — but he took exception to Shontell's comment, even if he shared her opinion. 'Just because she doesn't swear and smoke, it doesn't mean she's stuck-up.'

Christobel was sitting in a plastic chair outside the caravan door, grumpily chewing gum and leafing through a magazine. She'd tried to get her father to take her to Pisa, but he'd been tipped off by Nola. On account of their non-smoking status, Shontell, Cushla and Demi slept in one of the two bigger caravans. Christobel shared the other with Lateesha and Farrah. It wasn't a happy place. She spoke up: 'You're both right.'

'About what?' Shontell replied drowsily.

'April being stuck-up and the major not being interested.'

'What would you know about the major, Christopher Columbus?' she said with a sneer.

Christobel flipped a page. 'I know he spends more time ignorin' April than he does lookin' at you. And wearing a pair of shorts that shows the cheeks of your bum isn't going to change that.'

Nola studied Shontell's shorts: they barely covered her crotch. 'You didn't wear those in the orchard today, did you?'

'How else is she goin' to get him to notice her?'

'Shut up, Christobel.'

Christobel recounted what had happened that morning …

The shorts belonged to petite, fifteen-year-old Cushla. On Cushla they were brief, but on her twenty-seven-year-old aunt they were minuscule. The back view revealed two fleshy half-moons of buttock. Brad nearly fell off his ladder when Shontell appeared in the orchard wearing them. *Everybody* stared. The major looked as if he wanted to court-martial her.

Sensing that Tarn was about to erupt, and knowing that things were done differently in the civilian world, Smitty hurried to the packing house to get April. When Christobel heard that Shontell was involved, she went with them.

'Did you put sunblock on your bum before you came out, Shontell?' April asked tartly when she arrived.

Shontell's brows formed a vee over her nose. 'Beg your pardon?'

'We're expecting it to get to at least thirty-two degrees Celsius today. Your backside will look really attractive when it's sunburnt and peeling.'

Shontell's scowl deepened when Brad snorted.

'Aurora's last owner died from melanoma,' April continued. 'We expect the people working for us to take care of themselves.'

'What d'you mean "*we*"? The major owns this place — not you.' Shontell turned to Tarn. 'What do you think, Major?'

'I think you're a damned nuisance. Go and change.'

Christobel heard April mutter, 'Got more than you bargained for, Major?' before she stalked back to the packing house.

Christobel found it all very confusing, just like her parents' preoccupation with Latoya's friend and her resemblance to their family. The only explanation Christobel could think of was that her father must have had an affair with April's mother. However, she had immediately discounted that theory for two reasons: if Barry had, Nola would've shot him; and Heather Ritchie, according to Carole Elliott, was a stuck-up bitch who wouldn't look twice at a man if he didn't have a few million in the bank.

Christobel unparked the gum from her cheek and began chewing again. 'I talked to Carole. April's parents used to own this place. She ran off with her boyfriend when she was seventeen. Caused a real stink because she nicked some files from the local hospital when she took off.'

Nola didn't know about the files. 'She must've had a good reason to run away.' What was wrong with the Ritchies? Why hadn't they gone after April?

'What else d'you know?' Barry asked Christobel.

'That the boyfriend was the son of the owner of the biggest orchard around here, and they got married but it wasn't legal. April suddenly turned up again a few months ago, after years away. The big orchard owner has been causing trouble for her and the major.'

'What sorta trouble?'

Shontell got up and brushed grass from her buttocks. 'This is boring. I'm going to find Lateesha and Farrah.'

'Unless you want to get sacked, you'd better change out of those shorts,' Nola advised her daughter as Shontell sauntered away. Nola turned again to Christobel. 'What else did Carole say?'

'Quite a bit.' Christobel chewed like a placid cow. 'Why d'you wanna know?'

Barry and Nola shared a look.

'We can't tell you,' Nola said.

'Why not?'

'Because we need to talk to somebody else first.'

'Who? Lady April?'

Nola wouldn't be drawn. 'Seriously, Christobel, I need you to tell me what you know and not blab to the others.'

Christobel joked, 'Are we secretly related to the Ritchies? Have you found out we've inherited a million dollars?'

Nola and Barry snorted.

She pulled a face and chewed. 'Thought it was too much to hope for.'

Clarence called Rosamund to tell her about his lunch at Aurora. Rosamund had confided to him that April wasn't Heather and Grant's daughter, but not the details of how they had got the wrong child. Clarence knew she'd want to hear the latest developments.

'Nola Gutsell's husband, Barry, was there too.'

'And?'

'He groped his wife under the table, and rubbed his hands together and told Carole he was looking forward to trying French food when she said she was serving lasagne. It sounds like they live on hamburgers and fish and chips from their shop.'

'Dear God,' Rosamund murmured faintly. 'How is April?'

'Doing a good job of running the packing house and managing the inmates inside it. They might be rough around the edges, but the Gutsells are good workers.'

'How is Tarn?'

'Running the orchard with military precision. He and April aren't the best of friends, but they make a good team.' Clarence chuckled with glee as he added: 'Ivan is spitting because April enticed another orchard owner to use Aurora to pack their crop instead of Mount Pisa like they usually do.'

Rosamund nodded with satisfaction. She expected no less of her granddaughter. 'Is … the youngest Gutsell girl there?'

'Which one's the youngest? I can't keep track of them all.'

'Her name is Latoya.'

Clarence thought for a moment. 'Can't remember one called that. There's a Christobel, a Lateesha, a Farrah, a Shontell, a Cushla and a Demi.'

Rosamund shuddered.

'Why don't you pay a visit?'

'I don't need to visit. I get regular reports from Tarn on the orchard and from you about the other things that interest me. My presence is unnecessary.'

April asked Clarence to help her train Christobel as a quality controller in the packing house for next season.

'Why? Won't you be here?'

'No, I'm leaving at the end of the season, and Christobel and her girls have already asked if they can come back next year.'

Christobel was pleased. Her husband wasn't always in work, and they had three other kids besides Cushla and Demi; they were staying with Toni, the second Gutsell sister. Christobel would earn extra money next year if she was a quality controller, plus her eldest son would be old enough to work by then, too.

'That was nice of you,' Nola said warmly. 'Christobel and her husband have trouble making ends meet.'

April shrugged. 'That's OK.'

Nola wished she could find a way past the barrier that April had erected against her. She was glad she didn't have to share her caravan with anybody except Barry when he visited. He was the only one who got to see her cry about April.

'I've got a favour to ask.' Nola saw the flicker of alarm in April's eyes right before the gates clanged shut.

'Oh?' she enquired politely. 'What is it?'

'Would it be OK if Latoya came and stayed for a week? She can sleep in the caravan with me.'

April's stomach plunged. She'd spoken to Latoya since her family had arrived, chatting about her mother and sisters and the work they were doing, but every time Latoya tried to steer the conversation to the real reason Nola had come to Aurora, April had changed the subject. She ignored the hurt in Latoya's voice, just like she ignored the longing in Nola's eyes and the alert, bright curiosity in Christobel's.

She couldn't face having the truth exposed. Her old concern about driving a wedge between Latoya and her family and usurping her place reared up again, making it impossible for April to let Nola, Barry and the rest of the Gutsells get close to her. She had no understanding of a normal family, or that such a thing as unconditional love existed. Knowing she was hurting good people, and worrying about it, was making her miserable.

Tarn appeared not to have noticed, but April knew nothing got past those shrewd, observant eyes. She longed to talk to somebody. Under different circumstances, she might have spoken to Latoya. Years ago, she'd have definitely talked to Courtney, but their relationship was still undergoing repair. The only person she wanted to talk to, who she knew would really listen and whose judgement she trusted, was Tarn. But his coolness towards her stopped April — that, and knowing that if she did talk to him, his message would be the same: she had to front up and face the music.

Nola was still waiting for an answer about Latoya.

'You'd better ask Tarn,' April said. 'He's the boss.'

# Chapter 19

*It's not what you are that holds you back, it's who you think you're not.*

**Anon**

'Why is April going to leave at the end of the season?'

Tarn looked up from his laptop at Nola. 'Because she wants to.'

The major was definitely a cool one. He irritated the hell out of Nola, who preferred loud laughter, loud arguments and noisy reconciliations. She came further into the study and stood beside his desk, frowning.

'Is there anything else I can do for you, Nola?'

The corners of her lips were turned down, deepening the lines running between her nose and mouth. 'I'm just about ready to give up. *How* do I make that girl talk to me?'

He dropped his pen on the desk and sat back. 'I'm probably not the best person to ask.'

'Yes, you are. If anybody can make April talk, it's you.'

Tarn would argue with that. His way of doing things didn't fit with civilian life. 'I think your confidence is misplaced.'

'I think my confidence is placed right where it oughta be,' Nola retorted. 'You're a bastard to get on the wrong side of, but people look up to you.'

'Thank you.'

'Try not to be a smart-arse all your life, Major.'

Tarn got up to close the door of the study and gestured to the shabby chairs in front of the fireplace. 'Have a seat.'

Nola chose the burgundy wing chair her daughter so hated, and Tarn took the other.

'April's got black circles under her eyes and she's losing weight,' she said.

'I noticed.'

Mealtimes were one of the worst times of the day because they had to sit together. Night-time was marginally better because he was alone and didn't have to hide his feelings, but then there was the added complication of knowing that April was just down the hallway. She was wound as tight as a spring, and it was painful to see.

'It's my fault,' Nola said.

'Not just yours; I have to shoulder most of the blame.'

'She's only angry with you because you asked us here.'

'She's angry,' Tarn clarified, 'because I overstepped the mark. April knew the day would come when she'd have to face up to you and Barry and Latoya. I made her do it sooner than she wanted. I forgot she's had people interfering in her life ever since she was born, with disastrous results. She feels betrayed.' He moved his shoulders in a gesture of regret or resignation — Nola wasn't sure which. 'She's got a right to feel the way she does.'

'It'd help if Shontell would stop flashing her bum at you. It makes April jealous.'

'April isn't jealous, and I haven't been looking at Shontell's bum.'

'Crap. My girls are all pretty, and you're a guy — you've looked. And April *is* jealous.'

Tarn smiled, and Nola saw what had attracted April and Shontell.

'I've found with April the direct approach is best.'

'What do you think I should say?' she asked sarcastically. 'April, I'm your mother; these are your sisters. Come give me a hug or, even better,' her eyes got suspiciously bright, 'let me hug you.'

Tarn searched for and found a box of tissues, and handed them to her. Tissues weren't something he'd kept handy in his office when he was in the army.

Nola blew her nose. 'If I could get my hands on her, I'd strangle that bitch Heather Ritchie.'

'You'd have to get in the queue,' he said drily. 'I don't know what advice to give you, Nola. April is a tough nut to crack, but on the inside she's soft as butter. It took me a long time to understand that. You'll have to be patient with her, but it won't hurt to throw a few brickbats her way to shake things up — April expects them.'

'What does that mean?'

'If you want to tell her you know who she is, then do it. But only you — nobody would survive a simultaneous attack by half a dozen Gutsells.'

Nola couldn't argue with that. 'Christobel knows, and Lateesha and Farrah are beginning to look sideways at April.'

'Will they keep their mouths shut?'

She snorted. 'They might've moved out, but I'm still their mother.'

'What about Shontell?'

'Shontell hasn't got a clue. She's too busy looking at you and your helicopter.'

The elusive smile appeared again. 'I'll make more of an effort to keep her attention.'

Nola leaned over and jabbed him in the arm. It was a good, solid arm, like him. 'You stick with the Gutsell you've got. She's the one who needs you.'

His smile faded.

'I forgot, Latoya asked if she could come stay. April said I had to ask you.'

Poor April, she was being attacked from all sides. Tarn wished she'd talk to him; that he could talk to her. 'It's fine by me as long as April doesn't have a problem with it.'

Nola studied the interior of the shabby, genteel study: the antique white marble mantelpiece, the ornate plaster cornice edging the ceiling, and the wide Georgian windows overlooking the driveway and orchard. 'Look at this place. It's no wonder she looks at us like we just crawled out of a swamp. What's Latoya going to think when she sees what she missed out on?'

Tarn said impatiently, 'If you're going to worry about that, then leave. When you look at Latoya and April, who looks happier?' He returned to his desk and booted up his laptop. 'If you're looking for sympathy, you've come to the wrong person. I'll see you in the morning.'

Nola realized she'd been dismissed. 'You really can be a prick.'

'Your daughter worked that out a lot faster than you did.'

He was the only person who referred to April as her daughter. Nola smiled, and blew her nose again.

Carole didn't kick up a fuss when Tarn told her that Latoya was coming to stay. All she said was, 'Another one? How many of them are there?'

'Nola and Barry have got seven kids.'

'Goodness, didn't they know about the pill?' she joked.

Tarn smiled fleetingly and Carole's heart squeezed. She'd been so wrapped up in her own misery, she'd forgotten he was unhappy too. Even as a little fella, he'd been self-contained and serious yet at the same time deeply contented. The contentment had been missing since he'd left the army. It had reappeared briefly weeks ago, giving Carole hope that Tarn was finally starting to enjoy living at Aurora, but it hadn't lasted. She despaired of him ever being happy in civilian life. Running a cherry orchard didn't offer the same challenges and responsibilities.

Carole wanted Tarn to be happy — like she was.

Barry had visited again and been unable to keep his hands off his wife; they'd even held hands when they went for a walk. This time, Carole was less offended and more envious. When she'd hesitantly voiced the opinion to Gerald that Barry and Nola were acting like teenagers, he'd replied, 'Sex isn't just for youngsters, y'know.'

His look and those words had given Carole the courage to splash out on new underwear and ditch her three-quarter pants for skirts and dresses. Gerald's eyes followed her around the kitchen as she served lunch each day. It was a delicious feeling having a man desire her, and knowing that it was she — not Gerald — who had the power to take things to the next level.

The day she reinstated their coffee-and-cake sessions, Carole wore a new dress the same shade of pink as the jumper Gerald liked. It was covered in sprigs of tiny green flowers, buttoned down the front, and had a V-neck and short, bell-shaped sleeves that helped cover her batwings. She was glad she'd worn one of the new bras that lifted her breasts when she caught Gerald looking at them as she bent to put the coffee plunger on the table.

Their eyes met. For once, Carole didn't look away.

Neither did Gerald.

He was wearing shorts. As she straightened, the skirt of Carole's dress brushed against his bare calf. His throat looked brown and strong and his shoulders brawny under his T-shirt. His hair was damp from where he'd run his wet hands through it in an effort to remove the sweat that had accumulated over the morning.

Carole took a step closer and drew a deep breath. Gerald watched her breasts swell against the bodice of the pink dress. He looked into her brown eyes and saw how nervous she was. He reached up slowly and cupped one of her breasts in a calloused palm, and touched her cheek to coax her down for his kiss.

Their lips clung. Carole allowed Gerald to unbutton her dress but stopped him when he reached inside it to release the clasp at the front of her mocha-coloured lace bra. She rested her hands on his shoulders and asked unsteadily, 'Where are you supposed to be?'

Gerald caressed the sides of her waist and looked at the bounty of her breasts overflowing the pretty lace bra and the hard points of her nipples denting the centre of the cups. 'Having coffee with you and then checking the pump at the dam.'

He watched Carole waver between what she wanted to do and what she should do. He'd wanted her for such a long time, he didn't know what he'd do if she turned him down. His hands tightened on her waist. He pulled her forward, and suckled her.

Carole gasped, and dug her fingers into his shoulders. At any moment, somebody could walk into the kitchen and catch them. The thought left her feeling exhilarated — and terrified. She caught Gerald's head in her hands and drew him away. 'We can't! Not here!'

His face was flushed and his mellow hazel eyes intense. 'Where then?'

She took his hand and led him from the kitchen up the stairs to her bedroom.

'Are you sure Tarn won't come back?' Gerald didn't care for himself; it was her he was worried about.

Carole felt young and reckless. She couldn't believe she was leading a man to her bedroom in broad daylight solely for the purpose of having sex with him. Right now, she didn't want to think about Tarn or consequences. 'I said I might go to the supermarket. He'll never look up here; I only come upstairs during the day if I'm cleaning.'

She made herself leave the curtains open. They undressed each other slowly.

There was a roll around her waist, dimples on her thighs and her breasts were no longer firm. Gerald didn't notice.

The hair on his chest was turning grey, his skin was no longer taut and he had the beginnings of a paunch. Carole thought he looked perfect.

They lay facing each other on the bed. He cupped her breast and ran his hand down her ribs and over the generous curve of her hip. 'Do we need to worry about a condom?'

She hadn't even considered it. 'If you mean can I get pregnant — no, I don't have to worry about that anymore.'

'It's not just that. Things are different now, Carole; I think we're supposed to ask who we've been with.'

'Oh! Of course.'

They exchanged smiles tinged with sadness.

Gerald said quietly, 'Bronwyn.'

Carole cupped his cheek. 'Murdo.'

He turned his head and kissed her palm. 'Reckon we're alright then.'

She smiled. 'Yes.'

Gerald parted her knees and covered her.

Carole lifted her hips in greeting, and welcomed him.

April knew the day of reckoning had come, that Nola had grown impatient with waiting for her to talk about the real reason she'd come to Aurora. Nola had kept inviting April to the caravan for a cup of tea and April had kept finding excuses not to go.

Eventually, Nola had cornered April in the chiller room in the packing house. 'We can do this the easy way or the hard way. If you won't go somewhere private, I'll chase you around the orchard shouting what I want to say. It's up to you.'

By the time she fronted up at Nola's caravan, April was sick with nerves. She'd taken special care with her appearance and was wearing a floaty, white broderie anglaise top that gathered beneath her breasts, a short, faded denim skirt and a pair of white rope-soled shoes that tied around her ankles. Her hair was secured in a knot at the back of her head with a blue-and-white scrunchy. April felt like the head girl making sure her school uniform was perfect before she went to see the principal, which was ridiculous because Nola wasn't exactly a follower of high fashion.

Christobel was outside in the plastic chair, chomping gum and reading an article about recognizing pests and fungi that attacked cherries. April knew Christobel was in on the big secret, and that Lateesha and Farrah were beginning to suspect the truth. Christobel saw April's white face and said, 'You look like you could do with a cigarette.'

'You know I don't smoke.'

'Now'd be a good time to start.'

Nola came to the door of the caravan. 'Haven't you got something to do, Christobel? Like check where your kids are?'

'I know where they are: they're with Shontell.'

Nola raised her brows. Loving her children hadn't blinded her to their faults. Shontell wasn't baby-sitter material or a good role model for two impressionable teenage girls.

'OK! OK!' Christobel muttered. She closed the magazine and stood up. As she passed April, she handed her a piece of gum. 'Here, you look like you need this more than me.'

April was oddly touched. Right now that nicotine gum was more precious to Christobel and her sisters than gold bars. 'Thanks.'

'If you don't use it, I want it back,' Christobel called over her shoulder. 'Don't give it to Farrah or Lateesha.'

She was mad if she thought April would get in the middle of a range war between the Gutsell sisters. They fought dirty, but were quick to circle the wagons if one of them was threatened.

Inside the caravan, Nola pointed at the bed. 'It's the most comfortable place to sit.'

April knew that.

'It's OK to sleep on if there's just one of you, but it's too small for two.'

She knew that, too. It was the reason she'd slept on top of Tarn the nights he'd stayed. April huddled on the bed, fighting memories.

'Don't worry, I got some decent coffee from Carole.'

That was unexpected. Carole liked Nola about as much as she liked April.

Nola spooned coffee into the plunger. 'You just have to pick the right moment. She's been a lot happier lately — I think she's getting some.'

*Tarn's mother is* having sex? *Who with? Herself?*

'That's ridiculous!' April exclaimed.

Nola spilled some coffee grounds on the tiny sink bench. She was so damned nervous. 'Yeah, yeah — you're probably right.' She took milk from the small fridge, added just the right amount to April's mug and handed it to her.

'Thank you.'

April sipped the coffee and smoothed her skirt over her knees. One of Nola's battered wedge shoes lay on its side beneath the table. April looked at the lollipop-pink nail polish on Nola's toenails, and the chain and kiwis dangling from her ankle, tried to imagine both on Carole, and failed. Nola and Carole were chalk and cheese.

Nola leaned against the sink and took a swallow of coffee to steady her nerves. She winced when it burned her mouth; she'd taken care getting April's coffee right, but neglected to put enough milk in her own mug. For so long she'd imagined this moment and thought about what she'd say and how she'd say it. Now it was here, she didn't know how to begin.

The silence was getting embarrassing. She cleared her throat.

April was surprised to see that Nola was even more scared than she was.

'I wish Barry was here.' Nola saw the incredulous arch of April's brows. 'I know he's like a bull in a china shop, but at least he gets on with things.'

*Runs over things* would be a more accurate description.

'He wanted to be here, but he couldn't get away. He's going to call me later to find out how things went.' Nola tapped her wedding ring against the side of the coffee mug. 'It's better if I just come out and say it: it's pretty obvious that me and Barry got given the wrong baby at the hospital; Latoya should have come here, and you should have come home with us. We're your mum and dad.'

April froze.

Her lack of response confounded Nola. When one of her kids was angry or upset, they reacted with tears, shouts and tantrums, not this frozen immobility. 'We know you don't like it, but there you go. You must've heard the old saying about being able to pick your friends but not your relatives,' she joked weakly. 'And you must've been curious, too — otherwise you wouldn't have come looking for us.'

April swallowed twice to try to get some moisture into her mouth. 'I was …' she croaked, '… I wanted to see Latoya.'

Nola's mood took another nose-dive.

'I'm sorry, that was rude.'

''S'alright. It's better that you're honest.' Nola put her mug on the sink and frantically patted the pockets of her jeans and shirt. She needed a cigarette — *now.*

April held out the piece of gum Christobel had given her. 'Here.'

Nola looked distractedly at the gum. Her shoulders slumped. Suddenly she looked old and sad, and like she wanted to cry. She took the gum from April. 'Not quite what I was looking for, but thanks.'

April could handle her own pain better than Nola's. She'd come to terms with not being a Ritchie, and with being alone. Nola, Barry and the girls thought she was being a snob, but she wasn't — she simply didn't know how to be part of a family. She couldn't go with the flow when she'd been swimming against the current all her life.

'Nola, what do you want from me?' April burst out.

Nola covered her face, and squeezed her eyes shut. She *mustn't* cry.

April jumped up. 'Just tell me what it is you want!'

Nola whipped her hands from her face and flung them out, palms out. 'A hug! I want a hug!'

April's lips parted. She blinked.

'Never mind,' Nola said wearily. 'Forget I said—'

She started when April closed the distance between them and put her arms awkwardly around her shoulders. Nola's arms automatically closed around her. It wasn't like hugging one of her other kids; hugging April was like hugging a board, but Nola didn't care. She held April and stroked her hair and felt the terrible empty space in her heart fill and begin to heal.

Her baby … her beautiful baby …

April pulled away and put her hand on the door. She stared at her hand and muttered, 'I'm sorry, Nola.'

Nola saw how distressed she was. She swiped her eyes, put the gum April had given her in her mouth and threw in another piece for good measure. She shook her hair back from her face and blinked rapidly at the ceiling. 'Stop saying that! None of this is your fault, or Latoya's, or mine and Barry's. It's that bitch Heather Ritchie who's to blame.'

April wouldn't look at her. She fiddled with the door handle. 'What about Latoya?'

Nola frowned. 'What about her?'

'What if she goes looking for Heather? Latoya is too nice; Heather will tear her to pieces.'

*Nobody* hurt Nola's kids and got away with it, and that included the eighth one. 'When Latoya gets here, you're going to have to sit down and tell her about Heather and every nasty thing she's ever done to you.' She intended to listen in on that conversation whether April wanted her to or not.

April fumbled to open the door. She was poised to do one of her ballet leaps when Nola asked, 'Do you know why she did it? Why she swapped you two?'

'I was blonde.'

The door closed. April was gone.

Nola drummed her palms against her thighs and looked aimlessly around the caravan. She spied one of her wedge heels beneath the table. She crawled under it to retrieve the shoe, but a monsoon of tears blurred her eyes and slipped across her nose, making it impossible for her to see. Nola groped around until she found her shoe, then whacked her head on the underside of the table as she backed out.

She clutched her head, hurled the shoe away and sobbed, '*Fuck! Fuck! FUCK!*'

# Chapter 20

*You can close your eyes to the things you don't want to see, but you can't close your heart to the things you don't want to feel.*

**Anon**

The house was dark and silent when April let herself in. Her disastrous meeting with Nola had hammered home the thing she'd been trying to ignore: it was time to leave.

Knowing that she was the cause of the anguish on Nola's face tore at her, but knowing how Tarn would react, and what he'd think of her if she ran away, was a million times worse.

April was too upset to go to bed so she went to the study and booted up Tarn's laptop. She'd watched over his shoulder when he was logging in once and seen his password. There was no avoiding it: she needed to find out what the John Smith jewellery was worth and the best place to sell it. Besides, she would have happily surfed for information on paperclips if it meant she didn't have to head upstairs to bed and spend the night thinking about Tarn just along the hallway, and Nola upset in her caravan. Frankly, April didn't care if Tarn caught her. It would be easier if he did and threw her out. The reason she'd left the overhead light off was in case Carole saw it and decided to investigate.

She immersed herself in research on John Smith. He'd been

an incredibly gifted jewellery designer, with a complicated name that nobody could pronounce or spell, which was why he had changed his name to John Smith. He had risen to fame in the late 1800s, become the darling of the rich and famous, and died young. Smith had been notorious for telling clients they had bad taste, ignoring their requests when they commissioned him, and then producing something a thousand times more gorgeous than what they'd originally requested. He'd infamously told one woman: 'God didn't bless you with the gift of beauty. Instead he blessed me with the ability to make you something beautiful.' Smith had asked that the remark be engraved on his headstone.

'Nasty, arrogant shit,' April murmured. 'I probably would've married him if I'd been around in the 1800s.'

She continued to surf until she found the image of a silver JS locket. It was smaller than Rosamund's and decorated with amethysts and pearls — and it had sold for a hundred and seventeen thousand dollars at auction the year before. April nearly fainted at the price. It was rare for JS pieces to come up for sale because there were so few of them, and people were reluctant to part with them — but when they did, there was huge interest and large sums of money exchanged hands.

What *had* Rosamund been thinking when she'd placed such rare and expensive jewellery in the wardrobe door? What if the house had burned down? And why had she given it to April? The pieces were Dreyfuss family heirlooms. By rights, they belonged to Heather, or, even better, Latoya.

Tarn's desk was like him, tidy and organized. There wasn't a lump of multi-coloured Blu-Tack stuck to the corner or an old cup with a broken handle for storing pens and pencils — his pens lived in a plastic tray in the top drawer and he didn't own any Blu-Tack.

April found that out when she went searching for a pen and paper to take some notes. She was about to shut down the laptop when she saw a shortcut on the desktop to Tarn's financial accounts.

Her fingers hovered above the touch pad. Exactly how much debt was Tarn carrying? They'd never talked money, but she knew he hated having an overdraft and struggled with the concept. The army hadn't prepared him for the big overdrafts orchard owners routinely carried until they received payment from the exporters at the end of the season. She suspected he had a hefty mortgage, and the helicopter wouldn't have been cheap either. Tarn might not have a meltdown on a regular basis like her, but it appeared he'd had a real doozy when he left the army. By now April knew him well enough to know how badly he would have taken losing his men and Aaron's injury. As their leader, he was supposed to have foreseen potential problems and put things in place to stop them happening. To Tarn it would seem like he'd failed at his job, and failed his men.

April tapped the touch pad and pulled a face. She might have known his accounts would be password protected.

'What are you doing?'

Her bottom parted company with the chair and her feet parted company with the floor. April came back to earth and pressed a hand to her chest. She peered past the backlit screen of the laptop into the shadows beyond. Tarn was standing just inside the doorway, wearing only a pair of cargo shorts and with his arms crossed over his bare chest and tucked beneath his armpits. April couldn't make out his expression, but could tell from his voice that he wasn't too pleased to find her poking around his laptop.

'Don't do that!' she cried.

She stabbed at the touch pad to hide the guilty evidence of what she'd been up to, but Tarn was one step ahead of her. In seconds, he was across the room and behind the chair. He leaned over April's shoulder and in a few quick taps brought up the history of what she'd been looking at.

April was reminded of the night months ago when he had caught her trying to pick the lock on the wardrobe door. From out of her mouth popped the same excuse: 'This probably looks really bad.'

Tarn's hand stilled on the keyboard.

The light from the screen cast just enough light to see his expression. April risked a peep at his face, and slowly released the breath she'd been holding as his anger faded and was replaced by a look of amusement. He'd remembered.

April swayed towards him, and everything he represented: tenderness, passion and security, and an unswerving belief that April Ritchie, town pariah and failed kiss-o-gram girl, deserved not just better, she deserved the best.

Understanding of what had happened smashed its way into April's consciousness like a gate-crasher at a party: she'd fallen in love with the major.

'Can you explain?' Tarn asked gravely.

This was a disaster. Her bottom lip wobbled and her eyes filled with tears. When would she stop falling in love with the wrong men?

He'd only ever seen April cry the night they'd bumped into Berryman at the hotel; even after spending the night in jail she'd emerged unrepentant and dry-eyed. He touched the scrunchy holding up her hair. 'April, love, I was joking!'

Her nose prickled. She screwed it up and pressed it against the arm he had extended towards the laptop. 'Don't call me that!'

'Would Gertrude be better?'

She shook her head against his arm and wailed, 'Don't be nice to me! I was trying to look at your finances!'

'It doesn't make for good reading: I'm worth bugger-all of stuff-all.'

A possible cause of her distress occurred to him. Tarn squatted beside the chair and caught April's chin so she was forced to look at him. 'Where've you been?' Her eyes threatened to spout geysers again. 'Have you been talking to Nola?'

She looked away and swiped at her nose.

'How'd it go?'

'Wonderful.' Her voice caught. 'She apologized for not breast-feeding me, but I told her not to worry about it because Heather didn't either.'

'April,' Tarn waggled her chin gently from side to side, '*talk* to me.'

The dam broke. 'I can't f-feel for her what sh-she wants me to, T-Tarn! I just c-can't! I even m-made a mess out of hugging her.'

He suspected it was more a case of wouldn't than couldn't. When April watched the Gutsells bickering and laughing together, she looked like a little kid with her nose pressed against the sweet-shop window.

'Aw, love ...' He held her face and ran his thumbs beneath her eyes to wipe away the tears.

April shook her head slowly from side to side and mouthed, *Don't call me that!*

He picked her up and carried her to the chairs beside the fireplace. A three-quarter moon cast enough light through the windows for them to see each other's faces.

'N-not that one!'

He changed direction and sat in the chair opposite the burgundy one, with April on his lap.

She pulled up her knees and huddled against him. 'You must think I'm a basket case.'

Tarn put his arm around her shoulders and cupped the backs of her knees. 'No, I know you are.' He was relieved when he felt her smile against his bare chest.

April was silent for a moment. 'I'm sorry I hit you.'

'That's OK. I deserved it.'

'Yes, you did.' She tilted her head back and looked at him. 'Don't you have something to say to me?'

Tarn studied her damp, puffy face. 'Like what?'

'Like "I'm sorry I interfered and hired the Gutsells without telling you, April".'

'I'm not sorry I hired them, but I am sorry meeting them has been so hard for you. You know though, April, it had to happen sooner or later.'

His answer put the final seal on her leaky tear ducts. 'You think you've got all the answers,' she snapped. 'Why don't you start a column in the *Pisa Press*? You could call it "Ask the Major".'

'Don't be a bitch, April.'

She didn't appreciate having her own line thrown back at her. April tried to climb off Tarn's lap but he held onto her, and let her wear herself out with some undignified wriggling. 'I promise you'll get sick of this a lot sooner than I will. I'll let you up as soon as you give me some answers.'

'This is employee harassment. I'm phoning Rob Sturmley first thing in the morning to lodge a personal grievance.'

'Rob Sturmley doesn't handle employment cases, but I'm pretty sure Emma Murfitt does. Call her instead.'

April felt something hard poke her in the bottom and understood why Tarn wasn't in any hurry to evict her from his lap. She crossed her arms and her legs. 'What do you want to know?'

He drew circles on her back through her thin white blouse and coaxed, 'Tell me why you hate that chair so much.'

April shrugged. 'I was sitting in it when Heather dropped her little bombshell about me being a cuckoo in the nest, and when Grant phoned Dr Giles.' She arched a brow. 'Happy?'

He studied her thoughtfully.

That was another one of his bad habits: looking at people like he could read their thoughts, which invariably made them blurt them out, but April was wise to him now. 'What else do you want to know? I haven't got all night.'

'What were you doing in here?'

'I didn't come in here to look at your financial records. They caught my eye and I'm nosy.'

'You won't get any argument from me about that.'

'Why are you only nice to me when I'm upset?' April asked petulantly.

'When you're upset you're incoherent, and this *is* me being nice. Why did you come in here?'

She told him about the jewellery and how much it was worth.

Tarn's brows shot into his fringe, which she noticed needed cutting again. 'Shit! How'd it get there?'

'Well …' April crossed her legs the other way and turned towards him. It *was* a good story. 'Rosamund put it in the door when she came to Grant's funeral and sent me a letter saying if I wanted it, I had to come back and get it.'

'Rosamund? Sneaking around the house hiding jewellery? At a funeral?'

'Rosamund doesn't sneak anywhere. She's like you: bossy.'

'I'm not bossy.'

April snorted.

'I'm surprised you're still here. I thought you'd be gone the moment you got what you came for.'

She sighed inwardly. So did she. 'In this heat? It's a long walk to Queenstown.'

'You'd only have to smile at Tecklenberg and he'd take you anywhere you wanted.'

Tarn didn't look too pleased as he said that. Was he jealous of Brad Tecklenberg? April smiled smugly.

'Try not to look so pleased with yourself.'

She decided to test the waters. 'Legally, the jewellery is probably yours.'

'Probably.'

Her smile vanished. '*Morally*, it's Latoya's.'

'And where does April fit in all this?'

She relaxed onto him, hit bedrock and snapped her pelvic floor muscles to attention when they began to hip-hop with anticipation. It was so much worse because she knew exactly what she was turning down. 'Don't you worry your handsome old head, Major. I'll make sure I do OK.'

Taking into consideration that she was on a misguided mission to right all the wrongs that had been done, Tarn seriously doubted that.

April yawned ostentatiously. 'It's been lovely sitting here in the dark talking to you about old times.' She patted him on the chest. 'Your muscles really look nice in the moonlight, but I need to get to bed.'

'I haven't finished yet.'

She looked bored. 'I can't take you seriously when you're almost naked. It reminds me you were once my sex toy.'

'Really?'

'Yes, really.'

'Not interested, huh?'

April looked him in the eye. 'No, but I can lie there and think of New Zealand if you insist.' She jumped when Tarn suddenly stuck his hand up her denim skirt and into her panties, and revealed what a crock her 'I'm not interested' excuse was. April made a half-hearted attempt to fight him off. 'That personal grievance claim just got a whole lot more serious, Major.'

He hooked his fingers in the top of her underwear and gave a tug. 'I'll take these.'

At least she didn't want to cry anymore. 'Tarn, we can't. What if Carole comes in?'

'She won't. She's been sleeping a lot better lately.'

They'd have been surprised if they knew why.

Tarn nipped April on the neck and soothed it with his tongue. At the same time, he lifted her hips and skimmed her underwear and skirt down her legs and over her rope-soled shoes.

He eyed the white ribbons laced around her ankles. 'I like the bondage sandals.'

'They're not bondage sandals.' She heard the soft sound of her underwear and skirt hitting the threadbare Aubusson rug. Tarn propped one of her sandals on the arm of the chair and bent her knee outwards. 'My loose morals get even looser when I'm with you.'

'It's one of the things I most love about you.'

April's eyes turned glassy with tears.

Tarn didn't see. He was intent on sliding his palm up her calf, around the curve of her knee and down her thigh to the damp centre of her. 'Beautiful,' he murmured.

She inhaled sharply as he touched her. Tomorrow she would go. This was the last time — a memory to take away with her. April gave herself up to the pleasure. In the morning she'd deal with the pain.

Tarn leaned forward and kissed her breast where it rose out of her floaty, white broderie anglaise top. He looked up and frowned when he saw the sheen of tears in her eyes. 'Are you OK?'

She tried to catch her breath. 'Of course. What … what flavour condom do you have?'

'There's some vanilla ones in the desk.'

She forced a laugh. 'You keep condoms in your desk?'

'I come prepared.'

Her laughter faded when Tarn leaned forward and began to kiss his way down the inside of her thigh. 'Oh!' April fell back against his arm. 'Ohhhh …'

He got up and carried her over to the burgundy chair.

April clutched his neck. 'What are you doing?'

'Giving this chair some new memories.'

He made her kneel on the chair with her arms over its high back. 'Stay there.'

April waited anxiously while he got a condom from his desk. 'I don't think I can do this, Tarn. This chair is a mood-killer for me.' She heard him unzip his shorts.

'Think of New Zealand.'

She was enveloped by the warmth of his big body as he tilted her and pressed against her.

'Sorry, this won't be pretty; I promise I'll do better the next time.' He made a sound halfway between a growl and a groan as he sank into her.

April closed her eyes and gripped the chair.

'I've missed you,' Tarn murmured.

She turned her face and found his lips. She'd missed him, too. She was already missing him again. He was more of a threat to her sanity than all of the Gutsells combined.

April slept in Tarn's bed that night. When he expressed surprise, she mumbled sleepily, 'You said you'd do better next time.' And fell asleep before he could make good on his promise.

They were both too exhausted to spend the night making love, and it was too hot to sleep close together. Tarn slept with a hand in April's hair, and she kept the toes of one foot against his calf. Halfway through the night, they both kicked off the sheet.

Apart from her U-turn on the sleeping arrangements, there was nothing to indicate that April was planning to leave. Tarn was disappointed, but not entirely surprised, when she left his bed before sunrise. He thought that she'd gone back to her own room before Carole got up. And he wasn't unduly perturbed when a quick check of her room revealed she wasn't in there, and she didn't come in for breakfast. She often went down to the packing house to check things over before they ate.

With the temperatures soaring as high as 36 degrees Celsius by early afternoon, they made the most of the early sunrise and cooler mornings and started work early. Between 2 p.m. and 3 p.m. they had to stop picking because the fruit got too soft to handle and it was too hot to work.

It was Nola who alerted Tarn that April was missing when she asked him where April was.

'Isn't she in the packing house?'

'No. I haven't seen her yet this morning.'

A cloud of dust approaching along the driveway heralded the late arrival of Brad in his rusty blue truck, and behind him Clarence in his Volvo. Clarence wasn't expected. April had her accreditation, and didn't ask him to help very often because she worried about him standing at the tables and getting tired.

Tarn began to feel uneasy. Nola followed him as he walked over to where Clarence and Brad had parked. 'Morning, Clarence. We weren't expecting you.'

Clarence frowned. 'No? April called early this morning and asked me to come.'

'Did she?' Tarn's uneasiness grew. His eyes pierced Brad. 'You're late.'

Brad looked nervous. He held out two envelopes. 'April said to tell you it's her fault and to give you and Nola these.'

Nola took the envelope with her name on it. 'What's her fault?' she demanded. 'Has something happened to her?'

'No.' Brad cleared his throat. 'She was fine when I left her.'

'Left her?' Nola's voice rose. 'Left her where?'

'Queenstown.' His eyes slid between her face and Tarn's. 'She called me before the sun was even up and asked me to give her a lift. I thought you knew.'

Nola looked like she'd taken a king hit to the head.

Tarn reached out and took the other envelope from Brad. 'They're starting on the 'Samba' today. Smitty'll be waiting for you.'

Brad made himself scarce.

'What's going on, Tarn?' Clarence asked.

Tarn gripped the envelope tightly. Out of consideration for Nola, he didn't say aloud what he was thinking. 'I'm not sure. Thanks for coming, Clarence. Why don't you grab a cup of tea with Mum in the kitchen while I sort things out?' He touched Nola's arm. 'Come into the study.'

Inside, Nola read her letter.

*Dear Nola*

*I'm sorry. You didn't do anything wrong. I'm a trouble-magnet — just ask Tarn. You and Barry are great parents, and care about your children. I will get in touch again; I just need some time to sort myself out. Try to dissuade Latoya from going to see Heather. If she insists, contact Rosamund Dreyfuss, Heather's mother (Tarn has her number), and make sure you and Rosamund go with her. I hope you'll consider staying at Aurora until the end of the season. The girls need the money, and Tarn needs the help.*

*Best wishes,*

*April*

*PS: If you do see Heather, don't shoot her. She's not worth going to jail for.*

Nola slumped into the burgundy chair with the letter in her hands. She looked at Tarn sitting behind the desk, and the unopened envelope by his hand. Nola understood why he didn't want to open it. She held out her letter. 'Do you want to read it?'

'It's between you and April.'

'There's no such thing as privacy in the Gutsell family.' Nola read out the contents of the letter. Tarn's lips tightened when she got to the part where April said he needed them, but otherwise he showed no reaction. 'That girl thinks a lot of you, Major.'

He didn't answer.

'Was it me? Did I push too hard?' Nola asked forlornly.

'No.' He came to stand beside her. 'I orchestrated things.'

There was a tap on the door. Carole poked her head around it and came in carrying a tray. 'I brought some coffee.' She placed it on the table between the two chairs and looked between Nola and Tarn. 'Has she gone?'

Tears spilled over Nola's heavily mascaraed lashes.

Carole rubbed her back. 'I'm so sorry. April didn't have a good time … here … growing up,' she explained awkwardly.

Nola blotted her eyes with a tissue. 'Latoya gets here today. What am I going to tell her?'

Tarn had forgotten about Latoya. He wanted privacy to read what April had written, but wouldn't attend to personal business until he'd taken care of Nola.

'If you or the girls want to leave, Nola, I'll arrange for your wages to be paid into your account.'

'We're not leaving. We like the work and need the money.'

He attempted a smile. 'It might be a good idea to get the girls up to speed with what's happened. Why don't you take your coffee to the kitchen and call them in?'

'Yeah — yeah, I will.' Nola moved like an old woman as she followed Carole from the room.

Tarn opened the envelope on his desk.

*Dear Tarn*

*Don't sack Brad: he thinks you know I'm leaving. I know you'll think I'm a coward, but I'm not like you, I really am shallow, fickle and flawed — it isn't an act. Aurora has started to feel like home again, and you're starting to look less like my boss which would eventually become embarrassing for both of us. I usually have lousy taste in men, so be thankful you've had a lucky escape. I'm sorry to leave you in the lurch, but Nola is capable of running things in the packing house, and Christobel can take care of quality control, provided Clarence oversees things. He's been dying to come back; I think he's bored. I'll call Lionel to tell him I'm gone and let him know how to contact me when my court date comes up. I've left something for you and Latoya in the top right-hand drawer of your desk. It might be better to get Rosamund to handle things if you sell them, in case Heather tries to take legal action. I know you miss the army and think you made a mistake buying Aurora, but you're wrong: you were the right person to take over the place. Thank you for all you're done for me — seriously.*

*Love,*

*April*

'Love, April'

It was the kind of thing his mother or aunt put at the end of his birthday and Christmas cards.

Last night he'd told her that he loved her, but she hadn't answered. Tarn read the letter again, but still couldn't make sense of it. What did 'you're starting to look less like my boss' and 'you've had a lucky escape' mean? A lucky escape from what? Was it April's screwed-up way of saying that she loved him?

Tarn put the sheet of paper on his desk and stared out the window. One of the Israeli pickers rode past on the quad bike. In the distance, Tarn could see Smitty driving Clarence on the tractor while they discussed the part of the orchard to be picked today.

He felt hollowed out. Empty. The urgency and sense of purpose he'd greeted each day with was gone. He felt like he had before April came, when he hadn't cared if a single cherry grew. He wished he could walk away, too, but that wasn't possible: there were people relying on him.

The burgundy wing chair mocked him with memories from the previous night. April wasn't the only one who hated the sight of it now.

Tarn knew what he'd find in his desk drawer, and only opened it because April had said there was something for Latoya. Of course, being April, she managed to surprise him.

There were two envelopes in the black velvet bag. One had his name on it; the other had Latoya's. Neither of the envelopes was sealed. In his, Tarn found an exquisite silver locket. It was set with a fat emerald surrounded by marquisette diamonds and, although he knew nothing about jewellery, Tarn could tell it was a quality piece.

An antique diamond and emerald peacock brooch and matching bracelet slipped from Latoya's envelope onto the desk.

April had given away all the jewellery.

# Chapter 21

*If you mess up, 'fess up.*

Anon

Hours later, Tarn was still no closer to finding an answer. He was out in the orchard when his cellphone rang. He snatched it from his pocket, but it was Frank Jepson calling to say that Aaron had disappeared.

'I went to visit him at his new place in Wellington, and he hasn't been seen for a week. I was worried he might have had a fall and injured himself, but the security guy wouldn't let me in. It is *some* place. How can Aaron afford a penthouse apartment in the middle of Wellington's CBD?'

Frank and the rest of the men didn't know that Aaron was one of the Cinnsealach winery Kinsellas. Aaron kept his private life and his army life separate. Tarn was his best friend, but even he didn't know all the details, hence his surprise when he'd found out Aaron had a wife.

Tarn was almost relieved to get the call. He was better at sorting out other people's problems than his own. 'Is there a cleaning service?' he asked.

'The woman from the service said she hasn't seen him since last Tuesday. I think Warrant Officer Kinsella has done a runner, Major.' Frank wasn't joking. 'I called some of his women friends —

the ones I know about — but none of them has seen him.'

'I'll call his wife and see if she knows where he is.'

There was a prolonged silence.

'His … wife?' Frank repeated slowly. 'Aaron has got a wife?'

'I was as surprised as you. I met her once: her name's Harmony.'

'How the hell did he keep that quiet? And why am I looking up his old girlfriends if he's got a wife?'

'Aaron says his marriage is a business arrangement.'

The day Tarn had met Harmony Kinsella, Aaron was at his worst: moody and careless. He seemed fond of his wife, but Harmony's pinched white face led Tarn to believe that her feelings for her wayward husband were based on more than a business partnership.

Tarn heard Frank muttering under his breath. 'What bullshit. How long has he had her? What's she like?'

'Not what you'd expect. I'll call her, and get back to you. And don't tell any of the guys about her, Frank — if you do, Aaron will find you and shove his prosthetic limb up your arse.'

As soon as he'd rung off from Frank, Tarn called the Cinnsealach vineyard. He asked to speak to Mrs Kinsella, not realizing it was Harmony who'd answered the phone.

'Dinah?' she replied politely. 'If you'll wait a moment, I'll transfer the call to her room.'

'No, not Dinah.' He had no idea who Dinah was. 'I want to speak to Mrs Aaron Kinsella — Harmony Kinsella. Is that you?'

'Oh … yes.' She seemed unused to being called Mrs Kinsella. The whole situation just got more bizarre. 'How can I help you?'

'This is Tarn Elliott. We met at Aaron's apartment.'

'Major Elliott. Hello.' She paused. 'Is anything wrong with Aaron?'

Tarn heard the concern in her voice. 'Have you heard from Aaron recently?'

'The last time I saw him was a few months ago at the limb-fitting centre. I can give you the address of his apartment in Wellington if that would help?'

Her husband had returned home with his foot blown off and she couldn't even be bothered to visit him regularly, let alone call him. If Aaron wouldn't return home to Marlborough, his wife should have moved to Wellington to be with him. Disapproval turned Tarn's voice cool. 'I already have the address. Most of the men from Bravo keep in touch with Aaron. That was how we discovered his apartment is empty and he hasn't been seen since last Tuesday.'

Harmony could do cool every bit as well as Tarn. 'Thank you for telling me, Major. I'm sure you know Aaron will turn up when he's good and ready. In the meantime, why don't you contact his current and old girlfriends? I suspect that's where you'll find him.'

Tarn was astonished; he repeated the conversation to Frank later.

'What kind of wife *is* she?' Frank growled.

'I'm sure she was worried at first. She got on her high horse when I climbed on mine.'

They shouldn't judge. Aaron had been a first-rate soldier, and a superb warrant officer, but under no circumstances was he husband material.

'I'll meet you at Aaron's apartment in Wellington. He gave me a key.'

Tarn was taking a risk leaving Aurora in the hands of his mother, Smitty, Clarence, the Gutsells and an assortment of seasonal workers. Ivan Vincent would be rubbing his hands together. He needed April now more than ever.

'Are you OK?' Frank Jepson asked. 'You look like you spent the night in a foxhole.'

Tarn had a thumping headache. 'I'm fine. Let's go take a look at Aaron's apartment.'

He introduced himself to the security guard at the apartment building as Major Elliott. Even without a uniform, Tarn still looked and sounded like an infantry major, and when he revealed he had a key, the guard allowed them to take a look around the penthouse apartment.

'Jesus!' Frank breathed when he saw the view of Wellington Harbour and Oriental Bay from the windows of the living room and master bedroom. The chef's kitchen, and the sauna and personal gym off the deck, weren't too shabby either. 'I didn't know a warrant officer's pay was so good.'

Tarn didn't answer. Aaron's family was his business.

The security guard watched them carry out a systematic search of each room. Aaron's crutches were in the wardrobe off the bedroom, along with an array of prosthetic limbs. They counted four different types.

Frank picked up a curved blade of steel that wasn't attached to a socket. He pressed the blade and watched it spring back again. 'What's this?'

'I think it's a running blade.'

'Be careful with it,' the security guard piped up nervously. 'Mr Kinsella just got it. I was downstairs when the courier delivered it.'

'Looks like a fancy clothes hook to me.' Frank examined the blade closely. 'This thing must've cost a bomb.'

Tarn shrugged. 'He's got no dependants.'

'He's got a wife,' Frank said pointedly.

The guard leaned closer. 'Mr Kinsella is *married?*'

He'd probably witnessed Aaron's harem parading back and forth through the downstairs foyer. Losing half his leg hadn't affected Aaron's love life one bit.

'Yeah,' Frank said irritably. 'For all we know, he's got half a dozen kids tucked away, too.'

Tarn understood how Frank felt. When you were stationed abroad in dangerous territory, you relied on knowing the men serving with you, on understanding what made them tick. Frank thought he'd known Aaron; now he wasn't so sure.

'He's still Aaron, Frank.'

Frank shrugged.

They checked the rest of the apartment but came up with nothing. Outside, they reviewed their options.

'Has *Mrs Kinsella* called?' Frank asked sarcastically.

'No.'

'Figures,' he muttered.

'Aaron might've been a first-rate warrant officer, but I doubt he's much of a husband.'

Frank grunted. 'Now what?'

Tarn tucked his hands in the pockets of his cargo pants and considered. His head was beginning to clear. He felt better away from Aurora.

'It still seems weird seeing you in civvies and calling you Tarn,' Frank said.

He summoned a smile. 'When I'm with one of you, it feels weird. Let's get something to eat.'

Courtney heard about Tarn leaving for Wellington when she

dropped something off at her mother's house. Mrs Murfitt had heard about it from Tarn's mother when they'd bumped into one another at the supermarket the day he left. She hadn't been a fan of Ivan Vincent's ever since Stefan had got away with smashing April's car and almost breaking Courtney's wrist. She wasn't a fan of April's either, but she liked Carole and still had hopes Tarn might become her son-in-law.

'April Ritchie picked a fine time to stage one of her disappearing acts. Carole said they really need her now. You know what a vulture Ivan Vincent is: he's probably perched up there at Mount Pisa Cherries waiting to swoop down and put a spoke in Aurora's wheel.'

Courtney startled her mother by crying, 'That's wonderful news!'

April had called at an ungodly hour of the morning, when only police officers getting ready for a morning shift and mothers of teething toddlers were awake and coherent, to tell Lionel she was leaving and give him her contact details. Lionel almost parted company with one of his prominent ears when Courtney snatched the phone away from him and demanded to know why April was running away again.

Kieran was clinging to his mother's pyjama leg as April started to give some wimpy excuse about her real mother and a truckload of sisters turning up at the orchard. Courtney spoke above her son's grizzling: 'I don't believe you.'

'It's true. My birth mother and four of her daughters are staying at the orchard.'

Courtney jiggled her leg and Kieran quietened. 'How'd they find you?'

'Tarn invited them.'

'Stop lying!'

'I'm not lying! Go up to Aurora and take a look for yourself. You can't miss them — Tarn says we look like a set of Russian dolls. I have to leave. Heather's daughter, Latoya, is arriving today.'

Courtney stopped jiggling. *'Really?'*

'Tarn said she could come.'

Kieran began to wail again.

'What's wrong with him?' April asked.

'Teeth — hold on.' Courtney picked Kieran up and handed him to Lionel, who was about to walk out the door. *Five minutes*, she mouthed.

Lionel headed in the opposite direction with Kieran balanced on his arm, muttering, 'Those new teeth of yours will probably come through and fall out again during those five minutes.'

'You told me you were good friends with Latoya. It can't be much of a friendship if you think she's going to blame you for Heather being a basket case and playing swapsie at the hospital — that's hardly your fault.'

'I've had enough of this from Tarn. I don't need it from you, too.'

His name kept on coming up. 'Are you sure it's Nola Gutsell you're running from?' Courtney asked slowly.

'Of course it is,' April insisted. 'I don't feel comfortable around her. I don't know what to say to her or her daughters.'

'April, you can talk your way out of anything. What aren't you telling me?'

'I've got to go. I haven't got much credit on my cellphone.'

'It's Tarn, isn't it? You've fallen for Tarn.'

'I've got to go. Brad's dropping me at a backpackers in Queenstown.'

Courtney did a little dance of excitement. Why hadn't she thought of it? Why hadn't she *seen* it? April and Tarn were perfect for each other: Tarn was the rock that was missing from April's life; April was the spark Tarn needed in his.

She went looking for Lionel. He was trying to persuade Kieran not to chew one of his epaulettes.

'How could I have been so dense? April has fallen for Tarn. She's perfect for him.'

Lionel brushed baby dribble from his shoulder. 'I thought Emma was perfect for him.'

'That's just Mum's opinion. We've got to get April back here.'

'There's no "we" about it.' He handed over Kieran. 'I'm going to work.'

After seeing her mother, Courtney wasted no time dialling April's phone.

'Tarn had to go to Wellington to see a soldier who lost his leg. Carole's having kittens and Ivan is waiting to swoop. You'll have to leave the splendour of the backpackers. You've got to come home.'

Tarn planned to grab a bite in Cuba Mall, but Frank had other ideas. He liked fine food and wine almost as much as he liked a good single-malt whisky. It used to amuse Tarn when he saw Frank barking out orders to the men on the parade ground, and imagined what their reactions would be if they knew Staff Sergeant Jepson was a gastronome.

Frank turned his nose up at Tarn's suggestion of takeaways. 'I want something better to eat than a burger and fries.'

Tarn had no choice but to follow him into a restaurant. While Frank checked out the wine list, Tarn tried to find the cheapest thing on the menu and not think about how large his overdraft was. April's disappearance had sent his appetite AWOL, but he didn't want to disappoint Frank.

'I'll have a bottle of the Cinnsealach Reserve Chardonnay,' Frank told the wine waiter.

It seemed ironic that Frank was ordering a bottle of wine from Aaron's family's vineyard.

When the wine had arrived, and their glasses were filled, Frank tilted the bottle and studied the label. 'Have you ever looked at one of these labels?'

Tarn had because Aaron had drawn his attention to it. He almost never spoke about Cinnsealach, so Tarn had been surprised when Aaron had asked him to help him celebrate when one of the wines won a gold medal at an international wine competition. While they were drinking it, Aaron had held the bottle up next to his face and pointed at the label. 'That's Bacchus, the Roman god of wine and partying. Who does he remind you of?'

Tarn had studied the Rennaisance-style figure beneath the purple Celtic lettering for Cinnsealach. Bacchus was tall and semi-naked, with broad shoulders and rippled abs, and pointed ears. He was wearing a garland of vine leaves and grapes in his flowing blond hair. 'A Vulcan male gigolo.'

'Take a closer look at the face,' Aaron had urged.

Tarn had and had recognized Bacchus's heavy-lidded, slanted eyes, large nose, prominent cheekbones and the derisive smile curving his wide, thin-lipped mouth. Tarn had laughed. 'Did you pose for it?'

'Of course I fucking didn't. The label was redesigned after I left. If my old man hadn't died, and wasn't ham-fisted and un-imaginative, I would've blamed him.' Aaron had tossed the bottle in the rubbish bin. 'This was done by somebody subtle and clever. One day, I'll find out who it was.'

It felt like *déjà vu* as Frank pointed to the label and said, 'He's supposed to be Bacchus, the Roman god of wine. Every time I buy a bottle of Cinnsealach I think how much he looks like Aaron.' He studied Tarn intently. 'Cinnsealach is Celtic for Kinsella.'

It wasn't Tarn's place to deny or confirm his suspicions. 'Aaron probably buys a case as a goodbye present for all his girlfriends.'

Frank snorted. 'Where d'you think he is?'

'In bed with a woman.' Tarn took a hefty gulp of wine as he remembered falling asleep in his bed with April last night.

'Are you OK, Boss?' Frank asked.

'Never better,' he replied caustically, and refilled his glass.

Frank had to be back at the base by the following afternoon. They spent the morning fruitlessly searching for Aaron before agreeing that it was unlikely he was dead in a ditch somewhere and that he'd turn up when he was ready to.

Tarn called Carole with the intention of telling her he'd be home as soon as he could get on a flight to Queenstown.

'April is back,' Carole said.

It was the last thing he expected to hear.

'Tarn? Did you hear me?'

'Yes. I heard you.'

'She found out you'd been called away and came right back.' Carole waited for him to say something. When he didn't, she asked, 'Did you find Aaron?'

'No.'

'When are you coming home?'

Tarn felt utterly confused. 'I'm going to keep looking.'

'Oh. In that case, I think I'd better give April the password to the accounts. Gerald and I are no good at that kind of thing.'

'If you want to. Who's Gerald?' he asked indifferently.

'Smitty is Gerald. His real name is Gerald Smit. Where will you stay?'

'I'm not sure yet. If you want me, leave a message on my phone.'

The cost of the flight from Queenstown had strained his meagre finances. He couldn't afford to stay another night at a motel, so he returned to Aaron's apartment building. The same security guard who had let Frank and him into the penthouse yesterday was on duty. He jumped up when Tarn walked briskly into the foyer carrying his old kit bag.

'I'll be staying at Mr Kinsella's apartment for the next few days.'

He strode past the guard to the elevators and pressed the button for the penthouse. Thankfully, the doors opened almost at once.

'OK, Major,' the guard called as the door closed.

The elevator ascended. Tarn watched the numbers above the doors light up. April and Aaron weren't the only ones who could run away.

# Chapter 22

*If you don't get lost, there's a chance you may never be found.*

ANON

April returned to Aurora to find she was in trouble with just about everybody except Latoya, Smitty and, amazingly, Carole.

'Thank you for coming back, April.'

April saw the look of approval Smitty gave Carole, and her tentative answering smile. Her head rattled like a one-armed bandit as the penny dropped: *Carole and Smitty! Nola was right. What will Tarn think?*

There was a variety of reactions to her disappearance and subsequent return.

Brad thought she should have stayed away. 'The major was really pissed off.'

'What did he say?'

'Not much; it was the way he looked. You know what I mean.'

Christobel was angry. 'You've really hurt Mum, Dad and Latoya.'

Lateesha, Farrah and Shontell unanimously condemned April for thinking she was too posh to be part of their family. 'Gutsells aren't *gutless.*'

'Oh, for goodness' sake …' April muttered.

Demi asked if she was supposed to call her Auntie April now, and Cushla wanted to know if she could borrow April's white rope-soled sandals. 'Our feet are the same size, and they're really kewl.'

Nola told them all to shut up and leave April alone, and stayed away. Her silence made April feel worse. She'd rather Nola jumped on the bandwagon and abused her the way her daughters had. April didn't try to say sorry. It wasn't enough.

Latoya was willing to forgive April because she understood how she felt. She was overwhelmed by Aurora. 'I can't believe I've got anything to do with this place. Are you sure I'm really Heather's?'

'You have to be, unless Lionel Prescott is really a girl.'

'Who's Lionel Prescott?'

'One of the local cops. He was born at the hospital the same night we were. I suppose you're angry and think I'm a chicken, too?'

'I'm too mixed-up to know what I think,' Latoya replied tiredly.

'Ditto.' April studied her closely. 'Are you feeling OK?'

In a rare show of temper, Latoya snapped, 'I've already got Mum and the girls hovering over me, worrying I'm going to have a seizure. I don't need you to join in.'

April and Nola wouldn't allow Latoya to work in the orchard or packing house, so she helped Carole in the kitchen instead. April escaped by throwing herself into work, but was only so successful. Things happened and cracks kept appearing in her protective walls.

She overheard Carole say to Smitty, 'I don't know how somebody as rotten as Heather produced a daughter as sweet as Latoya.'

'She's sweet because Nola and Barry raised her,' April retorted.

Shontell kept asking Carole when Tarn was coming back.

Carole looked at April before answering, 'He hasn't found Aaron yet. I'm sure he'll be back as soon as he does.'

It had been a mistake taking the coward's way out and running away like she always did. April wanted to apologize to Tarn, and when she remembered what she'd written in her letter to him, she wanted to curl up in a ball and hide. She wouldn't blame him if he threw her off the property when he got back.

One day stretched to two, two days stretched into four, and still Tarn didn't call. Nor could Carole reach him on his cellphone. They were united in their worry about him, and kept telling one another he was alright.

'It isn't like him to not call,' Carole fretted.

She gave April the password to the financial accounts. 'I'm no good with accounts; neither is Gerald.'

April roused herself to ask, 'Who's Gerald?'

'Smitty.' Carole turned pink. 'His name is really Gerald.'

She was touched by Tarn's mother's bashfulness, and by how happy she looked. April hoped Smitty — no, *Gerald* — wouldn't hurt Carole the way Murdo had.

When she went to the study to work on the accounts, April noticed that the burgundy chair was missing. 'Carole? Where's the burgundy chair?'

'In one of the garages. Tarn put it out there before he left.'

Tarn slept in Aaron's guest room, drank some of his wine, watched most of his DVD collection, and ordered in so much pizza he got to know the delivery boys by name. He ate it for breakfast and for dinner. Lunch was a non-event. He showered, and shaved if he felt like it, and didn't bother to recharge the battery on his cellphone. He was taking a vacation from his life.

He couldn't have made it any clearer how he felt about April, but she'd run away. And then when he'd left, she had returned. The big drawcard for her had to be Aurora — she loved the place. Well, April, Smitty, and his mother could worry about things by themselves for a while. April kept telling him he wasn't in the army anymore, and that she wasn't one of his men, so Tarn was through interfering.

After four days, Aaron still hadn't shown up and Tarn was sick of his own company and a diet of pizza and wine. Brooding alone was overrated, which was probably why he'd never done it before. He wasn't cut out to sit around on his arse feeling sorry for himself.

He showered, shaved, threw a load of washing into the machine and squeezed himself into one of Aaron's handmade shirts, a pale blue paisley affair that really did look like it belonged on a gigolo but was the only thing that fitted. Aaron was a couple of inches taller, and leaner than Tarn, but provided he didn't take any deep breaths the shirt buttons were probably safe.

There was a different security guard behind the desk downstairs. He came out from behind it as Tarn emerged from the elevator, and tried to stop him. 'You must be the gentleman staying in the penthouse apartment.'

'Yes,' Tarn agreed curtly and stalked out the revolving door.

He ordered brunch at a café, which he couldn't eat, and sat outside in the sunshine drinking coffee, trying to decide if he wanted to take a walk to the Beehive and watch the politicians slugging it out or ride the cable car up the hill above the city and look at the views. In the end, he flipped a coin. The politicians won.

As he tossed back the last of his coffee, a late-model sedan pulled up across the road, and a man with grey hair got out.

It was Ralph Berryman.

Tarn slowly returned his coffee cup to the saucer.

Berryman disappeared into the office block beside the café.

April had told him not to interfere. She would hit the roof if he did it again.

Tarn got up, and followed Berryman.

Berryman's Cereals was on the seventh floor. The company slogan shone in gold letters on the wall outside his office: *Berryman's … Berrygood*. As the CEO and major shareholder, Ralph Berryman had a corner office with views of the Beehive and old Parliament Buildings, and a personal assistant who guarded his door like a prison warden with Hannibal Lecter under lock and key.

She bristled when Tarn said he didn't have an appointment, then looked doubtful when he gave her his name and included his army rank. Tarn figured that the paisley shirt made it difficult to believe he used to be a major in the New Zealand Army.

'Mr Berryman has a very full day.'

'I'm sure he does,' Tarn replied.

'If you give me a message, I'll make sure he gets it.'

The prison warden jumped when Tarn rapped out, 'Tell Mr Berryman Major Elliott would like to have a word with him about April Ritchie — we all met recently in Queenstown.' He took a seat. 'I can wait.'

The PA didn't seem to recognize the name of her boss's ex-wife, but did get the message that Tarn wasn't going anywhere until he'd seen Mr Berryman. Wearing a frown that was one furrow short of a scowl, she went and tapped on the door behind her and disappeared into her boss's office.

A few minutes later she emerged and folded herself into her chair. 'Mr Berryman will see you. *Ten minutes.*'

Ralph Berryman didn't get up from his desk when Tarn entered his office. Tarn saw a flash of recognition in his eyes before they stalled on his shirt. The muted lighting in the foyer of the hotel in Queenstown had been kind. Up close and in daylight, Berryman looked older and greyer than he had that night, but he was still a well-preserved silver fox heading for his sixtieth birthday safe in the knowledge that business was good and he was in the best of health. Tarn studied the face he'd seen smiling broadly on cereal boxes. He wanted to punch it.

In a corner opposite the desk, there were two brown leather sofas with buttoned backs that looked like they belonged in a London gentlemen's club. Tarn imagined meetings being held there over a tray of coffee and knew Berryman wouldn't be offering to move their discussion there; he'd stay behind his desk to give the appearance he was in control. It suited Tarn. If he got too close to Berryman, he might not be able to keep his hands off him. He didn't wait for an invitation to sit but picked up a chair in the same brown leather as the sofas, moved it in front of the desk and sat down.

Berryman's eyes flickered warily. 'What do you want, Major Elliott?'

Tarn came straight to the point. 'When April divorced you, she was too traumatized to ask for a settlement.'

His lip curled. 'You want money.' He had Tarn pegged as a blackmailer.

The sneer in his voice made Tarn want to pluck him from his throne and throw him against the wall, but that wouldn't help April.

'Yes — for April.' His gaze bored into her ex-husband. 'I've seen what you did to her back.'

Berryman's eyes shifted guiltily. He tried to regroup. 'What happened between me and my ex-wife is personal and none of your business.'

'It is when your personal business is written on her back.'

'There's always two sides to a—'

'So what's your version?' Tarn asked curtly. 'That you were working out with your belt and she walked into the buckle half a dozen times?'

Berryman shifted some papers around on his desk. 'It was an accident.'

Tarn's head started to throb. 'It wasn't an accident.'

'Are you trying to blackmail me? Did April put you up to this?' he demanded belligerently. 'I suppose you thought that now, when my wife is about to have the baby, was the perfect time.'

*Don't hit him. It'll make you feel better, but it won't help April.*

Tarn got up, placed his hands on the desk and leaned towards him. 'April has photos,' he said very carefully. 'If she'd wanted to blackmail you, she could have done it years ago. She took them because she was scared you'd come after her.'

Berryman wilted. 'I'd never have done that. I loved her.'

'You call that love?' Tarn asked in disgust. 'You sick bastard.'

'You've no idea what it was like. She was allergic!' Berryman jerked a thumb at his chest. '*To me!* Then I bumped into her mother and—'

'You listened to her.' Tarn's face hardened with contempt. 'You paid attention to lies spun by a woman you'd never met before. You believed her over your wife because it gave you an excuse to get out all your anger and frustration because April couldn't get pregnant. You'd made a deal and you felt short-changed. When you said in sickness and in health at the church, I bet you were thinking about your healthy young wife looking after your sick old carcass.'

Berryman's eyes slid away. 'It wasn't like that,' he muttered. 'I still can't believe that it happened.'

'Would you like me to send you the photos to jog your memory?'

'Of course not!'

Tarn stared at the thinning, grey hair on top of Berryman's head, which his expensive haircut couldn't disguise. 'Did you ever bother to find out if she was alright? Or wonder how she was supporting herself? If she needed help?'

Berryman had no answer. He was a pathetic, middle-aged man who'd purposely married a much younger woman so she could help him retain his youth by giving him babies. Tarn bet Berryman had already been thinking about finding a way out of his marriage to April before Heather spoke to him. April had done him a favour when she ran. After the divorce, and when he was certain she wasn't going to tell her story to the press or embarrass him in any way, Berryman wasted no time finding a replacement wife and getting her pregnant. He'd had April's trust, and all of her kooky, generous heart.

He was too stupid to know what he'd lost.

Berryman was the kind of man who'd suffer more from being outed than being thumped. Tarn grabbed a pen from the desk and scrawled Rob Sturmley's name and details on the blotter. 'This is April's lawyer. I'll tell him that your lawyer will be calling to arrange the transfer of some money to April.'

Berryman glanced up. Down again. 'Do we have to involve lawyers?'

'Yes,' Tarn said flatly, 'we do.'

The older man's shoulders sagged. 'How much do you want?'

Tarn hadn't thought that far. He'd expected Berryman to put

up a bigger fight. Tarn was no expert on divorce settlements, so he just plucked a figure from the air: 'Two million.'

April's ex looked cagey instead of outraged, which made Tarn think he'd probably sold her short. Taking into consideration that they'd been married for four years and Berryman was a multi-millionaire with extensive business interests, two million dollars probably wasn't much. That didn't stop him trying to cry poor. 'I haven't got that sort of money available.'

'Get a loan from the bank, liquidate some assets — I don't care how you do it.' Tarn threw the pen on the desk. 'And work out a payment plan with April's lawyer so that she gets at least half of the money before the end of January. If you try to weasel out of the agreement, I'll give her lawyer copies of the photos and ask him to lay a complaint with the police.'

Berryman paled. 'My wife is due to have the baby next week.'

'Then you'd better get cracking.' Tarn helped himself to one of Berryman's business cards. 'And if you ever feel tempted to take your belt to wife number two, stop a moment to imagine the inside of a jail cell because I promise that's where you'll end up.'

Aaron returned home at four-thirty one morning nearly two weeks after he'd last been seen by his cleaner. He crashed into the apartment, clattered his car keys onto the glass-topped table in the hallway, dumped his kit bag on the living room floor, removed his prosthetic limb and left it by one of the sofas, and hopped into the kitchen to noisily investigate the contents of the fridge.

Tarn got the message. He climbed out of bed, pulled on a pair of jeans and walked barefoot into the kitchen. Aaron was leaning on the top of the fridge door, drinking orange juice straight out of the carton. He looked seedy — like he'd been on a week-long drinking binge.

He dangled the half-empty carton from his fingers. 'It really is you. When security called to say there was a major staying in my apartment, I thought they were kidding.'

'Where've you been hiding?'

'Here and there.' He returned the carton to the fridge and hopped over to the sink to fill the coffee maker. 'Sounds like I'm not the only one who's been hiding.'

Tarn averted his gaze from the empty space at the bottom of Aaron's trouser leg. He didn't think he'd ever be reconciled to the sight of that missing limb. 'You want me to get your crutches before you break your neck?'

Aaron threw coffee into the percolator. 'Nope.'

'I'm sorry I gate-crashed without asking.'

'My casa is your casa.'

Aaron had butchered the Spanish phrase, which told Tarn how black his mood was, or that he was still drunk. Aaron spoke Spanish, French and German fluently, and had been the first to pick up the local lingo whenever they'd been posted abroad. Tarn had exploited Aaron's talents to the full.

He tucked his hands into his armpits. 'You've been drinking too much.'

'By the look of my wine rack, so have you.'

'I hope you didn't drive home like that?'

'Somebody gave me a ride.'

Tarn bet the driver was female.

Aaron glanced around the kitchen. 'Has the cleaning service been through? I'd expect the place to look like this if Sled had been staying, but not you.'

'I'll replace the wine, and the cleaning service is coming in the morning. I was going to tidy up before I left. I borrowed one of your shirts, too, but I washed and ironed it.'

Aaron studied Tarn's burly proportions as the water boiled. 'Did you use a shoe horn to get into it?'

'I picked the worst one I could find in case I ripped it — an ugly, blue paisley thing.'

'That one?' His blue satyr's eyes gleamed. 'Shit, you must've looked like a truck driver turned gigolo.'

'Better than a big blonde fairy.'

Aaron laughed and tipped water into the coffee maker. He used the kitchen counter to hop over to a cupboard and get out two mugs. He held one up to Tarn, who nodded. Why didn't the reckless fool let him get his crutches?

'So what's eating you? Got sick of playing orchard owner?'

'I'm taking a brief sabbatical.'

He cocked a brow questioningly. Tarn didn't take sabbaticals.

'What's your problem?' Tarn asked. 'Have six of your girlfriends found out about the other half dozen?'

'No, I'm taking a brief sabbatical from all that,' Aaron mocked.

Tarn snorted. The only time Aaron took a sabbatical from the opposite sex was when he was too busy with work, or they were posted somewhere too remote and dangerous to have anything to do with the local women.

Aaron indicated the mugs of coffee on the counter. 'You can carry them into the living room. I'm legless.'

When they'd finished their coffee, Tarn said, 'I'll go back tomorrow.'

'Do you need to?'

'Of course I do. We're in the middle of the picking season.'

With his family background, Tarn expected Aaron to understand.

'How much do you know about running a cherry orchard during the picking season?' Aaron asked Tarn bluntly.

'I'm learning,' he replied shortly.

'Who did you leave in charge?'

Tarn looked at the prosthetic leg propped against the sofa next to Aaron. 'Somebody who knows a lot more about growing cherries than I do.'

'Good. Let her get on with it — you look like you need a break.'

'What makes you think it's a she?'

'It explains why you're holed up in my apartment playing hooky. Normally, you're the most responsible person I know.'

Aaron tucked his hands behind his head, tried to prop his missing ankle on his knee and toppled slightly sideways. He sat up again. Even after all these months, he still sometimes forgot it wasn't there anymore. Usually this lapse happened when he was with one of the guys — when he'd been with them, he'd been whole.

He saw the sympathy and guilt on Tarn's face before he looked away. It was what made it hard for him to be around his former colleagues. They were soldiers, they didn't make a fuss, but the bond between them meant that they felt each other's loss or pain personally. Things got even more complicated when it came to Tarn. Aaron knew Tarn blamed himself for what had happened on the patrol. He made himself relax back against the cushions. 'Is she a girlfriend?'

'No,' Tarn was stiff, standoffish. 'April isn't a girlfriend.' He couldn't say what she was, or when she'd stepped over the line from being a nuisance to become the centre of his life.

'You got married and didn't tell me?'

'No, but I wouldn't be the first.' Tarn gave him a pointed look: 'How's your wife?'

Aaron grinned. 'Last time I spoke to her, fine. Tell me about April. What's she like?'

'A bit like you — blonde, charming and irresponsible about her personal life — but unlike you, she isn't promiscuous.'

He didn't bat an eyelid. 'How long have you known her?'

'I met her when she was eleven. She's twenty-six now.'

'A younger woman — even better.'

'Funny, I never think of April as being nine years younger.'

'You would if she slipped your discs every time you took her to bed. Was she at the orchard when you bought it?'

'No. She gate-crashed the birthday party the guys arranged for me. She came as a kiss-o-gram girl and tried to break into my wardrobe and steal something.'

Aaron stared. 'Right … and what did you do?'

'Took her to the police station. The local cop knows her. He kept her overnight because she didn't have anywhere to stay.' Tarn still felt bad about it.

Aaron tried to imagine his stern former OC driving a kiss-o-gram girl to town. He hadn't been to Pisa, but knew exactly what it would be like. 'Why didn't I hear about this from Sled or Wylie?'

'Because you haven't been interested in what was going on.'

He couldn't argue with that. 'What kind of kiss-o-gram was she?'

The corner of Tarn's mouth kicked up in remembrance. 'A red devil.'

The major had been hooked by a kiss-o-gram girl wearing a red devil costume?

'Was she still wearing her costume when you took her to the police station?'

'No.' Tarn turned the tables. 'Does your wife run Cinnsealach for you?'

'Who?'

'You know who: Mrs Kinsella — Harmony.'

Aaron's smile had a big 'Stop' sign attached. 'Yes, she does — admirably.'

'So how long have you known her?'

'A while.'

'How long have you been married to her?'

'A while.'

'You're not going to talk about her, are you?'

Aaron grinned. 'No. Are you going to tell me more about April?'

'I've already said more than I intended to.' Tarn carried his empty mug towards the kitchen. 'I'm going to bed.'

Aaron stretched out on the sofa and called, 'Stay a few days longer. I won't try and make you talk about the red devil, as long as you don't try and make me talk about my wife.'

# Chapter 23

*I don't have to attend every argument I'm invited to.*

**Anon**

Unaware that she was about to become a wealthy woman, April juggled the demands of overseeing the packing house and the pickers with help from Nola and Smitty. Two of the Taiwanese workers had to return home unexpectedly, but they got lucky when an experienced picker filled one of their places. Or at least April thought they'd got lucky — until Courtney and her mother volunteered to share the other vacancy, and Mrs Murfitt identified the new guy as a regular at Mount Pisa Cherries.

April's initial reaction was to ask him to leave, but she couldn't — they needed him. Instead, she left Nola in charge of the packing house and Clarence in charge of quality control and went into the orchard to keep an eye on things and to help pick the precious white 'Rainier' cherries that fetched such a high price in the Asian markets.

'Rainier' cherries were notoriously tender, and had to be treated like nitroglycerin. Only half a bucket was picked at a time; and the bottoms of the buckets were padded with rubber to stop the fruit bruising. There was always a trade-off between planting more of this premium-priced variety versus the extra time it took to pick and pack the crop. Also, it took five years before a new tree, or 'rod', produced its first crop of cherries. For all of these reasons, 'Rainier' was Aurora's smallest crop, but April felt it was worth planting more of that variety provided that she, Tarn, Smitty and the Gutsells could do the picking when the time came.

April was at the top of a ladder, with a bucket strapped to her front, picking the cherries when she realized she was making plans for five years from now, plans that included Tarn and herself. She stopped, and leaned her forehead against her arm.

Lateesha was on a ladder on the other side of the tree. She peered at April through the branches. 'Are you OK?'

She nodded slowly, and resumed picking.

It was exhausting work. Each row of trees was 180 metres long, which meant the pickers did a lot of walking. A full bucket of cherries weighed about five kilograms, and the harness the buckets slipped into placed a lot of strain on the picker's shoulders and back. Add lifting ladders in and out of trees and working in sweltering temperatures, and it was easy to understand why picking cherries weren't everybody's cup of tea.

But April loved it. She loved finishing a tree, picking up her ladder and moving it to the next one in the row. She loved looking back and seeing green branches missing their glossy, deep red earrings of fruit, and looking forwards to see luscious splashes of red amidst deep emerald-green, framed by a brilliant, cloudless blue sky. She loved the old, white house shaded by towering chestnut trees on the rise above the orchard, the frilly heads of lavender bushes waving around its knees, and the ducks paddling and squabbling on the pond between the kitchen door and the glasshouse.

Maybe if Aurora's stiff-necked, granite-faced owner had remained stiff-necked and granite-faced, she wouldn't love him, too.

Things started to go wrong. Little things that didn't add up, and couldn't be traced to anybody. A cigarette butt was found in one of the buckets. Lateesha, Farrah, Christobel and Nola all swore they hadn't smoked for weeks and it wasn't theirs. One of the exporters heard and called to ask if everything was under control, and wouldn't say how he'd found out.

Rain at harvest time was a big enemy because it made the cherries swell and split, but there were products that could be sprayed on the fruit to prevent this from happening. April had made sure they had a supply of spray ready, but when rain was forecast one night and she went to the garage, the containers were miraculously empty. She made a frenzied call to the supplier.

'I saw that new guy in the garage yesterday,' Shontell told her.

'Doing what?'

'I dunno.'

'Why didn't you tell me?' April cried.

'What'd I do?' Shontell asked blankly.

'Jesus, Shontell!' Christobel snapped. 'You're the reason there's so many blonde jokes!'

'April told us to keep an eye on the new guy and let her or Smitty know if we saw him doing anything out of the ordinary!' Farrah shouted.

'How was I to know he was acting out of the ordinary?' Shontell shouted back. 'I thought Smitty had sent him to get something.'

'You could've checked!' Latoya yelled.

April stuck her fingers in her ears.

They were still spraying as the rain began to fall. In the morning, April surveyed the dreaded 'smiley faces' on the cherries and estimated that twenty-five per cent of the crop had been lost. She felt like she'd failed Tarn.

Nola, Latoya and the rest of the girls were almost as upset as April, Carole and Smitty.

They stood in the sunshine amongst the rain-washed trees and discussed what to do.

'I'll get rid of the new guy,' Smitty said grimly.

April stopped him. 'I've already done it.'

The new guy only shrugged when she told him he wouldn't be needed anymore. She wished she was bigger and taller and could punch like Muhammed Ali. The best she could come up with was to tell him to pass on a message to Ivan. 'Tell Ivan he's a mean, lying, short-arsed old fool and that he's picked the wrong fight.'

He finally looked worried. 'I can't do that!'

'Then go get drunk and blab it to your friends instead. The bush telegraph at the pub is better than the Internet,' April replied nastily.

'You shouldn't have spoken to him alone, April,' Carole reproved.

'He didn't care. It's not as if we can prove anything.'

Carole turned towards the house. 'I'm going to call Tarn and tell him he's got to come home.'

April grabbed her arm. 'No — don't!' Everybody dumped on Tarn and expected him to put things right. When they all looked at her like she was nuts, she added more calmly, 'We can manage.'

April racked her brains for a solution. What was she good at? Dressing up in an angel costume and singing in rhyme, and causing trouble. Yeah, she was *great* at causing trouble.

Nola had seen Ivan strutting his stuff in Pisa and hated him on sight. She asked April if she'd really married his son, to which April replied, 'Not legally, and in my defence Stefan is taller and better-looking than his father.' Nola nodded understandingly. She knew about youthful mistakes just like she knew that she loved all her kids but they were all different. For instance, April and Latoya were smart, but Shontell didn't have the brains to shout in a shark attack.

'What are we going to do about Ivan the Arsehole? We can't pick, pack and fight the little weasel at the same time.'

April chewed her lip thoughtfully. 'I think it's time we called in the big guns.'

'Our biggest gun is in Wellington,' Christobel pointed out.

'Tarn's not our only big gun. We've got another older, more experienced model called Rosamund.'

'Rosamund?' Carole thought she must have misheard. 'You're going to call *Rosamund?*'

'Who's Rosamund when she's at home?' Nola asked.

'Heather's mother,' Carole replied.

Nola's eyes lit with anticipation. She couldn't wait to meet her.

Carole continued, 'You've heard how April used to get called the Princess of Pisa?'

April grimaced; Nola nodded.

'Well, Rosamund was known as the Duchess of Aurora.' Carole looked at April. 'You really think you can get Rosamund to leave her swanky retirement home and come down here?'

'Of course.' April noticed Latoya's troubled expression and realized she wasn't the only one worried. The Gutsells closed ranks.

'Don't worry about the old bat, Latoya,' Shontell said. 'There's only one of her and seven of us.'

Nola rubbed Latoya's arm comfortingly. 'It's OK, Toots. Granny won't give you any trouble.'

Rosamund didn't appreciate being called away from her mah-jong four and told she had to get on a flight to Queenstown.

'That's not how you issue an invitation, April. Call me back when you've remembered your manners.'

'Don't you dare hang up on me, Grandma!'

It was the 'Grandma' that made Rosamund stay on the line; she'd given up on ever hearing April call her that again. 'Would you care to explain that comment?'

'One of Tarn's soldiers has gone missing and he's away trying to find him. Ivan is making the most of his absence to cause trouble.'

'Is he? How?'

April explained about the cigarette butt, the exporter calling, and losing twenty-five per cent of the crop.

'You know there's nothing you can do about the weather, April. Take it on the chin and move on.'

'Of course I know, but Phil Northcott has made things really difficult by giving Tarn a pitiful overdraft. I want to be able to give him some good news when he gets back.'

*Ah, so that's the way the wind blows. Excellent.*

'You're supposed to be Tarn's partner. You should be helping, not sitting on your bu—'

'April!'

'Not playing mah-jong all day.'

Rosamund was already planning what she'd pack. 'Why do I need to come all the way to Aurora when I can simply telephone Phillip Northcott and remind him how long the bank has had my business?'

'Because you'll have a lot more fun swanning around Pisa flipping the bird at Ivan.'

'I have no idea what "flipping the bird" means, April.'

'Yes, you do, Rosamund. The only difference between you and

me is that you wear gloves when you do it. Oh, and one other thing: your granddaughter is here.'

'I know that. I'm not senile.'

'I mean your *real* granddaughter is here.'

April was her real granddaughter. 'Do you mean Heather's daughter?'

'Yes. Her name's Latoya. Apart from Courtney Murfitt, she's my closest friend. She's very sweet and terrified of meeting you, so you'd better be nice.'

Rosamund tangled her fingers in the jade beads around her neck. Latoya wasn't the only one who was scared.

As usual, April didn't see the potential flaws in her plan until it was too late to change it. She really did think Rosamund was the best person to help. She just hoped there wasn't going to be a blood bath when Rosamund met Nola and the rest of the Gutsells.

'You do realize things could quickly turn pear-shaped when Rosamund gets here?' Carole asked.

'I'll make sure it doesn't. Or do you have a better idea? Other than calling Tarn?'

'I don't understand why you're so dead set against calling him.'

'He needs a break,' April insisted. 'Everybody expects him to sort out their problems. Who got called when Aaron went missing?'

Carole conceded she had a point, and that maybe she relied too much on her son.

'I'm going to ask Gerald to move into the house. I want to know there's somebody we can call on if all hell breaks loose.'

'Why don't you have done with it and ask Smitty to move into your room?' April asked.

Carole pointed at the back door. 'Get out of my kitchen!'

April came back later to apologize. 'I'm sorry, Carole. I shouldn't have said what I did about you and Smitty.'

'I don't want to talk about it.' Carole was emptying cutlery from the dishwasher basket into the drawer in the dresser.

'I do. I think Smitty's a great guy and that it's nice you two have got together.'

Hearing Gerald praised chipped a hole in Carole's bad mood. 'What makes you think we're together?'

'I keep bumping into him on the stairs when he's sneaking out of your room at night.'

If Tarn had still been here, there was a good chance she'd have bumped into Smitty on the stairs when she was creeping out of Tarn's room.

Carole slammed the dresser drawer shut.

'There's nothing wrong with it, Carole. You look happy. Much happier than you did with Murdo.'

'You shouldn't have lied about Tarn being in the packing house with Heather.'

It came out of nowhere, catching April unawares.

'I didn't know what else to do. Dad needed Murdo and I didn't think Tarn would care.'

'Of course he cared. *I* cared.'

'Then why didn't *you* speak up? Why did you let Tarn take the blame?'

Carole picked at the cutlery basket. 'I'd been trying to turn a blind eye to what Murdo did for so long … Tarn was always stronger than his father.'

April nearly blurted, *You're his mother! How could you have hurt him like that?* But then, who was she to criticize?

'If it makes you feel better, give Smitty the downstairs bedroom and put Rosamund in my room.'

'Where will you sleep? There aren't any beds in the other rooms and the caravans and bunkhouse are full up. Latoya's had to squeeze in with Shontell and the younger girls.'

'I could sleep in Tarn's room while he's away,' April suggested. 'I've already robbed the wardrobe — and put back what I took again.' She'd returned the jewellery to the door because it seemed safer than leaving it in Tarn's desk drawer.

'I don't understand you, April.'

'Me neither. Are you going to kick up a fuss if I move into Tarn's room?'

'I don't have the energy.'

'Hard work and good sex tends to do that.'

Carole scrubbed at a non-existent mark on the front of the dishwasher. 'There's something I need to ask you that I really don't feel comfortable about. I know you think I'm an old fuddy-duddy, but that's the way I was raised and I can't help it.'

April thought of, and dismissed, all kinds of things. Carole was too old for an unplanned pregnancy. Did she want to borrow April's so-called sex manual that wasn't a sex manual at all? Had she found the flavoured condoms when she was doing the dusting and wanted to know who they belonged to? April would have to say they were hers. Carole wouldn't have any trouble believing that.

'Are you sleeping with Tarn?'

Her mouth fell open in shock. The night before she left was the first time they'd done any sleeping. 'No.'

'None of your stories now,' Carole warned. 'I want the truth.'

Half a truth seemed better than a whole lie. 'Only once — I was drunk and Tarn felt sorry for me.'

Carole obviously didn't believe her.

'OK, I wasn't drunk.'

April waited for her to ask why, if it had only happened once, there were opened boxes of chocolate- and strawberry-flavoured condoms in Tarn's desk/bedside drawer/army boots or wherever else he stored them. She should have thought ahead and stuffed them in the wardrobe door with the jewellery. Would Carole believe her if she said she'd bought a flavoured-condom franchise and was waiting to get her new company logo printed on them?

'Do you ever tell the truth?' Carole asked.

Wasn't *that* a loaded question? April avoided answering it. 'What made you ask about Tarn and me?'

'Gerald hinted.'

*Good old Gerald.*

'You can sleep in Tarn's room as long as you move out the moment he gets home.'

April's heart sped up. 'Have you heard from him?'

'He called last night to say Aaron was back.'

'Did he say when he was coming home?' She wished she didn't sound so pathetic and needy.

Carole's forbidding expression softened the tiniest bit. 'No.'

April's mood plummeted further.

'I'm sure he'll come home soon. It's Christmas in two weeks.'

'Is it?' She was surprised by that, and that Carole had almost sounded comforting.

'Yes, April — it's the same day every year. I've ordered the meat for the spit roast and I'm putting the trees up in the drawing room and by the stairs tomorrow night. Demi and Cushla are going to help me decorate them. How could you forget about Christmas?'

Carole studied April more closely. She flew in and out of the kitchen without finishing meals and whizzed around the orchard so fast it was hard to pin her down. Carole clicked her tongue impatiently: April looked like a bag of bones. 'You've been working too hard. You're skin and bone.'

'I'm watching my figure.'

'You haven't got a figure to watch.'

'That's the nicest thing you've ever said to me. Apart from "Happy birthday, here's your cake; if you don't like it, I'm not making another one."'

Carole flushed. Little brat. Naughty, neglected little brat. She and April would never be bosom buddies, but at least they were learning to be civil.

Before things got too uncomfortable and somebody broke out the hearts and flowers, April said, 'You know that book I was reading about French women's attitude to sex?'

'Yes?'

'It isn't a sex manual. It's about how our culture and upbringing affects our attitudes to things like sex. If I lend it to you, maybe you'll stop acting like Queen Victoria — who, I might add, apparently had a very hot sex life with Prince Albert — and let poor Gerald stay the night in your room and get a decent night's sleep.'

Carole considered her offer. 'Do I have to read it by headlamp?'

# Chapter 24

*Families are like fudge: mostly sweet with a few nuts.*

**Anon**

It was eleven years since April and Rosamund had seen each other. Neither of them was prepared for how much the other had changed.

The spoiled, rebellious teenager had been replaced by a lovely young woman with a tough exterior and haunted blue-green eyes.

'You're too thin, April.'

The tall, autocratic matriarch had shrunk and her hair had turned silver. She used a walking stick now and looked frail and old.

'Thank you, Grandma.'

Nola had automatically taken against Rosamund because she was Heather's mother.

Rosamund took in Nola's short skirt, wedge heels, thick blue mascara and the pink scrap of material holding back her long, faded blonde hair. She thought Nola looked like an ageing Amish hippy.

Despite the heat, Rosamund wore a biscuit-coloured trouser suit with a lemon-yellow blouse and a double strand of pearls. Her hairdresser had permed and set her hair before she'd left, and her make-up was limited to a good foundation, a touch of peach blusher and lipstick. Nola thought Rosamund looked like she'd dressed to be laid out in her coffin.

'Mrs Gutsell,' Rosamund said distantly when April introduced them.

'Duchess,' Nola replied and pulled Latoya forward. 'Let me introduce my daughter, Latoya. She's the baby your nutcase daughter swapped with April.'

Carole and April exchanged panicked looks.

Rosamund didn't seem to notice Nola's rudeness. She stared at Latoya's anxious face and gripped her walking stick tightly. Her throat worked. 'You remind me of Edwin,' she said at last.

Nola's hostility faded. Latoya relaxed slightly.

Smitty had collected Rosamund from the airport and unloaded a small mountain of luggage next to the front door. 'I'll take your cases upstairs, shall I?' he suggested.

April dived after him as he went towards the stairs. 'I'll help!'

Latoya was hot on her heels. 'It's like meeting the queen!' she whispered. 'Who was Edwin? Her husband?'

'No, her brother. If she'd said you reminded her of Donald, you'd have been in trouble.'

They grabbed a case each.

April waved Smitty grandly up the stairs. 'This way, my good man.'

Behind her, Rosamund said tartly, 'I see there are some things that haven't changed about you, April.'

Carole got brave and let Smitty move into her bedroom. He stayed most nights, and when he didn't she sometimes stayed at his place. On those nights they got up early so that Carole was back in time to make breakfast.

Rosamund took the downstairs bedroom because the stairs were too much for her. Her frailty disturbed April; she'd always seemed so indomitable. April nagged Latoya to move into her old bedroom so that she was closer to Rosamund and could spend more time with her, but Latoya's gentle nature and Rosamund's brisk abrasiveness weren't a good mix.

April cornered Latoya about it in the caravan that Christobel shared with Lateesha and Farrah. It was blissfully smoke-free, although the Pisa chemists were still doing a roaring trade in nicotine gum.

'Where will you sleep?' Latoya asked.

'In Tarn's room.'

Christobel was sitting on her bed, eating a yoghurt. She snorted.

April ignored her.

'I don't know what to say to her,' Latoya said nervously.

'I don't know what to say to Nola either, but I talk to her.'

'Mum isn't scary like your grandmother. She doesn't bang her walking stick on the ground when she's pissed off.'

'Like Nanny McPhee,' Cushla interjected.

Christobel licked the spoon. 'Put a sock in it, Cushla.'

'She's your grandmother, too,' April said.

'And Mum's your mother, too,' Latoya retorted.

Christobel piped up again. 'Grow some balls, Latoya.'

Cushla giggled. 'Tim wouldn't like that.'

'Put a sock in it, Cushla!' April snapped.

Cushla looked at her mother indignantly. Christobel calmly continued eating her yoghurt, and Cushla flounced out.

'Brat,' Christobel yawned, and fired her spoon into the sink. 'Can you two take this somewhere else? I want to get some shut-eye before I have to go back out into that oven of an orchard.'

Rosamund contacted Phillip Northcott. He extended the overdraft.

She arranged for the father of the exporter who'd called about the cigarette butt to come for lunch at the house.

'Something cold served outside, Carole. My mother's dinner service is somewhere in the kitchen dresser and I'll select the wine.' The walking stick thumped twice. 'I'm not blind, April! I can see you tugging your hair and curtseying. And stop laughing, Latoya — you'll only encourage her.'

'What about Ivan?' April asked. 'What do you have planned for him?'

'Calling him names didn't do your case any good, April, and speaking of cases—'

April didn't want to talk about her court case. 'You're right, I shouldn't have — which is why I called you. I knew if I didn't, I'd start scrapping in the sandpit and throwing my play dough.'

Latoya stared off into the distance with her mouth all bent out of shape.

Rosamund sighed sharply. 'Clarence said there's a meeting of the Pisa Round Table this afternoon to discuss the arrangements for the cherry festival. As the chairman, Ivan will be there — and so will we. I want you girls to put on your nicest dresses and do your hair and make-up.'

'I don't have time to go to a meeting of the Round Table!' April protested. 'I've got cherries to pack. Take Latoya — she's nicer than me.'

Latoya gave her a daggers look.

'You're coming, April,' Rosamund said firmly. 'Smitty and Carole can manage for an hour or two, and you need to take a break.'

Latoya's look made her cave in. 'Alright, but I'm not wearing a dress.'

'Fine, wear a smart suit,' Rosamund said crisply. 'Now hurry up; I'm getting older by the second.'

Falling asleep on the garden seat and banging a walking stick on the floor kept a girl busy, April concluded sourly.

She didn't own a 'smart seeyute', as Rosamund called it, and even if she did, it was too hot to wear one. She dug out a white sleeveless dress with a blue pattern on the neckline and hem, and tried to take back her bondage sandals from Demi, but they were covered in dust.

'Get those sandals into the washing machine, Demi!' Christobel yelled when she saw them. 'Are you nuts? Why did you lend them to her in the first place?' she asked April.

In the end, April had to wear a pair of Rosamund's navy-blue court shoes and stuff toilet paper into the toes to keep them from falling off. She screwed her hair into a bun, refused to wear any make-up, and passed when Rosamund offered to loan her the handbag that matched the shoes. Latoya borrowed April's turquoise dress with the satin ribbons. It looked better against her olive skin and dark hair, but was a little short.

'I want you to look businesslike, not like you're off to a discotheque.' Rosamund eyed the hem of Latoya's dress disapprovingly. 'That skirt is too short. Bend your knees.'

'Don't let her get to you,' April consoled Latoya. 'We're just window dressing — she's the main feature.'

Rosamund looked regal in a white-spotted navy silk dress and her pearls.

'Where're your gloves?' April asked. 'We're going bird-flipping, remember?'

At the Pisa District Council offices, Rosamund was given a warm welcome by the members of the Round Table. Ivan's smile looked like it had been chipped into his face with an ice pick when she was ushered to his seat at the head of the table and proceeded to take over the meeting.

Rosamund pointed her stick at April. 'I'm sure you remember April.'

'Hardly likely to forget her,' somebody muttered.

She pointed to Latoya. 'And this is my other granddaughter, Latoya Gutsell.'

Latoya reddened as every eye turned her way.

'Your *other* granddaughter?' Ivan inquired archly.

'Yes. There was an unfortunate mix-up at the hospital the night Heather gave birth.' Rosamund smiled fondly at Latoya. 'Fortunately, April found Latoya for us.'

Ivan leaned forward. 'How is Heather?'

'She's spending Christmas in London with her husband.' Rosamund's smile didn't waver. 'How is Stefan?'

'Good,' Ivan replied shortly. 'So how did the mix-up happen at the hospital?'

'It's a long story, Ivan,' April said curtly. 'And extremely painful for Grandma to talk about.'

She sounded just like Tarn when he was putting somebody in their place.

'Thank you, dear.' Rosamund made a performance of propping her walking stick against the table. Ivan had to swallow his suspicions and innuendos or risk looking like he was bullying a frail old lady.

'Now, about the cherry-pip-spitting competition held on New Year's Day,' Rosamund continued. 'I'd like to host it at Aurora this year.'

All eyes turned to Ivan.

He smiled tightly. 'But Charmaine and I always hold it at Mount Pisa. We look forward to it.'

April watched in fascination as Rosamund smiled sadly back at him. She'd never seen her grandmother act weak and helpless before, and was certain Rosamund would put aside the tissues and get out the knuckle-dusters if Ivan didn't come to heel.

'I'm eighty-four years old, Ivan. You may not know this, but the competition was originally my husband Donald's idea.' *Which she'd hated.* Rosamund wilted slightly. 'I'd very much like to hold it at Aurora in his memory.'

'Weren't you the junior champion when you lived here, April?' one of the other orchard owners asked.

She nodded. 'Grandad coached me by teaching me to spit at the water tank.'

Rosamund's nostrils flared with distaste. *Odious man.*

The members of the Round Table were all fed up with Ivan and knew what Rosamund and April were up to. One of them put forward a motion to hold the competition at Aurora. It was seconded and passed unanimously.

Ivan didn't vote, or answer when Rosamund expressed the hope that she'd see everybody there on the day.

As she walked away from the council offices flanked by her granddaughters, Rosamund enquired, 'Was the bird flipped to your satisfaction, April?'

Tarn stayed one more day at Aaron's apartment to reassure himself that his friend was alright before Aaron kicked him out.

'I don't need a nanny. If I did, I'd hire one much better-looking and more fun than you. Go home.'

'And get a call from Frank or Sled or one of the other guys because you've disappeared on another two-week binge of drinking and sex?' Tarn retorted.

'What's it to any of you if I do? I'm not in the army anymore, and neither are you, Major Elliott.'

Tarn would be the first to admit that Aaron was a complicated character — he didn't understand how somebody so meticulous about his work could be so careless about his personal life. Aaron had a gift for getting the best out of the men and recognizing which way the wind blew in army politics. If he'd been willing to tidy up his personal life and make better use of his political instincts, he'd have risen higher than the rank of Warrrant Officer. But he simply wasn't interested in doing either.

'Aaron, you can't keep on pushing yourself like this. You've got way too many skills to waste your days boozing and screwing.'

'Some days I screw before I booze.'

Tarn lost his temper. 'I'm sorry I sent you up the hill and you stepped on the land mine! I know you wish you'd died like the others, but you fucking didn't!'

Aaron grabbed one of the crutches he always left lying around and threw it across the room. It flipped end over end and crashed into the wine rack when Tarn ducked, smashing the necks of some of the bottles. They watched as two bottles of Merlot that had cost Tarn a ridiculous amount of money spewed onto the kitchen floor.

'Shit!' Tarn grabbed a dishcloth and tried to staunch the flow. 'Stay over there!' he ordered when Aaron moved towards the growing puddle of red.

Aaron was wearing his leg. He edged around the puddle and grabbed a couple of glasses from a cupboard. Leaning over, he began to fill one of the glasses. 'It's sacrilege to waste good wine.'

Tarn shook his head. Just like that, Aaron's explosion had ended without a whiff of smoke to show for it. He pulled the other bottle from the rack, stepped over the mess on the floor and stood it on the kitchen counter.

Aaron put the other glass under the broken bottle and held out the one he'd filled to Tarn. The flow of wine began to slow as Tarn took it. They sipped from their glasses in silence.

'You can't grow me another leg, or sort out my problems, Tarn,' Aaron said quietly. 'You're not to blame for me standing on that mine, or for the others dying. We were in a war zone — it happens.'

Tarn stared unseeingly at the red puddle on the floor. Aaron knew he was no longer in the apartment, but miles away in the dust and heat of the desert. 'Why are you hanging around here when you've found what you want?'

Tarn roused himself to say, 'What do *you* want? Apart from your leg and your old life back?'

'I don't know, but you'll be the first to hear if I ever do. Enough about me — you know what you want. April's nine years younger; if you don't get a move on, you won't have a hope of running after your kids and catching them.'

'She thinks marriage is a dirty word. She's done it once — almost twice — already.'

Aaron was fascinated. An almost-twice-married twenty-six-year-old kiss-o-gram girl wasn't the kind of woman he'd pictured for

Tarn. He started to ask how a person could almost be married twice.

'It's a long story,' Tarn said. 'And there won't be any children: April's allergic to sperm.'

Aaron sat down. 'Now I've heard everything.'

'I didn't believe her either.'

Tarn told him about the visit he'd paid to Ralph Berryman.

'So the cheery-faced cereal millionaire is a wife-beater?'

He tossed back some wine. 'He took a belt to her. I wanted to kill him, Aaron. I still do.'

'I'm sure April would rather have two million dollars than you in prison.' Aaron linked his fingers and rested his hands on top of his head. 'I can't wait to meet this kiss-o-gram girl.'

Tarn snorted softly. 'She probably won't have me. She ran away when I told her how I felt, and only came back because I left.'

'So what? Wear her down.'

Tarn finished off the last of his wine. 'I can see why you were the go-to man when it came to problems with girlfriends.'

'And you were always the expert on wives. I'll keep that in mind if Harmony ever gives me any trouble.'

On the drive from Queenstown airport, Tarn stopped for petrol in Pisa. Jacinta Woodall was serving on the cash desk at the petrol station. She'd plastered her mouth with bright-orange lipstick — her lips looked like a couple of satsumas.

'Major! You're back!'

He'd only been gone ten days.

'I'm only here one day each weekend,' Jacinta explained. 'I would have much preferred to work at Aurora, but I'm allergic to cherries. Can you believe it? A Pisa girl allergic to cherries?'

He'd heard worse. Tarn handed over his bank card and looked at the display of lollies next to the cash desk.

While she completed his transaction, Jacinta commiserated about the cigarette butt that had been found in the bucket of cherries at Aurora and the exporters who'd threatened to pull their orders for the season, and said nobody blamed April for calling Ivan Vincent a mean, lying, short-arsed old criminal. She gave Tarn his receipt and card, and smiled complacently. 'I'm sure Mrs Dreyfuss will get things sorted out now she's here.'

Tarn's brown eyes were flat and unfriendly as he picked up two bags of lollies and dropped some coins onto the counter. 'You made the right choice working here. You would have hated working at Aurora. There'd be no chance to dish the dirt.'

The heel of his hand thumped the glass door as he left.

It was late by the time Tarn reached Aurora. This far south it stayed light until almost ten o'clock, so some of the workers were sitting outside the bunkhouse and caravans talking or reading. Christobel was outside her caravan. She waved when she recognized Tarn's white truck and waited for him to drive past. As soon as he was out of sight, she put aside the Organization Systems Manual she was reading and hurried down the driveway to the packing house to tell April he was back.

Tarn drove past the front door and around the back of the house to the garages. On the way he saw a green wreath trimmed with a red bow and gold-sprayed pine cones on the front door beneath the ornate fanlight, and remembered it was almost Christmas. He parked the truck in the garage beside the helicopter hangar, collected his kit bag and walked to the back door.

Carole wasn't in the kitchen. Cushla and Demi were there loading the dishwasher, and pounced on the bags of lollies Tarn had bought them at the petrol station.

'Where's April?'

They screwed up their faces as if he'd asked them to describe how to split an atom.

'It's not a trick question.'

'I think she's in the shower.'

'I think she went out.'

His future happiness relied on finding April and talking to her — and the only intel on her whereabouts was coming from very unreliable sources. His mother would know where April was. If not, he'd tear the place apart until he found her. 'Do you know where Carole is?'

The girls looked at each other and back again. 'Smitty's.'

Tarn pinched the bridge of his nose and tried one more time. 'What about Mrs Dreyfuss — Rosamund? Do you know where *she* is?'

'Oh yeah,' Demi said brightly. 'She's out with Clarence.'

He stalked out the kitchen door into the hallway, muttering to himself.

Cushla slammed the door on the half-emptied dishwasher. 'You moron!'

Demi threw the dishcloth she was holding at the table and missed. 'Dork!'

They clattered out the back door and raced off to the caravans to alert the rest of the Gutsell women.

Tarn checked out the study, powder room and upstairs, but there was no sign of April. He headed back downstairs. The scent of pine filled the hall from the big Christmas tree next to the stairs, but he barely noticed the tree, or the fat garland of green trimmed with red and gold bows, and tiny white fairy lights that wound around the balustrade. If April wasn't in the house, then she was probably in the packing house. He walked out into the warm night.

April was in the packing house. She was in the office with a box of cherries open on the desk, checking them through the Maggy lamp for blemishes and any signs of pests. Tarn hadn't anticipated that the blonde mafia would be there too. They were all crammed into the small office with April and a tall, slender dark girl he guessed must be Latoya.

They turned together when he came in. He paused and looked around the circle of faces. They weren't exactly hostile, but they weren't friendly either. Cushla and Demi must have sounded a Code Red. Tarn felt like a lone stormtrooper pitched against The Force.

His eyes sought and found April's in the middle of the circle. She looked like she'd shrunk. She was all big eyes and cheekbones. Her collar bones looked sharp against her pink spaghetti-strap top. He wanted to snatch her up and spirit her away from her bodyguards.

Tarn rounded on Nola. 'Couldn't you see she was losing weight?'

Nola bristled like a hedgehog. 'She wouldn't have *lost* weight if you hadn't run off to play Lawrence of Arabia!'

Farrah's eyes flashed. 'She's had to handle all the crap you should have been dealing with, like dodgy pickers—'

'And Ivan the Arsehole,' Lateesha interrupted flatly.

'You don't look so hot yourself, Major,' Shontell chimed in.

In a family crisis, even Shontell remembered where her loyalties lay.

April glanced at the dark girl and bit her lip. The dark girl began to giggle.

Nola wasn't amused. 'Latoya! This *isn't* funny.'

'I'm not laughing.' Latoya grabbed April and dragged her towards the door and Tarn. 'I have to talk to April.' When she reached Tarn she shoved April at him and gave him a push.

'Where are you—' Nola began.

Latoya slammed the packing-house door behind her and leaned against it. 'Don't try and bust it open!' she yelled. 'I'm leaning against it!' She looked at April and Tarn and whispered, 'Better make a run for it while you can.'

They didn't go far, just around the side of the building and to the fence next to the front gates. Tarn lifted April over and whisked her into the trees. He sat down and pulled her onto his lap. 'Christ, you're skin and bones.'

April let him tuck her beneath his chin. She squeezed her eyes shut as the hard knot of pain and loneliness loosened and forced its way from her chest. It didn't go in one big, easy piece, but in hard, tiny lumps. 'I'm not the only one who's lost weight, and why do you look so pale? Did you stay in a cave while you were in Wellington?'

Tarn put his face against her hair. She always talked more when she was nervous; he used to think it was because she was being cocky.

Darkness had fallen. The branches of the trees drooped to the ground around them, hiding them from view. They listened to the clang of the packing-house door and the sound of the Gutsell women arguing. Their voices faded away. Tarn assumed they'd gone to search for him and April, no doubt sent in the wrong direction by Latoya.

‘So that’s Latoya,’ he said.

April nodded. ‘Now you’ve seen her, you’ll understand why Heather swapped us.’

‘I’ll never understand that, April. If you make a mistake you have to face the music — just like you’ve been doing the last few months.’

‘I’m sorry I ran away, Tarn.’

‘You came back.’ He paused. ‘Why?’

‘Courtney told me to.’

‘Come on, April, you can do better than that.’

‘Oh, alright,’ she muttered. ‘I guess I knew you needed to run away more than I did; you were riddled with guilt and all mixed up about the men you lost and Aaron’s injury. So, did you find him?’ Tarn nodded against her head. ‘Did you fix him?’

‘I can’t.’

‘Hallelujah, Major, I do believe you’ve seen the light.’

He shut her up by kissing her.

‘If I can help you along the path to redemption, then go ahead, feel free to take what you need,’ April breathed when Tarn let her up for air.

He nibbled her neck. ‘I stopped in Pisa for petrol on the way home.’

She purred like a kitten.

‘Your friend Jacinta was serving on the cash desk.’

April pulled a face. ‘What did she have to say?’

‘Quite a lot. She’s a bitch.’

She looped her arms around his neck. ‘Why, Major, that’s the nicest thing anybody has ever said about her.’

Tarn snorted. She would always be two parts honey and three parts vinegar.

He recounted what Jacinta had said, and April told him about the cigarette butt, the empty containers of spray and how she'd fired the worker from Mount Pisa Cherries.

'How did you manage all that in ten days, April? Even for you, it's impressive.'

His willingness to hear her side of things and not instantly jump to the conclusion that she was to blame gave April the courage to tell the truth instead of the half-lies she usually did.

'Rosamund invited the father of the exporter to *luncheon* — not lunch — in the garden. She got Carole to get out her mother's best china, and made Latoya and me wear our best dresses and pretend we were demure and sweet. I swear if there'd been crinolines in the attic she'd have shoved us in them. Latoya pulled off being demure and sweet — Grandma has taken a real shine to her — but Mr Bradshaw remembered me and wasn't fooled. Your mother's food sealed the deal. He was disappointed not to meet Major Elliott, but Grandma promised you'd be here next time she invited him. I warn you she'll expect you to wear your uniform. Can I wear your medals if I'm good?'

Hearing her talk about a future with them both in it gave Tarn hope. 'No, but I promise to give you a private viewing. Is it true there's a range war going on between you and Ivan Vincent because you called him a mean, lying, short-arsed old criminal?'

'No.'

'Good.'

'I didn't call him a mean, lying, short-arsed old criminal …'

Tarn sighed. He sensed a 'but' coming.

'But …'

He knew it.

'I did call him a mean, lying, short-arsed old fool and said that he'd picked the wrong fight. Or at least, I told the worker I sacked to tell him that.'

'April, if you're going to insult somebody, have the sense to do it yourself. Don't send a bloody carrier pigeon.'

'I was *busy*.'

'You were *stupid*.'

'Not all of us are as perfect as you, Major,' she said huffily.

That reminded Tarn he hadn't told her about his meeting with Ralph Berryman yet. 'April?'

A mosquito whined by.

'Yes?'

'Have you heard from Rob Sturmley recently?'

'He left a message the other day, but I forgot to ring back.' April slapped at her cheek. 'Why?'

He told her briefly what had happened.

She sat like a stone in his lap. Even the mosquitoes didn't make her stir.

'I know you hate me interfering, but I promise that will be the last time.'

She didn't answer.

'You deserve the money, April. You won't have to see Berryman, just sign the papers.' Tarn caught her knee and wiggled it gently. 'For God's sakes say something.'

Her voice was clogged with tears. 'You did that for me?'

'Are you OK about it?'

'Am I OK about getting two million dollars?' April asked in a reedy voice. 'Ah — yes.' She caught Tarn's face in her hands and leaned her forehead against his. She was crying. 'Oh, Tarn ... *thank you* ... Not for the money, but for doing that for me.'

Tarn stroked her back.

'This is so romantic — just you, me and the mosquitoes. Shall we get married?' April asked.

Was she serious? He tilted his head and tried to see her face, but it was too dark.

'I'll understand if you say no, because I've screwed up once — twice, if you count Stefan — and I can't have kids. But I'm loaded and you like sleeping with me and I love you enough for both of us.'

'I *told* you I loved you that night in the study!'

April leaned back to look at him. 'When I said I had loose morals and you said it was one of the things you loved about me — *that* was it? I thought you were joking.'

'No, I bloody wasn't!'

'Is that really the best you could do?'

'Why'd you always have to jump the gun? Couldn't you even let me do the proposing?'

'If your declaration of love is anything to go by, you'd probably make a mess of it.'

'Shut up. Do you want to marry me?'

April put her chin on her shoulder, held the pose and sighed. 'Oh alright, Major — if you insist.'

He laughed. Even though it was dark, he knew she was batting her eyelashes at him.

# Epilogue

*Life isn't about waiting for the storm to pass … it's about learning to dance in the rain.*

ANON

The annual cherry-pip-spitting competition was held on New Year's Day in the grounds at Aurora. The place was packed with people from town, and orchard owners and workers, including a tight-lipped Ivan and Charmaine Vincent.

Rosamund held court with Clarence in the porticoed seating area on the eastern side of the house. She was kept busy introducing Latoya and her fiancé, Tim, to everybody; especially to the exporters who'd accepted her invitation. She had split her share in Aurora equally between Latoya and April.

'Make sure your sister keeps on sleeping with the biggest shareholder,' Nola kidded Latoya.

Barry chewed on one of Carole's marinated chicken drumsticks as he watched the Duchess of Aurora hold court. 'It's like watching the Queen open Parliament.'

Nola adjusted her blue-and-white gingham headscarf and big white sunglasses. 'She's a pain, but she's good to Latoya and April so we have to put up with her.'

'I'd put up with her, too, if she was handing out diamond and emerald brooches and bracelets and shares in cherry orchards.'

'And not just any brooches and bracelets — John Smith-designed ones.'

'Who's John Smith?'

'Google him.'

Nola sipped her drink. She had nothing in common with Rosamund, but had developed a grudging respect for her, and appreciated the way she'd welcomed Latoya into her family. They'd combined forces and gone to Roger Prescott to explain what had happened the night April had stolen the medical records, without revealing what Heather had done. It seemed likely that April would get some sort of community service as a punishment.

In Nola's opinion, the greatest injustice had never really been addressed — never *could* be addressed. She and Barry would always feel cheated because they'd never had a chance to meet Heather and tell her exactly what her terrible act had done to their family. Still, Latoya and April's happiness was more important than trying to settle an old score. They'd had to settle for telling Rosamund what a lousy mother she'd been.

Rosamund had apologized.

'If you asked to see Heather, she'd only meet with you because she'd be curious to see what you and Latoya are like, but she wouldn't care. She doesn't have the capacity for it — as her husbands keep finding out. Already the plastic surgery is less effective and the men she attracts aren't as young or handsome or rich as she wants them to be. She'll eventually end up alone, and there's nothing I can do about it.'

Tim didn't want Latoya to meet her birth mother, and eventually Latoya lost interest. April had told her how Heather hadn't coped with her wearing glasses, so she was hardly likely to cope with a daughter who suffered from epilepsy. Keeping herself well was more important than meeting the woman who'd swapped her for another child because her hair was the wrong colour. She had a wonderful man, a good family, a tidy inheritance, and an extra sister.

Nola's short skirt and ankle-chain drew eyes as she wandered up to Rosamund. 'It's time to present the prizes for the cherry-pip-spitting competition.'

Rosamund eyed her. Wretched woman — but she was a good mother and an excellent worker. 'Yes, I'll be there soon.'

Nola lingered, chewing her gum. 'Your granddaughter won the women's title,' she said loudly.

Rosamund smiled thinly. 'So I heard.'

'You must be so proud.'

'*Thrilled.*'

April was waiting with the champion male cherry-pip-spitter and the junior male and female cherry-pip-spitters. She'd won with a distance of eight metres, to wild applause from the Gutsells, Brad Tecklenberg, Courtney, Lionel, Kieran and Tarn. The winner of the men's title got two air tickets to the cherry-pip-spitting competition at the Cherry Harmony Festival, which was held each year in Manjimup near Perth, Australia.

'I knew all that talking would pay off somehow,' Tarn said.

Carole and Gerald passed by with fresh platters for the food table. They were preparing to move into the manager's house in the New Year and planned to marry in the autumn.

April had broken the news to Tarn that his mother and his orchard manager were a couple. Once he got over his shock, Tarn was pleased. He liked Smitty and could see how happy he made Carole. He was touched when Gerald asked him whether he minded if he asked Carole to marry him.

Tarn followed Gerald's lead and asked Nola and Barry if he could marry April. Nola cried and Barry pumped Tarn's arm up and down as if he were a one-armed bandit.

They'd accepted that April might never call them Mum and Dad, but were happy that she seemed to want to include them in her life and be part of their family. She was getting better at being hugged, and the Gutsells were all invited to April and Tarn's wedding in the autumn.

Tarn jumped as somebody thumped him on the back.

'Congratulations, Tarn!' Tom Giles exclaimed jubilantly. 'Wonderful news!'

'April hasn't won the trip to Perth, Tom.'

'I'm not talking about the cherry-pip-spitting competition. I meant the *other* good news!'

'Oh — that!' Tarn nodded briskly. 'Yes, thank you, Tom.'

He glanced across at April waiting in line to collect her prize from her grandmother and saw her laughing at him. She'd guessed what Tom was saying.

On Christmas Day she'd sabotaged a strawberry-flavoured condom with a needle from Carole's sewing kit and taken Tarn to bed. He didn't know the condom was faulty or why April wound her arms and legs around him and kept him talking after they'd made love until she checked the clock on the bedside table and gave him a cat-got-the-cream smile.

'Merry Christmas, Tarn.'

'Merry Christmas, love,' he murmured sleepily.

'Guess what?'

'What?'

'I'm not allergic to your sperm.'

Tarn dived off her and saw what she'd done to the condom.

'Christ, April! Are you mad?' he roared.

She looked up at him with her big blue-green eyes and said innocently, 'It's OK: Dr Giles is on standby. If I'd had a reaction, he had everything ready at his place.'

'Tom Giles *knew* about this?'

She nodded.

'He *knows* what we're doing at this moment?' Tarn demanded sternly.

April smoothed the lines on his brow and said soothingly, 'He's a doctor, he won't tell anybody. There's only one thing he wants.'

'What?'

'His flavoured condoms back.'